Praise

'I loved *The Male Gaze* . . . It takes a lot of nerve to
write a novel about suicide bombers, police brutality, clashes
of civilisations, and even more nerve to nest all of those
interests within the domestic context of a marriage.
It's a sad, funny, wistful, angry book'
Robert Macfarlane

'The novel's greatest success is its portrait of the
relationship between David and Rebecca. Joe Treasure
takes an intelligent, nuanced and sympathetic look at the
complex and rewarding process of crossing the boundary
between looking on and taking part in a new life'
Times Literary Supplement

'A slick, authentic modern tale . . . Like all
satisfying reads, there is resolution in its final pages.
I needed no coaxing to get there.'
Five Live Book of the Month

'A fast-paced plot and wry humour . . . an entertaining,
intelligent read, with just enough wit'
The List

'Compelling . . . Enabled by intelligently witty dialogue and
memorably observed detail, the narrative reflects resonantly
upon the uses and abuses of post-modern media and the
difficulty of remaining emotionally centred amidst its chaos'
Publishing News

'Funny in a wry, grim way redolent of Graham Greene . . .
His limpid, understated prose is absorbing to the point that
I could easily forget I was reading a novel. Treasure indeed'
Book Magazine

THE MALE GAZE

Joe Treasure was born in Cheltenham and studied English at Oxford. He has lived in California and in Wales, and is a graduate of Royal Holloway's Creative Writing MA. He divides his time between Santa Barbara and London. This is his first novel.

Joe Treasure

THE MALE GAZE

a novel

PICADOR

First published 2007 by Picador

First published in paperback 2008 by Picador
an imprint of Pan Macmillan Ltd
Pan Macmillan, 20 New Wharf Road, London N1 9RR
Basingstoke and Oxford
Associated companies throughout the world
www.panmacmillan.com

ISBN 978-0-330-44831-4

Typeset by Intype Libra Ltd
Printed and bound in Great Britain by
Mackays of Chatham plc, Chatham, Kent

Visit **www.picador.com** to read more about all our books
and to buy them. You will also find features, author interviews and
news of any author events, and you can sign up for e-newsletters
so that you're always first to hear about our new releases.

for Leni Wildflower

one

What wakes me is the scream. It comes from inside the apartment. I'm sitting at my desk out on the deck. Across the rooftops, towards the ocean, the sky is gathering for a violent sunset. There are other noises not associated with the scream – a passing siren, a door banging somewhere below in the building, wind chimes. From the apartment, though, there's only the scream. No breaking glass, no thud or clatter to indicate a fall. So the damage is probably not physical. Which doesn't stop my heart from pounding. This is the way I seem to be, right now – jumping at every disturbance. Awake half the night, dragging myself through the day. We've been here three weeks – I can't go on calling this jet lag.

At least I've been busy in my sleep. I've filled a hundred and thirty-eight pages with the letter b – must have dozed off with a finger on the keyboard. b for bloody thing won't write itself. My hand shakes as I drag the cursor, blackening the screen. b for buggered if I know how else it's going to get written. Perhaps it's time for a drink.

Rebecca's in the bathroom, rubbing at the front of her skirt with a flannel. I stand deferentially in the doorway.

She doesn't raise her head. She just says, 'What are you looking at?'

I've learned not to answer this sort of question. A question like this is a trap. What I'm looking at, of course, is her

– my lovely, excitable wife – head down, hunched over her scrubbing, an action that twists her torso to the left and raises her left leg so that only the toes are in contact with the floor. The pose puts me in mind of a Degas ballerina, though Rebecca is built on a different scale. Apart from the skirt, she's wearing a bra and a ribbon to hold her hair back and nothing else. Her action emphasizes the muscles in her upper arms and shoulders, the bulk of her thighs. Chunky is the word that comes to mind.

To calm myself, I do my butler impersonation. 'You screamed, ma'am?'

'Look at this skirt,' she says.

'Very nice. I've always liked that skirt.'

'Oh, for God's sake!'

Chunky is not a euphemism. I don't mean fat, though there is an appealing softness around the waist. And it's not some leering code, either, for . . . I don't know . . . huge-breasted or something. It's just that there's a breadth, a heft, a solidity about her that makes me want to go on looking. I don't say any of this, of course. I've learned not to flirt with this kind of language. You could be dead before you'd adequately explained the various distinctions.

It doesn't help that we've come to the land of thin people. I read somewhere that Americans are getting fatter. Well, *fat* Americans might be getting fatter, but we don't live where the fat people live. Where we live, as Rebecca observed the other day, fat is what comes out of a liposuc-tion pump.

She's finished with her skirt, and mopped the spilled lotion from the rim of the basin. Now she's attending to her face, massaging cream into the eyelids with smooth sym-metrical movements of the hands, outwards from the bridge of the nose to the temples, only the middle and ring fingers touching the skin.

'Please don't,' she says, 'you know I hate it.'

She doesn't like to be looked at, and even with her eyes closed she knows I'm still there. She's working on her wrinkles. She's been talking a lot about wrinkles recently. It's nothing, I tell her, you can hardly see them. And anyway they give your face more character. This doesn't seem to help. She's only thirty-five, seven years younger than me, but already worried about getting old. When I turned forty, I had a sense of settling into adult life, of feeling more on top of things. Being with Rebecca helped, of course. We'd been married three or four years already, but I still couldn't get over my luck. I still can't.

'Can I get you a drink?'

'Don't be ridiculous. Anyway, we don't have time.' She opens one eye. 'Are you going like that?'

'Going where?'

'Bloody hell, David!'

I'm wearing my favourite jumper, darned at the elbows, unravelling at the neck. 'I've been working.'

'I told you about it. It's important. It's on the calendar.'

'Ah, well, if it's on the calendar . . .'

'What's that supposed to mean?'

'They'll all be wearing black, I suppose.'

'I should hardly think so, it's a university thing. It'll be academics, mostly art historians. It's a chance for me to meet the department. Just try not to look so . . .'

'So . . . what?'

'So hopelessly English.'

'They like it that we're English.'

'But you don't have to wear it like a medal.'

English is shorthand, of course, for a cluster of insecurities. Maybe it means not being up on Foucault.

'I'll change,' I say.

'That'll be the day.' The joke signals a truce.

'It'll be fine, you know, this job – you'll do fine. Every-one'll love you. They obviously like what you've published, and they'll find out soon enough what a great teacher you are. By the time your six months is up they'll be begging you to stay . . .'

'Maybe if you'd drive . . .'

'. . . and if they ask, you can tell them you won me in a raffle.'

'I'm not up to this. I feel such a fraud.'

I can't resist her anxiety, the bunched lines on her fore-head. I move towards her and put my hands on her shoulders. They tense up then relax. She leans her head back. I like the feel of her weight against me. I lift her hair and kiss her lightly on the nape of the neck.

She puts her arms round behind me and gives me a squeeze. She hums ambiguously. 'Not now, David,' she says.

'I'll get you a drink.'

'There's that open bottle of red by the cooker.'

I go back to the deck to shut my laptop. Another day of measurable underachievement. Why is this suddenly so hard? It's not as though I've got to astound the academic world. It's just a bloody RE textbook, for God's sake. All I've got to do is explain in language accessible to a not very bright fourteen-year-old the difference between Lent and Ramadan. But everything suddenly feels like shifting ground. Categories keep bleeding into one another.

The sun is sinking towards the ocean. It broadens through the smog into spectacular orange streaks. It's still comfortably warm. There's a clatter down in the alley. An old woman is pulling bottles and cans from one of the bins, piling them into her shopping cart. She's very neat in her work, very orderly – bottles at the back, cans at the front. Nothing wrong with her categories. She's got a piece of string round her waist to hold her jacket together. She moves along the sun-bleached wall to the next bin, past startling splashes of crimson bougainvillaea.

I take Rebecca a glass of wine. I reckon I need it more than she does, but since I'm driving I shall have to stay sober. She's in the bedroom, buttoning her blouse. She's put her hair up loosely so that it straggles at the neck and around the ears.

'I'll put it here,' I say, 'on the dressing table.'

'Thanks.'

I take my sweater off and put on a jacket. I find my wallet and my driving licence on the dressing table. The car keys are hanging by the door. I busy myself, shutting windows and rinsing a few things in the sink.

We leave the apartment through the carport and drive onto a dusty side street. At the end of the block we take another turn and are instantly caught up in five lanes of mayhem. We've descended to the city's natural terrain, the roadscape, out of which the squat buildings rise, back into which they might at any moment sink. I read somewhere this city has more cars than people. For all I know, it's got more bloody drivers than people. You meet them, these drivers, moored and car-less, selling clothes, buying fast food, waiting in banks and post offices, and they're not quite themselves, they're on their best behaviour, smiling like the pages of an orthodontist's catalogue. They urge you to have a nice day, to be well, to take care now. But here, down in the roadscape, they relax into murderous aggression. This is one-handed driving – one hand for the wheel and the horn, the other free to juggle the phone and the coffee cup, to turn up the music, to express flashes of rage.

We might have gone to New England, where the trees apparently turn lovely shades of brown and orange this time of year. I could just as well have not written my book there as here.

We pass through a forest of billboards. They advertise TV shows and weight-loss programmes, and Live Nude Girls. There are advertisements in Spanish for lawsuit specialists and instant loans no questions asked. Rebecca's got the map. She's got the printout of an email with directions. She's got good ideas on how fast we should go and when we should indicate. We're nerving ourselves for a left-hand turn. Of the five lanes, it's the odd one, the one in the middle, you have to watch. This is where jeeps and SUVs and pickup trucks and Cadillacs hurtle towards each other. I pull out and find myself playing chicken with a tank. The teenage girl at the wheel is on the phone planning her weekend. I brake sharply, but she's gone without warning, cutting across two lanes of traffic with a squeal of rubber. I wouldn't mind some of that certainty. But I'm too middle-aged to feel immortal. We're stranded for five minutes before I find the gap we need.

And we're on the slip road, at last, crawling up onto the freeway. We begin to inch forward and there's nothing to watch but the darkening sky and the traffic shifting restlessly from lane to lane.

Rebecca hits a button on the dashboard, and we're listening to the polite voices on National Public Radio. There's an embassy building somewhere with a hole in its side and up to seventeen people dead. They call them unconfirmed fatalities. A White House spokesman says enough to make it clear that he has nothing to say. Back in the studio, the newsreader announces a heightened terror alert, and I'm wondering what this information means, if information is what it is, and what we're meant to do with it. Are we expected to pull into the side of the road and crouch at the wheel with our heads in our hands? Should we go home and barricade the windows? The news is terrible, and it's no more than we already know. It's an existential dread alert – the psychic equivalent of a pollen count. Expect people to be freaking out, exhibiting signs of strange, undirected hostility. But we're driving through LA, so what else should we expect?

By the time we're back on surface streets it's dusk and the lights are coming on. There are cheap clothing stores and furniture warehouses and rundown apartment blocks. We cross a major junction and the housing is more affluent. After a while, we stop at a red light and it's Sunset Boulevard, and the neon signs and the floodlit hoardings are screaming fashion at us and movie stars and sex. And Rebecca is explaining who these people are that we're about to meet, these people who are hosting the party. The driver beyond her is playing drums on her steering wheel and tossing her hair – sleek, blonde, shampoo-commercial hair – and I'm thinking how perfect she looks, with her even features and her perfect skin and her Porsche, and how happy I am with Rebecca, whose skin is comfortably imperfect.

'Which means, in effect, that Frankie's my head of department,' Rebecca says. 'Max works in television. He makes documentary films. Apparently he's got some series he's been busy with that's about to start, so you could ask him about it if you're stuck for conversation.' She says this because she knows I'm not good at parties, even back in England, and would rather be at home reading a book.

Horns blare from the cars behind the Porsche and I see that it's in the lane for turning right and it isn't turning.

'So they're a gay couple, are they, Max and Frankie?'

'David, please, please try to remember this, because it really isn't that hard. Frankie is Chair of Art History. Max is her husband. If we ever get to this party, it would be nice if you could pretend to recognize them, because they're the people who picked us up at the airport.'

Before I notice that the lights have changed, the Porsche has dodged out ahead of us. I lift my foot off the brake and we lurch forward after it. Then I hit the brake again, because there's a bang and a grinding sound, and the Porsche is moving sideways, dragging an SUV by its front bumper. They turn as they move, the Porsche spinning the SUV around and away from us. All the cars at the intersection seem to be out of alignment with each other, pointing at odd angles. For a moment I sense the arcane order of these movements, as though everything is happening according to local custom and only my surprise is surprising. The SUV has gone into a huddle in the far corner with a gold-tinted Mercedes and a U-Haul van, and the Porsche sits in the road like a discarded cigarette packet. The door opens, and the driver rises unsteadily to her feet. Something is attached to her hair above one ear like a spray of roses, and I see that it's blood. She takes a few steps towards the pavement. Then other people are there, taking hold of her. And the horns begin, or I begin to hear the horns. And my wife, who screams when she drops face cream on her skirt, is gripping my arm and murmuring, 'It's all right, we're all right, everything's all right . . .'

Cars are manoeuvring around us, finding their way past the wrecked vehicles to turn left onto Sunset Boulevard, or accelerating on up the hill. Other cars have begun to move, encroaching on us from either side, and I see that the lights have changed again. I just about remember how to drive. We shoot forward out of the flow of the traffic, and we're heading up into the canyon where Max and Frankie live.

'Are you all right?' Rebecca asks.

'More or less. How about you?'

'Do you think we should have stopped?'

'I don't know. It didn't occur to me.' And I realize that I have thought of all this, if I have thought of it at all, as a foreign cock-up on a foreign road to be sorted out by foreigners. 'There were plenty of people about.'

'Yes, you're probably right.'

I'm still shaking when we reach the house. It's a single-storey building, with alternating panels of glass and wood, and a roof with overhanging eaves. The light from the windows is unobstructed by blinds. I see angular furniture and art objects and vegetation. Max seems excited to see us. He greets me as though I'm an old friend, shouting a version of my name from the hallway.

'Dave! How the hell are you?'

And he pulls me into a bear hug. I am conscious of his ear against mine, of a sharp musky smell, and of my arms rising awkwardly to return his embrace.

'Frankie will be so excited to see you.'

He releases me and turns to Rebecca. He takes her hands and holds her first at arm's length, as though admiring how much she's grown since they last met. Then she gets the full-body treatment.

Frankie appears. 'We're in the back yard,' she says. 'Help yourself to anything you want.' Frankie's got a New York accent and New York hair – short and dark with silver-grey highlights.

She and Max lead us through the open-plan kitchen living room towards the garden. There's more glass than wood on this side of the house, and the distinction between indoors and outdoors seems more provisional. The room is stylish, but looks somehow un-lived-in. There are books and journals left open on a coffee table and chess pieces distributed on a board, but none of the artless clutter of ordinary life. You can't imagine anyone here lifting a pile of newspapers off a chair and dumping it on top of the dirty-clothes basket so you can sit down.

A guy with the physique of a body-builder approaches with a tray of drinks – white wine and orange juice and sparkling water. As he presents the tray to us, balancing it on one hand, the muscles of his chest and upper arm shift under his shirt. Rebecca takes a glass of wine.

Frankie's arm is around her shoulder. 'These earrings are so great,' she says.

I reach for a wine glass, manage to pick it up without toppling the others, and take a few gulps.

Max has gone on ahead, arms wide, to spread the word of our arrival.

'Excuse me,' I say to the body-builder. 'I'm sorry, but I don't suppose you've got anything stronger, have you, by any chance?'

He smiles, and says, 'I'll see what I can do.'

I turn back to speak to Rebecca, but she and Frankie have moved out into the garden. I see her comfortable figure retreating into a little wilderness of shrubs, where lights shine discreetly from the foliage, and I wonder if the body-builder will find me if I follow her. He's left his tray behind, so I pick up another glass in case he doesn't make it.

'We should talk.' The woman who says this is passing on her way to the garden. I don't realize she means me until she turns her head. A mass of reddish-brown hair sways and settles on her shoulders and I find her eyes on mine. The expression is serious, almost stern. 'Make sure you don't leave too soon.'

'Do I know you?' I ask her. 'I mean, should I remember you from somewhere?'

She shrugs. 'Who knows? An earlier life, maybe?' She smiles, steps lightly into the garden and moves out of sight. She looks about thirty. Perhaps she was a student of mine, longer ago than I can remember. But I don't attract many international students in my line of work, and the hair would be hard to forget.

As soon as I'm outside, I hear Rebecca laughing, and I'm glad she's begun to enjoy herself. I pass an olive tree and there she is, standing with Frankie, both of them looking towards the pool. There's a young man, sleek and tanned, making his way towards them, holding a glass. He's giving Frankie a sideways look and his mouth is easing into a smile. And now Frankie is laughing – a thinner, more brittle laugh, not as earthy as Rebecca's.

'Frankie,' the young man says, as if the name has a secret meaning. Then he does a similar thing to Rebecca's name, stretching it suggestively. 'You girls look so great.' He starts kissing cheeks, making little noises of pleasure and pain. He looks at them both appraisingly. 'How about a threesome later on?'

'Really, Amir,' Rebecca says, 'you're impossible.'

Frankie is still laughing. 'I saw you arrive but I had my hands full.'

'Yes, Max said you were dealing with food or children or something.' He gestures languidly, to suggest a longer list of unnecessary preoccupations. Then he notices me. 'You must belong to Rebecca,' he says.

'Yes,' I tell him, 'I'm her entourage.'

'Her entourage!' He savours the word, enjoying its Frenchness, and rewards it with a slow throaty chuckle.

Smiling, Rebecca takes my arm and starts stroking it in a way that looks affectionate but means *Behave*. 'This is David,' she says. 'Amir is one of Frankie's students.'

'Amir Kadivar,' he says, and we shake hands. 'So what's it like for the two of you being so far from civilization?'

'Do you mean do we miss Tufnell Park?' I don't know why he annoys me except that he's good-looking, in a pampered kind of way, and so superfluously pleased with himself.

'Not one of my haunts, Tufnell Park. Is it far from London? It sounds gloriously leafy.'

'It's fine,' Rebecca says, tightening her grip on my arm, 'but it's great to be here for a change – isn't it, David.' She borrows my wine glass, sips from it, and leaves it on a stone plinth just out of reach.

'Is this a new suit, Amir?' Frankie is stroking it, down along the narrow lapel and out over the breast pocket.

'Is it too much?'

'It's gorgeous.'

A child runs past me, giggling – a little boy with dark curls and chubby knees. An older girl follows him, reaches out to touch him on the arm, and retreats, breathless with laughter, to rest her head against Rebecca's cushiony hips. The little boy does his monster impersonation, wobbling towards us on tiptoe. The girl starts squealing.

Frankie waves at her to turn down the volume. 'Now, Laura, it's grown-up time. Play quietly, you two, or Daddy'll put you to bed.'

The children run off, squabbling noisily about which of them is making the most noise. Rebecca straightens her skirt.

'So, Amir,' Frankie says, 'who have you been talking to?'

'Your hatchet-faced friend over there seems to think I'm an Arab.' Amir nods towards the group by the pool. 'He was boring me about his trip to Syria.'

'That must be Stu Selznick.'

'Well, Stu Selznick's been on a fact-finding mission to Damascus, apparently. Damascus, I said, that must have been an eye-opening experience. Naturally he missed the joke and assumed he'd found an ally. Then he tried to get me involved in a fund-raiser for the Palestinians. I said I'd contribute to a fund to airlift decent French wine into the West Bank if he thought that would help.'

'I don't believe you said that.'

'Well, it might have a civilizing effect . . .'

'Amir, you're outrageous,' Rebecca says, unsettled but not outraged.

'What did he say?' Frankie asks.

'He looked puzzled, thanked me for my interesting suggestion and went off to harangue someone else.'

'Poor Stu. Now you've probably made him uncomfort-
able. He's a good guy, you know. Does a lot for the ACLU.
You only had to tell him you're Iranian – he knows where
Iran is.'

'Frankie, I'd just told him I'm researching Persian art.
What do you want me to do, hang a sign round my neck?'

'And how about the redhead?'

'The redhead?'

'Looked like a pretty intense conversation.'

'You saw that?'

'Was it private?'

'Who *is* she?'

'I was going to ask you.'

'It's your party.'

By now we've all located Amir's redhead, who is also
my redhead, the woman who thinks we might have met in
an earlier life. She's standing with her back to us, listening
to an elderly black man with stooping shoulders and a tight
frizz of white hair.

'You don't know her, then?' Rebecca asks.

Frankie shrugs. 'She must have come with someone.'

I'm relieved to see the body-builder walking towards us
with the drinks tray. He hands me a glass. Whatever he's put
in it, it's nearly full. He tops up Frankie's wine glass, then
Amir's. Rebecca puts a hand over hers, and gives me a look.
I console myself with a couple of gulps, as the body-builder
moves on towards the pool. It's bourbon, which wouldn't be
my first choice, but I feel it doing its job, loosening the knot
in my stomach.

'I think she might be a lunatic,' Amir says, 'but entertaining in small doses. She, at least, divined my origins.

Obsessed with Islam, unfortunately. Why do people assume I want to talk about religion? Do I look religious?'

'It's probably a recognized condition,' Frankie says. 'A masochistic thing. Like this fashion among movie stars for the Kabbalah. There must be a name for the kind of person who's drawn to exclusive faith-systems . . .'

'Fag hag?' Amir says, which is apparently so funny it makes Frankie snort wine up her nose. This sets Rebecca off. Amir's smile broadens.

I'm inclined to defend this woman, who isn't here to defend herself. 'There's nothing wrong with being interested in religion,' I say. 'It's rather a good thing to be interested in.'

Amir frowns thoughtfully. He starts nodding as though I've said something profound. 'And I hear stoning is great fun,' he says, 'as long as you're not the one being stoned.'

'But hang on a minute . . .' It's taking me a moment to catch up. 'That's hardly fair. I mean, you can find excesses in any religion, and abuses, of course you can. But that doesn't negate all the good things.'

'All the good things.' Amir repeats the phrase slowly, as if probing it for meaning.

'Yes, like, you know . . . tolerance and wisdom and respect for human life . . .'

'Ah, yes,' Amir says, 'Mullah Lite. The trouble is we think we can handle it, but in the end the rage-aholics always get drawn back to the hard stuff.'

Before I can think of an answer to this, before I've worked out exactly what it means, Rebecca asks Amir how his research is going and Frankie and Amir both laugh, Frankie more sardonically, which suggests that being a PhD student might not involve doing any actual work in Amir's case. And then they're all talking about the male gaze in seventeenth-century Persia, which is Amir's subject, apparently.

I wander out among the trees and bushes, following a

meandering line of stones. I regret my ponderous interven-
tion. Let these people think what they like – what do I care?
It's not as if I know what I think myself most of the time. I
step out of the way of the children, who still haven't been
put to bed, and cut across a patch of gravel to avoid another
cluster of grown-ups making grown-up conversation. There's
an area of paving and a table with some food on it, and some
glasses and an open bottle. I put down my empty bourbon
glass and pour myself a glass of wine. Then I put a piece of
celery in my mouth for my teeth to bite on. I find myself at
a fence, looking down into the darkness of the canyon. I'm
wondering why I let a boy like Amir get up my nose.

Fragments of conversation reach me from different parts
of the garden and become one conversation.

'Hey, Joel, did you hear this about Schwarzenegger?'

'She was screwed by the ethics committee – two years
of research down the tubes.'

'He's a Taurus, right, but he's on the cusp, which really
sucks.'

'The way I heard it, De Niro wasn't available so they
rewrote it for DeVito.'

'Give me a break, the guy's a moron.'

'Are you kidding me – Nietzsche was a huge influence.'

'But isn't he a neo-con?'

'She's got a retrospective at the Zuckmeyer – the critics
are going crazy.'

There's the gasping laughter of the children, playing
their chasing game.

'Do you know the weirdest thing?' This question isn't
part of the conversation. There's a woman standing next to
me. It's the woman with the hair. It's rust-coloured and
unruly.

'I doubt it,' I say.

'See that guy over there.' She points back through the

garden toward the pool. The smooth surface of the water seems to glow with its own light. 'Bald guy with a beard.'

'The one who looks like Freud.'

'Hey, you're right, he does look like Freud. Isn't that something!'

'Just add a cigar. He's not a therapist, is he?'

'Hell, no!' She leans towards me to confide her secret, and I can smell her perfume, which is dark and herbal with a trace of jasmine, unless the jasmine is from somewhere in the garden, or wafting up from the wilderness beyond the fence. 'I have a rule, not to stand next to therapists at parties.'

'That's an unusual rule.'

'I've been felt up by enough therapists to last a couple of lifetimes.'

'At parties?'

'On couches, in parking lots . . . So anyway, the bald guy is smart. You'd like him. A physics professor. There's nothing sexier than a physicist talking physics, don't you think?'

'I never really thought about it.'

'First time I really got relativity – I mean, got it viscerally, like I had a sense of space bending – I was wet. Practically came right there in the car. I was on a date with a guy from MIT.'

'You're right – that is unquestionably the weirdest thing.' I raise my wine glass to my mouth and I'm surprised to discover that I've emptied it already. The children are squatting by the pool, dropping pebbles into the water. I catch a glimpse of Rebecca and Frankie with some other people over by the house.

'But I haven't told you yet. It's about electrons. Apparently you can know where an electron is, okay. And you can know how fast it's going. But you can't know both. Isn't that just wild? Turns out it can be anywhere. I mean, just anywhere. One minute, there it is, buzzing about, doing, you know, whatever electrons do – its little subatomic thing – Jesus! it could be part of you – part of your ear . . .' She touches my ear experimentally, rubs the lobe between her finger and thumb, as though feeling for an electron. My breathing suddenly feels unnatural, a strange movement of air in and out of my mouth. 'There it is, zipping about in your molecular stuffing, or whatever, and suddenly, zap, it's on the far side of Jupiter. And vice versa. Some electron from . . . God! you know . . . the Amazonian rainforest is suddenly part of your central nervous system.'

'That is surprising, isn't it.'

'It's a percentage thing, of course. The odds aren't great, but, Jesus, the implications are limitless, don't you think?'

'I think I'm beginning to.'

'I mean, for God's sake, our neurons are plugged right into the space-time continuum. And people wonder about autistic savants. People are so linear, so three-dimensional. The cosmos is buckled like a pretzel, and they're all trying to cram it into their little Cartesian box. Did you try this dip? It's fat-free. Wow, think about it, though. Makes sex seem pretty tame, huh!'

'It certainly is an exciting thought.'

'We're talking total interpenetration on a multi-galactic scale. How do you like that for an orgasm?' She puts a stick of carrot in her mouth. Her nails and lips look purple in the leaf-filtered light. 'You can file that one,' she says through the carrot, 'right under cosmic ecstasy.'

I'm surprised to see the body-builder coming my way with a glass. The ice clinks as he hands it to me. 'Thought you might be ready for another,' he says.

'Thank you,' I say, 'thanks very much.'

'My pleasure,' he says.

The woman with rusty hair laughs. 'Your accent really is the cutest,' she says.

'I've had years of practice.'

'I knew we should talk.'

'Why did you say that?'

'Because you looked interesting.'

'Like Amir.'

'Amir?'

'The Iranian student. Over there, studying Persian art.'

She rolls her eyes. 'Looks can be deceptive. Is that ginger ale?' She takes hold of my drinking hand. 'My God, you're shaking. Are you okay?'

'Yes, absolutely. I'm absolutely fine.'

'You want to talk about it?'

'Not particularly, no.'

She raises the glass to her nose and sniffs. 'Thank God. We're surrounded by recovering alcoholics.'

'I've no intention of recovering,' I say, and take another swig.

She laughs excitedly. 'You're smart. I knew you'd be smart. I'm Astrid.' She holds out her hand.

'David,' I say, 'David Parker.' She has a firm handshake. The gesture seems oddly formal now that she's fondled my ear.

There's a gust of wind. I feel the cool air on my neck. Astrid's dress, which is blue and billowy, shimmers as it moves. It follows her figure where the wind touches it, gathering elsewhere in generous folds. I swallow a couple of mouthfuls and turn to watch the people grouped under the trees. I recognize Max's expansive gestures, dark against the light from the house.

'It's just that I can't quite take any of this seriously. I keep thinking it's an illusion. Do you think you might possibly be an illusion?'

She laughs. 'Well, sure I am, who isn't?'

'And any minute I'm going to wake up and discover I'm dead, because my body's lying in a mangled heap down there on the road.' I hear myself saying this and I'm startled that this thought has been squatting in my head. I raise my glass and find there's nothing in it.

'Well, you feel like flesh and blood to me, sweetheart,' she says, taking my hand.

'Sorry. We just had a near-miss on our way up the hill. No serious injuries, I think.' It's the grinding of metal against metal I can still hear, and metal against tarmac.

'Sounds like the universe just did one of those little bifurcations it's so fond of.' She's standing close to me, holding my hand, looking towards the canyon. And I wonder if it's her perfume or the bourbon that's brought on this feeling of weightlessness. As I watch, the glowing surface of the swimming pool detaches itself and hovers among the trees where the people merge and multiply, and their chatter blurs with the squealing of children. I tell myself I probably shouldn't be doing this, holding hands under the trees with this nicely scented stranger, and I wouldn't if we were in Tufnell Park, but this is another place where normal rules are suspended and people walk away from collisions.

'We just happen to be on this plane,' Astrid says, 'having this conversation. Why shouldn't there be another plane where you didn't make it, and a third one where . . . I don't know . . . you've won the Nobel Peace Prize?' She laughs, and I laugh, and my laughter feels weak and disconnected. 'It's string theory, honey, and you've just gotten hold of one of the strings.'

'And you learned all this from whatsisname . . . Freud over there, or . . . the other one.'

'I've dated a lot of physics professors.'

'How nice for the physics professors.'

'As well as a couple of macro-biologists. And this guy
who practically invented Chaos Theory – boy, what a control freak he turned out to be. I guess I've always wanted to
get up close to where the world is changing. It wasn't, of
course.'

'Wasn't what?'

'Changing. Not for the better, anyway, that's for sure.'

'From all the deceits of the world, the flesh, and the
devil, good Lord, deliver us.'

'No kidding. Turned out I was looking in the wrong direction. You'd think these ideas would explode in people's
heads, and make everything . . . you know . . .'

'Orgasmic?'

'. . . fresh and innocent and new. Instead, everywhere you
look they're crawling back into the darkness.'

'I know what you mean.' Strange things are happening
at the edges of my vision – a spiralling of lights and the darkness between the lights.

'Which is why I'm getting into Islam.'

'That's a pity, because you won't be able to wear this nice
blue dress anymore.' I put my hand out to touch the collar,
to feel the silky texture of it between my fingers.

'I won't?'

'Not when you're a Muslim.'

'Are you just a little bit drunk?'

'How can you tell?'

'You're so cute when you're drunk. No one else at this
party is drunk.' She turns to face the garden. 'Look at them.
All too scared to lose control.'

'You won't be able to get drunk either, not even a little
bit, not when you're a Muslim.'

'Honey, I'm not converting. It's research. I'm probably on
some CIA list by now, the number of radical Islamic sites I've

checked out. Not that I can make much sense out of any of it.' She sighs impatiently. 'I've got so many questions.'

I'm thinking about my desk out on the deck, the tinkling wind chimes, the bright line of distant water between the buildings. Now I'm away from it, writing seems so easy.

'The day they started knocking down the Berlin Wall,' Astrid says, 'I was fourteen. It was my birthday. I thought it was a birthday present from the universe. It was like we were all holding hands, stepping into the sunlight. Now we seem to be in the middle of some kind of psychotic breakdown. And maybe it's something to do with religion, and maybe it isn't, but people are killing each other, so I suppose it has to be about something. Whatever it's about, it makes you want to weep.'

The little girl is chasing her brother round the pool. Their curls light up like halos as they pass the window. 'It's enough,' I say, 'to make the angels weep.'

'Isn't that the truth.'

'One little paragraph on Ramadan. One little chapter on Islam. Half a dozen questions for class discussion. You wouldn't think that would be beyond me. I sit in front of my laptop, and what comes out. A hundred and thirty-eight pages of bollocks – bollocks with a b. This book is very slowly doing me in.'

'Which book?'

'My book.'

'You're writing a book on Islam?'

'Well, only partly on Islam.'

'Jesus! How synergistic is that!'

'No, no, you don't understand. It's just a textbook . . .'

'I'm bursting with questions and I meet the guy – my God! – who's writing the textbook.'

'And I'm just the writer. Someone else is doing the

pictures and the graphics. I mean, it's just a Key Stage Three thing.'

'That's a stage of enlightenment, right?'

'No!' I hear laughter across the garden, and the sound of water splashing. 'Well, yes, in a way, I suppose, but not really, to be honest, no.'

'Is it related to Jung? I love Jung.'

The little girl is suddenly still, standing awkwardly by the pool with one finger in her mouth. I'm trying to clear my head, so that I can explain the unimportance of what I'm writing, of what I'm not writing.

'So, Islam. What's the difference between the Sunnis and the Shias, theologically I mean? And tell me about the Wahhabists.'

'The wha . . . ?'

'Wahhabists – they're huge in Saudi Arabia.'

I leave my mouth open, hoping something intelligent will come out. There's a scream and one of the women leaps into the pool.

'Something's happening,' Astrid says.

Water spatters on the stone and against the window. Max is running through the trees.

'We're missing the party.' She pulls me by the hand. 'We'll do lunch.'

I tip towards her and find myself stumbling forward, over gravel, through the shrubs.

'This is going to be so great!'

There's a man kicking his shoes off. It's my friend the body-builder, who brings me drinks. He's about to dive as we reach the stone paving. It makes me warm to this place that even the waiter is not excluded. As he slides into the water, Astrid jumps, whooping with anticipation. I have time to see her blue dress billowing up around her waist. I have time to regret my Englishness, to regret that I must always stand at the edge and watch. But the water, sparkling with fragments of light, is tilting towards me. It throws itself at my face, washing over me with an intimate commotion. The old sounds of shouting and splashing are muted. Twisting in this low-gravity element, I see legs that might be Astrid's legs – green and distorted – and other women's legs, and legs in trousers. I see an arm waving frantically across my face and I see that it's my arm. I break the surface, struggling to breathe. There's a clatter of voices. Through a blear of water, I see my friend the body-builder on his knees, dripping. A woman kneels holding the little girl. There's a blur of shocked faces. The curly-headed boy is lying on his face and the body-builder is pressing on him with his big hands. Only Rebecca is looking at me, shouting something as she pulls her jacket off.

two

It's an uncomfortable journey home. Rebecca's driving, of course. I'm in some transitional stage between drunk and hungover, and focusing on not throwing up. Max has lent me some dry clothes, so I'm up to my neck in designer labels.

At some point Rebecca decides to speak. 'That woman's conversation must have been really fascinating.'

'It was all right.'

We're waiting at a light. 'So what was it you talked about actually, for so long?'

'Nuclear physics . . .'

'David!'

'. . . and Islam, with particular reference to the Wahhabists.'

'You sad, pathetic liar.'

She turns the corner rather too fast while she's saying this, and I have to close my eyes and take a deep breath before I feel able to respond.

'That's it. Honestly. That's what we talked about.'

'With her neat little cleavage on display, she might as *well* have been talking about nuclear physics for all you cared.'

'Well, the physics part was just small talk, as it turned out.' I draw in a breath carefully through my nose, and let it out. 'It was the Wahhabists that really interested her.'

'Honestly, David, you haven't even got the decency to feel embarrassed.'

I do, though. I'd say this to her if I had energy for the debate. If a capacity for embarrassment is a sign of decency, I must be one of the most decent people I know. And right now I'm reliving my stumbling entry into the water and my floundering exit. I remind myself that for most people at that party, as for most people anywhere, my existence is a passing thought at most, but it doesn't dispel the feeling.

Rebecca's annoyance, on the other hand, I don't take too seriously. Rebecca doesn't go in for jealousy. Envy is in her repertoire all right. Envy is part of her academic baggage, and it's jumbled up with all the usual bodily insecurities. It doesn't pass me by, for example, that she not only observed Astrid's cleavage but considered it to be neat, neatness not being one of her own virtues. She can do cleavage, no problem, if cleavage is required. Neatness eludes her. But whereas Astrid's trim figure might annoy the hell out of her, on past experience I'd say she's not likely to worry too deeply about the effect it has on me.

A passing reference a few days later to *the trollop* reassures me that, though her annoyance lives on, it's moved into a phase of self-parody. Trollop is one of her grandmother's words for the celebrities whose antics fill the tabloid press.

I'm sitting at my desk in the afternoon sun, thinking about all this, when my laptop tells me I've got mail. There's a message from astro@spinmail.com. I'm holding the mouse, with the cursor hovering over the delete icon. Astro doesn't sound like anyone I know and is probably selling some virility-enhancing drug. But curiosity gets the better of me. There's no greeting. *jazzed about our talk*, the message reads. *so many questions. hope you dried out ok. am i forgiven? are you writing? gathering in moonglow cafe malibu. join us in 45 mins? if writing write. otherwise how about it? astrid. ps say*

25

no if you like but i went through all six degrees of separation to get your info. say no only if writing. a.

I write a reply. *Dear Astrid, It was very nice to meet you too. Thanks for the invitation. I'd love to come, but unfortunately I haven't got a car. Rebecca takes it to work. I'm trying to write, without much success to be honest. Keep in touch. David.* Then I delete the bit about Rebecca having the car, because it sounds like a plea for sympathy, or just too much information. Then I wonder if I've deleted it so as to delete Rebecca. So I add a postscript – if Astrid can have a postscript why can't I? *PS. Rebecca is out at work.* Then I delete the postscript, because it's irrelevant. Then I delete the whole message and write, *Can't come. No car. Sorry.* I send the message, and I'm immediately invaded by a sense of loss. Nothing is happening again. Astrid was at least something.

I'm struggling to construct a simple sentence about the religious purpose of fasting that is uncontroversial without being soporifically boring, when Astrid's reply arrives. *in the shop? no injuries i hope. i'll send the boy. give him 30 mins. a.*

I read the message a couple of times. I understand the last bit, anyway. It's not just my email address Astrid has got hold of. I'm to give the boy thirty minutes. That leaves me plenty of time to wonder how I feel about this, to consider what I should wear, to consider whether the fact that I'm considering anything so unlikely as what I should wear is a clue that I'm getting into deep water. And who's this boy? Is Astrid old enough to have a son who can drive? How old do you have to be to drive in this city, though – twelve? Perhaps the boy is some kind of household servant, in which case he might be older than I am. Will he wear a uniform? I read the message again. *in the shop? no injuries i hope.* I note the assumption that a collision is the only imaginable reason for someone to be without a car. I note also that the thought of replying, *Can't come anyway*, has only just occurred to me, and now it's too late because the boy is already on his way.

Sitting at the top of the apartment steps, I watch the car turn into our road. It pulls up and the dust settles behind it. It's sporty, or was once. The front fender is lopsided. One of the headlights is held in with duct tape. There are tide marks on the body where the paint has peeled and only the passenger door, an obvious replacement, is uniformly red. I stoop to look in through the open window.

The boy peers back at me from under the peak of his baseball cap. 'So you're Astro's latest.'

'I'm David,' I say, and hold my hand out.

'Jake,' he says, pumping it a couple of times. It's like a child playing at being a grown-up, the way he does this. He doesn't smile. He's revving the engine, checking the mirror.

He gives me a hard look. 'You don't have Asperger's, do you?'

'Asperger's?'

'Asperger's.'

'Not as far as I know.'

'No offence,' he says, 'I was just thinking.'

I get in and sink back against the worn leather. There's a smell of incense. As I pull the door shut, the seat belt judders towards me, tightening across my chest, and we catapult forward. At the end of the street, he finds a narrow gap in the traffic and shoots us into it. He makes jerky movements with one hand on the wheel, resting the other hand on the gearstick, and the car darts with disconcerting suddenness, like a fish in its own element.

Jake is in his late teens or early twenties and he *is* wearing a kind of uniform – T-shirt, baggy knee-length shorts, trainers. It's the favoured style of the skateboarders on the boardwalk and the aspiring screenwriters at their laptops in the sidewalk cafes, and all the kids from thirteen to thirty for

27

whom, I have found myself resentfully imagining, cloudless-
ness and endless sunshine have become the empty skyscape
of the mind.

Jake's mind is neither cloudless nor empty, it turns out.
He doesn't talk much at first. I thank him for picking me up.
I ask him what he does and he tells me he's a student. He's
at junior college, hoping to transfer to a four-year college in
the spring, planning to major in sociology. He's working on
some project that's more than a paper and not exactly a dis-
sertation and might turn out to be a multimedia thing. Bits
of it might be danced or sung.

'I thought originally it might be a book,' he says, 'but shit,
do we even know if books will exist five years from now?'

'So what is it so far?' I ask. 'What is it right now?'

'Right now? You know . . . it's like pain. Some days it's
like this humungous thing that's eating me up. Today's one
of those days. I'm just trying to hang in. Trying to be present
to who I am.'

'And who are you?'

'An incredible, beautiful human being in a world full of
pretence and dissonance and bullshit. Whatever it turns out
to be, it's basically waiting to come out. I just have to allow
it to take whatever form it has to take. My job's to get myself
out of the way, you know? I just have to sit with the process.'

'I know what *that* feels like,' I tell him. I'm not sure I do,
actually, but there's something about Jake that I warm to,
and I'd like to help him relax. I wonder if I'm making him
nervous, or if he's like this all the time. How can anyone live
at such a level of lip-chewing intensity? When he talks about
his project, the red peak of his baseball cap, which is frayed
and blackened at the edges, bobs up and down.

'There are days,' he says, 'when I'm just invaded by
This Isn't Working, and sabotaged by Everything's Fucked.'
He raises both hands for a moment to make those rabbit's

ears in the air that mean quotation marks, and my stomach lurches.

In the moment before he yanks the wheel to avoid a wide-sided truck, I have an exaggerated awareness of the road, of these acres of traffic all hurtling towards the scrapyard, of the crushable softness of the human body. I become aware also, in a new visceral way, of his style of speech. I find myself listening for the kind of phrase he might want to put in quotes and I'm ready to take defensive action.

'Which is kind of ironic, you know,' he says, 'because that's basically what I'm writing about, the fact that basically everything *is* fucked. Like the way, you know, indigenous people are fucked by global business, and love is fucked by ambition, and the ice caps are fucked by a million miles of freeway.'

I latch on to the second of these propositions because I'd rather hear Jake talk about himself than about capitalism or global warming. 'You think love is fucked by ambition?'

'Sure it is. Don't you? You see a guy in a bar with a girl or whatever and he's telling some dumb joke about his European ski trip, or explaining what's great about being a corporate attorney, and she's laughing and showing off her dental work, and they carry on like they're looking for love or something . . .' Without warning, he puts *love* in quotes, stretching it out like the chorus of a song, and I'm bracing myself against the dashboard and staring at the drifting white lines and the starbursts of brake lights, until his hand drops again to the wheel. 'Meanwhile she's checking out the size of his bank balance and he's feeling for her zip code, and that's all that's going on.'

'And sex?'

'Yeah, I guess, whatever, but sex is just another commodity, and it's all mixed up with power and money.'

He makes a movement like an angry gesture, and we're

swinging left across the traffic. I shrink in my seat, as though this will help squeeze us through. We accelerate into a side street with the sun in our eyes and the horns fading behind us. I have to admit he's good at this.

For a few blocks the ground rises. We pass clothing stores with angular mannequins in the windows. Then there are real people labouring at treadmills or lying back to have their toenails trimmed. The road dips and the ocean jumps up at us between buildings, a deep blue rectangle, and it's like something I've never seen before, it's so bright and touchable. We turn north again, and the ocean slips down below us to our left, on the far side of a strip of grass. The palm trees curve their slender, scaly trunks towards the sky. Weaving among them, down near the roots, are the joggers, and the walkers who work their hips and elbows like salsa dancers. There are also crazy people and people doing business on the phone, all jabbering and gesturing at invisible listeners.

'Look, Jake,' I say, 'I don't know what impression Astrid gave you, but . . . you called me her latest. I'm not exactly sure what that implies, but I think it's probably inaccurate.'

'So what would you call yourself?'

'An acquaintance, I suppose. I've only met her once. I mean it was just a conversation at a party . . .'

'Yeah, and you jumped in the pool and some kid nearly drowned. I heard all about it.'

'Oh, you did.' This is unsettling. 'Well, I don't know what Astrid said about it, but at least she managed to carry it off with some kind of style. I hope she gave herself some credit for that. I'm afraid I made a bit of a fool of myself.'

'Because you live on an abstract plane.'

'I do?'

'Which is Astro's way of saying you're too bright to know what's going on half the time.'

'I don't know if that's entirely fair.'

'Don't let it swell your head, or anything. Astro likes to have some genius in tow. You're just her latest.' He snatches a look at me. 'They're usually dorks,' he says, 'or brainiacs with one foot in the grave. You don't look so bad.'

I decide to take this as a compliment. 'So we're going to the Moonglow Café.'

'Moonglows, yeah.'

'Which is where, exactly?'

'A mile or two up the coast. Where Mom and Astrid hang out.'

'And Astrid's a friend of your mother's.'

'Her only friend, pretty much. They met at Overeaters Anonymous. Now Astro's a kind of part-time lodger.'

'Over-eaters . . . ? That's hard to imagine. Astrid is hardly . . . I mean I can't picture her . . .'

'Fat is a state of mind, according to Mom. Astrid's usually in New York. She's got her own apartment on the Upper West Side.'

'So when she's here, the three of you live together.'

'Four, with Natalie.'

'Who's Natalie?'

He hesitates before answering, as though he wants to get this right. 'Natalie's a very special person. She's probably the most incredibly gifted person I know. She's not easy to be around sometimes. But she's deep, you know, and authentic as hell.'

'Not ambitious, then.'

A shadow crosses his face and I'm annoyed with myself for this clumsy reference to his thesis.

'There are different kinds of ambition. You better be ambitious if you're an artist or you'll shrivel up and become nothing. Or else settle for some corporate job and be worse than nothing.'

A gap opens up in the grass where the road swings downwards, and there's the water again, bright and glistening. It rolls along beside us for a while then disappears between low buildings, reappearing from time to time like an extra piece of sky. Following the road to our right is a stretch of cliff that towers and falls back, dips into canyons and rises again, before opening out into hillside. A few of the buildings that block our view of the ocean stand alone with stylish facades. Most look like shacks or garages or motels strung out in a line. And all the front doors open within yards of the road like beach huts on the edge of a motorway.

Without warning Jake pulls the wheel to the left, and for a breathtaking moment we're spinning sideways. I'm looking out the side window at the grinning radiators of two vehicles, and there's nothing between me and them but a car door and shrinking length of road. Then we're facing the way we came and stopping sharply, almost filling the narrow gap between the road and the row of buildings, and the traffic is hurtling past us.

three

Moonglows is a hut with a neon sign in the shape of a crescent moon. There's a row of portholes facing the road. I follow Jake up the steps. He pulls the door towards him. It creaks open and swings shut behind us with a clunk of wood against wood. The noise of the traffic is shut out, and I hear the ocean. The iron counterweight, dangling at the end of a cable, knocks the doorframe as it settles. There's a bar and tables and chairs and the whole place is a nautical stage set, with ropes and fishing nets and lobster pots and hunks of coarse-grained timber. Along the far side, there's a row of windows opening on to water and sky, and people at tables. I see a mass of red hair against the blue of the water and recognize Astrid. There are two other women sitting across from her, and there's Jake, hovering between me and them, as though he can't relax until I've been delivered. It's the youngest of the three women who sees me first. She looks fragile and undernourished. Her eyes are too big for her face. The startled look she gives me makes me feel I've stumbled into something illicit, a conspiracy or the meeting of a coven. Then Astrid is standing with her arms out ready for a hug. Her dress is black and artfully ragged. I remember her scent. She turns to introduce me to the others – Mo and Natalie. Mo, who must be Jake's mother, is plump. She's exuberantly beaded and bangled. Natalie doesn't look any more relaxed now that she knows who I am.

Astrid pulls me down on to a chair beside her. 'Okay, so like I told you, David's a genius,' she says. 'He's gonna give us the low-down on the Islamists.'

'Look, Astrid,' I say to her, 'I want to clear this up before we go any further, I mean I don't want to feel I'm here on false pretences . . .'

'I hear that, you know, David,' Mo says, 'I really hear that.' She reaches her hand across the table to rest it on my arm and her bangles clatter on the table. 'What you've got to know about Astrid is that she thinks love and under-standing will solve everything and like you say it's a false pre-tence. You can't love suicide bombers.'

'But you can try and understand them, sweetie,' Astrid says. 'We're nowhere if we don't try to at least get under their skin.'

'You can't love wife-beaters and bullies.' Mo's grip on my arm tightens as she talks, though it's Astrid she's talking to now.

'And what about torturers?' Astrid says. 'What about the guys in the Pentagon with their smart bombs and their col-lateral damage? Can you love them?'

Mo considers this. 'I see it like a cosmic lesion, you know – you can only sit it out, and wait for it to heal. What do you think, David? Do you think some of them will eventually get it after maybe another dozen lifetimes – something'll finally sink in?'

'Well, to be honest I'm not thinking that far ahead,' I tell her. 'I'm hoping I'll make it through to the end of the week.'

Mo's eyes widen. I feel her nails through my shirt. 'What have you heard? Are they planning something?'

'No, I mean . . . It was a kind of joke. Sorry.'

'Well, you should be. This isn't a joking matter.'

Astrid is laughing.

'No, really, Astrid.'

'Not even a joke, in fact,' I tell her. 'Just the way things are at the moment.'

Mo softens at that. 'It's like the world's diseased,' she says. 'You can smell the evil seeping out of its pores.'

'Please,' Astrid says, 'not the E-word. Jesus, let's leave the E-word to the government.'

'You sound like Saint Paul,' I tell Mo. 'For we know that the whole creation groaneth and travaileth in pain.' There's silence. Mo gives me an odd look, and Astrid laughs.

There are glasses of water on the table, and cutlery, and a video camera – one of those older ones that use miniature tapes.

Natalie is still looking at me with her large eyes. 'So you're Astrid's friend.' Her voice is quiet and she chews her thumbnail as she speaks. 'You seem sad. Don't you think, Mo – there's something sad in his aura?'

I don't know what to say to this. Sad isn't quite right. I could deny it. I could suggest an alternative – anxious, perhaps, or distracted – but I don't feel like being bounced into therapy.

'David's okay, honey,' Mo says, 'he's a bit stiff is all. He's from England.' And she strokes Natalie's hair.

Jake has pulled a chair up to the table, and sits looking at the menu.

'You wanna eat?' Astrid slides a menu towards me. 'We ordered already.'

'I don't know,' Natalie says. 'Wounded somehow.'

'He might not be wounded, honey,' Mo says. 'It's just there's a lot of dark energy manifesting right now.' She turns to me, and takes both my hands in hers. 'If you're not in touch with your shadow side, there's no knowing what might show up in it. The cosmos is heading for a crisis, you know, which might be terminal, or might be a breakthrough to another level.'

My phone starts ringing. It's a number I don't recognize. 'Sorry,' I say, releasing myself from her grip, 'I should probably take this.' I stand up, moving away into a space by the bar.

'David. It's Rebecca.'

'Oh, hi. How's it going?'

'Fine. Am I interrupting you? Are you writing?'

'No, not really. I keep getting stuck.'

'Bad luck.'

There's a burst of noise from a nearby table.

'Just a moment, let me just . . .' I move further along the bar. 'Rebecca, sorry, what's happening?'

'Nothing much, I just wanted to talk. Where are you? I thought you'd be at home.'

'I just came out for a bit.' I'm caught off guard. I should just tell her – but why complicate things for no reason?

'Is there someone with you? We could talk later if you're with someone . . .'

'No, now's fine. Really. So . . .'

There's an open door that leads on to a deck. Outside I feel the air moving in off the water. The line between the ocean and the sky is blurred and the sun is ringed by haze.

'What did you want?'

'David? You sound on edge.'

'I don't think I'm on edge.'

'I wasn't accusing you. I was just saying. Maybe this isn't a good time.'

'Has something happened?'

'No. Look, are you going to be home soon? I might try and get back early if you're going to be there.'

'What's wrong?'

'Nothing's wrong. I just thought perhaps we could talk. Can't I phone you unless something's wrong?'

'I didn't say that.' I lean over the rail, and watch the

water swirling below, breaking into foam against the boulders and timber struts. 'So when do you think you'll be back?'

'If you're going to be out, there's not much point, is there. It's not as though I haven't enough to do.'

'I could be home before too long if you're going to be early.'

'Where are you now, then?'

'I'm not sure.'

'What do you mean? How can you not be sure?'

'By the water.'

'On the beach?'

'Yes, on the beach.'

'Are you with someone? It sounds like you're with someone.'

I hesitate. She doesn't need to hear I'm with Astrid – she's upset enough already, without that. 'It's just people in the bar.'

'I thought you were on the beach.'

'In a bar on the beach.'

'Are you drinking?

'Is that why you phoned? To ask if I'm drinking?'

'Oh, David, this is pointless.' I can hear her voice thickening as she begins to cry.

'I'll see if I can get home.'

'Don't bother, David, if it's that much of a problem.'

'Well, call me if you need to talk.'

She's gone. I think about calling her back. But to say what? You're right, I am with someone, but it's not important – would that make it better?

I walk back past the bar to the table, still jangled by this broken conversation.

'He would have been dead if it hadn't been for the

caterer.' Astrid is talking about the boy who fell in the pool. 'You should've seen the guy move.'

'The guy's a healer,' Mo says. She's holding the video camera, filming Natalie, who stares into her water glass.

'He's done some paramedic training,' Astrid says, 'and he's worked as a lifeguard – you know, in between jobs.'

'Paramedic, whatever – he's a healer.'

'Catering jobs?' I ask, not because I care, but because I feel I'd like something somewhere to be clear and definite.

'No,' Astrid says. 'Acting jobs.'

'He's an actor?'

'He's a healer.' Mo keeps filming while she talks.

'Something's come up,' I say, 'I probably ought to think about going.'

'Not necessarily, as a matter of fact,' Natalie says. 'Children have this amazing thing with water, like this affinity thing. Most of us lose it, like we lose wisdom, you know, and this closeness to nature that we have from the womb. But children don't drown.'

'Maybe Jake could drive me home.'

'Jesus,' Jake says, 'I've got to eat. Am I going to be allowed to eat?'

'It's like the water knows who they are.'

'Children drown all the time,' I say. 'Babies can drown in the bath.'

'I don't know,' Natalie says. Her big eyes flash towards me and away again. 'How many babies drown compared with those who don't?'

'I don't understand. Is that a question?' I feel all my agitation focusing on Natalie's slithering logic.

'You know what I mean, Mo?' Natalie says. 'How do we live in the womb, floating in like fluid and all? We have to retain some memory, some affinity for all that.'

'Sure,' says Mo dropping the camera, 'you've got a point there.'

'Has she?' I ask. 'Has she really?' But Mo's looking at Natalie with a kind of delight, as though Natalie is a precocious child. And Astrid's staring at the ocean and I can't see her face. Then Mo raises the camera again and I can't see hers either.

'I'm going to order a burger,' Jake says, getting up from the table.

Natalie leans towards the camera to confide a secret. 'I used to hide in the swimming pool when I was a small child. When my parents were fighting and my dad was beating up on my mom, which was like all the time practically, I'd hide out in the swimming pool. Just sink to the bottom and stay there for hours. I did this thing like with my metabolism, slowing my heartbeat and everything, and just went into a trance.'

'While the pool was full of water?' I ask her.

'Of course.'

'That would be an amazing talent.'

Mo has pulled back, turning the camera to follow Natalie's profile.

'No,' Natalie says, looking at me for a moment, then looking down at the table, 'an ordinary thing for a child.' She scratches at the wood with her fingernail. 'Amazing only that I managed to stay in touch with it so long.'

'So you're saying, basically . . . what you're saying is that you can defy the laws of nature. I mean, for God's sake, there are people who train for years to stay under water for five minutes.' I regret beginning this speech, long before I've got to the end of it. What do I care what these people believe?

I'm horrified to see Natalie's eyes filling with tears. 'I don't think you know necessarily about children,' she says, 'however smart you are. Smart people know less about certain things.'

She puts her hand up against the camera and Mo lets it drop. 'I don't even want to sit here anymore.' She knocks her chair over as she gets up. 'It's like something's happened to the energy in here – like someone's channelling my dad or some-thing . . .' She pushes past Jake, who's on his way back from the bar.

'Jesus, what the fuck did you say to her?'

'I'd better go after her,' Mo says, 'see she's all right.'

'Look, I'm sorry,' I say, 'I didn't mean anything.'

We're all standing now, except for Astrid. Jake is follow-ing Natalie towards the door. Mo is putting the video camera into an embroidered bag. 'It's not you, sweetheart,' she tells me. 'Nattie's working through some deep issues. It's like she's an electric storm just now, and you show up like a lightning rod. Come back to the house and we'll see if we can work through it.'

'I'm afraid I can't stay, though, you see. I should be get-ting home. That was my wife on the phone.'

Mo puts her bag on the floor and looks at me. 'You're kind of wired, aren't you, David – always rushing on to the next event. How about sitting with this one? It might be a chance for growth.'

'Perhaps some other time.'

'No such place, sweetheart. Now is where we live.' She puts her hand on my arm, and looks into my face as though she's searching for something. 'If I can speak frankly for a moment, there's this huge thing in you called judgement, am I right? Your border guards are never off duty, sweetheart.' She stares at me for a moment, with a sorrowful expression, then she pulls me into a hug. 'I'm not making you wrong for that – it's who you are.'

I strain for a moment against this unwanted intimacy. Then my resistance gives way, and I find myself unexpectedly comforted by her bosomy warmth. 'It's just that my wife's expecting me.'

She lets me go. 'It's up to you. The thing you need to know about Natalie is she's a kind of cosmic receptor. That's the way she came in. She's carrying the darkness of the world in her psyche. I've been helping her get in touch with her shadow, but it sure isn't easy for her, combating the darkness. There are whole nations swallowed up by it.'

I watch her leave.

Then Astrid takes me by the arm. 'Hey, you.'

'Do they have taxis in Malibu?'

'I'd take you myself, but my car's being fixed.'

'I seem to have upset everybody.'

'Honey, they're just running their numbers. Don't take it personally.'

She's looking at me the way she did in Max and Frankie's garden, but it's somehow too much now I'm sober. 'You can't go yet, anyway,' she says. 'There's something I have to show you.' She pulls me towards the door.

'Where now?'

'Home. Two minutes from here. It's practically next door.'

'Hey, Astrid, what's up?' A tall blond guy is standing by our abandoned table with three plates of salad.

'Put them in boxes, Jason,' Astrid says, 'I'll come by later and settle up.'

So I follow Astrid along the dusty strip of tarmac beside the highway to the place where she lodges with Mo and Jake and Natalie. She strides ahead of me, looking like a Victorian waif in her ankle boots and her flimsy black dress. We're hemmed in by single-storey frontages of stucco and painted wood, and by vehicles that pass us at terrifying speed.

Astrid pushes open a door and I follow her in. She kicks the door shut behind her, and it's calm again. There's a shadowy hallway with doors leading off it and a downward staircase. The room ahead, beyond the archway, is draped with fabrics, fringed and tasselled, gathered into swags, faded by sunlight. There are mirrors with lengths of silk hanging from their frames. Moth-eaten Persian rugs overlap on the floor. There's a bronze Buddha and some gongs. There are candlesticks and candles. There's a huge Celtic cross on the wall carved in wood. The room opens straight on to a deck, which is where all the light comes from.

'The kitchen's through there,' Astrid says, pointing to an alcove off to one side. 'Help yourself to whatever. I'll be right back.' She puts the back of her hand against my face, as though checking the temperature. 'Don't stress, okay. They're all crazy – but who isn't, if you think about it?' She moves back towards the hall and out of sight, leaving me with my mouth open and a *yes, but* forming in my head.

With the front door shut, there's nothing to suggest that we're anywhere near a road, nothing to distract from the mesmeric washing of waves on the beach. After a moment, I hear a murmur of voices from below and footsteps on the stairs. I walk through to the deck, and look down over the wooden railing to a narrow strip of sand and rocks and the churning water of the Pacific. I'm still worrying about Rebecca. It's not like her to phone from work.

'We need tea.' It's Mo in the kitchen, putting the kettle on.

I leave the deck and stand in the kitchen doorway. 'Anything I can do to help?'

'I'll let you know,' she says.

'Is she feeling better?'

'She was disturbed on my behalf, I think. Nattie's attuned at the deepest level.'

'On *your* behalf?'

'Because I'm Irish.' She takes hold of my hand and squeezes hard. 'I don't expect you to get it, but there's a sea of ancestral pain, right here in this room, washing between us.'

'What part of Ireland? You must have been young when you left.' I'm surprised I haven't detected an accent.

'My people are from Donegal.' She's gone back to her tea-making. She's putting bags in a pot. 'My great-grandparents were driven out during the famine.'

'The great potato famine?'

'I don't suppose you know much about it. The English have written it out of the history books.' She empties the kettle into the teapot. A cloud of steam rises to the ceiling. 'Famine is, in any case, a romantic word for genocide.'

'Your great-grandparents?'

'Across the Atlantic to Ellis Island.'

'All eight of them?'

'All eight?'

'Great-grandparents.'

She's holding a tray with the teapot and two mugs on it. Her eyes are intense. 'What makes you think they all made it?' she says.

When she's gone, I wander back into the sitting room. I trip on the edge of the rug, and stumble against an armchair. I see where the edge of the rug is rucked up against the leg of the couch. I get down on my knees to pull it straight, and find myself looking at some sort of totem. It's a black face with huge hollow eyes and a protruding howl of a mouth. I reach under the couch to pull it out. It moves six inches before it snags on something. I give it a gentle tug and it slides out towards me. It's a gas mask, an ugly-looking thing. Tangled in its straps is a small handgun. I wonder if these are Mo's, if this is how she intends to sit out the period of cosmic darkness. I hold the gun, just to feel it in my hand. Then I

push it back under the couch, and take a closer look at the
gas mask. On an impulse I pull it onto my face, and tighten
the straps at the back of my head, standing up to watch
myself in the mirror. There's a smell of canvas and rubber.
The mirror behind me reflects a series of cylindrical snouts
and rubber straps obscuring each other to infinity. I turn my
head to one side and then the other, testing the limits of
my vision, wondering what it would be like to be running,
stumbling in a panic, and wearing such a thing.

When I look again at my reflection, a dark form has
complicated the pattern of images. I spin round. There's a
woman in a burka facing me. No part of her is visible. She
has stepped silently into the room from somewhere – from
another room, or up the stairs from the lower level. Her stillness and her anonymity are unnerving. I pull at the gas mask,
but it catches on my ear. I smile, and feel foolish for smiling,
because she can't see my smile. My hands are fumbling at
the straps on the back of my head.

'Sorry about this,' I say. My voice is muffled. 'I can't seem
to get it off. I'm a friend of Mo's. A friend of Astrid's, really.
Sorry. Didn't mean to startle you.'

Giving up on the straps, I put my hands up to indicate
friendly intentions. The woman doesn't seem startled, but
it's hard to tell. She might be frozen with terror under all
that black material. She might be smiling back at me. She
might be indifferent, or bemused, observing the inexplicable
antics of a foreigner. It occurs to me that her English might
be limited, that she might not speak English at all. But it
would be patronizing to act on that assumption, without
more evidence.

'So you must be staying with Mo. Jake explained to
me on the way over that it's quite a commune.' Over the
woman's shoulder, I see my gas-masked head tilting and
nodding in a grotesque parody of small talk.

Then something odd begins to happen. The woman takes hold of the skirts of the burka and begins pulling it up, exposing her feet and ankles. Her toenails are purple. Her knees appear, and there's a trace of a flimsier material shadowing the rising burka like the lining of a dress. Her skin has a mellow, sun-warmed look. Her thighs are unexpectedly toned. She crosses her arms, letting one side of the garment slip down almost to the knee. Then she catches it, bunching it again around her hips. There's a glimpse of leopard-print underwear, before the lining tumbles free of the heavier fabric and slips down to cover the tops of her legs again. And I see that it's Astrid's dress, lopsided at the hem, Astrid's face appearing from the blackness and her red hair straggling free.

She drops the burka beside her. 'God, it's a weight, though,' she says.

'You scared the life out of me.'

'What about you?' She's laughing as she crosses the room. 'What the hell are you doing with that thing?' She starts fiddling with the buckle.

'Is it yours?' I ask her.

'God, no.'

'You could have said something.'

'But that's the point, isn't it.' She's giggling with excitement and I feel her breath against my face, as the mask comes off. 'I mean it's like the ultimate passive-aggressive power trip. I could be anyone I like, wearing that. It's a prison, but it's a fortress too if you think about it.' She fluffs my hair while she talks, to obliterate the impression of the straps. 'I mean, you can look at a hundred pictures, watch Arab women on CNN, you know, or in airports – you can make all sorts of judgements about it – but get inside that thing and it's another world. You're sort of invisible.'

She's gone to gather up the discarded burka, and I'm left with an impression of her physical proximity.

'I'm so jazzed by this. I wanna wear it out somewhere. Walk up and down Rodeo Drive or something.'

'Is it new?'

'Arrived this morning. I bought it on eBay.'

The murmur of voices in the room below has become louder. There's a crash of breaking glass or china, something thrown or dropped, and Natalie's voice rises in a thin wail like a kettle on the boil.

'Things are kind of crazy around here just now, huh,' Astrid says.

A male voice cuts in, cracking in anguish – Jake must be down there as well – and there's the answering hum of Mo's voice, soft and soothing. For a moment the two overlap and interweave like backing vocals. Then the wail turns into a scream, silencing the other voices, and the scream is the first of a series of screams. A door bangs and there are footsteps on the stairs.

Jake appears, wild-eyed and haggard. 'Why the fuck doesn't she ... I don't fucking see why she can't just ... Why does it always turn out to be so ... fucking ... fucked?' For a moment it looks as though he might be waiting for an answer, then he's gone, slamming the front door behind him.

Downstairs the women's voices rise, then diminish until we can no longer hear them above the noise of the water and the rattling of pebbles down on the beach.

'I need a drink,' Astrid says.

'I take it Natalie is Jake's girlfriend.'

'Not principally. Principally she's Mo's client. Jake's like besotted, but that's kind of Jake's thing, his gift – to be besotted, I mean. He was besotted with me once, which was kind of creepy, as a matter of fact. Natalie is at least more age-appropriate.'

I follow Astrid into the kitchen. 'Mo's her agent, then, or what?'

'Mo's her therapist, honey.'

'And they live together?'

'Mo's got boundary issues – what you gonna do?' She shrugs and turns to open the fridge. 'Red or white?'

'Not for me, thanks. What's she got, then, Natalie? What's Mo treating her for?'

'She's bipolar, I guess, and OCD – you know, obsessive-compulsive – hand-washing and all that, which goes along with the touch-taboo thing. She's bulimic obviously, I mean look at her.' She hands me a bottle of red wine and a corkscrew.

'I really should be going.'

'So you said. Have a drink. Jake'll be back soon enough. He's like tied to this place with an elastic band.'

'Because of Natalie, you mean.'

'If it wasn't Natalie, it'd be someone else.'

She reaches past me and takes two glasses out of the cupboard and puts them on the counter. I'm conscious of the way her dress shifts and rearranges itself as she moves, of what it shows and emphasizes and conceals from one moment to the next.

'They were sort of engaged for a while, when she was here before, then it all broke up and she moved out. He kept the ring on a shelf in his bedroom. Put it in a coral dish under her photo – a kind of shrine. Then Ramona showed up. She was a whole other thing. Christ, was she crazy! A walking encyclopaedia of addictions, and a bit of a klepto as it turned out. Mo likes to have a project. Are you opening that bottle or what?'

'Yes, sorry.' I'm glad to have something to do, and suddenly in need of alcohol.

'Ramona also had a crazy appetite for sex. Screwed everything in pants, including Jake. Poor kid, he didn't know what hit him. After months of waiting to be allowed to hold

Natalie's hand, he's suddenly got Ramona all over him. No wonder he thought it was love. Then one day she's gone, disappeared with a random selection of other people's stuff, including his ring – Natalie's ring.'

The cork slips out with a satisfying pop, and there's that gurgling in the neck of the bottle as I tip it, just before the wine begins slopping into the glass.

'Even then Jake thinks it's some kind of a message – how fucked up is that? – like she's telling him she loves him back.'

She clinks her glass against mine, and we drink.

'So he's waiting for the happy ending, the phone call, whatever, and he runs into this hunk on the beach, this local surfer guy, and the guy's wearing the ring on his pinkie. Naturally, Jake goes berserk and the guy punches him in the mouth. Of course, if you think about it, that's the happy ending Jake was sort of waiting for all along. He's never happier than when some woman's stomping on his self-esteem.'

'Poor Jake.'

'Yeah, poor Jake. Do you wanna watch the sunset?'

'Why not?' I follow her out onto the deck.

'That's the thing about guys, though, I sometimes think. When it comes down to it, they either want to hurt you or be hurt by you. And some of them swing both ways, if you know what I mean.'

I'm standing beside her, leaning on the railing, and our arms are not quite touching. It's still warm, but there's a breeze stirring. There's a big red sun streaked with cloud, and it's just losing its lower edge as it sinks into the ocean. And I'm breathing uneasily, because I'm not sure what's supposed to happen next, and I'm hoping it won't be anything much.

Natalie has appeared below us on the beach. She's changed into a white cotton dress – a flouncy thing like a peasant frock in an opera, with flowing sleeves, and a wide flaring skirt. And there are long white ribbons trailing from her hair. She's facing out to sea, staring into the sun.

'It's what I was thinking about earlier,' Astrid says, 'when I had that thing on. What's that about, I mean really? Do you get it, because I sure as hell don't. There's some weird S&M shit going on there I can't unravel. Something obliterated, someone abased – but what and who?'

'Something more than keeping women in their place, you think?'

'In their place, sure, but what a place to keep them in. I was in Florence earlier in the year. There were these two women on the Ponto Vecchio – identically veiled, only the eyes showing. One of them had a camera. They took pictures of each other, one after the other, and I thought, What's the second picture for?' She giggles. 'Was that bad of me?'

'Wicked.'

Natalie turns and looks up the beach towards the house. I look down and see the video camera and the top of Mo's head and Mo's foreshortened body progressing unsteadily towards the water. Natalie spins round to face the ocean again, setting everything in motion – her frock and her hair and the ribbons in her hair. She walks on tiptoe down the beach until the water is washing around her ankles. Mo circles behind her, solid and maternal, shuffling bare-footed through the sand.

'What's this thing with the video camera?'

'Some kind of therapy. Nowness Enhancement Work, she calls it. It's her own invention. She likes that it spells New.'

'Does it help?'

Astrid shrugs. 'Must do. She's thinking of going digital.'

I laugh as though Astrid's made a joke, and Astrid laughs, so maybe she has. Unless it's just being here that's making us both laugh, with the day holding its last breath and the horizon tilting towards us.

Natalie is holding up her right hand the way evangelicals do when they're channelling the Holy Spirit. The sleeve has fallen to the elbow. Now the water is surging around her knees, sucking at the hem of her dress. She twirls more sluggishly, slowed down by the waves. A couple of steps later, they're lapping at her waist. Her left hand, which has been swaying at her side, suddenly begins to move through the air in a wide circle. There's a glint of something in it that catches the sun as it moves, and I think for a moment of Jake's ring, but that's long gone with Ramona and the surfer guy. The moving hand reaches the raised arm like a violinist's bow brought down against the strings. There's a convulsive movement of the shoulders, and blood spurts from the raised wrist. There's blood on the dress. I watch without moving as Natalie sinks, and she sinks as though there's nothing inside the dress, as though it's a costume from a magician's wardrobe after the magician's assistant has slipped away. And then there's only a fan of hair swirling in the discoloured water. Then only the water. I hear a scream and see Mo running, and I hear the soft impact of the video camera hitting the sand and the crash of Astrid's wine glass.

four

The cab pulls away and the road is empty. I can hear the wind chimes in the next-door garden. I climb the stairs, feeling in my trouser pockets for the keys. They're still there, though the trousers have been in and out of the ocean and hung up to dry. It's not yet day, but the sky is opening up towards the east, grey and cold behind the rectangular shapes of the city. I take my shoes off, stiff from their soaking, and unlock the door to the apartment.

I fill a glass of water from the cooler and listen to the bubbles glugging in the plastic bottle. I drain the glass and fill it again, feeling slightly queasy. I've been sitting in that cab in a kind of stupor, conscious of the stale smell of leather and heated air, wanting to be home and in bed. It occurs to me that I must be an unusually callous person. Perhaps it's a male thing to be so untouched. Perhaps it's an English thing.

There wasn't time, of course, while it was happening, to indulge in anything that could be identified as an emotion – the three of us up to our waists, up to our chests among the rocks, Natalie tossed and flipped by the waves – a missed footing and there could so easily have been another death. And our hands reaching for her – Astrid's first, then mine and Mo's – finding an ankle, a knee, dragging her up the beach, a skinny arm dragging, the head flopping weirdly, and a gash of blood along the sand. Then phone calls, and a space like falling, and knowing you're falling but not having hit the ground, before the technicians turn up, the paramedics and the police. People who know what to do with a dead person, who have their languages for keeping things in order. And for a while you answer questions and do what they tell you, and there's sympathy and suspicion and more questions, and someone at some point gives you a leaflet on grief counselling and that's feelings taken care of. Except that Jake must be found, and I've nothing to contribute to the search; not knowing this place, and then, not knowing Jake, must leave it to Mo and Astrid to find words for this unspeakable thing. So I pick up the broken pieces of Astrid's wine glass from the deck, and wash some dishes, and tidy the kitchen. And eventually there's nothing left for any of us to do but stare into the horror of the event. And even then some watchful corner of my brain distances itself from the hysteria and the grief and the incredulous retellings of what just happened.

As I open the door into the bedroom, Rebecca mutters something. Her voice is throaty with sleep. She says my name like a question, and I tell her not to wake up. She yawns, with little moaning noises, and I hear her lips and tongue working and then settling again with a sigh. An arm pushes its way up onto the pillow, dragging the sleeve of her nightie, and her body shifts languidly under the quilt. I am aware of my own exhaustion. I want to be lying next to her. There's this longing for warmth and physical comfort, and then a sexual feeling, like a pulse of energy. The sky has brightened behind the blinds, and pale bands of light follow the contours of her hips and her shoulders.

Her eyes open drowsily, and she says, 'What happened to you?'

'Go back to sleep.'

'I thought you'd gone off somewhere.'

'Gone off?'

'Walked out, left me.'

I sit on the bed, and gently touch her face. She looks different somehow.

'Unless that was a dream,' she says. 'I think that was a dream.'

'Where would I go?'

'Is that why you don't – because you've nowhere to go?'

'I love you. You know that?'

'Mmm?'

'It isn't time to get up yet.'

'Time to get up? Am I late?' She's dragging herself awake. 'What time is it?'

'It's not even six.'

'Bloody hell, David.' She supports herself on one elbow. 'Have you just got back?'

'Did you get my message? I phoned and left a message.'

'I was in the bath. I called you back but I couldn't get through.'

'I'm sorry. My jacket was still on the deck, probably. There was so much going on. Look, go back to sleep. I'm sorry I woke you.'

'What deck? What's happened to you? Did you have an accident?' She puts her hand on my cheek and turns my face as though looking for signs of damage.

'No, really. It was nothing.' Why am I saying this? It's the opposite of nothing. It's so big I can't get my mind around it and the words that might describe it stick in my throat.

'David, your shirt's damp. It's not raining, is it?'

'No. We'll talk about it in the morning.'

'It is the morning.'

'But you can stay in bed for a bit.'

'You look wrecked. Where were you, for God's sake?' She pushes the quilt back and gets to her feet.

'There was an accident – not me, somebody else. I was just helping out.'

She's walking towards the bathroom with her hands up in a gesture of surrender, and this is when I realize what's different about her.

'What did you do to your hair?'

She turns round, fingering it self-consciously.

'Oh, yes, what do you think?'

'I don't know. You've always had it long.' It's cropped to a few inches below the ears, and it's flat on one side and sticks out on the other. 'Is that what it's going to look like?'

She covers it now with her hands. 'David, I've just got out of bed.' She walks into the bathroom, slamming the door behind her.

I listen to her peeing, and the rush of water as she flushes the toilet. I don't want to fight with her. I make myself stand up. 'Do you want some breakfast?'

She shouts back, 'Of course I want some breakfast.' And I hear the shower running.

I put some bread in the toaster and set the table. The smell of the coffee as it brews makes me feel sick again. I was looking at a menu in that place called Moonglows when Rebecca phoned, and then we all left without eating. And what have I had since? A bite of a sandwich is all I can remember. The toast pops up. It can't be more than sixteen or seventeen hours since I left here with Jake. It's hard to put in order everything that's happened.

Rebecca's using the hairdryer. After a few minutes she comes out of the bedroom buttoning her blouse. It's all right, actually, her hair. It's a bit startling that's there's so little of it, but it spikes out evenly around her face now she's given it some attention.

She moves with a kind of defiance, challenging me to

criticize. 'I'm sorry – it just took me by surprise,' I tell her. 'It looks fine, actually.'

'I wasn't asking for your approval.'

I pour her a mug of coffee. 'Yesterday, when you phoned, what was bothering you?'

There's something evasive in the way she laughs. 'Nothing much. Why, what did I say?'

'Only that you wanted to talk.'

'Yes, well obviously you were busy, so I just got on with it, I suppose.'

'You got on with what?'

'With whatever it was.'

'You sounded upset.'

'I wasn't expecting to have to make an appointment.' She looks at me, narrowing her eyes. 'There's something weird about you.'

'And you've only just noticed?' It comes out like a line from an old routine, but I mess up the timing, or the tone's wrong – she doesn't get the joke, just more of the weirdness.

She smears a piece of toast with low-fat spread. 'Among other things, Frankie's worried about Max. He's been getting threatening messages and phone calls about this documentary he's producing.'

'Can't his secretary deal with that kind of thing? I assume he's got a secretary.'

'What's his secretary got to do with it?'

'To answer all these messages. I mean *you* have to deal with admin all the time.'

'They're anonymous, David. Somebody's threatening him.'

'You didn't say that. You didn't say anonymous.'

'Well, I'm saying it now, all right. He's getting anonymous messages. He's being threatened.'

'What's it about, then, this documentary?'

'It's part of a series called Women Speak Out. They're all based in LA. This one's about Muslim women who are in conflict with their families over something or other. One of them wants to be a stand-up comic. One of them's left her husband because he beats her.'

'Sounds like campaigning stuff.'

'Are you being sarcastic?'

'No. No really, I'm not. I'm just wondering about the timing of it.'

She has the corner of a half-slice of toast in her mouth and she looks at me in a challenging kind of way.

'You know, it just seems like a rather obvious target these days. Moral outrage against the men in beards is sort of main-stream.'

'So you *were* being sarcastic.' She starts eating again.

'I was just wondering . . . I don't know . . . who's going to watch it. What effect is it meant to have?'

'So we should put all this stuff on hold, you think. Just because America seems to have it in for Islam, Muslim men are suddenly exempt. They can do what they like.'

'Hang on a minute . . .'

'Just because you're stuck into some alpha-male conflict with the American government, honour killings and genital mutilation are suddenly off the table, no longer our business.'

'I didn't say any of that.'

She takes a gulp of coffee. 'No, I don't suppose you did.'

I get up and walk towards the sink, and then to the window. I'm too agitated to eat.

Rebecca says, 'I'd better go.'

'You've got hours yet.'

'I can beat the traffic for once.' She's on her way to the bedroom.

I feel panic at the thought of her going. I look out at the neighbouring yard – overgrown palms and eucalyptus trees crowding the space between the barbecue and the plastic hot tub – and along the lines of shallow roofs, the stucco walls with aluminium windows, the scruffy patches of vegetation. It all feels dusty and arid and foreign. The fear of being alone here comes to me as a cluster of physical sensations, a speeding of the heart, a tightness in the throat, a prickling that starts at the back of my neck and spreads up over my scalp. I feel an intense resentment that I've followed her to this place where I suddenly don't want to be without her.

'You look awful.' She's standing in front of me again. She's put on some make-up around her eyes and a mauve linen jacket that I haven't seen before. She's offering an olive branch, I know that. She's also asking a question. But what I have to tell her needs more time – I can't just toss it out as she heads for the door, like *A funny thing happened to me on the beach last night*.

I shrug and try on a smile. 'Must be the thought of genital mutilation.'

'It isn't all about that stuff. I told you, it's a series. It's not all about Muslims.' She turns away and walks over to the coffee table. I've disappointed her.

She's leaning over to pick up some books and folders and I see it's a new skirt as well – shorter than she usually wears. It shows off her legs, the softly muscled bulk of them, so much more than I can get my hands round. Natalie's not twelve hours dead and all I can think about is sex – what's the matter with me?

'The others are about all kinds of other things. Just women speaking out – that's what it's called.'

'That skirt suits you.'

'Thanks.' I've made her self-conscious again.

'Have some more coffee before you go.'

'No, you finish it.' She's arranging things in her bag.

I start clearing the table. 'So what else are they speaking out about?'

'All sorts of things.'

'Such as?'

She looks up. 'Are you really interested?'

'Of course I'm interested.'

'Well, for example . . .' She hesitates, looking at me as though she's searching for something. 'For example, one of them deals with women who work part time in the sex industry – prostitution, stripping, that kind of thing. All the crap they have to take from their clients and pimps and boyfriends and so on, and how they cope with it.' She pauses.

I know she's talking partly because I'm not talking. In a minute I'll just say it – someone died, I was there. Until I say it, it's a pressure in my head.

'Another one's about cosmetic surgery, women who have it done, or are in conflict with someone over it. There's a woman whose pea-brained husband is forcing her to have implants. And there's a seventeen-year-old – a bit of a star, apparently – in the documentary, I mean – whose father offers to get her a nose job for her eighteenth birthday, but their rabbi tells her it's anti-Semitic. That's one of the lighter stories.'

'That's ridiculous.' My irritation takes me by surprise.

'What? What exactly is ridiculous in your opinion?' She drops a book on the table. 'The nose job? The objection to the nose job? The plight of a young woman stuck between male authority figures?'

'Plight? Have you been writing the blurb for this show?'

'I knew you'd be insulting about it.' She slings her bag over her shoulder and makes for the door.

'Well, come on, Becca, you've got to admit it all sounds a bit shallow.'

She turns on me with her hand on the doorknob. 'You're determined not to like these people.'

'These strippers and nose-job people, you mean, or these LA people in general?'

'Max and Frankie, I mean.'

'What difference does it make to you whether I like Max and bloody Frankie or not?'

'I have to work with them.'

'With Frankie. Not with Max, as far as I know.'

'Yes, with Frankie, who helps Max from time to time because he's her husband.'

'This argument is stupid. I don't even know what it's about.'

'Well it's not about this, that's for sure.'

'Not about what?'

'About whatever it is we're talking about. It's about you picking a fight because you feel bad because you were out all night and apparently can't tell me what the hell you were doing.'

'You only had to ask.'

'You only had to tell me.' She's waiting with her eyebrows raised and her mouth slightly open and her hands and shoulders halfway to a shrug.

'This girl killed herself.'

She's appalled. 'Which girl?'

'A woman, a young woman. She used a razor blade. Or she drowned, or hit her head, or something.'

'She killed herself but you don't know how?'

'I saw it happen – all right?'

'Who was this? You said you'd gone for a walk on the beach.'

'I was with Astrid.'

'Who?'

'The woman at the party, the one who jumped in the pool.'

She lowers her bag to the floor. 'So that's it.'

'No, she just wanted to ask me some things. It's not important . . .'

'I'll decide what's important.'

'I watched this girl cut her wrist with a razor blade. It wasn't very nice. And I feel somehow responsible, which is absurd because I know I was just an accidental part of it, but I can't help feeling it needn't have happened if things had gone differently.'

'Things? What things? Christ, David, what did you do to her? Who is this girl?'

'Just a girl who was living with Astrid and Mo.'

'Who are these people? What were you doing there?'

'I told you. Astrid's got hold of this idea that I can tell her all about Islam. She wanted to show me her burka.'

'I bet she did.'

Rebecca's humourless snigger ignites something in me, a kind of outrage at the injustice of her assumptions, a knowledge of how close to the mark she is without knowing it, a frustration at my inability to explain. I'm saying things out loud without knowing what I expect them to mean. 'Why can't you just, for once . . .' I begin to say. 'Why assume that I . . .' But I don't know how to finish either of these sentences, and anyway I find myself unable to speak, because something odd is happening to my breathing. I'm staring at Rebecca as though the intensity of my expression will make words unnecessary and my view of her is suddenly obscured. I look away. The light from the window is a blur, and the tears are wet on my face, and the catch in my breath has developed into a sobbing, a series of juddering spasms that drag air into my lungs and push it back out again. There are strange monkey noises coming from my throat. I taste the saltiness of tears and diluted mucus around my mouth.

My body has taken control of itself, leaving my mind free to register discomfort at the fraudulence of this behaviour. I have a sense that I could stop this any time if I really wanted to, except that, having started, there seems no particular reason to stop. All this thinking is slow and placid, as though taking place in some meditative corner of my brain.

Rebecca has drawn me down onto a chair. She holds my head and pulls it towards her shoulder, murmuring things like 'Poor David' and 'It must have been awful for you' and 'I'm so sorry' and other things I can't quite make out because one of her hands is moving across my left ear and my right ear is pressed against her breast. But I can tell that she's crying too, and I'm not sure if she's crying out of sympathy, or because she has her own private things to cry about, or out of frustration that I've somehow usurped the role of victim by this uncharacteristic display of feeling.

Then my phone makes the noise that means someone has sent me a text message. Nothing happens for a while, except Rebecca rocking me back and forward, my strenuous sobbing, her silent stream of tears. Then the other phone rings – the landline – and Rebecca picks it up.

'He can't talk right now.' She's dabbing her eyes with her handkerchief, and wiping the purple streaks from her face. 'Yes, he got home okay. Who is this?' She rolls her eyes. 'Well, I suppose you'd better tell him yourself.' She hands me the phone, and sits on the other side of the table with her head in her hands.

I blow my nose and clear my throat.

'Hey, I hope I didn't wake your wife.' It's Astrid. 'She seems kind of crabby.'

'No, we're both awake.' My voice feels sore, as though I've been shouting.

'You sound rough.'

'So do you.'

'We're all still in shock, you know. Don't expect too much of yourself. Take some time out for repairs.'

'I'll see what I can do.'

'This is huge, sweetie. Huge is the only way to describe what this is.'

'You're probably right.'

'Jake's a complete mess.'

'That's hardly surprising. How's Mo?'

'Hard to tell. She wants to do something – some sort of ritual. I've told her it's too early, but she seems pretty definite about it. We've got to help Nattie move on, Mo says. Wherever she is just now, she still needs us. It's Nattie's trauma, Mo says, before it's ours. And I don't know if it's a good idea or just Mo having one of her crazy moods, but either way, I figure it can't do any harm. We thought Thursday night on the beach.'

'On the beach?'

'Where she died.'

'To do what, exactly?'

'Whatever it takes, I guess.'

'Are you talking about some sort of exorcism?'

'Could you do one of those?'

Rebecca's staring at me with her mouth open.

'Definitely not,' I say.

'But you can come.'

'You want me there? Does Mo want me?'

Rebecca gets up and starts clattering plates and mugs into the sink.

'I think it would be important – don't you?'

'She hardly knows me. I was with Natalie for ten minutes.'

'You were there, David. We went through this experience together. We need completion.'

Rebecca's got her bag over her shoulder, and she's on her way out the door as I put the phone back on its stand.

She gets back later than usual. I'm rinsing vegetables at the sink, and I'm relieved to hear her car pulling into the garage. She comes in looking tired but otherwise all right, carrying a piece of board under her arm. As she manoeuvres it through the doorway I see that it's a block-mounted poster.

'It's from the museum shop,' she says. She drops her book bag onto the table and carries the poster into the bedroom.

I follow her, drying my hands on a tea towel.

'I thought over the desk, or there by the window.' She rests the poster on the floor and looks around, considering the options.

Generally I like this about her, that her response to an emotional problem is just to get on with things. It's not so comfortable when the emotional problem she's responding to is me. There's something unnerving about this jaunty manner after all that happened this morning. It puts me on the lookout for signs of hostility. The hair doesn't help – cropped like that, without any warning, as though to remind me that she's her own person.

'Can I be of any hindrance?' I ask.

She holds the poster above the desk. 'I thought we needed something to brighten up the room.'

'You brighten up the room.'

'Very funny,' she says, meaning it isn't very funny but she doesn't mind that I said it. She drops the poster on the bed and I give her a hug. She clings to me, digging her fingers into my back, and I'm not sure whether she's comforting me or asking for reassurance. We stand like that for a moment, then she pulls away, tilting her head to look at the poster. 'What do you think?'

It's a Turner with some lettering advertising an exhibition. I squint at it and make a show of massaging my jaw. 'What's that supposed to represent, then?' I ask her.

'At a guess,' she says, playing along, 'I'd say it's a sunrise between two headlands.'

'Blimey, how d'you make that out?'

'Well, don't you think this orange smudge looks exactly like a headland?'

'To your highly trained eye, maybe.'

'And this darker smudge? Obviously another headland, dark because it's in shadow. And this burst of yellow in the middle? Couldn't be anything other than the sun rising over the sea.'

'And does it have a title?

'Yes. It's called – ' she lifts it up to read the label on the back – 'Sunrise Between Two Headlands.'

'Uncanny.'

'I do my best.'

'Well, it's certainly colourful.'

She raises an eyebrow, as though colourful might be a coded insult.

'No, really, it's nice.'

'Well, among those who know about such things . . .'

'Like you.'

'Like me, Turner *is* generally considered to be nice and colourful . . .'

'Just the thing, then.'

'So. Over the desk? Or where?' She picks it up and carries it to the piece of blank wall between the window and the bathroom. 'Is it lost here, maybe?'

'Perhaps it is a bit lost.'

She lowers it and looks around, biting her lip. Her face lightens up as she remembers something. 'The boy who sold it to me, you'll never guess what he said. First he said, Isn't Turner just the best, which made me think he must be really intelligent. But then he spoilt it by saying, Have a truly outstanding day.'

'And are you?'

'Am I what?'

'Having a truly outstanding day?'

She watches me while she lets out a breath. 'Well, it stands out, I suppose, though not so far in a particularly good way.'

'And is there anything I can do?'

'I don't know. Is there?' She frowns, and there's something cautious, almost fearful, in the way she looks at me. She holds out the poster for me to take. 'Try it over there.'

'Wait till I take my shoes off.'

'Okay.'

So I'm standing on the bed, holding the poster above the headboard, while Rebecca turns her head this way and that, as though finding a place for this poster is all that's happening. And I'm wondering if it's honestly the bedroom that needs brightening up. The room is spacious by London standards and inoffensively blank – white walls, stained wood doors and windows, the kind of blinds with vertical strips you see in offices. The desk is nominally mine, though I tend to wander these days, like a dog circling for a comfortable place to lie – it's one of the marks of my unease. The telly's in here as well because this is where we found a cable socket that worked. There's a door to the bathroom and the French windows opening on to the deck, around which gather the gnarled branches of an avocado tree and sprays of shabby, brown-edged palm fronds. The vegetation filters out some of the heat, which is good, and a lot of the light, which isn't so good.

'Six inches lower,' Rebecca says, taking a step back.

So this is mainly where we work and sleep, which leaves the other room for everything else. Kitchen at one end, living room at the other, with a transitional dining table; it's all pale wood and glass in the international flat-pack style. There's a patch of hallway by the front door, and what the landlord quaintly calls the powder room, and that's our apartment. No reason why we shouldn't be as happy here as anywhere, if we chose to be, if I could forget how far it is to the nearest Tube station, if Rebecca could overlook my various shortcomings and misdemeanours. And choosing to be happy is the meaning of her sunrise between two headlands, I'm assuming – which is fine, unless it also means that she's preparing to be happy in spite of me, in spite of my gloom, in spite of my new friends.

'No,' Rebecca says, 'it's going to have to go over the desk.'

'So we'll be able to see it from here.' I lower the picture and rest it on the pillows at my feet. 'You can wake up to it every morning – Turner's sunrise.'

'That's true.' She's turned her back, eyeing the space.

'Do you want me to put it up?'

She faces me again with a determined look that I don't like. 'What I want you to do, actually, David, is to change your plans for Thursday evening.' So that's it, then.

'How do you mean, change my plans?'

'I don't see why you have to go to this exorcism thing.'

'It's not an exorcism.'

'Whatever it is, I don't see why you have to get mixed up in it.'

I'm not sure how to respond. I feel committed. I can't back out now. And I don't want to back out, even if I could.

But before I've worked out how to explain any of this, she says, 'I might need the car anyway.'

'So you can work late on Max's documentary?'

She glares at me for a moment. 'I'm going to get the hammer,' she says.

So I'm back in the kitchen, lifting a pan off the draining board, pouring some olive oil in the bottom, turning on the gas. I'm angry at Rebecca, angry at being made to feel petty, angry at myself for being petty. Rebecca's probably wishing she had some heavier work to do with the hammer than knocking in a picture hook. I'm sorry Turner had to get dragged into this. There are some things we've never argued about. Sex, for example – we've never once argued about sex. And where we go and who we meet, that's another thing we've never argued about. And we've never argued about what we put on the walls. We usually like the same things, and when we don't, I assume Rebecca's right. I've always trusted her when it comes to art. It's what she does. It was what she was doing the first time I saw her.

I'd been wandering through the Tate. There was an empty bench in front of Millais's *Ophelia*, so I sat and watched the water pulling at the edges of her ballooning dress, and that odd gesture as she sinks, like a priest praying. People came and went. Then this woman was in the way. After a bit, she backed towards the bench and sat down beside me. I guessed she was in her late twenties, younger than me but not too much younger, with a lovely expressive face. She scrabbled in her canvas shoulder bag for a bit, and fished out a notebook and a pen. She wrote a page of notes in big bold letters. Then she bent forward to pull off her shoes – ankle boots with low heels. With her knee still raised, she began massaging her foot through the nylon of her tights.

'Hard work,' I said, 'all this culture.'

She turned and looked at me. 'Culture?' She repeated the word as though she was unfamiliar with it.

'Looking at art. Hard on the feet.'

'Oh, I see what you mean. Culture.' She was teasing me, but I didn't mind it. She waved her notebook at *Ophelia*. 'This is your kind of thing, is it?'

I shrugged. 'It's okay.'

'I read in *Time Out* that it's one of Britain's best-loved pictures. Doesn't that strike you as odd?'

'By a British painter, does that mean, or just any painting most British people like?'

She pulled a face. 'How should I know?'

'Best loved – that's nonsense anyway. It just means two people mentioned it, unlike all the other paintings that just got one vote each.'

'What are you talking about – who said anyone voted?'

'Britain's best loved picture, you said.'

'One of. Anyway it's just someone's impression, probably, some journalist. But they might be right, look. There's a crowd round it now.' We looked at the cluster of backs. 'Odd, though, don't you think? A woman doing herself in, and it's one of our favourite pictures.'

'I suppose it's the Shakespeare connection. A double helping of culture.'

'Ah, yes.' She looked at me again, with one eyebrow raised. 'Culture.'

'Look, if there's something about that word that bothers you, I'm not attached to it.'

We were both laughing by then, there was something so outrageous in the way she was going for me, as though by sitting in front of this picture I'd made myself responsible for it, answerable for its iconic status. She told me later that it wasn't like her at all, to talk so freely to someone she didn't know, but I'd invited it somehow – both the teasing and the openness.

'Seriously, though,' she said, 'it is sort of weird, this thing people have for the Pre-Raphaelites, don't you think? I mean what's it all about? The brooches, the ribbons in the hair – my God, the hair!' She gestured around the room. 'And those dreamy, faraway looks. Don't you find it all a bit . . . I don't know . . .'

'Chocolate-boxy?'

'Fetishistic.'

'I'd never really thought about it.'

'Well, you know, those lutes, or whatever they are, the hands in those manipulating postures, playing with themselves, yards of fabric, everything in beautifully contrived disorder . . .'

'Tell me something—'

'And the eyes, so lost in thought, but so perpetually conscious of being looked at.'

'It sounds as though—'

'So many surrogate objects, eroticized extremities, fingers and ankles and throats.'

'You don't really like them at all.'

'Like them?' The question seemed to take her by surprise.

'Well, do you?'

'Not much. They're all a bit naff, aren't they, to be honest.'

'And you're here because . . . ?'

She shrugged apologetically. 'They get a mention in my thesis.'

'Naff is a technical term, then, is it?'

She laughed and I laughed. And she offered to show me what she called the real thing. Naturally, after the women's studies lecture, I thought we were heading for Gwen John, but she led me to a room full of Turners. 'Don't they knock you out?' she said. 'Imagine seeing them for the first time. Paint had never looked like this before.' And that's when I knew I really liked her, when I saw she was more interested in the art than in the argument.

five

The sun has set. Half the moon is showing and a scattering
of stars. We're on the beach, close to the spot where Natalie
did her last dance. We're sitting around the edge of a piece
of woven material that might be a shawl. There are things
on it, things belonging to Natalie, that once belonged to
Natalie – books, jewellery, items of clothing. At the centre
is a cluster of fat candles, their flames dipping and flickering and righting themselves as the wind shifts. The tide is
going out, but it's a steep beach, so the water isn't far away.
In the distance, a late surfer comes into view, bouncing down
the face of a wave. It looks easy until the board swings up
and he flips over and out of sight. Closer to the shore, a wave
tilts towards us, swells and unravels. I watch the fragments
scurrying among the pebbles to reconnect, sucked back
into the body of the water, and I'm struck by the illusion of
coherence, that the ocean, which is just a coincidence of mole-
cules drifting around with whatever is dissolved or suspended in it, appears to act as one thing, like an animal
breathing or stretching in its sleep.

For Mo, the ocean is something you can talk to, like a
goddess, who might listen and respond. She's talking to it
now – looking out towards the horizon, and talking about
Natalie's love of water, her instinct to return at the end to
its embrace, asking it to soothe Natalie with the rhythm of

71

its tides. Mo's voice is insubstantial. She looks ten years older than when I first saw her in Moonglows.

Behind her are the ramshackle frames that hold up the backs of the houses, hunks of timber rising fifteen or twenty feet into shadow, and crude wooden staircases twisting up among them.

Mo has turned her attention to mother earth. She's speaking about the dissolution of Natalie's body. And I'm thinking, Lord let me know mine end, and the number of my days, that I may be certified how long I have to live, and I'm feeling a long way from the Church of England. Astrid sits across from me with her hands in her lap, rocking forward and backward. Her face is wet with tears. It's hard to see Jake's face because he's wearing his baseball cap, and the peak casts a long shadow, but his shoulders are hunched and he holds himself tight. Mo is talking to the moon and the stars. She's talking to Natalie, calling on her spirit, asking us who sit here on the ocean's shore, which is also the border of the earth realm, to open ourselves to Natalie's pain, urging the objects in the circle to open themselves in spirit to Natalie, to whatever it is Natalie is moved to ask of us, anxious to tell us.

Some of the books look like journals. One of them has pressed flowers on the cover and the pages are frayed at the edges like homemade paper. There's a book called *The Path of the Mystic* and one called *How to be Extraordinary* and one called *Act Real*. There's a paperback copy of *Jane Eyre* and a hardback copy of *Goodnight Moon*. They all have the battered look of books that have been read and reread and carried from place to place. There's a large woven shoulder bag, embroidered with poppies. There are scarves and ribbons and half a dozen floppy hats. There's a rag doll. There are some pebbles and a lump of quartz and a chess piece, and a handful of photos with bent corners and holes where drawing pins have been – Natalie in a boat, on a mountain, with Mo, with a couple of friends, with a man who could be her father. There are pictures of other people, but most are of Natalie alone, or looking alone even when she's with other people – unless that's just the way it looks now. But if she had friends, why is it just the four of us sitting round this shawl – her therapist, her housemate, her would-be boyfriend and me?

Astrid is clearing her throat. She has a book open in front of her. She begins reading in a subdued voice, stops to control her breathing, and carries on. She's reading from *The Tibetan Book of the Dead* about the suffering that comes from attachment and regret, and I'm wondering if I could have corrected Natalie's first impression of me if there had been more time. I'm thinking about the conversations we might have had about *Jane Eyre*, which I've read, about what the path of the mystic might be, which ought to get a mention in chapter seven of my book if I ever get that far, about chess, which I can play but not very well. Was she a chess player? Was she interested in chess? In my imagination I'm befriending her, in an avuncular kind of way. I'm saving her life. But I know nothing about her except her unhappiness, and her bizarre story of breathing underwater, and the way she died, and this collection of things laid out on the beach.

Mo is moving a bowl of something in circles over the candles. She sets light to it and I see that it's charcoal. She drops a handful of incense into the bowl and the smoke rises between us in a grey cloud.

Astrid is reading something by a Sufi poet about life flowing towards death as the river flows into the sea, and I'm wondering if things will get easier with Rebecca once this is over, and what else is worrying her apart from the threatening messages Max has been getting, and whether I've been unfair about Max's documentary series, and what it is about Max that I just don't like. And then there's silence and Astrid and Mo are looking at me. They're all holding hands – Jake stiffly, sullenly maybe, it's hard to tell because his head's down. Mo is holding her hand out towards me, with a questioning look. I raise my hand to take hers, pushing my other hand more awkwardly towards Jake's, which lies between us on the edge of the shawl.

'David?' Mo says. Her grip is intense.

'Mo wanted to know if you've got anything to add,' Astrid says.

'Or questions, David. Anything to send out into the spirit realm.'

'Yes, sorry.' I cough a couple of times and feel the phlegm in my throat. 'Questions.' A couple of the candles have gone out. The others are spilling their wax lopsidedly. The yellow light flickers across Natalie's things. I look at *Jane Eyre* and the straw hat with the blue bow and the ebony chess piece. It's a pawn, though it would rival the queens in any set I've played with. It makes me sad to see it, limbless in its ridged skirt, tilting with the slope of the beach, oddly placed among these girlish objects. This sadness is like a weight pressing on me.

Mo's head is down, but her ear is turned towards me. She squeezes my hand, waiting for me to speak. Astrid's eyes move between us.

'Was she a chess player?' I ask.

Now they're all looking at me.

'A chess player?' Mo says.

'Did she play chess?' I drop Mo's hand and reach for the pawn. My fingers fit between its smooth ridges. I'm wondering what it might have meant to Natalie. 'Is this part of a set?' I ask. 'Or just something she had, like a souvenir or an ornament? It's big for a pawn.'

Astrid has this quizzical look on her face. Mo's face is all compassion, as though I've said something profoundly sad. Jake's eyes are fierce, fiercer than usual, and he isn't looking at me any more but at the pawn or at nothing.

six

I'm beginning to get a feel for the grid – the almost reliable logic of it. Which is to say I'm getting a feel for the obstacles – the malls and freeways and studio lots that have you dead-ending and U-turning, the maverick boulevards that snake across the map, tempting you into oblique angles, the sudden escarpments that buckle the adjacent streets. There's a river that has no name, concrete banks rising up out of a smudge of water. People tell me it's called the LA River, which sounds like no name to me. There are no bridges – nothing you'd call a bridge – just places where the buildings end and the ground drops beside the road and rises again and there are more buildings. Somewhere further inland there's the desert I've never seen, whose emptiness, I read somewhere, is already measured out in virtual blocks ready for limitless future development. From time to time, they tell me, when the Santa Anas blow in from the east – the hot winds that drive the smog out over the ocean and dry the skin until you feel you could shed it like a snake – hills leap up behind the buildings to the north, startlingly close.

And always there's the ocean, or the knowledge of the ocean. It's somewhere, ahead, behind, to one side – at the edge of your mental map. You see the tilt of the palm trees, all of them in lines, straining towards moisture. Then you make a westward turn and the road dips and it's suddenly there. It has this way of taking you by surprise. And when you see it like that, when you come face to face with it, you have a sense of its impact. This is where the road trip that is America's history hits the obstacle of water, and the urge to keep moving turns in on itself. I begin to understand this, as I hadn't understood it before. This is the place where the elements collide, where people come to be nurtured or transformed, where bodies must be worshipped or punished into new shapes. I begin to see the pattern underlying this stew of physical indulgence, and psychic exploration and vague cosmic yearning.

I've had an email from Jake. He's asked me to meet him. It's Natalie's car I'm driving. It was Mo's idea. I had to get home after we'd finished doing whatever it is we were doing on the beach, and the car was cluttering up the narrow space between Mo's house and the highway. I felt odd about it, but Mo insisted, and Astrid couldn't see what my problem was.

'Whose is it, actually?' I wanted to know. 'What about her next of kin?'

'If you're talking about her parents, forget it,' Astrid said. 'Her father could buy and sell the lot of us. The bastard could hardly remember where she lived, let alone what she drove.'

'Legally, though. What about . . . I don't know . . . probate, that kind of thing.'

'Look at it,' Astrid said, 'it's a piece of junk.'

We looked at it – an old VW Beetle, with flakes of rust along the trim. The lumpy paintwork was a grey lilac colour under the streetlights.

'Nattie loved it, though,' Mo said, putting out one hand to touch it, and raising the other to her mouth. 'She called it her flying machine.'

Astrid took Mo in her arms and spoke gently across the top of her head. 'Sure she loved it, Mo, I know she loved it. But she loved it for what it is, which is a piece of junk.' That made Mo laugh and then it made her cry.

Rebecca wasn't so happy about it. She didn't say much, but I could tell. In daylight the car is unmistakeably pink, with little stencilled flowers in purple on the doors. There's nothing neutral about it. It's far from anonymous. It's hard not to read it as a statement, that I'm driving it – a statement of what, I couldn't say for sure. But as far as I'm concerned it's a car, and I need a car.

Things are not good between me and Rebecca. She works long hours. I sit at my laptop in the bedroom or out on the deck or at the dining table, trying to work, not working. I feel up and down but always, somehow, on edge. What we were for each other, not so long ago before we came to this place, was a doorway we could walk through any time we felt like it – this way and that, as thoughtlessly as if a door were a chance product of nature, not a constructed thing – as if the world were full of heavy obstacles made weightless. Suddenly it's all drag and resistance. We're becoming unhinged.

I brake sharply because the traffic has stopped. There are a couple of police cars by the side of the road and a crowd of people on the pavement. Something's blocking the street up ahead, an accident maybe. I can't be more than a few hundred yards from the place I'm looking for. There's a sign pointing to Venice Community College, which must be where Jake studies the distorting effects of capitalism on personal relationships. The driver in front of me does a U-turn, edging his way into the line of oncoming traffic. I follow him, backtrack for a couple of blocks, pull into a strip mall and park. The engine of Natalie's flying machine coughs and judders and falls silent. The printout of Jake's email is lying on the passenger seat. I pick it up and read it again.

> dave, your probably still mad at me and maybe i
> deserve it but somebody shd know what ive found and

i cant think of anyone else, and maybe you sort of owe
me? on my way to 2 lips on vnc and 20th by the college,
ill be there from 11 on for maybe an hour. im googling
this fucker, im trying not to make him wrong, but he shd
know what he did to nat. sorry im not thinking strait,
please be there.

I guessed that vnc must be Venice Boulevard and I seem
to have got that right. But I'm wondering what kind of place
2 lips might be. I've see the billboards advertising places with
names like all4you and Xposé, but I don't suppose Jake
wants to meet me in a strip club.

I walk past a flower shop called Darling Buds and Mike's
Liquor Store and Starbucks and a place called Dreamboat
Sushi, and back towards where the traffic stopped.

The plaster columns that mark the entrance to the college rise up behind the crowd and the queues of traffic. In
front of the building, and blocking half the street, there's
a fire engine and a cluster of ambulances. More police cars
straddle the pavement. The building is set back from the
street. As I get closer I catch glimpses of grass, and I see
the barriers that have been set up around it, a system of plastic rails and bollards. My eyes are drawn to the figures in
white, to their bulky plastic overalls and beekeepers' head-
gear – protection against hazardous material. One of these
white suits emerges through the double door, and another
one behind. Between them they carry a stretcher. There's a
young woman rolling on it, clinging to the edge. They shuffle
down the steps, manoeuvring their load between the hud-
dles of people.

They're lying on the steps, these people, and on the
grass, and others squat over them. Some of the medics, if
that's who they are, wear gas masks and protective clothing.
Someone's shouting orders through a megaphone. My view

is obscured by heads. It's a student crowd, looking on, noisy and curious. I make my way further up the street until my way is blocked by an ambulance. I'm standing next to a young black woman. I ask her what's going on. She opens her mouth to answer, and I find myself pushed up against her. I turn to see a stretcher swinging past. There's a teen-age boy on it who might be Korean or Vietnamese. For a moment I'm looking into his face. He looks back indiffer-ently, whistling. He winks at me. Did I see him wink? He's wearing a green armband. The wounded wear armbands in different colours like members of competing militaristic parties. I turn to apologize to the woman.

She shrugs. 'Hey, it's no problem,' she says. 'It's an exer-cise. They're testing the emergency services, so they say, in case of an attack.'

'Are you a student here?'

'A teacher.' She gives me a lovely smile. 'I was supposed to take the day off. There was an email, apparently, but not everybody got it.'

'So you've had have a wasted journey.'

'All the way from Eagle Rock. I just made my feelings known to the principal. And do you know what he said? He said, Doris, you won't get an email when Armageddon's due. Isn't that something? I said, Harold, you sure do have a way with words. Don't you think that could be the first line of a song, though?'

'It certainly should be. It might be a huge hit.'

'Say, you should come into my English class, so my students can hear what Wordsworth ought to sound like.'

I take Jake's email out of my jacket pocket. 'I don't sup-pose you know a place called two lips?'

'Sure I do, the two lip café, it's practically part of the college.' I hear the tulip as she says it, her lips opening and closing around the word. She nods up the street. 'But I think you'll find it requisitioned, like everything else.'

I push my way round behind the ambulance and walk past half a dozen cars.

Jake's voice reaches me, before I see him. 'This is bull-shit. What the fuck is this? Jesus!' The greasy shade of his red baseball cap bobs in and out of view like the beak of an exotic bird.

Leaving the street, I nudge through the crowd towards him. On the other side of the barrier, a policeman in a short-sleeved shirt is coming our way. His chest and buttocks are ready to burst out of the uniform. Hanging from his hips are the tools of his trade – nightstick, radio, a surprisingly bulky gun in a polished holster. His face is handsome in a brutal kind of way. He strikes me as a walking parody – a cartoon cop, a gay pin-up – but he's the genuine article. The wounded are student volunteers, the hazardous materi-als are imaginary, but the cops are real. Behind him, inside the barriers, is the Tulip Café. The outside tables are full of people in uniform, drinking coffee, eating muffins. The place has been commandeered.

'You,' the cop says, 'step back from the rail.' He's talking to Jake, a scrawny figure with his backpack bulging behind him.

'Man, this is fucking surreal.'

'What did you say to me?'

'I said surreal.'

'I don't appreciate you cursing at my officers, young man.' A black policewoman has appeared. In build, she's not unlike her male colleague, except that she's six inches shorter and the bulges are more rounded.

Jake looks murderously angry. 'Fuck this.'

The cop squares up to Jake as though he's preparing to wrestle him to the ground. 'You got a problem?'

'Damn straight I got a problem.'

'Well, take your problem the fuck out of here.'

I put a hand on Jake's shoulder. 'Stay calm, Jake.' People around us are looking to see what happens next. We're suddenly street theatre, reality TV. Further off, the traffic crawls past. Drivers with their elbows out take in the scene, rocking their heads to conflicting rhythms.

'You're the problem, man,' Jake is saying to the cop, 'you're the fucking problem.'

'What did you say to me?'

'You heard what I said.'

'Jake, let's go. You had something to show me.'

He turns to me, too agitated to stop his body moving. 'This is fucking shit, you know?'

'Don't worry about it. It's not the only cafe in town.'

'I'm warning you, young man.'

'He's upset,' I tell the policewoman. 'A friend of his just died. Practically one of the family.'

'Who the fuck are you to say why I'm upset? You didn't even know her. She didn't even know who the fuck you were.'

'Come on, Jake, let's go somewhere and talk about it.'

I can't get his attention. His head is down, moving from side to side, his eyes fixed on some inner picture.

'Look, I got your email.' I'm reaching in my inside jacket pocket for the folded piece of paper, when I'm jostled from behind. I stumble against the barrier, colliding with Jake. There's a rush of movement and a noise like a ratchet, and then a sudden stillness. Six inches from the bridge of my nose there's a gun, and the handsome brutal face of the policeman is staring at me over the top of it. At the edge of my vision I see people crouching, edging away.

'Don't move the hand,' he says. There's a dangerous rasp in his voice. 'The hand stays just where it is.'

'Easy, Dougy, easy,' the policewoman says. The sounds of the megaphone, of the oblivious bystanders, of the car engines, are still there, but muted. What I hear mainly is the rushing of my own blood. She's reaching under the lapel of my jacket, feeling past my wrist, past my knuckles, with the plump pads of her fingers, into the pocket. Her head is turned as though she's breaking into a safe. I get a close-up of the freckles on her cheek, the steady, watchful eye. Slowly she pulls out Jake's email. I can sense the tension going down around me. I hear the long outward breaths. But the gun is still in my face.

'Easy, Dougy,' the policewoman says, no louder than a murmur.

He lifts the gun so that it's pointing into the sky and, without taking his eyes off mine, adjusts something with both hands, making that ratchet sound again. He's putting the safety catch back on, or uncocking it, or doing whatever it is you do to a gun to stop it from killing someone. I watch the thing sliding into his holster, and feel my breath coming out.

'Yo, Dougy,' some joker calls out, 'take it easy, man.'

'Hey, Dougy, what you doing with that gun in your hand?'

Suddenly everybody knows him by his first name and they're all giving him advice.

'Take a break, Dougy.'

'Do what the boss says, Dougy.'

'Hey, Dougy, time to kick the Prozac.'

And the name ripples outward through the crowd. Dougy is looking at me as though he regrets not pulling the trigger while he had the chance, pouring all his rage, all his humiliation into this look.

I find I've still got my left hand out in front of me, an instinctive defence, or a learnt posture of submission that came to me so naturally that I've only just noticed it. The policewoman has her hand on Dougy's shoulder. She steers him away from the barrier, towards Tulip's, and at last he's looking somewhere else.

She turns to me. 'I suggest you get your young friend out of here before someone gets hurt.'

I feel inclined to hug her, to kiss her on both freckled cheeks, this woman who has saved my life, with whom I've shared a moment of intimacy. I resist the impulse. 'Come on, Jake, let's go.'

A space has cleared around us. Jake seems to set off in three directions at once. Decision is beyond his reach, but the inactivity of indecision is killing him. I take his arm and draw him away through the crowd. 'Where I left the car,' I tell him, 'there's a Starbucks.'

'No way,' he says, 'no fucking way.'

'You're right, coffee is probably not what you need right now. Do you realize, do you have any idea how close to death I was back there?'

'A Starbucks on every corner – what a vision of the future. Piped straight to your car is actually what the fuckers have in mind. A spigot grafted into your fucking bloodstream, and a charge on your credit card every time your heart beats. No fucking way.'

'Not Starbucks, then. A bar, maybe. You need a stiff drink, something to slow you down. I need a drink, anyway.'

He stops and faces me. 'Jesus, Dave, I'm nineteen, we're in the middle of a fucking LAPD rally. What planet are you on?'

We're passing a Mexican fast-food place, with tables on the pavement. I steer Jake towards a plastic chair. He takes his backpack off and drops it on the ground. I sit down opposite him. 'So tell me what's going on. What was it you wanted to see me about?'

'I should hate you, you know that?' He isn't ready to make eye contact. 'I think maybe I do hate you, as a matter of fact. Natalie was always being screwed over by old men.'

'Well, that's fine, as long as you don't point a gun at me. I've never had a gun pointed at me before. That may seem strange to you in a man of my advanced age, but it doesn't happen so often where I come from.' I find myself unaccountably at ease with his anger. There's something so unguarded about it.

A waiter appears with a basket of a chips and a bowl of salsa. He turns our water glasses over and fills them from a jug. He takes two menus from under his arm and puts them on the table. He says, 'Buenos días, Señores,' and moves away.

Jake's still studying the pavement. He's got his legs apart and he's jiggling one of them up and down. As I pick up my glass of water, the ice rattles, and I see that my hand is shaking.

'Tell me something,' Jake says, and his eyes dart towards me, and away, and back again. 'Why did you come?'

'Oh, I don't know, I suppose I've always been a sucker for exotic travel.'

'Today, I mean. Why did you come?'

'Because you asked me to.'

'Do you always do what people ask? Do you think that somehow makes you a better person or what?'

'No.'

'No, what?'

'No, I don't always do what people ask.'

'So?'

I drink some water. I'm beginning to feel calmer. 'Look,' I say, 'we all feel bad—' I want to talk about Natalie, but he cuts me off, holding his hand up in a stop sign and shaking his head.

'You don't get to say we. What the fuck is that *we* about.

You were never part of any *we* as far as I'm concerned. You just showed up one afternoon.'

'I – all right? – I feel bad about Natalie – sad, sorry, regretful – for all the obvious reasons, and for various other complicated reasons of my own. And I'm going to make a guess – and I'm sure you'll put me right on this if I've got it wrong – that you, for all your own complicated reasons, probably feel a hundred times worse.'

'You can't begin to imagine . . .'

'No, I can't. I can't imagine what it's like to feel so angry at Natalie, at Mo, at me, at yourself, at the world, at all these old guys who were forever screwing her over. What are you supposed to do with all that anger? Who are you supposed to hit?'

He looks at me, then his eyes drop to the table and are hidden again under his cap. The words come out slowly, and only just audible above the noise of the traffic. 'There was this . . . connection between us, though, like this . . . real deep . . . thing. You can't understand, nobody can.' He's squeezing his hands together. 'And the last thing I said to her was, You're so up yourself you can't even see the fucking leaves. Which doesn't even make sense.'

'Do you think she cares about that, wherever she is now? Do you think she's worried about a moment of anger, or the fact that you got your metaphors in a twist?'

'Do you believe all that, then, like Mo and Astrid, that she's off somewhere on the edge of some new adventure? Glimmering out towards the event horizon, like Astrid says?' There's scorn in his voice as he quotes their words, though I realize it doesn't follow that he doesn't share their belief, or that he doesn't want to.

So I think carefully before answering. 'I don't not believe.'

'What does that mean?'

'It means, I suppose, that I've never met an explanation of why we're here and what happens to us afterwards that doesn't fill me with incredulity.'

He reacts impatiently, as though I'm trying to trick him with words. 'You don't believe any of it, then. You're an atheist.'

'Yes, well, I suppose I would be, if the atheists' explanation wasn't as impossible as all the others. This floating chemistry lab that just happened to turn up in the middle of what I suppose had not yet become space, giving rise to an entirely random series of experiments, conducted by no one, that resulted, by chance, among other things, in human consciousness and a sense of good and evil and, I don't know, Mozart. Doesn't it make your head spin to think about it?'

'I guess.' I can see he's lost interest.

'Have you eaten?'

'Why?'

'Did you have breakfast? Are you looking after yourself?'

'You were right, by the way, what you said. I wanted to kill you. Or someone else. Or I wanted to do what she'd done, to make it even. Then I started reading her journals. Turns out there was this guy.' In a sudden movement, he lifts his backpack onto his knee and pulls out one of Natalie's books.

I recognize it from the evening on the beach, except now there are yellow Post-its sticking out around the edges.

'The thing is you've got to read it backwards. I worked out that that's what you've got to do, otherwise you can't tell what's important. Not that anything at the end makes much sense, not right at the end. Are you interested in this?'

'It's why I'm here.'

'Look, there are bits you can read, but you can't tell what

half of it's getting at. It's like she's yelling at someone in her mind, but you don't know who it is most of the time.'

The waiter's standing, waiting for us to order something. I wave him away.

'There's some stuff about her father.' He turns the book towards me, so that I can see what he's reading. '*Daddy don't you even care that I hate you and I've made an incredible life for myself WITHOUT ANY HELP FROM YOU.* Those last five words are all in capitals, see. And this might be her father as well, or I guess it might be anyone. *I know I'm an unbelievably extraordinary person and too bad for you that you don't.* Then this guy begins to show up.' He flips backwards through the journal, looking for something. 'I knew there were other guys in her life. I'm not stupid. I just never thought . . .' He stops looking. 'I just always thought that she'd get it eventually, that there's this person standing for her, who's extraordinary, as extraordinary as she is, this human being that I know myself to be, who can blow people away he's so huge inside and so authentic, even if he isn't some cut body with a bulging bank account. I thought she'd see that one day. And she would've done, I totally know that.' He looks lost for a moment.

The waiter's still hanging about, so I point to something on the menu. 'One of those,' I say.

'Enchilada?'

'Yes, an enchilada.'

'Two?'

'One will be fine.'

'One each?'

'We'll share.'

'Chicken or beef?'

'I don't care. Either. Chicken.'

'Si, señor.'

I turn back to Jake. 'So this other guy.'

'Yeah, this guy.' He finds the page. 'Look, here. *So much for making me famous, so much for launching my career, some file, you fucking horrible fucking creep.* Look, she's so angry she digs a hole in the page and into the page behind. This is all messed up with other stuff, most of which doesn't make any kind of sense that I can see. But then you go back a week and there's this story. It's not clear, because she doesn't bother to explain everything. There's something about a key, and I didn't pay any attention at first because it was one of her words. This thing or that thing was always key for her. Who you know is key in this town, or whatever. It made me mad when she said things like that, when she tried to sound like she was all grown up and in the biz. But sometimes it was good – real spiritual, you know, like when she talked about acting. She said to me once, Stanislavsky's still key. Turns out he's behind everything. And I didn't even know who Stanislavsky was, so she told me, and I was blown away, it was like this real deep thing happened, like energy flowing between us. She once said, Finding out what's inside you, that's what acting's all about, and that's what life's all about. And she smiled like it was a conjuring trick or something, like she'd pulled a flower out of her mouth. It was a way she had of looking sometimes, with her hands open like this, like she was showing you they were empty, and that shrug of the shoulders, and her eyes wide. She was so unbelievably beautiful when she did that. And we talked about being authentic and how shallow and fake most people are, and scared of what they'd find if they looked inside, or of finding nothing at all. We used to climb up into the hills, you know? And the higher you get, the bigger the ocean gets and the smaller all the cars and the buildings and whole fucking movie industry that carries on like it's God or something. And we'd smoke a joint or whatever, and there'd be this real, you know, connection between us, like I'd never felt with anyone. And for her too. I know it. It was like you could touch it.'

'So what about the key?'

'Yeah, so the key turns out to be the key to this creep's office. And he's got something in there that really freaks her out. She wrote this, see, a few days before she killed herself. *Why did I look? It was all ok until I looked. And now I've spoiled everything. Why do I always spoil everything.* See, she's blaming herself for looking, but what was it she looked at?' He flips back through the pages. 'And this was more than a week ago. *I should have hit him. There was a golf club and I should have hit him with it, and he'd be dead. Standing there in his robe scratching his hairy chest, trying to make out it was all nothing.*' He stops. He's breathing hard. 'Here, you read it,' he says, and pushes the book across the table.

I take my reading glasses out. The writing wanders across the page. You can feel the intensity in the changing slope of it.

Not like a teddy bear after all, just an old grey baboon, fat and hairy. What makes him think he can judge me? I'm an extraordinary person. I'm beautiful inside where he can't see. Who is he anyway with his shelf full of girls names? A sad old man jerking off in front of a tv screen, which is probably what he does. I should turn his camera on HIM. Film him jerking off and put it on the internet and he'd be DEAD. He'd be dead inside.

I look up and Jake's eyes are on me.

'Right? Right?' he says. 'I read that and I thought, Jesus! What the fuck did he do to her?'

A woman turns to look at him as she walks past, and then over her shoulder at me.

Jake doesn't notice her. 'So then I found this, from a

couple of days earlier.' He reaches across and turns the page
to another marker. 'There, see?'

It's horrible what he did, and like the totally horrible
part is that I can't ever tell anybody because of how
horrible it is. Looking at myself doing it I nearly
threw up.

The waiter has come and gone, leaving an enchilada that
looks like a boat sinking in a grey sea of beans.

Jake pushes it aside and leans across the table towards
me. 'He filmed her, see. He filmed her having sex with him.
Okay, now read this.' He takes the book and turns to another
marker. 'This is two weeks ago, right?' The table begins to
resonate with a frenetic rhythm under his fingernails.

Asked again about auditions – if he's fixed any up for
me. And he starts off about phonecalls and emails and
publicity shots, and I should see the file he's got on me,
which he's always telling me about this file, like I should
care how thick his file is! So I ask him when we'll be
together, and he laughs and says, We ARE together,
which is what he always says. But then he's like, You're
special, you know, you're one of a kind. Which I don't
even want to hear, because it sounds like a LINE, and
I know he's better than that – really beautiful and
loving when he isn't trying to hide it. And he has to hide
it so much of the time because they're all sharks in this
business – it makes me sick, to be honest. So I'm like,
I know I'm special, cos I can see right thru to your sad
sad heart, like it's just an act. And he laughs. But I
CAN! Nobody really gets how sad he is but me. And he
SO gets that I get it, but acts like he doesn't. So then
he's in the shower – this is REALLY bad!!! – and I go

in the back of his closet, behind all his business suits,
and get the spare keys to his office – 2 keys on a plain
silver ring. I know it's there because I saw him get it
once when he didn't know I was awake. I'll probably
never use it. But it's a kind of fun to know I could if I
wanted. And romantic too, being so close to him, closer
to him than he knows. He's so sweet, my Rochester, and
he so doesn't get how sweet he is!

'Get it? See, that's when I first saw the name. Rochester.'
'His name's Rochester?'
'That's what it says – my Rochester. So then I could go
back and look for the name again, and it goes back to June.
Look, here, here's one of the earlier ones.' He takes another
journal out of his bag, lays it on the table, and opens it where
he's marked the page.

Lunch with Rochester! At Chinoise on Main in Santa
Monica!!! How wild is that! I think maybe Rochester's
got a crush on me. It was kind of gross when they
brought that fish out with the head still on, I always
hate it when the eyes stare up at you. But Chinese is
totally the best, because you get to share, and no one
can tell how much you eat. I let him eat all the fish, for
example. And most of the prawns and most of everything
else, apart from some of the Chinese chicken salad,
which you can't get fat from eating half a plate of
Chinese chicken salad with the dressing on the side!

Jake's flipping through a yellow file pad, filled with his
own writing. 'I'm guessing he's in the business, right, because
she thinks he's going to help her. Do you have any idea how
many movie producers there are in this town? Everyone's a
fucking movie producer, or wannabe producer. Producers,

actors and screenwriters, that accounts for more or less everyone you can see. Everything else is just people doing things to fill time and get money, pretending to be attorneys and limo-drivers and shoe-store managers and waiters, until they make it in the biz.'

The waiter's eyeing me. 'Food okay?'

'Yes, it's fine, thanks,' I tell him. I haven't touched it. Even if I was hungry, Jake's energy would give me indigestion. 'Closet screenwriter?' I ask Jake, nodding towards the retreating waiter.

'Doesn't apply to Mexicans. Mexicans are the only people doing real jobs in this town. They're the only real people, you wanna know the truth. None of these people are real.' He pushes the pad towards me. 'There's a John Rochester, see, who works for HBO, and Rochester Brampton Junior – Jesus, what a name! – who's some kind of big-shot at Miramax. There's also a Stevie Rochester, but she turns out to be a woman. Here's a guy called Roy Chester, and a whole bunch of Roachesters – weird name. All related probably, part of the movie mafia.'

'But Jake. What are you thinking of doing? If you find this Rochester, I mean.'

He stops for a moment. He moves his face as though he's trying to get the answer right. 'Sometimes I just want to punch him out, and sometimes I want to have like this totally authentic conversation with him. And sometimes I want to do both. And if I hit him, maybe I'd be dead, but maybe I could like say to him, this is what you did, you know? And I'd be a clearing for something to happen, like some change in the world.'

'So you're assuming Rochester's his real name, then?'

He struggles to make sense of the question. 'How do you mean? You're thinking he'd give her a made-up name? Why would he do that? She went to his house. She must know all kinds of stuff about him.' He reaches across to find something in the journal.

'I just thought maybe it's a name she uses, a private thing between them, or just a private thing of her own.'

There's this puzzled look on his face. 'Why would you say something like that? I'm trying to do something here. I'm been up all night Googling these fuckers. What the hell have *you* been doing?'

'It just occurred to me . . .'

'Yeah, it occurred to you to pour crap on all this, because you haven't got a better idea. She calls him Rochester, so Rochester, as far as I'm concerned, is the guy's name.'

'Okay, I was just asking a question.'

'You always have to put people down, you know? You can't stand not to be the smartest guy in the room.' He's begun gathering Natalie's journals and his file pad, stuffing them in his backpack.

'Look, Jake . . .'

'No, you look, Dave.' He puts his finger up in front of my face. His hand is shaking. His face is buckling in on itself as though he's about to cry. 'Fuck you, Dave.' And he's off along the pavement, with his backpack swinging behind him.

Heads turn to look at him, to look at me. In this town, people don't shout at each other in the street, not unless they're safely inside their cars.

'Food no good?'

'The food was fine,' I tell the waiter, and I take out my wallet to pay.

seven

When I've calmed down a bit, I call Astrid. She tells me she's at the office. I'm wondering what kind of office could contain her – I can't picture her in a cubicle. But she explains that the office is just her private name for the Bluegrass Café on the corner of Joshua and 2nd, one of the places where her friends might expect to find her during the working day. I'm surprised to find myself resentful of these friends, which is ridiculous because obviously she has friends, probably hundreds of friends. I also have friends, though none of them are available just now, not even by phone – where they live it's eleven o'clock at night.

It's nice to see Astrid again. It's the hair I see first, the edges flaming in the afternoon sun. She's sitting at a table on the pavement with her fingers on the keyboard of her laptop. Her reading glasses, perched on the end of her nose, look like a prop for a photo-shoot. She pulls the glasses off when she sees me coming and waves them at me. The frames and the fingernails are in coordinated shades of blue.

It's a bohemian crowd at the Bluegrass Café. They spill out onto the pavement, where they lounge at tables, and lean against parking meters. At the table next to Astrid's there's a hairy guy with a guitar. Something about the way his hand grips the fretboard suggests that he isn't a musician. As I get closer, it occurs to me that the bald guy painting him in acrylics might not be a painter. A lot of these people look

like students, but I'm guessing there are also movie types
trying to look like bums and bums trying to look like the kind
of eccentric millionaires who don't care what they look like.
I don't feel out of place in my frayed tweed jacket.

'Hello, gorgeous,' Astrid says, in a passable English
accent. 'I got you tea. You sounded like you needed tea.'

'That was thoughtful of you.'

She relaxes into her own voice. 'Hey! You're a long way
from home. Someone should be looking out for you.' And
it's not just sympathy I see in her face but her own sadness.

I sit down, with my elbows resting on the table, and she
puts a hand on my arm in that casual way of hers. 'I love this
place, you know,' she says. 'I really do . . .'

'This cafe?'

'This town, this city of aspiring angels. It's where I live
for six months of the year, and it's not like I don't have a
choice. But God almighty, some days I wonder if it isn't just
the loneliest place on earth – most talented, maybe, most
pampered, for sure, but radically disordered in spirit. I've
been checking the statistics on it . . .'

'On loneliness specifically, or on disorders of the spirit in
general?'

'On everything, honey, starting with where not to live.
Look at this. Someone's done some research into it, believe
it or not.' She twists the laptop towards me, and scoots her
chair closer to mine. I'm conscious of the swaying of her hair
against my shoulder. 'LA's in the top fifteen per cent of
unhappy places. We're beaten out by Detroit, see.' Her man-
icured fingernail hovers over the list. 'And Salt Lake City and
Phoenix, and a dozen others, but we're up there. Look at
what's at the bottom of the list, though. I mean, Jesus, who's
gonna move to Anchorage or Des Moines on the outside
chance that your neighbours might cheer you up? Because
the problem, as a statistician once explained to me . . .'

'On a date?'

'I was white-water rafting and he was in the same raft, which was just as well because otherwise I'd be dead.'

'You're telling me you owe your life to a statistician?'

'I know! What are the odds on that?' She laughs as though the joke is an unexpected gift. 'But the point is you've got to distinguish cause from effect. For all we know Des Moines just attracts happy people. The odd depressive who shows up there is going to be doubly miserable with no one to talk to. Suicide rates, on the other hand . . .' She's scrolling and clicking.

I start paying attention to the tea. 'Astrid, your search for knowledge is truly impressive.'

She gives me a doubtful look as though she thinks perhaps I'm teasing.

'No, really. There's something exhilarating about it.' I can see that it's also her own way of dealing with what's happened.

'Well, I figure we may as well know.' She's still searching for suicide figures.

'Jake's been reading Natalie's journals.'

'He told me.'

'Did he tell you about Rochester?'

'In upstate New York?'

'No, some boyfriend of Natalie's. Jake's trying to find someone to blame.'

'He's one up on Mo, then.'

'In what way?'

'She's just holed up in the apartment beating the crap out of herself.'

I'm about to ask Astrid what form this takes, Mo's self-flagellation, but I notice she's crying – not in a demonstrative way, just spilling tears.

'Are you all right?' I put a hand on her forearm where it

rests on the table. There's an awkward fumbling as our hands move and settle, and she's leaning against me with her brow pressing the side of my head. The sigh, as her tension eases, hums in my ear. I feel the warmth and moisture of it.

Her voice isn't much more than a whisper. 'We got the autopsy report. Did Jake say?'

'No, he was probably too busy with other stuff.'

'No surprises. It was what the paramedics thought. Her neck was broken – that's what killed her. She wasn't under water long enough to drown. We could've saved her, if the waves hadn't thrown her about, if there hadn't have been so many rocks.' She allows herself a few sharp intakes of breath. Then she shakes her head, taking out a paper handkerchief to dab her eyes. She straightens up, and the street scene reassembles itself – the bald painter who can't paint joking with a girl whose dog has wrapped its lead around his table, the guitarist who can't play tilting back on his chair to borrow a light.

Astrid's handkerchief has left dark smears under her eyelashes. 'Okay, here's what I was looking for.' She's working the mouse again, bringing up lists of place names and numbers on the screen. 'There are almost four hundred suicides in LA every year, give or take – it looks like the figures dip after earthquakes. That's a whole lot of misery.'

'It certainly is.'

'But it turns out to be pretty much the average . . .'

'For America?'

'I guess. My God, can you believe it, though – four hundred a year. Must be just America, because see this – so many of them involve firearms. Jesus! That's something the National Rifle Association could make more of – your inalienable right as a citizen to do yourself in.' She talks to the screen, scrolling through graphs and tables. 'It *is* just the US, because look at these national figures. America's not so bad. Look at Switzerland. My God, look at Slovenia.' She's minimizing and exposing boxes faster than I can follow. 'State by state, Arizona's way up, look, higher than California – which figures, with Phoenix being so high on the unhappiness chart – not to mention the climate and the general absence of any positive qualities to speak of whatsoever. Look who's doing it, though – three times as many women try to kill themselves – three times as many men succeed. I guess I sort of knew that. But wow! – this I didn't know – look at the age gap. We seem to get better at it as we get older. For under-sixty-fives there's a one-in-seven success rate – for seniors it goes up to one in two. You've gotta turn the concept of success on its head to make sense of this stuff.'

'It's not a fair comparison,' I say. 'They've had more practice, those old people.'

'And they've really, really had it with the alternative.' She laughs and then she's sad again.

'So Natalie was unlucky, if you look at it that way.'

'Oh, David, was she ever. One in three, one in seven, whatever – do the math.' She takes another tissue and holds it under one eye and then under the other. She blows her nose. 'She's in the right demographic ethnically, though. Look at this. More Caucasians than blacks or Hispanics. More Protestants than Catholics or Jews. Why do you suppose that is?'

'No idea. What about Muslims?'

'Good question. You don't suppose they've included the nineteen hijackers . . . ?'

'Somehow I doubt it. It'd be an insignificant blip, anyway.'

'Conceptually, though – is the suicide bomber a suicide, or just a bomber – or some other thing entirely? And aren't all suicides also suicide bombers to some extent? Maybe they mean to have an impact, maybe they're too overwhelmed to think about the impact they're going to have. But either way, look at the collateral damage. Look at Mo.' She breathes in. The outward breath sounds like a deflation. For a moment she stops talking and she stops clicking and scrolling, and she looks at the screen without seeing it, as though she's run out of steam.

'You're really worried about her.'

'She hasn't been this bad for a long time. And there isn't much to do, but sit it out.'

'Is there any way I can help? I don't suppose so, but let me know, anyway.'

She looks up at me. Her eyes have filled with tears again. 'You could come visit, I guess.' She does some more mopping. 'She doesn't do friends. She's pretty much a hermit at the best of times . . .'

If I hesitate, I suppose it's because I hadn't thought of making another trip to Malibu. By which I mean, I suppose, that I have thought of it and I've also thought of all the reasons why it wouldn't be a very good idea.

'It's a lot to ask, and you've got your book to write.'

It's the thought of the book that settles it. 'Of course I'll come.'

'Can I email you about it?'

'Yes, let me know what'll work for you.' Because why shouldn't she email me? And why shouldn't I take a few hours out of my non-working day to visit Mo, even if that mainly means visiting Astrid, Mo being pretty much a hermit at the best of times and these not being the best of times for Mo – not even close.

'Thanks,' Astrid says, and it's the easy way she touches my face with the tips of her fingers that tells me it's time to leave. I get up, scraping my chair back. And she's on her feet giving me a hug.

'You're such a good person,' she says.

'How do you mean?'

'Looking out for Jake, helping me with Mo, being you.'
The words vibrate in her throat, a murmuring that I seem
to inhale with the scent of her skin. Over her shoulder I
glimpse the bohemians of the Bluegrass Café, not quite in
focus, posturing along the pavement. She holds me for the
comfort of friendship, because I'm a good person. I respond
with a blur of disorderly sensations, a racing heartbeat, a
redistribution of energy that weakens my limbs and makes
my head swim. I'm acutely conscious of the shifting pressure
of her body as she breathes, and of mine as it prepares itself
indecorously for sex.

We separate, promising to be in touch, and I turn away,
carrying with me the tingling memory of contact.

The car is parked down the street, nose to the kerb outside the health-food store. I've reversed out, and begun to
pull forward, when my phone starts ringing. It's Rebecca.
She seems to be developing an instinct for my Astrid
moments. I take the call, cruising towards the stop sign at
the end of the block.

We're invited to dinner this evening at Max and
Frankie's, Rebecca tells me, and she's going straight from
work. Low key, she says, no pressure, but maybe I can behave
like a civilized human being this time. She says this like a
joke, but I allow myself to bristle anyway. And I don't really
want to hear that Max and Frankie are making an effort to
normalize things after the swimming-pool incident. I restrain
an impulse to identify *normalize* as a Max word, and the call
ends without conflict.

I'm putting the phone away as I turn the corner and
somehow I miss the pocket. Over the engine noise, I hear
it clattering to the floor. Up ahead the traffic lights are
changing to red. When I've stopped moving, I lean forward,
feeling under the seat. Then I put my head down beside the

steering wheel. I can't see the phone, but something glints under the accelerator pedal. Whatever it is, it's just within reach. I straighten up and look at what I've got – two keys on a ring. Light-headed at the sudden movement, I take a second to focus on the label. It says *Office Spare*. The horns are clamorous behind me and the light is green.

eight

I accelerate past the garbage truck and swerve back towards the kerb. I pass a jeep and a sports car and a battered pickup full of gardening tools, and there's Max at the edge of the road, cool in black linen, with his hand inside his mailbox. He turns as I steer into the drive. He's clutching a bundle of mail, and there's a look on his face so intense that, though I catch it only for a second, it's still visible to me as I sweep past the house and pull up by the car port. If I had to put a name to it, I'd call it fear. I remember Rebecca talking about death threats and anonymous messages. But the mail in his hand, as I picture it, is unopened, a bundle of envelopes lifted that moment from the mailbox.

He's hurrying after me, a flicker of movement in the mirror. When I push open the door, a change comes over him, a change of pace, a mellowing in his expression from fear – or anger, as it occurs to me now it might have been – towards puzzlement. Almost at once, he's recovered his poise. At ease again in his loafers and stylish suit, he lets his face relax into a grin. He lopes towards me, head tilted, arms opening, the left hand bulky with mail.

'Dave,' he says. It's a long, slow sound he makes of my name, of this single syllable of my name, as though he's teasing me or responding to being teased.

I'm preparing myself for the hug, but the tilt of the head

has turned into a question mark, with raised brows and half-closed eyes, and the gesture is taking in Natalie's car.

'The Bug,' he says, 'kind of took me by surprise. To see a man of your intellectual stature . . .'

'It is rather pink, isn't it.'

'People take liberties. Not to make social judgements, but to see such a car turning onto your property. I find I'm watching my back just now.'

I look at the car, at the lumpy paint job, at the purple flowers spiralling across the door. 'You're worried about hippies?'

'A man in my position, Dave, has many enemies.'

There's an awkward pause. I look at him talking about his enemies, and I have no reason to think I should be one of them, except that there's something about Rebecca's loyalty to him that bothers me. Her capacity for ironic detachment in the face of certain kinds of bullshit is usually reliable. But I've been invited here, apparently, to help normalize things, so I attempt small talk.

'So I hear women are speaking out.'

'About what?'

'Isn't that the name of your documentary series?'

'Oh, sure. Women Speak Out.' I can see he's still distracted by the car.

'So how's it going?'

'Not to flog a dead horse, Dave, but where would a guy like you get such a vehicle? You bought this thing, or what?' He's studying it closely, as though he might be in the market for one himself.

'I borrowed it. Someone lent it to me. I needed a car, they had one lying around.' I don't feel like explaining the whole process. This girl topped herself and I got the car. It comes to me that way, I know, because I feel awkward about it. Awkward is probably an understatement. But there's a more positive aspect to it that I've hardly acknowledged, even to myself – a kind of privilege in getting close to this person whose life so narrowly overlapped with mine, in being allowed to get to know something about her car, at least – to have a sense that this is who she was, or chose to be, in this city of drivers. I'm already spoilt by our leased automatic. You can't drive stick-shift across this town in early evening traffic without forming a relationship with your gearbox. Following Max into the house, I still feel the bulge of the clutch pedal like a bruise on the sole of my foot. The repeated tensing has left an ache in my left calf. You get to know the roads more intimately – the ruts and potholes, the disused tramlines – rattling over them on worn suspension. You feel the vulnerability of sitting in something so obviously crushable. And there are the reactions of other drivers, the smiles and the peace signs and the fingers.

Max has led me in through the front door, into the lounge, and offered me a glass of wine. I'm perched on the tan leather couch, looking at the glass-topped coffee table, with the expansive chessboard and the Japanese coasters, and beyond that to the low-level fireplace – the horizontal lines of tile and timber, the softer verticals of potted vegetation, indoor and outdoor so subtly differentiated that's it hard to tell transparency from reflection. The tall fat books by the fireplace have the names of artists and art movements on their spines. There are candles at eye level along the mantelpiece, square black candles, each on its own silver dish.

Max hands me a glass of white wine, and slides a coaster towards me. 'Junk mail,' he says, tossing one envelope at a time onto the coffee table. 'Do you get this in England? All these time-sensitive offers, zero-percent credit deals, charitable solicitations? Here's one from a politician. You support these schmendricks, send them off to Congress, they roll over and play dead. They're already bought and paid for.

Your thousand bucks is strictly the icing on the cake. But what are you gonna do? Two-party democracy's the only game in town. Meanwhile we're being governed by wackos. Herman Munster goes to Washington.'

I've been grunting and nodding to hold up my end of the conversation. Now Max has dealt with his mail, there's an awkward silence.

'So this Women Speak Out series,' I say, 'are you happy with it?'

He laughs. 'I'm always happy. It's keeping everyone else happy that's killing me. At least with a series you get to cover all the bases. Three's an interesting number, you know? I think of it like a sandwich. The meat's in the middle.'

There's the sound of a car on the drive, car doors slamming, and a second car, and female laughter, and I realize how grateful I am that Rebecca's about to walk through the door.

'The gang's all here,' Max says.

First to appear are the children, the little boy running at Max's legs, an airplane making a crash landing, the girl shy at the sight of me, then Frankie with a briefcase and a pair of brightly coloured backpacks. She passes the girl, who hovers in the doorway. To my surprise, it's Rebecca, last through the door, to whom the girl turns, snuggling against her without turning or raising her head to make eye contact, because her young eyes, curious and doubting, are still on me. I wonder how Rebecca is taking this. Rebecca doesn't usually disguise her indifference to children. But this one seems to have charmed her, or else she's making a special effort, to please Frankie, to please Max. She rests her hand on the child's head, squatting now to reassure her that it's okay, it's only David. She draws a straggle of hair off the child's face, curling it gently back behind the ear. Her posture has drawn the hem of her skirt up – part of her new wardrobe. Her thighs are a shade darker after weeks of casual exposure to sunshine.

The boy, meanwhile, has bounced off his father's legs and hurled himself, head first, into my groin.

Frankie is apologizing and saying hi and wanting to know how my book's going. 'Slow down, buster,' she says to the boy, as he pushes past her on another suicide mission.

Across the room, the girl is imitating Rebecca's hand movements, the two of them in mirror image adjusting each other's hair.

'Come on,' Rebecca says, 'come and say hello.' She stands, taking the girl's hand, and leads her towards me and Frankie.

Max has the boy's head trapped between his knees. 'Guantánamo for you, kiddo,' he says, tickling the boy's ribs. The boy squeals with delight.

'Hi,' Rebecca says, holding my arm, raising her lips to my face, 'are you okay?' She looks at me almost shyly. Something in this unbalanced circumstance constrains us, but shifts us also out of our recent hostility. I'm getting used to the haircut. The shortness of it does something to her eyes and makes her seem more animated.

'Hard day at the office?' I ask her, and return her kiss, putting my hand on her waist, which feels warm through her blouse.

'You know how it is,' she says, 'art history's a dirty game, but someone's got to do it.'

And with this exchange of meaningless phrases we establish something. I'd forgotten how good you look, I might have said to her, when you think nobody's looking. And she might have said, Let's have sex tonight.

'She's a godsend,' Frankie says. 'To me, personally, I mean. And she's wowing the students.'

'I'm foreign,' Rebecca says, shrugging off the compliment. 'That's mainly what it is, I'm a novelty.'

'That'd get you a dime and a cup of coffee in this town, if you couldn't back it up.'

The child is tugging at Rebecca's hand. 'Oh, Laura, this is David. He's actually much nicer than he looks.'

'Hi, David.'

'Hi, Laura.'

'This is my new friend, Laura,' Rebecca tells me.

The child is looking up at me solemnly. 'Are you Becca's boyfriend?'

'I'm her husband.'

'You talk funny.'

'Rebecca talks funny too, though, doesn't she?'

'Not as funny as you.'

'These monsters eaten?' Max asks Frankie.

'Juanita fed them. They just need a bath.'

'I'm not a monster,' Laura protests.

'I had a bath at Nita's,' the boy says. 'Nita put me in the tub and scrubbed me and scrubbed me, and the dog, and the turtles.'

'The hell she did,' Max says. 'Bathroom in three. Hi, Becks.' And he moves in for a full-on hug with Rebecca. I'm conscious of the spread of his dark hands, their muscular boniness against the pale blue of her blouse, and of his nose nuzzling her hair, while Laura talks at me.

'Becca picked me up from Nita's, and I would've ridden in her car, 'cept her car doesn't have a booster, but she's gonna take me in her car another day when she does have a booster, and we're gonna have donuts.' By the end of the speech she's put her hand in mine as easily as an adult would rest an elbow on a table.

Rebecca has meanwhile disentangled herself. 'Daycare's on the way here from college,' she tells me.

'So you were travelling in condom,' I say. And suddenly there are all these eyes on me, and I have this vertiginous sensation as the words repeat themselves in my head.

Max is grinning. 'You wanna run that by us again?'

'I mean . . . convoy.' I laugh awkwardly. 'You were travelling in convoy.'

Everyone laughs. Then Frankie is talking to Rebecca about something someone said in the funding meeting, and Max is on his way out of the room with the children, and I'm left reaching for my wine glass. And convoy is perhaps what I meant, unless the word I had in mind was tandem. Was I thinking of tanks or bicycles? Neither, apparently. Apparently what I was thinking of was something else entirely.

'So what did you do today?' Rebecca sits next to me on the couch. Frankie is on her way to the kitchen.

'This and that. Bit of writing. You look wonderful in that skirt, by the way.'

'Not too short on me, then, you think?'

'As long as it isn't too distracting for your male students.'

'Not very likely.' She takes my glass, drinks from it, and hands it back. 'So you got some work done.'

'I had an email,' I tell her, 'from Jake.'

'Jake who?'

'Natalie's boyfriend. The girl who killed herself.'

This lowers the temperature a bit. 'What did he want?'

'He wanted to show me her journals.'

'The dead girl's?'

'Yes.'

'Isn't that a bit creepy?'

'I don't know. He's trying to understand why she did it.'

'Did you look at them?'

'Edited highlights.'

'Don't you think, maybe, that's an invasion of her privacy?'

'Seems sort of academic at this point.'

'So he came round to the flat?'

'No, I met him at his college.'

'Just the two of you?'

'Just the two of us, yes. It wasn't much fun, if you really want to know. I had a gun pointed at my head.'

'He threatened you?'

'No, not him. There was something going on at the college, some kind of exercise. The place was crawling with police. One of them thought I looked suspicious and drew his gun.'

'My God! Are you all right?' She puts her hand on my face.

'It was rather upsetting, actually.'

She draws my head towards hers until our foreheads touch. 'Poor love. You're not safe out.'

'I usually seem to get by okay.'

'Are you sure you should get mixed up with these people? They sound like bad news. And that car puts you under an obligation.'

I draw my head away. 'It's nothing to do with the car.' How can I explain this? 'I was there when it happened. This boy Jake is upset, and you can't blame him. He emailed me. I think I have a responsibility. He's nineteen.'

'He's not one of your students.'

'A human responsibility.'

'And the trollop? How old is the trollop?'

'Her name's Astrid.'

'How could I forget?' She looks over her shoulder towards the kitchen. She's angry suddenly, but she hasn't raised her voice. She doesn't want us to argue in front of Frankie.

The light is fading. There's a reddish glow across the pale furnishings.

It irritates me that she should be on her best behaviour for these strangers. 'That thing about the car . . .'

'What thing?'

'That thing you said about the car putting me under an obligation. That's not like you. It's the sort of thing your mother might say, if the neighbour offered to lend her a lawnmower or something.'

Frankie appears, carrying a tray.

Rebecca is glaring at me. 'You should have complained,' she tells me.

'Who to?'

'I don't know. Whoever was in charge.'

'Nothing happened.'

'Even so.'

'Complained about what?' Frankie puts the tray on the coffee table and kneels beside it. Despite her delicate build, she moves awkwardly, like a grounded bird.

'Some policeman drew a gun on David.'

'Jesus! Why?'

'It was just a misunderstanding. There was a crowd of people. I think I made him nervous.'

Frankie watches me for a moment. Then she slides the chessboard aside to make space on the table, and begins to unload the tray.

'It'd probably mean a stack of paperwork,' I say. 'Complaining, I mean. Pointless interviews and form-filling. Why bother?'

'Well, obviously,' Rebecca says, 'to stop it happening to someone else. You would if it happened back home.'

I shrug. Maybe she's right.

'What did he look like?' Frankie has put the wine bottle on the table, and two glasses, each on its own coaster. There's also a dish of olives, some hummus in a pot, a plate of carrot sticks and a pile of cocktail napkins. 'How would you describe him?'

'I wouldn't need to describe him. I heard his name. Everyone in the crowd heard it. It was quite amusing, in retrospect.'

'What happened to his face, though? How would you describe his expression?'

'What a strange question. I suppose he looked mean.'

'How, mean? What did mean look like in his case?'

'I don't know. Hostility mixed with intense concentration, I suppose.'

'So if you'd only been able to see his face, if you couldn't see the gun, would you have known he had one?'

'I'm not sure I understand.'

'Could he have just been a guy concentrating on a video game, for example? If you saw his face out of context.'

'Hard to say. I wouldn't fancy being the video game, though, I can tell you that. Particularly if he was losing.'

She's refilled my glass, and poured wine for herself and Rebecca. She strikes a match from a box on the mantelpiece and begins lighting the candles.

'I don't mean to bug you about it.'

'No, that's okay.'

'If it's a painful subject. It's just that I'm curious about expressions . . .'

'It's what she's working on,' Rebecca explains.

'. . . what's spontaneous, what's socialized, and what's merely contextually determined, that sort of thing. I'm convinced that the influence of context on our reading of expression is considerable. If you think about the iconography of portraiture, there are the classic indicators of occupation and status, and going back to the Middle Ages any amount of religious symbolism. So the virgin's lily is replaced

by the huntsman's gun. And certain kinds of photo-portrai-
ture are in a direct line with that – the distinguished academic
pictured in front of a wall of books, for example.' She adjusts
the lighted candles as she talks, spacing and grouping them
unevenly along the mantelpiece. 'The unposed portrait puts
a new emphasis on spontaneity, the subject captured on the
move, unaware that the picture's been taken. But the iconography's still there. The jazz singer elated at the microphone,
or despondent in some anonymous backstage corridor.
There's this whole narrative of public affirmation and private
loneliness. And we read that story back into the face of the
subject. It gives us the illusion of immediacy, of moment-
ariness. As though the picture's given us some kind of
unmediated contact with the subject's joy or pain.'

She clicks a button and flames start up in the fireplace.
The warmth has gone out of the sky. The images of candle
flames and gas flames flicker over the garden and inside the
bushes, displaced and duplicated by double glazing. Around
the coffee table, the shadows become deeper and more restless. Frankie is talking about the decontextualizing of images
and the mutability of meaning. Rebecca has curled her feet
up on the couch and is eating a carrot stick, happy, apparently, to hear her boss on what must be a familiar theme. I'm
happy too, in a minimal sort of way, not to be in conflict with
Rebecca, not to have told her yet that I saw Astrid today, not
to have told her that I didn't, not in so many words.

'Point a camera at a couple of girls at a party,' Frankie
says. 'They smile, lean towards each other to compose a picture – their socialized conception of what a picture ought to
be. We value spontaneity, here, now, more than any time or
place you can think of. Everything's got to be spontaneous.
So spontaneity itself becomes an elaborate construct with its
own iconography.'

The chess game, which has been slid to one side to make

room for wine and olives, has come alive in the candlelight. The shadows shift among the pieces. A game has been temporarily abandoned. In this elegant room, the unfinished game is the liveliest sign of previous habitation. And it's easy to imagine that the chessmen have been distributed across the board for visual effect, to create the illusion that chess is played – part of the iconography, as Frankie might describe it, of the reflective life. I find myself thinking of Natalie's chess piece, standing oddly among her stuff on the beach, and of my feeling that that too was no plaything, but a sacramental object. Then the physical resemblance strikes me – Natalie's piece must have been part of a set just like this one.

Rebecca is talking about an exhibit at the museum of modern art, but I'm counting black pawns. Somewhere between five and six I lose count. I need to apply a system. I start again, moving row by row from left to right. I make it six. With the two that stand off the board, the ones that have been taken already, that makes eight. It's a complete set. The similarity is accidental. There might be dozens of identical chess sets in this city, now I think about it. There might be hundreds. There's probably a store in Beverley Hills that's cornered the market in outsize chess sets for the executive home.

'Hey, Becks.' It's Max padding bare-footed across the wood floor. 'Laura says you promised her a bedtime story.' His hand drops lightly onto her shoulder.

'So I did,' Rebecca says, getting up off the couch.

'I'll put her off if you're busy.'

'No, I'd love to.'

'It'll give me time to deal with Noah.'

And Rebecca follows Max back into that part of the house where the children are bathed and put to bed. The voices diminish. Doors swing on their hinges. There are squeals and murmurs, and the hushing sound of flames curling around artificial logs.

'Which raises the question of orgasm,' Frankie says.

'Orgasm?'

'No, perhaps you're right – sexual pleasure in general. Various states of arousal, let's say, and all the facial expressions associated with them.'

'I'm sorry. I wasn't really concentrating.'

'Orgasm particularly, though, surely, because this is where we're at our most spontaneous, our most private, closest to our animal nature. Which is nonsense, of course, because it's hard to imagine a more codified activity. Do you have any idea how many simulated orgasms the average American watches in her lifetime?'

'Do *you*?'

'I could look it up. But I'd rather stay here with you, if that's okay.' She picks up her glass.

I'm thinking of Astrid gathering up the skirts of her burka – the tanned, athletic legs and the glimpse of underwear – and I'm wondering what state of arousal would have registered on my face, if my face had been visible.

'Sorry,' Frankie says, 'I'm talking too much. You can see these ideas excite me.'

'Yes, I can see why they would.'

The glass stops, poised just below her mouth. 'David, are you flirting with me?'

'I don't think so.'

She watches me steadily over the rim of her glass, as though she can see more than I mean to reveal. 'It's okay if you are. I hope that's understood. Flirting's kind of expected in these circumstances.'

'These circumstances?'

'A man, a woman, candlelight, a bottle of wine. It's a long-standing convention.'

'I wasn't intending to flirt with you.'

She takes a sip of wine and places the glass carefully back on its coaster. 'Can I ask you something, David?'

'I don't see why not.' For something to do, I lift a pawn from the chessboard, hold it in my hand for a moment, and put it back on its square.

'Is your marriage monogamous?'

'Yes, of course it is.' I pick up a second pawn. 'I've always assumed so.'

'You don't want to know how I'm defining monogamy?'

'How are you defining it?'

'The question is how are you defining it?'

I pick up a third pawn. I'm counting, but I'm feeling as well. I have a memory of Natalie's chess piece lying in my palm – a tactile memory of the bulges against my hand. 'Being faithful, I suppose. Not sleeping with anyone else.'

'There's sleeping and sleeping.'

'Well, obviously I'm not talking about sleeping.'

'Well, obviously. Kissing, though. How about kissing?'

'Not advisable, I'd say.'

'I'm not asking for advice. I'm asking for definitions. Is kissing adultery?'

'No, not adultery, of course not. It might, I suppose, be what some Christians call an occasion of sin. But I'm not really an expert.'

'On kissing?'

'On moral philosophy.'

'And how about non-penetrative sex?'

'You mean . . . like . . .'

'Hands, mouths . . .'

'I wouldn't call myself an expert on that either, exactly.' I laugh to cover my embarrassment. 'An enthusiastic amateur, perhaps.'

'But would you call it adultery?'

'Definitely.' I have pawn number four in my hand. 'Though I seem to remember there were some prominent American Baptists ready to agree with Clinton that he hadn't really had sex with that woman.'

'How about if you talked dirty to me right now?'

'I'm not sure I'd be very good at that.'

'But say you were and say you did, and say I came, without touching.'

'Me touching?'

'Or me. Say I just came, spontaneously.'

'Is there such a thing as spontaneity?'

'Would that be adultery?'

'Well, obviously not.'

'Obviously?'

'It could hardly be my fault. Or yours, come to that.'

'So it's only sex if it's someone's fault.'

'I don't think I said that.'

'I think perhaps you did.'

'Then I take it back.'

'You're withdrawing your implied definition.'

'All right, I'm withdrawing it.'

'So kissing is okay, though inadvisable, but oral sex, for example, is out, whereas coming without touching is . . . what would you say?'

'Nobody's business but your own.'

'Exactly, but what if I sat in your lap, and you came, and what if I rubbed my hand between your legs while you were fully clothed and you didn't come, and what if I just talked to you like I'm talking to you now and you just got turned on. Which of those, if any, is adultery, and which is just flirting, and which is something in between?'

'I'm not sure I could say.' My breathing is beginning to feel constricted. 'I've never really thought about it.'

'What a narrow fantasy life you've led.'

'In terms of definition, I mean.'

'So in other terms . . . ?'

'In other terms?'

'You *have* thought about it?'

'From now on I might.'

'You see, David, in my lexicon, flirting is not necessarily a prelude to fooling around. Flirting, at its best, makes fooling around redundant.'

'Yes, I can imagine.'

'I'm sure you can.'

I pick up the fifth pawn mechanically, and put it back in its vulnerable position towards the white end of the board, ringed by enemies, ripe for sacrifice. I'm aware of Frankie's eyes on me, as she swallows a mouthful of wine. My hand shakes slightly as I lift the pawn again. I didn't imagine it – this pawn is heavier than the others, and rougher at the edges. I tilt it towards the candlelight. It's not made of ebony, but clay. And it's not symmetrical – I see that now. I would have spotted it immediately in daylight.

'You've discovered my secret.' Max's voice makes me jump. His hand lands firmly on my shoulder. 'It's a replacement. I was kind of upset at losing the real thing.'

'Everyone tucked up?' Frankie asks him.

'Party time. How are you kids getting along? Dave, you've stopped drinking.'

'I've been telling David about my research.'

'Imagine that, Dave – slicing up photos for a living.' He empties the bottle into my glass.

'David gets it, don't you, David.' She looks at me, while she says it, and the way I read her expression is significantly informed by context.

Max seems oblivious. 'So who's cooking?' He thrusts a piece of carrot into the hummus and scoops out an unstable glob, lowering his chin to meet it halfway.

'I am. David's offered to help me in the kitchen.'

Max looks at me as though to check I'm up for this.

'Tell me something,' I say, weighing the pawn in my hand. 'Why did you have it made in clay?'

'How do you mean?'

'Why not wood like the rest of the set?'

'The whole thing was Evie's idea,' Frankie says.

'Evie was this young woman, this art student, who was coaching Laura for a while. Laura's got a real talent for art, by the way.'

'Max was asking everyone if they'd seen it, checking the vacuum-cleaner bag, accusing Noah of eating it.'

'Come on, I wasn't that bad.'

'You were going crazy.'

'Well, it's a nice set.'

'So one evening Evie has the kids messing with clay, and she does this on the side. Fired it at college. Came round next day in person to deliver it.'

'Can you believe that? Found a pretty good colour-match for the wood too. What a sweetheart.'

'Well, good for Evie.' The words sound hollow in my mouth. My mind's on a separate track.

'Who's Evie?' It's Rebecca, back from her child-minding duties, sinking into the couch next to me.

'You don't know her?' Max asks. 'She's one of Frankie's kids.'

'No reason why you would,' Frankie says. 'This year she's pretty much focusing on ceramics.'

'What a sweetheart, though.'

And suddenly I can't look at him. I understand his strange behaviour by the mailbox when I pulled into the drive, his reaction to the car. He thought I was Natalie back from the grave. Maybe he doesn't even know she's dead. Why would he? Here's her car, and here's Natalie, turning up to embarrass him five minutes before his wife's due home, to create a scene in front of his guests.

Rebecca's saying nice things about the children, how sweet Laura is, how she listened wide-eyed to some story about witches. She takes my arm and rests her head against it. She's so good at making people happy, my wife. And her affection makes me feel mean-spirited for resenting her efforts – she seems such an innocent in this company. Remembering the way Max summoned her, leaving Frankie to catechize me on sexual ethics, it comes to me in a wave of heat that maybe swapping's what they have in mind. If so, they're wasting their time. I can't imagine either of us going for that.

Max is talking about his blood work, which is apparently perfect, except for his cholesterol, which remains stubbornly high, in spite of a low-fat diet and a killer workout regime. He wants to know about my cholesterol.

'I've no idea,' I tell him. 'I've never thought to ask.'

'Jesus, Dave, a man your age.'

'Max worries about his health,' Frankie says, 'but he's healthy as a horse. Aren't you, dear. Your problems are all in your head.'

'That's true as a matter of fact, but not necessarily in the sense you mean.'

'You're going to split hairs now. Max is a hair-splitter.' She says this with wry amusement and a kind of pride, as though hair-splitting is a party trick.

'Truth is I've got this thing with my corpus callosum.'

'My God, Max, where d'you get that from all of a sudden?'

'Really. My corpus callosum is sort of attenuated.'

'Corpus . . . ?' Rebecca asks.

'Callosum. The fibrous connection, you know, between

the left and right sides of the brain. Mine's sort of attenuated.'

'You know this?' Frankie challenges him, her eyes wide
with comic outrage. 'He says it like he knows it. You've had
it measured, or what?'

'I'm telling you. I have an attenuated corpus . . .'

'Callosum,' she says. 'Yeah, so you keep saying. And so
what if it's sort of attenuated?'

'It's a definite disadvantage, you wanna know the truth,
in certain contexts.'

'You're going to apply for food stamps now, or what?'

Max laughs. 'Materially, okay, it's not a disadvantage.
Maybe it's useful in the business sphere, to be frank.'

'To be frank is not often useful in the business sphere.'

'Unless you're firing someone.' Max laughs in anticipation of his own performance. 'You're useless, to be frank, so
get the fuck out of my office . . .'

'But wait, what is this exactly?' Rebecca is feeling left
out. I can see she wants to be part of this banter. 'What is
this corpus . . . ?'

'Callosum,' Max says. 'It's what enables the two sides of
the brain to communicate.'

'He does this.' Frankie points to him like an exhibit.
'He runs these numbers and we're supposed to sit here and
listen.'

'They experimented on severe cases, you know.'

'He gets hold of some scrap of information and, poof,
he's an expert.'

'This psychotic I was reading about, for example – way
back, when they did this sort of thing, this nut who'd had
his corpus callosum severed.'

'Neurosurgery, now.'

'He could still recognize a colour, for example, and he
could still name the colour, but suddenly not both at once.

He couldn't negotiate between one side and the other. It's blue, he'd say, looking at a rose. No, red. Because until he'd heard his own answer he had no way of knowing it was wrong.'

'So your corpus callosum is severed, you're saying?' Rebecca sounds bemused, as though a real conversation is taking place.

'No, no, no, not severed.'

'Extruded,' I tell her.

'Attenuated,' Frankie says.

'That's why I make films.'

'That's why you make films? We've been married fifteen years and finally he's going to tell me why he makes films. So Max, if you're going to tell us, tell us already.'

'I just did. So the left half of my brain can see the right half thinking and I can get a handle on what I'm looking at.'

'Like how can I know what I think till I see what I say,' Rebecca suggests.

'Not think, though, Becks. I always know what I think.' He rests a hand easily on her arm. 'That's my point. Ask me anything – American foreign policy, gay marriage, Derrida's impact on the way we watch movies. I'll tell you what I think.'

'I love you, dear, you know that,' Frankie says, 'but your understanding of Derrida is strictly limited.'

'What I know is beside the point. I'm talking about what I think. As opposed to what I perceive non-verbally.'

'Which is also – okay, I grant you – strictly limited.'

'No, not limited, not limited at all. That's not at all what I said. Which, if you were actually listening, you would know that. See what she does? She edits me. Nine-tenths of what I'm attempting to communicate lands on the cutting-room floor.'

'Poor baby.' Frankie strokes his shoulder. 'He has such castration anxiety.'

'Not necessarily limited. Huge, maybe, as a matter of fact – the perceptions I'm capable of. Potentially overwhelming. But not accessible as data, not available in their full . . . you know . . .'

'Immediacy?' I suggest.

'You see?' He turns to Frankie, as though a point has been proved. 'Dave understands.'

'Excuse me,' I say. 'There's something I need from the car.' And I'm getting up off the couch with no purpose in mind except to be somewhere I can think.

'Sure, Dave, no problem.'

'I'll be in the kitchen,' Frankie says, 'as soon as you're ready.'

Rebecca is looking at me oddly. 'What is it? What is it you need?'

'Nothing. Just something I meant to do.'

When I open the front door, the cool air stings my face. I must be burning up. I've paid no attention to how much I've drunk, to the warmth of the fire. I pull the door shut behind me and walk to the car. I've left it unlocked. Who'd steal this piece of junk in such a neighbourhood? I lower myself into the driver's seat, open the glove compartment and take out the keys, which might be the keys Natalie wrote about in her journal, which might be the keys to Max's office. Natalie had a pawn like the one Max lost, but it doesn't follow that Max was Natalie's Rochester. And if he was, why should I care? Natalie was old enough to make her own decisions, and Frankie certainly doesn't need looking after. I think about Jake, Googling all the Rochesters in town, hoping for an authentic confrontation. If I say nothing and do nothing, am I protecting Max from the consequences of what he's done? The keys sit in my hand, tempting me to use them. But I'm no cat burglar. I drop them back into the glove compartment. Frankie's preparing dinner and Rebecca will be wondering where I've gone.

nine

I've watched Jake do this – how hard can it be? It's the sense of time suspended that lifts the heart into the mouth. I'm at a dead stop in the fast lane with the indicator ticking, searching the distant traffic for signs of an opening. There's the kerbside parking space waiting for me, tantalizingly close. I'd like to move, preferably before I'm rear-ended. But misjudge the U-turn and I'll be shunted sideways into the most advanced medical care in the world, followed by a crippling hospital bill, and at some point, the inevitable interrogation, probably while I'm coming round in the ICU – what the hell did I think I was doing? The final body blow. It's Rebecca I hear asking the question, and it's not about my driving skills – it's about Astrid and Malibu and being miles from home on the Pacific Coast Highway for no reason that makes any sense. Visiting Mo? Because she's depressed? It's one of the seven acts of spiritual mercy, comforting the afflicted – but the afflicted are everywhere. I wouldn't have to walk far from my own front door to meet affliction in need of comfort. Me and Mo, we hardly know each other, and it seems unlikely that a chat with me is going to do anything to cheer her up. I'm responsible for the potato famine, after all. It wouldn't take Rebecca long to work out why I'm here.

I can see what might be an opening, way ahead where the road curves into view – both lanes clear.

It isn't that we've been quarrelling about Astrid. We haven't. Max seems to be off the agenda as well. We've been finding safer things to quarrel about – symbols and surrogates.

Here comes the gap, and after it, at frightening speed, the closing of the gap, and I lurch into my U-turn, foot to the floor. And within seconds I'm braking, with my tyres gouging grooves in the dirt.

The other night, for example, after we'd come back from our normalizing dinner party at Max and Frankie's, we both seemed ready for a bit of normalizing of our own. And I think we both sensed that care must be taken. So we showered, Rebecca lit some scented candles, I put on slow music, she put her diaphragm in, I turned the lights out, we got into bed. And there it was where we'd left it – sex – so companionable, so illogically exciting. How could we have forgotten to make space for this? After a while the biggest thought in my head was how good it feels to lie here with my face between Rebecca's legs and her hands in my hair and her taste in my mouth. I was ready for Rebecca's hips to begin lifting and rolling to their own rhythm and for the small familiar noises in her throat, but felt only a restless repositioning. There were noises too, but they were the kind she makes when she's writing an article and she's stuck for a word.

'It's me,' she said, 'I can't seem to relax.' And maybe it was her, I couldn't tell. 'You go on,' she said, 'don't worry, I'll be okay.' An odd phrase, I thought, crawling up alongside her, as though I was being urged to abandon her on a mountainside for the sake of the expedition.

It was me too, as it turned out. Rebecca was tense – I could feel it in the awkward way she shifted underneath me. But my mind was suddenly all over the place. All over Astrid, mainly – her blue dress floating and clinging in the Klein-mans' pool, her curious unrobing in Malibu – and vulnerable to other more disturbing images. When my head jerked back, it wasn't excitement, but the thought of Natalie's limp body hurled onto the rocks. And Rebecca was asking, 'Where did you go all of a sudden?'

We'd given up or were taking a break, I wasn't sure which – both of us staring at the ceiling – and she said, 'There are things we need to talk about.' She wanted to know how I pictured the rest of my life, and I said something about getting back to London, back to our regular jobs, and her promotion, and our catching up with old friends. 'Is that it, then?' she said. It seemed like an important question to which I should probably think of an answer. But when the phone rang, and Rebecca told me to ignore it, I picked it up anyway, saying, 'It might be from London. Something might have happened. It's morning in London.'

It wasn't London, of course, it was a student asking for Dr Parker – some kid, I assumed, who hadn't yet mastered the concept of bedtime. Rebecca was in the middle of answering questions about Dutch painting, which is one of her things, when she started giggling. 'Amir,' she said, 'really, you're impossible!' And I realized it was Amir bloody Kadivar, Frankie's PhD student with the Armani suit, who seemed able to relieve her tension when I couldn't.

'Isn't he supposed to be doing Persian miniatures?' I asked her when she'd hung up.

'He's just exploring some connections. Frankie told him I'd be the person to ask.' She sounded pleased that Frankie had thought to pass this chore on to her.

'Even household servants get time off,' I said. I knew it wasn't Amir that bothered me, and she knew it too. The reason didn't matter. If there'd been any chance of salvaging the evening I'd blown it. She put her earplugs in, snuffed the candles and curled up ready for sleep.

Astrid has her finger across her mouth when she comes to the door. She smiles, and invites me in with a small movement of the head. I step across the threshold, miming puzzlement. It seems we're doing sign language today. She shuts the door behind me, silencing the traffic, and we're in semi-darkness. I follow her through the archway from the hall into the lounge. The glass doors at the far end are covered by a curtain that mutes the midday sky. From one edge, a shaft of light cuts along the side of the room. It catches the head of a Buddha and the fluting on a candlestick, and bounces dazzlingly towards us from the mirror behind the couch. The television is on, beaming its own blue aura over the furniture.

'Are you all right, Mo?' Astrid says.

A hand rises from the couch, waving listlessly. Three of the chubby fingers are decorated with rings – a turquoise, an amethyst and a couple of silver bands. It's Mo's hand. As my eyes adjust, I see the rest of her – shapeless in grey fabric. Her face is invisible. She's wearing Astrid's burka.

'We've got a visitor, honey. David's here.'

The fabric stirs and I see the gauzy panel where the eyes must be. She turns the flat of her hand towards us.

'We could talk. You haven't seen David since . . . well, not since we sent Natalie on her way.'

At the mention of Natalie, the hand clenches and sinks.

'That was something, though, wasn't it, Mo? Guiding Natalie into the spirit realm? We did good, didn't we? We did the best anyone could've done.'

The figure shifts under its covering, shrinking into the

couch. I'm not sure if I hear a sigh, or just the sound of the water moving among the rocks.

'Heck, Mo, we have to talk about her some time.'

I take a step into the room. 'How are you, Mo?' There's no answer. In the mirror, now my angle has shifted, instead of the column of light I see the television screen. Natalie is dancing down the beach, swirling the skirts of her peasant dress through the waves. An arm snakes outward, hovering above the line of the horizon. The hand seems too large for the emaciated wrist.

Astrid waits for a response, then says, 'Can we get you anything, honey. I've got Thai food next door. The tom kha gai's good. Or maybe just a green salad?'

Mo's jewelled fingers rise and wave us away.

I feel Astrid behind me, taking hold of my elbow. She leads me back through the hall, past the top of the staircase, to a door. She pushes it open and I walk into the brightness of another room. Following me, she shuts the door, and leans back against it with her eyes closed.

'What's going on?' I ask her.

'Mo's going on.'

I haven't seen this part of the house before. It's as big as the lounge, and opens out on to its own deck.

'And on, and on, and frankly the sound of her saying nothing is beginning to drive me nuts.'

I wander towards the view, turning to take in the room. There's a desk in one corner next to a couple of armchairs and a loaded hat stand. The bed is decorated with silvery ironwork and piled with pillows. There's an antique wardrobe brightly painted. The floorboards have the pallor of old whitewash deep in the grain. It's a complete living space, airy and sun-bleached, with bold splashes of colour. Astrid in a canary-yellow dress is one of the splashes.

She's tipped herself forward with a growl, throwing her

hair down towards the floor. Now she straightens up again, to stare at the ceiling. 'God, I need a drink.' She looks at me. 'I'm so sorry,' she says, 'to drag you into all this weirdness.'

'It's fine, really,' I tell her, 'it's nice to be here,' though I'm not entirely sure whether she's talking about the specific weirdness of Mo's silence or the whole Malibu drama that's been blowing through my life since the first day I walked into Moonglows.

'You're a real pal,' Astrid says, and she comes up and gives me a hug. There isn't much of her when you get close. She has such an impact in conversation that I'm always surprised at how slight she feels. I'm so used to Rebecca's body – to the subtle yielding of substance under pressure.

Astrid kisses me on the cheek and moves away quickly. 'I've got some lunch out on the deck.'

She's laid two places on a low table with cutlery and glasses and paper napkins. At the centre of the table there are half a dozen takeaway cartons and a silver ice-bucket with a bottle of champagne in it. While I open the bottle and fill a couple of glasses, she takes the lids off the cartons. Then we lean back on cushions already warmed by the sun. We talk in a rambling way, and graze, and calm ourselves with alcohol. And the ocean does its thing down below us, throwing itself, wave after wave, onto the rocks and the sand, sucking itself back into wholeness, the global drag and sway of water, governed by a dizzyingly distant moon. The knowledge of this is freshly astounding to me.

'What's that look?' Astrid says.

'Just thinking about the tides. The fact that the moon can have such an effect.'

'The sun too. The sun's responsible for part of it.'

'I didn't know that. Makes sense. If the moon, why not the sun? Amazing, though, either way.'

'And amazing how long people have known – about

the moon, at least. The Ancient Egyptians, for example, thousands of years before we understood gravity. What an incredible leap of the imagination.'

'More incredible to us, maybe, than to them. We don't see the mechanism, so we find it mysterious. For them it was just like astrology. They didn't care so much about mechanisms – they had gods for all that.'

'Is this going to be in your book?'

I laugh. It's defensive laughter – a way of not answering. The gap between Astrid's notion of my book and the mundane reality seems increasingly hard to bridge. And it makes it worse that I'm not even working on the book right now.

'Is this a painful subject?'

'I open my computer,' I tell her, 'but we always end up staring at each other across the table. Then it puts on its screensaver and I feel completely shut out.' We've both drunk enough wine to find this funny.

As her laughter subsides, she says, 'It sounds like marriage,' which is another thing, right now, I'd rather not think about. So I ask her how Jake's doing.

'He told me the whole Rochester story,' Astrid says. 'Took me through the passages in Natalie's journal. He tells me you've got some theory that Rochester's an alias.'

'He's a character in *Jane Eyre*.'

'Hey, you're right.' She smiles, seeing the connection. 'William Hurt played him in the movie. And *Jane Eyre* was one of Natalie's books. How did you even know that, by the way, that she loved that book?'

'It was on the beach, remember, with all her special things.'

'Wow, and you noticed that. Jake thinks you're a genius, you do realize.'

'Sounds unlikely. Last time we met I thought he was

going to kill me.' I'm laughing off the compliment, but the truth is I'm relieved to know that I haven't alienated him. 'Tell me something, Astrid. How well do you know Max?'

'Max who?'

'Not very well, then.' This sets us off laughing again.

'Should I?'

'Max Kleinman. We met at his house.'

'Okay, *that* Max. I met his wife, I think. It was her house too, right?'

'Astrid, you can tell me. Did you gatecrash that party?'

She gurgles into her wine glass. 'Hell, no, I was on a date. Why do you care, anyway?'

'I have this feeling that Max might be Rochester.'

'I'm sorry, I don't get it.'

It's the first time I've spoken the suspicion out loud. 'This boyfriend of Natalie's might turn out to have been Max.'

She's wide-eyed now, sitting up, cross-legged, on her cushions. 'Natalie was dating your friend Max?'

'That's what I'm inclined to think.'

'And your friend Max was the screen-test freak, the guy with the non-consensual . . . taping . . . fetish . . . thing.'

'He's not exactly my friend.'

'How did she even know him?'

'That's what I was wondering.'

'So how did you come to work this out, David? Has he spoken to you about her?'

'No, absolutely not. It was the chess piece. You remember, I noticed it on the beach.'

So I tell her about Max's chess set, the replacement pawn – lumpy tribute from Evie the art student. I've begun to think of Evie as slightly lumpy herself, and I tell Astrid about this too – Evie as I picture her, timid and ungainly with chewed fingernails and a crush on her employer so hopeless that it can only be expressed in mute offerings. Then I tell her about the keys I found in Natalie's car, spare keys to someone's office – Rochester's presumably.

'My God, David, you've got the guy's keys?' She's on her feet – the movement is impressively effortless.

'They were lying under the accelerator pedal. I found them when I was driving away from the Bluegrass Café.'

'You think these really are the keys Natalie wrote about?'

'Unless she had an office of her own somewhere. They've got a tag on them that says Office Spare.'

'And you've had them for days, and never told me? I could strangle you.' She says it with a growl on *strangle*. Her excitement has brought her to her knees on the deck beside me. I hold her wrists to defend myself and her face hovers over mine. I have a disconcerting view down the front of her dress to a shadow of cleavage and a fringe of purple lace, all animated by laughter.

And I'm laughing too. 'I would have told you before . . .' I feel her arms go slack and I loosen my hold on her, and our arms drop without quite disengaging and for a moment we're just holding hands. 'But what does it mean, really?' I ask her, and I'm still talking about the keys – I'm not ready to think about what this hand-holding means or whether it means anything at all. 'What am I supposed to do with these keys? The fact that they exist doesn't settle anything.'

'David! Don't be so obtuse.' Her hands have taken off again, casual as birds, to make expressive shapes in the air. 'A key is for opening a door, for God's sake! Find some excuse to visit Max. Wait till he isn't looking. Have a snoop, see if the keys fit, pull Natalie out of the filing cabinet, or wherever he's got her. You settle the *Who's Rochester* question and we get to destroy the tape. That should make everyone feel a whole lot better.' She's on her feet, moving away from me around the low table with the wreckage of lunch on it and the empty champagne bottle. 'Jesus, we need it.'

'Have a snoop?'

'Jake needs it. Mo knows nothing about the Rochester question – she's got enough to cope with – but if she ever found out, she'd need it too.'

'I'm not sure if I can do that.'

She looks at me, standing with her back to the sky, as though I've said something funny. 'What is this, some gentlemanly code? A chap doesn't break into another chap's office?'

'Where did you learn to do that English accent, by the way? It's terribly good.'

'You're avoiding the issue.'

'It would be an invasion of privacy. Theft, even.'

'Natalie's privacy was pretty much invaded. And if there's a tape of her having sex, whose property do you think that is? Sounds to me like your only problem is getting into the house.'

'Oh, that's easy.' I get up, struggling out of my low seat, to join her at the railing. 'There's a party later in the week. Friday night. I'd give it a miss if it was up to me. But we all have to watch the opening night of Max's bloody documentary series.'

'You mean you're going to be there? And everyone's going to be glued to the TV?'

'Except for Max, of course. It's his film. He'll have seen it already.'

This is apparently the funniest thing I've said all afternoon. 'David,' Astrid says, while she's recovering, 'you really don't understand the artistic ego, do you.'

'Apparently not.'

A shadow crosses her face. 'I should check on Mo. I'll see if I can tempt her with some of this soup.' She picks up the paper tub, still half-full, and takes it with her, leaving the tang of lemongrass and coconut. I wonder if Mo's still watching Natalie's final dance. The same question must have occurred to Astrid, I realize, Mo being another film-maker who can't get enough of her own footage.

I watch the ocean for a bit. Facing north, I can see the westward curve of the coast before it's lost in haze. Much closer, there's a sandy outcrop with cactus plants above the waterline. I recognize the fleshy leaves of the prickly pears, discs of light and shade in the bright sunlight. There's another kind with longer leaves that point upwards or flop down towards the roots. They cluster on the bank, each plant a big clump of grey-green ribbon, like the bow on top of a birthday present. And once I've seen them this way, I begin to think of the prickly pears as green and yellow party balloons, turning in the air. Just for the moment, everything seems that simple.

I hear the door open and shut and Astrid comes out onto the deck.

'How is she?'

'Asleep, thank God. She sleeps a lot. I turned off the TV. I also unplugged the video camera. She'll probably just plug it in again, but with her energy level she might settle for a daytime soap instead.'

'And she's still wearing that thing?'

'I shouldn't have left it lying around.'

'Is she being a nun, do you think – reverting to the faith of her fathers?'

'It feels more punitive than that, like she's obliterating herself.'

'Isn't that what nuns do – mortifying the flesh, denying the will?'

'I don't know any nuns.' She sighs, and leans beside me, looking down at the toppling waves. 'I've seen her like this before, but not so bad. And soon enough she's going to bounce right back.'

'Well, that's an encouraging thought.'

She looks up at me. 'Don't joke about this. If you think this is crazy you should stick around.'

I'd like to explain that I wasn't joking, I just misunderstood, but Astrid is on her way back into the room. 'I just wish she'd chosen something less spooky to wrap herself up in. I mean, God, there's enough to choose from.'

I follow her through the doorway.

'Did I show you my collection?' She turns the latch of the wardrobe, and the doors burst open. The scarves expand into the space, swaying out on their hooks, and the clothes crammed along the hanging rail swing towards us. 'This one's from Pakistan. Look how beautiful it is.' She lifts from its hook a large rectangle of patterned silk and begins arranging it around her shoulders and over her head. 'What puts into people's minds that loveliness has to be beaten out of the world? Do you get that, because I don't? According to the Koran – okay? – men are supposed to cast their eyes to the ground when a woman passes. But the way I figure it they've got to see her coming to know not to look. This is your subject, David, so you can tell me if I've got this wrong, but it sounds to me like it's telling guys to quit leering and show a lady some respect, which is more or less what my grandfather once said to some punks in Times Square. When did that get distorted to the point that women have to make themselves invisible, starve themselves of air and daylight?'

She has the silk scarf wrapped as a veil around her face, its corners hanging almost to her waist. As she says, it's beautiful. And because it covers her hair, I'm conscious of her face in a way I haven't been before. Her eyes look larger. And though her teeth have been straightened and whitened to characterless perfection, her mouth moves in its own asymmetrical way, the lips parting earlier and meeting later on one side than on the other.

'I mean, Jesus, David, a scrap of hair like this, for example.' She reaches under the scarf at her temple to liberate a curling strand. 'Can you imagine that there are places in the world right now where I could get flogged for appearing like this in public? How terrified of a woman's body do you have to be?'

For some reason, I choose this moment to lean towards her and meet her slightly parted lips with my own. It's not a very long kiss and, since there's more stillness than movement, exploratory only in the sense of shifting us into uncharted territory. I draw back just as the absence of other contact is beginning to feel unsustainable. For a moment I don't move and neither does she.

I have a sense that everything is available. She's a gift waiting to be unwrapped. The bed invites us with its superfluous pillows. I only have to reach out a hand and one thing will lead to another and there'll be no end to it. Because for her too, I notice, there's a kind of suspension – eyes wide, heightened colour, visible signs of an accelerated pulse. Light-headed with the realization of what I've done, of what I might be about to do, I find myself at a dead stop in the fast lane, already gasping at the foreseen collision, the screeching brakes, the pummelling impact of bodywork and jarred frames, the painful return to consciousness and *What the hell did I think I was doing?*

When Astrid speaks, it's to ask an overlapping question, but one quite different in effect. 'Is this what we're going to do, then?' There's no hint of judgement in it, no rhetoric – just a request for information.

'I'm married,' I tell her, and feel stupid for saying it. She knows this, of course. She's seen Rebecca, spoken to her on the phone, commented on her grouchiness.

'Well, who isn't?' She laughs, impersonating her own

breezy style. 'Though in my case, it's something of a technicality.' She pulls the veil from her head, leaning back to shake her hair free.

I want to ask her about this technicality – it hadn't occurred to me that Astrid might have a husband – but she's got more to say. 'You know, David, how other people manage these things is kind of mysterious to me. I figure you're old enough to know what works for you. My only request is that whatever happens we keep it between the two of us.'

'Well, yes, obviously.' My mouth is dry and my voice doesn't feel entirely my own. 'Obviously I wouldn't breathe a word. I won't, I mean, about any of this.'

She's shaking her head. 'I don't mean that. I'm not asking for discretion. I mean right now. The room feels kind of crowded.'

'Oh.' She has this way of continually surprising me. 'Oh, yes. I see what you mean.'

'So do you want to open another bottle of champagne or is it time for tea?' She watches me open my mouth, close it and open it again. 'You know,' she says with a shrug, 'we can always keep the champagne on ice for another time.'

'To be honest,' I tell her, 'I could murder a cup of tea.'

She goes and switches on the electric kettle on her desk, and finds a box of teabags in a drawer. Although she's got her back to me, I see the care she takes and a kind of dignity that's almost a stiffness in her movements. And I'm already missing the subtle friction of lips. And I'm missing what this might have led to – the dream state of reflected adulation and the breathless reinvention of sex. But more than this I'm nostalgic for that earlier time, when we could sit on the deck, Astrid and I, in our prelapsarian state, when options hadn't yet been defined. Because I know about adultery – I've read books. I know about the stolen hours, the agonizing in hotel rooms. I'm not sure I'm prepared to make the commitment to a double life. I'd rather be at home – if I could only be sure where home is right now. The bedding is unrumpled beside me. Neat in her yellow dress, Astrid is making tea. I feel precarious and alone, and I'm thinking, If Astrid shuts me out what will I do?

To break the silence I ask her, 'Did your grandfather really say that – quit leering?'

'Sure he did. I was sixteen. That was Grandpa Leibowitz. He was very protective of me, probably because he'd had to give up trying to protect my mother from anything. If it had been old man Duvall, he would have had them horse-whipped, except old man Duvall probably wouldn't even have noticed. He was from the alcoholic side of the family.' By the end of this explanation, she's facing me again, which is a relief.

'And he was another grandfather, was he – Duvall?'

'Dad's father.' She holds her hands out, presenting herself as an exhibit. 'Astrid Leibowitz Duvall, that's me – a walking history of America.'

And after a while, we're sitting by her desk drinking tea, and she's telling me about her unusual upbringing. Eventually she gets to her estranged husband, Jeremy, who's cleverer and better read than anyone else she's ever met, with whom life was never dull, but who turned out to be kind of impossible to live with.

'For one thing, we could never get along with each other's friends. Mo was my matron of honour – this was just a few years ago. It was the first time they'd met and it was like a total disaster. He'd just written a piece for *Harper's* on the Kennedy assassination, and she told him it was so good he must have channelled it psychically, and he told her she was talking drivel, which was one of his words. She was really trying to be nice to him, you know? For my sake? And I thought, wow, it's like his intellectual capacity's this big' – she makes an expansive gesture – 'I mean huge, but at some level his learning button's stuck.'

'How long did it last?'

She hums, staring out towards the ocean. 'That's a really hard question,' she says. 'There's this bizarre thing in quantum physics. You get a pair of electrons. Some weird kind of entanglement develops between them. If one spins up, the other spins down. Because that's what electrons do, apparently – they spin up or they spin down – they can't seem to stop from spinning. It's like staying still isn't an option if you're an electron. And being entangled means doing this dance, where they're forever balancing each other. And here's the really weird bit – pull these electrons apart, and it doesn't seem to make any difference to this . . . whatever you call it . . . this state of entanglement. They just go on doing this dance – if one's down, the other's up. Isn't that incredible? They have this effect on each other, however far apart they are, and nobody knows why. Up and down they spin, as entangled as ever. They've got to be hooked up in some other dimension, if you think about it. Anyway.' She sighs into her mug. Then she looks up sadly. 'That's me and Jeremy.'

ten

I hear the soft clap of a liberated cork, the fizz and splash of the first pouring, and Max turns from the drinks table with a champagne bottle and a glass spilling foam from its tilted rim. His voice cuts through the chatter. 'Take a glass, guys, we're on in five.'

Applause and laughter ripple across the room. Behind Max, on the other side of the table, the body-builder has taken the bottle and is filling glasses. He's got a team of surfer girls distributing champagne while he pops some more corks. Max moves out among the guests, encouraging them to take their seats. The lounge has become a screening room. There's a huge television in front of the fireplace, and half a dozen rows of folding chairs. Venetian blinds block out the garden. There are artful displays of finger food on starched tablecloths. There's an ice-sculpture of the Venus de Milo decorated with shrimp impaled on cocktail sticks.

It's a different crowd from the faculty party – more flamboyant, more wide-eyed and open-mouthed, more whoopy. I don't suppose Frankie's art historians and assorted academics would have taken the same innocent pleasure in the progressively denuded Venus. I find myself watching these people like television, which is what they are. But today I'm watching everything like television. It all seems heightened and unreal. I'm not quite here, today. I'm in some kind of altered state. It's not that I'm without energy, but all the energy is on the inside, circulating like electricity. My outward movements have slowed down.

There's a lot of energy at this party, a lot of excitement. Excitement is something these people mention like an achievement or a professional credential. 'I work in scheduling,' some woman just told me. 'Scheduling,' I said, 'good for you.' 'Yeah,' she said nodding enthusiastically, 'I'm real excited.' Some of the women have the guarded, self-conscious look of women who are used to being looked at, a kind of sliding gaze that avoids the intimacy of eye contact. There are a couple of men with the exaggerated good looks of news anchors and chat-show hosts. Even the ugly people seem charismatically ugly, models of ugliness.

A glass of champagne is put into my hand. I'm stuck in a corner with a producer. I catch sight of Rebecca weaving among the crowd. She's wearing a black cocktail dress with a high collar and long sleeves. It looks good on her – where it clings and where it hangs – smoulderingly good. Satin smooth with gauzy panels strategically placed – a suggestion of cleavage, a shadowed line of legs above the hem. When she walked out of the bedroom earlier this evening and I saw it for the first time, I wanted to say how great she looked, but she cut in with *Just don't start, okay?* And I saw how much trouble we're in. Because she'd come through the door defiant, ready to fend off an attack. And in her mind it's all about Max, my inexplicable hostility to him, my snobbish disdain for his world. And to begin with it probably was about Max, but now it's about Rochester and his hidden camera, and it's about my suspicion that Max and Rochester are the same person, a suspicion about which Rebecca knows nothing. Which is why I have to find out. Once I know for sure, I'll be able to tell her. It won't be easy, but at least it'll clear things up. Because if this goes on much longer we won't be able to move for the clutter of stuff that can't be said.

The producer's telling me all about his TV show. The show's called *Animal Wackos*. Next week there's a woman who sleeps with her python, a family apartment converted into a tropical aviary, a guy trying to heal his brain-damaged squirrel with aromatherapy and acupuncture. The producer's excited about it.

'But won't they mind being identified as wackos,' I ask him, 'this python woman, I mean, and this squirrel-healing person? Won't they be hurt when they see themselves displayed for other people to laugh at?'

'Are you kidding? Every week the phones are jammed with wannabe wackos. The studio's knee-deep in home movies. Failure, for these jerks, is not being *enough* of a wacko.'

'It sounds like you really love your work.' I've lost sight of Rebecca. She was with Amir a moment ago, smiling at one of his stories. Now I don't see her.

'Sure I love it, but it can get pretty crazy sometimes,' the producer tells me. 'There was a guy a few months back who dressed his Doberman in a khaki tunic. Put a swastika armband on its foreleg and trained it to do a Nazi salute. He'd say Sieg Heil and the dog would stick its paw in the air and bark. After the show, some crazy bitch shot the dog. You probably heard about it – it was all over the evening news.'

'I don't think it reached England.'

'Really! It was quite an event here for a couple of days. This woman, the shooter, claimed her arrest was politically motivated. Invoked the First Amendment – I mean, like shooting a Nazi dog was an act of free speech. The animal-rights people went nuts. Demonstrated outside the courthouse, demanded the death penalty. Turned out she was a paid-up member of the Anti-Defamation League. The Republicans and assorted anti-Semites had a field day – reckoned it was the dark underside of political correctness – policing language today, shooting dogs tomorrow. Next the gulag, the salt mines, re-education for the middle classes. The League had to take a half-page ad in the *LA Times* to say they had nothing against Dobermans.'

There's a movement towards the seats. There's a scrum at the food table, people stocking up, or dropping off empty plates. My producer friend hurries to pluck some shrimp from the Venus de Milo's buttocks. I'm sorry to see him go. It was no effort to listen to his stories. I'm too distracted to generate small talk. I drift towards the kitchen, a bright space half-open to the lounge, gleaming with granite and stainless steel, and lurk by the breakfast bar, hoping not to draw attention to myself. Frankie passes me on her way to the fridge. Max is right behind her.

'Jesus, Frankie,' Max says through his teeth, 'I left it on the mantelpiece. Where the fuck is it?'

'How the hell should I know?'

'We've got a room full of people here.' He's looking among the empty bottles, and the unwashed glasses.

'I said we could do this, on condition . . .'

'Not now, Frankie, for chrissake.'

One of the surfer girls arrives with an armful of used plates and begins unloading them by the sink.

'On condition,' Frankie says, lowering the volume a notch, 'that I wouldn't have to be responsible . . .'

'We're on the air in two minutes.'

'That I wouldn't have to be responsible for any of it.'

Max's search has brought him to the abandoned plates and glasses on the bar. He sees me and nods. 'You see, Dave,' he says, 'how my work is treated in my own house. The remote's gone walkabout, my career's heading for the toilet and my wife's got more important things on her mind.'

My smile is forced – I'm going to be searching this man's

office as soon as I get the chance – but Max doesn't seem to notice.

'Christ almighty, Frankie, there are people in this town threatening to kill me.'

'Maybe *they* took the remote.'

'That's not even funny.' He's feeling his way along a windowsill lined with a collection of improbable-looking cactus plants. Nearby, the surfer girl is stacking the dishwasher. 'You'd withhold water from a drowning man,' he tells Frankie, 'if it wasn't in your contract.'

'Don't be melodramatic.'

'Is this what you're looking for?' The girl stands by the bin, an elegant container that has slid at her touch from under the counter. She's poised ready to scrape a plate full of shrimp shells and cocktail sauce.

'Fuck, Frankie, who put the remote in the trash?' Max reaches for it gingerly. 'Did Noah do this?'

'He was helping me tidy up for the party.'

'And he put the remote in the trash?'

'It's good, I think. He's getting the concept.'

'What concept? That it's good to throw stuff in the trash?' He walks past her, into the lounge. He raises his hand towards the television. 'Show time,' he says in his public voice. The sleek black screen is suddenly alive. Speeding cars collide silently and disappear in a spectacular yellow bonfire. 'Okay, everyone.' He goes towards the door. With his hand on the light switch he checks his watch. There's a last-minute scrabble for seats. Some woman yelps and says, 'Hey, watch yourself.' The heavyset guy who has stumbled over her feet apologizes noisily. I see Rebecca by the food table. She's eating dim sum without any sign of pleasure.

The volume rises on the TV and we're watching a preview of a gritty new cop show. The investigating officer is slamming the suspect's head against a wall. Max has found something sticky on his hand. He turns the remote over. Muttering irritably, he reaches for a napkin from a nearby table. The volume of the interrogation rises to a boom and falls as Max wipes. There's laughter. Heads turn to see what he's playing at. Suddenly we're watching another channel. '. . . sitting in this booth,' the pretty reporter says with satisfaction, 'in this very seat, eating a burger, when the shooting occurred.'

'I know that diner,' Frankie tells me, 'it's on Melrose.'

'You've eaten there?' I ask.

'It's next to my favourite bookstore.'

'How awful!'

'What the fuck . . .' Max is fumbling to find the channel button.

'Poor Max,' Frankie mutters. 'He's such a kid.'

'A hospital spokesman reports that her condition remains critical. Police are not ruling out . . .'

'. . . incest, the final taboo.' This new voice is a couple of octaves lower and takes itself more seriously. There's a sigh of relief from Max. We're back on the right channel again. 'But has it always been?' Sculptures of Hindu gods cross-fade into classical murals, while the voice-over, sonorous and intimate, promises a startling new look at the devious practices of the ancients.

Frankie touches my arm. 'Are you and Rebecca okay?'

'Why wouldn't we be?'

'Just asking.' She looks at me for a moment, then sets off towards the dim sum.

Human faces pop into view from around the screen. They fly towards the centre where they cluster to form the word Outreach, which immediately fragments again, spiralling outwards in sparks of light. The accompanying burst of sound consists mainly of African drums and a vast chorus singing in a language that might be Gaelic.

'Here we go,' Max says, as he dims the lights.

A male voice, grave and vibrant, introduces Outreach TV's groundbreaking weekend miniseries, 'Women Speak Out'. There's a bewildering collage of images, then the title of this week's film appears: *Pressing the Flesh*. Sporadic clapping breaks out around the lounge. Someone turns to acknowledge Max with a raised glass.

The title fades and the screen is full of coloured lights. The camera scans the plush interior of a bar until it finds a young woman gyrating in her underwear against a pole. The music dips, and someone, the woman presumably, begins to speak. 'I'd never thought of stripping, until my room-mate suggested it. I guess I was always athletic, like a cheerleader and all, which is good, because you've gotta be real confident to do this, like have a whole lot of self-esteem.' As she reaches behind with one hand to unhook her bra, the camera closes in. The face, pixelated, turns away. As the camera rotates, the unobscured breasts slide past, bathed in blue and orange light. 'I wasn't planning to tell my parents. We were fighting about, you know, the usual stuff and it just came out. My dad hit me. The bruises kept me off work. They don't like bruises. They don't like piercings. It's a very conservative industry.' The camera takes in half a dozen vacant male faces and pulls back to reveal the stage again, where the young woman now hangs upside down, gripping the pole between her legs, her long hair sweeping the floor. 'I lost two weeks' work. Which made my mom feel kind of bad, I guess, because later she came to see me dance, which I was glad she did that, you wanna know the truth, though it kind of weirded me out at the time.' She pulls herself up to take hold of the pole above her feet. 'She said afterwards I'd always been, you know, athletic, even as a child – good on the monkey bars and all. Which was important to me, because it was kind of validating.'

There's a burst of laughter on the back row, a response to the film or to some private joke. Max is restless. His eyes flit uneasily about the room and back to the screen.

Frankie stands with a hand draped round Rebecca's neck. She watches through half-closed eyes, with her head back, either because she's critically appraising the camera work or because she'd like to disappear. Rebecca is frowning, waiting perhaps for the feminist subtext to reveal itself. Amir joins them. He's whispering in Frankie's ear, making jokes.

We're listening to another voice. It's been distorted, this one, but the East European accent comes through. 'I am an artist, I work with my hands. This is not so funny, actually. I am talking of my real work. This is just how I live now, to get me through college, until I open my own studio.' We're following the woman along a city street. We hear the traffic noises, the horns and the sirens. 'Some of these girls say this, incidentally – that they are artists, that this is dance or theatre or so forth. This is bullshit in my view. For art there must be self-expression, as a matter of fact, not negation of self.'

I hear the Venetian blinds rattle and look across the room in time to see the glass door slide shut, the blinds settling back into place. Rebecca and Frankie have escaped into the garden. Amir, with his hands in his pockets, faces the screen sullenly.

The woman from Eastern Europe is saying she likes the hours, the freedom of being self-employed. She likes the money, of course. She walks briskly in a T-shirt and jeans, filmed always from behind, pulling a small wheeled suitcase. Her hair is tied in a ponytail with a pink ribbon. I'm guessing she's Czech. She turns between a pair of plaster nudes and exchanges a few words with the bouncer in the doorway.

I've seen them before, these plaster figures. For some reason they hold my attention. They're modelled on some classical image – Diana, perhaps, spied at her bathing by Actaeon. But it's in this form and in this setting that I've seen them, white against the black entrance with its heavy scarlet curtain, somewhere in my travels through the city.

We're looking at a couple of faces out of focus in shadowy light. The legs in the foreground, naked above pink ankle socks, flex and rotate. There's a small tattoo at the base of her spine. It's a bird – a swallow in flight. The focus shifts, blurring the legs. Now it's the men's faces that are sharp.

'It's not easy always to do this,' the Czech woman says. 'But to clean rich houses isn't easy. To sell things to strangers on the phone isn't easy. It's normal for people to feel like nothing, to be looked at like nothing. This work is not so different. I've had boyfriends, of course. One boy, you know, was special. He wanted to marry me. We used to talk about settling down. But he couldn't handle that I do this. He asked me to quit, actually. What am I going to live on? I asked him. It was him or me, I think. I had to choose me.' The performance is over. The girl crouches to retrieve the dollar bills scattered around the stage. 'It isn't art, but it is job. What does this mean, settling down, actually? Nothing is ever settled.'

Now there's a third woman speaking. 'So I've been doing phone work on the side,' she says. 'You've got to plan ahead, don't you. There's no money in it, but you get to work from home and no one cares if you look like shit.' She's older looking, a black woman, heavy in the belly and around the hips, but with the thickly muscled thighs of a sprinter. The music is suddenly raucous. The many-coloured light from the television flickers across Max's face, and across the faces of the guests, brightening and fading and brightening again as the woman dances naked on the flat television screen. And the television people with their glasses of champagne are thinking about ratings and rivalries and spin-off opportunities, royalties and residuals, and the unseen camera crew are thinking about the job, and the blurred figures hunched over their drinks and sprawled on couches beyond the stage are thinking about sex or power or nothing. Trailing a sequined dress from one hand, the heavy woman turns her back on the camera, and lowers her head and torso towards the floor, taking the strain in her thighs and the backs of her calves, and I feel the nudging of an erection as sex wins over sociology.

The woman is leaving the club. It's a different club, this one – no plaster nymphs – and a different street, littered and desolate. 'It don't apply to me,' she says, in voice-over, as she turns on to the empty sidewalk, ' 'cos any guy ever lay a finger on me again, they'd be dead – but no one can hurt you just talking on the phone, and that's a plus.'

I shift uncomfortably where I stand, crossing my legs at the ankles, letting one foot rest on the other, and I feel through my trouser pocket the scratching of Natalie's keys against my thigh, Rochester's keys. I shouldn't be standing here – I've got work to do. One of these keys has to fit a keyhole in Max's office. I imagine the slight resistance, the sliding and shifting of moving parts under pressure, the tipping point and the click as the lock releases. I back into the corridor. I take half a dozen steps on my toes, watching the heads silhouetted against the television. Then I turn to face the way I'm going.

There's a closet, then the bathroom – I remember the marble floor and the smell of rose petals. I pause by the third door, before turning the handle and easing it open. The bed is a slab of grey-green luxury, wide enough to sleep three or four considerate strangers. The bedside tables are symmetrically supplied with lamps and angled books and boxes of Kleenex.

I reach the next door in six careful steps. It swings open

silently and I'm in an office. A louvre window looks out into the garden. Beyond the overlapping slats of glass, there are dark vegetable shapes and patches of paler sky. I close the door behind me and lean back against it. I'm thinking of how little I've had to drink, some wine, a glass of champagne. I'm not drunk, I'm floating.

There's a black leather chair and a desk with banks of computer equipment. Lining one wall are shelves of books and tapes and DVDs. The facing wall has a pinboard and some movie posters. There are filing drawers under the desk. I take out Natalie's keys, and try each of them. They're too big. Next to the door is a fitted cupboard. The smaller key turns easily in the lock and the door slides open. Inside are shelves of box files, and some more tapes. Most of the tapes have printed labels. I'm having difficulty reading them. There's a spotlight on the desk. I angle it away from the window and switch it on. I see some handwritten labels on the bottom shelf, but the titles don't give me any clues. I wheel the chair from the desk. It swings and tilts as I stand on it. I steady myself against the door frame, and lift down a box file. As soon as it's out of the way, I see the tapes lined up behind. I slot the box file back in place and remove a different one. I see the name Nat, which must be Max's version of Natalie. She would have stood where I'm standing, I realize, teetering on the same chair. The tape next to hers is called Evie. It takes me a moment to remember why I know this name – Laura's art coach, of course, poor Evie, tongue-tied and lumpy. What the hell is she doing here? And there's another name that catches my eye. My heart is pounding. I feel slightly dizzy. I stumble and catch myself. Crouching, I wait while my vision clears, then stand up so I can breathe more easily. The third name is Becks. No reason to jump to conclusions, I tell myself. No reason to assume that this Becks is connected in any way with my Rebecca. The world must be full of Rebeccas and Beckys and Beckses, gagging for some onscreen action with a big-shot TV producer.

There are voices outside. I drop the three tapes onto the chair and slide the cupboard shut, pulling the key from the lock. Then I scoot the chair back against the desk. I nerve myself for the office door to open. I'm practising an explanation in my head. *I was just wondering*, I might say, waving towards the computer, *just wondering if I might check my email. Something important I was expecting . . . surprised they haven't phoned. I thought maybe . . . didn't want to interrupt the film . . .* There are the voices again, but they're coming from the garden with the stink of sage and eucalyptus. I turn the light out and wait.

'Are you sure you feel okay, honey?' It's Frankie.

'I'm much better, thanks,' Rebecca says.

'We don't have to go back in if you don't want to.'

'We should, though. Max'll be hurt if we don't.'

'He'll cope.'

Nothing happens for a moment. I hear Rebecca blowing her nose.

Then Frankie says, 'Why don't you talk to him?'

'I don't know. I want to. I keep waiting for the right opportunity.'

'Just come right out with it. What's the worst that can happen?'

'I don't know. He's so erratic these days. We've been married six years and suddenly I feel I don't know him at all.'

'I'll talk to him if you like.'

Rebecca seems to find that funny. 'Not a good idea,' she says. I love that earthy laugh of hers. I haven't been hearing it so often.

They're moving away. I listen for their voices along the side of the house. The door to the lounge slides open. A saxophone insinuates itself into the garden. The door slides shut, and the music slithers back indoors. They were talking about me. Rebecca has something to tell me, something I'm not going to like. And here's her name in Max's private collection. But Frankie's in on it too. I can't make sense of this.

I slide the chair away from the desk and look at the tapes. I feel ridiculous – wrong-footed. There are reasons not to snoop that I forgot when I was talking to Astrid. It isn't nice to be snooped on, but it's worse for the snooper, because the snooper is demeaned. And when the snooper discovers something to his disadvantage, the joke is on him. I've seen what I came to see – the tape with Natalie's name on it. Now I can put it back and leave. I can't possibly carry it out of here, in any case. To prove this to myself, I pick it up. I lift the back of my jacket and tuck the tape down into my waistband. My jacket covers it. Without a mirror, I can't tell whether the bulge is visible, though it's hard to imagine it isn't. I listen to the silence in the garden. Who am I trying to fool? I pull the tape out again and hold it in the lowest gap between the slats of glass. My fingers keep their grip for a moment. Then I let it go. It lands softly and the scent of sage reaches me like a receipt. Impulsively I take the other two tapes – Evie and Becks – and let them slip through, one at a time. I move away from the window. This is the moment of greatest danger. With the door open a crack, I listen for voices or footsteps. Melancholy strip-club music wafts down the corridor from the lounge. I step into the corridor, and pull the door shut behind me.

There's a pressure in my bladder, like a build-up of tension. I walk casually back towards the bathroom. I've opened the door and taken a step inside before I realize it's occupied. As I pull the door shut, with a murmur of apology, I have a clear sight of Amir's back, and his face in the mirror, mouth open, one finger to his gum, and his eyes suddenly alert. There's a pale smudge around his nose, and I see that he's not dealing with a dental problem.

Frankie's coming towards me along the corridor. I'm standing with my hand on the doorknob. 'Amir's in there,' I tell her, and feel foolish for saying it.

'How sweet, you boys going to the bathroom together.'

'No, it's just . . . that he forgot to lock the door.'

'And you're keeping guard?' She flashes her ironic smile and walks past me into the bedroom.

The television screen is full of men: middle-aged men in a bar, suited and prosperous; young Hispanic guys in unlaced hi-tops and baggy jeans gathered around a pickup truck; blond rangy types in shorts, all of them guilelessly exposing themselves, revealing their self-deceptions and their double standards, making incoherent moral judgements. The film is just beginning, maybe, to get its teeth into the hard centre of its subject.

I turn into the room and there's Rebecca – a stranger to me, dressed so stylishly and with her hair lifted and feathered. She sees me looking at her, and there's this uncertainty in her eyes, as though she's not sure whether to approach or what to say – conscious that she knows things that I don't know, perhaps, or fearful that I might know things she doesn't. She walks up to me and squeezes my hand. 'You okay?' she says and nuzzles against me.

I stiffen, and then feel myself go slack. 'I'm fine,' I tell her.

I like the warmth of her breath on me, the vibrations of her murmuring against my neck. I feel tears coming. She's waiting for an opportunity to tell me something I'm not going to want to hear. This is home, after all. I don't want to lose this. 'I just need some air,' I tell her.

I slide open the door into the garden, step through and slide it shut behind me. Light spills out towards the wilderness of the canyon in a line that widens and narrows as the blinds sway. I wait while they settle and the narrower stripes of light and shade sharpen on the paving stones. The sky is ash-grey. A glow rises from the city. The music from the lounge diminishes as I move along the side of the house. People are talking in one of these rooms. The conversation is quiet but intense. The louvre window of the office is easy to recognize. I scuff through gravel and bark, and squat by the wall. As I reach my arm behind the sage bush, my cheek collides with something, a protrusion with a rough edge. The wound stings. It's rough and warm to the touch. There are words unexpectedly close, but muffled and breathy. I move my hand back along the wall and feel the side of some kind of ventilator panel.

'You have to stop this.' It's Frankie.

The reply is just about audible, an angry male voice too distorted to decipher.

'I'm sorry, Amir, but it's not going to happen. Really, you should go back to the party.'

He's talking again, Amir, making woofly noises and little barks of rage. I'm thinking that she's caught him with his cocaine and is spelling out the rules of the house. But the next thing she says puts me right.

'Look, you're a sweet boy. I'm kind of flattered that you feel so strongly.'

I catch some of what he says. Maybe he's moved closer, or shifted his angle. He doesn't like the word *flattered*. He repeats it a couple of times.

'Sure I'm flattered,' Frankie says, 'and a little bored, to be honest.'

'Bored?' I hear that all right.

'Only today, only with you in this pestering mood, which is so unlike you. I'm sorry, really I am, that you feel I've misled you. But words are only words. We're not obligated to act on them. How would the world work, honestly, Amir, if we translated all representations into action – if our ability to conceive embraced only the mundane and practicable. Human imagination would be incalculably impoverished.'

'You are really incredible, you know that. You're pushing me out of your life . . .'

'Don't be histrionic.'

'. . . and you talk like that . . .'

'Like what?'

'Like I'm in your freshman class.'

'Let me ask you something, Amir. Did you imagine we were going to have sex?'

'Yes, of course.'

'I mean actual penetrative intercourse?'

'Among other things.'

'And did it give you pleasure to imagine it?'

'What kind of question is that?'

'It's the only question that matters. Because if it gave you pleasure, what do you have to complain about? The reality would probably fall short of your fantasies, in any case. There'd be disappointment and recriminations. Do we really need to put ourselves through all that?'

'You really are a cold-blooded bitch, you know that.'

I will myself to get on with what I came here to do. I edge forward, pushing my arm towards the dark shapes between the bush and the wall. The music of the argument is still present to me, but not the words. I pull the tapes out one at a time and stand up, avoiding the pipe, avoiding the bathroom window.

I make my way back to the path, and follow it round the corner of the house to the side gate, which is bolted, but not padlocked. I open the gate, and shut it quietly behind me.

The drive is full of cars, sleek and gleaming. Ours is at the bottom, by the mailbox. The boot gapes at a touch of the remote. Its pristine interior glows softly. I pile the tapes neatly in the corner. They won't stay in a pile, I realize, and Rebecca will wonder what the noise is, so I lay them side by side. I hesitate, then take my jacket off, and throw it on top. I shut the boot.

There's applause from the house. Cheering and laughter and conversation. If I go back, people will say *Enjoy it?* and *Whaddya think?* But I don't know what I think. I wander into the road. I face uphill and start walking.

eleven

There's a sound like rain. The gutters are awash. Water spills across the road, exposing its dips and crevices. All up the canyon, the automatic sprinklers are switching themselves on. We haven't been this way, Rebecca and I, uphill beyond Max and Frankie's place. It's steep walking. Then the view begins to widen. The properties clamour for attention – a medieval manor house, a Greek temple, a Spanish hacienda with a pantiled roof. Signs by the mailboxes say *Private Drive, No Trespassers, Armed Response*. I recognize all the elements of this landscape. The composite effect is weirdly unfamiliar.

There's a fork in the road and I turn at random, taking the narrower route. I've left the grid far behind, down below Sunset. Somewhere ahead, if I went that far, beyond the snaking crest of the hill, after a winding descent, I'd find it again on the arid plain that people call the valley. But there are no right angles up here. The road curves downward and my pace quickens without effort. After a while, I take another downward turn, and I'm descending a narrower gulley, my weight pulling me into a jog. The buildings have become smaller, more provisional. Some overhang the edge of the road propped up on stilts, or dig back into the rock walls. They have the undisguised screwed and bolted construction of tree houses. The timber casing follows the patterns of shiplap or bat and board, knotty planks with the joints showing. There isn't much traffic, so I keep to the centre of the road to avoid the parked trucks and the overgrown verges. It's cool, but the air is still heavy. I haven't thought where I'm going, only that I'm not ready to see all those people. The road falls away in front of me. At every step my ankles and my knees are jarred in a rhythm over which I seem to have no control. Anxiety is a knot somewhere up under my ribcage. This is what makes me pant – not the effort, but this knot. The noise, which is the air passing from my lungs and through my windpipe, dragging at my vocal cords, is a kind of singing, a kind of keening. It's some relief to make noise, to work my limbs, to feel myself on the move.

I went into Max's office for an answer, and I came out with more questions. What does it mean to me that Max has a tape labelled Becks? It might mean nothing. It *would* mean nothing if Max didn't also have a tape labelled Nat. If I hadn't read Natalie's journal. If Rebecca hadn't had her hair restyled and bought a dozen new outfits.

I've become increasingly aware of the pressure in my bladder. I could stop any time and pee among the under-growth. I begin to feel the need more urgently. There's a place ahead where the road turns and divides. It's a kind of shack with a covered deck like a veranda. The people sitting out might live there. They might be guests. But something about the way the place is lit up and the cluster of vehicles and motorbikes by the steps makes me think it's a bar or a cafe. They'll have a toilet. I could do with a drink. But I'm not ready to face anyone, to answer questions like *How's it going?* and *How are you today?* and *What brings you to this neck of the woods?* I should stop now, where there's some privacy. But my legs aren't ready to stop.

I hear an engine revving behind me and I swerve off the road towards the trees. It's a jeep. The driver puts his head out of the window to ask, 'Where's the fire?' as he accelerates past. He can see I'm no jogger, I suppose, with my shirt sleeves flapping. I could be a criminal, a grown man in grown-up clothes running down the road. I could get shot.

I don't see what it is that trips me. Fencing wire? A piece of tree root? A low branch? It feels soft against the top of my shoe as I fall forward. The verge is hard, though, toughened by drought. Either that, or I've hit rock or a concrete kerbstone. It catches my knee and forearm and topples me sideways, so I roll on my back on the tarmac. It's the road that knocks the wind out of me. For a moment I make no attempt to get up. I'm waiting to see what hurts most, where the damage is. The blood is pounding in my head. The sky flows between the trees like a grey river, then retreats and stops moving. I twist over onto my side, push myself up into a kneeling position, squat back on my heels. No harm done, I tell myself. Just a few bruises.

I close my eyes and open them again. Someone is running up the hill towards me. He's wiry and runs with a limp, twisting to his weak side at each step. He's wearing cowboy boots and holds a wide-brimmed hat in his hand.

'You took a tumble, sir,' he says when he's close enough. 'I saw you from Josie's and I said, Judas, that's some tumble.'

'Yes, stupid of me. I wasn't looking where I was going.'

'It's a dark stretch of road, and you was going at some lick, sir, I'll give you that.'

I'm leaning forward, resting my right hand on the tarmac, shifting my weight, steadying my left foot to take the pressure. Every move brings its own pain, but everything's still working.

'Here, take my hand.' His grasp is strong and he pulls me to my feet as though I'm no weight at all. 'Come sit down in Josie's. We'll get you something. Take a look at what that road done to you.'

'Thanks for coming out.'

'Glad to be of help. It's a dark road, and a tough road. You ain't the first person I seen on his knees. You live round here?'

'No, I was at a gathering somewhere further up the hill, a sort of party, with my wife and her boss and her boss's husband who makes films . . .' I stop talking. I don't know what I'm trying to say, but I notice I've got to Max's films pretty quick.

'And . . .'

'And that's about it, really.'

'And you just needed to run, I guess.'

'Yes, I suppose I did.'

'Well, I sure as heck know what that feels like. Been running most of my life. Running from one blessed thing or another. Finally figured out what I was running *to*. But not before I was out cold more times than I can say.'

'I don't make a habit of this, actually. I just needed to be alone for a bit.'

We've reached Josie's and he turns at the foot of the stairs and looks me in the eye. 'That's understood, sir. I did not mean to imply anything to your discredit. I want you to know that.' He's younger than I took him for at first. He might be younger than me, though his face is weatherworn and pale on one side where a patch of smoother skin has been grafted. He smiles and his eyes soften. 'I'm Wyman, by the way,' he says, offering his hand.

'David.'

He takes my hand in both of his and gives it a vigorous shake. 'Wyman by the way and David by the wayside.' He gurgles with pleasure at his own joke. 'You'll have to pardon me, David, I have a weakness for words.'

He pulls on the handrail, elevating himself from step to step with an easy rolling movement. I follow more awkwardly. He gives me a hand at the top.

'I reckon we must look like the cripple O-lympics,' he says, laughing.

The people sitting on the deck, a girl and two guys in leathers, are saying 'Hi' and 'Welcome' and I'm nodding and smiling as I follow Wyman through the door into Josie's. Some kind of rock anthem is playing at low volume. A couple of pool-players turn their heads from the table. 'What's up, Wyman?' one of them says. 'The spirit is up, brother,' Wyman tells him, 'the spirit is up.' A girl reading by the window laughs and drops her eyes again to her book. The door has swung shut behind us, and I have a premonition that I'm about to be mugged.

Wyman shows me where the restroom is, and I stand at the stainless-steel urinal, enjoying a moment of release as the pressure eases and the bright stream of urine sings and splashes into the trough. And I'm telling myself not to be paranoid. Wyman is a nice person. These are nice people. Niceness is their native language. It may be only skin deep, a culturally acquired mask for indifference, but I don't have to fear it. What I have to fear are my own irrational impulses. What am I doing here? I should be heading back. Will I even remember which way to turn? I'm vague about how far I've come, and it'll take longer uphill with a stiff knee. And there is, I can't deny it, something creepy about this place. I put my hand in my trouser pocket and I'm comforted by the feel of my wallet.

Then my legs begin to shake and the wall blurs, and I think about sitting down with a drink. I wash my hands, and throw some cold water over my face. There's a raw patch from the base of my little finger to my wrist where I've lost a layer of skin. The bruise on my cheekbone, where the ventilator panel caught me, is still tender – a purple smudge reaching nearly to the eye, and a crescent of dried blood at the centre. I dab around these sore places with a paper towel and return to the bar.

Wyman is carrying a plastic bowl full of water. He rests it on a stool, which rocks on a twisted floorboard, setting the water slopping to one side. Steam rises past him, as he sits drying his hands on the towel. The two mugs on the table are also steaming.

'Josie says the coffee's on the house. You should take plenty of sugar with that.'

I turn to Josie, who's drying glasses behind the bar, a fresh-faced woman in her twenties, pretty in a vacant, characterless kind of way. Her hair is tied up in a floral headscarf. 'Thank you,' I say, 'that's very kind of you.'

'Oh, you're very welcome, David.'

There's the rattle of balls colliding on the pool table, and the softer sound of a ball finding a pocket. I pick up the mug nearer to me. 'Perhaps you could put something in it – brandy, or something . . .'

She has a blank look on her face, as though I'm speaking a foreign language.

'Not on the house, of course. I'll pay, obviously, for the brandy.'

'You want brandy?'

'And something for Wyman as well. Whatever Wyman's drinking.' I turn to Wyman. 'I'm sort of shaken up. A stiff drink ought to do me some good.'

'Oh, I doubt that,' Josie says. She's looking at me in a sorrowful kind of way with her head on one side.

Wyman slings the towel over his shoulder. 'Josie don't serve alcohol, David. Do you, Josie?'

'No, David, I do not.'

'Let me look at your knee,' Wyman says.

'Never mind,' I say to Josie, 'coffee's perfect.' I raise my mug, meaning I know it isn't her fault that she hasn't got a licence, and I'm sorry I made her feel bad, and I lower myself into a chair.

Wyman rests his hands on my leg. 'I done first aid, I ain't gonna do you no harm, no sir.' He turns his head sideways as though listening for something, moving his hands to press in different places. Behind him there's a notice board with posters and handwritten messages and, hanging below it, a wooden rack for flyers and leaflets. There's a tear in my trousers, just below the knee, an L-shaped flap with a dark stain around it. 'Why don't you roll it up,' he says, 'and we'll see what's what.'

He seems to know what he's doing, so I pull the trouser leg up until it's bunched around my thigh.

'We'll need some ice, Josie,' he says, 'when you got a moment. Wrap it in a dish towel, will you.'

He's probing the knee joint gently with the coarse pads of his fingers. I gasp when he touches the bruising. 'I done first aid in the military. This is nothing to me. I seen death up close.'

'So you've been a soldier.'

'I was a marine. Proud to serve my country. I killed some folks and that don't make me feel good. They were infidels, I knowed that, but I'd sooner've saved their souls and let them live their lives to the glory of God almighty.'

And I realize I haven't been paying attention. It wouldn't have taken me this long back home. 'You're a Christian.'

'Yes, sir, I believe I am – a Bible-believing Christian.' He smiles at me and his eyes are eager and alive.

'And this place . . . ?'

'Josie's?' He wrings out a cloth over the bowl, and presses it against the cut. 'Josie's is an oasis in the desert.'

'Bless you, Wyman.' Josie puts a first-aid box and a tea towel full of ice on the table. She smiles at me with her hand on Wyman's shoulder, and returns to the bar. And I tune in to the song that's been playing since I sat down, the fervent voices, the devotional words: *Awesome as summer lightning, strike from above, conquer and crush me, Lord, that I may be raised up by love.*

'Can I ask you, David, have you read the news of your salvation?'

And the leaflets come into focus behind Wyman's head – *Christ Denied: The Secular Conspiracy, Seven Lies of the Gay Lifestyle, The Evolution Myth.*

It's not as though I'm unfamiliar with this stuff – I run into evangelicals all the time, it's an occupational hazard – though it doesn't usually come in this packaging. 'I've read the Bible, yes,' I tell him, 'I'm quite familiar with it, actually.'

He whistles, as though I've said something impressive, then his face relaxes into a grin. 'Would you say you're lukewarm, David? I'd say you're lukewarm for sure.'

'Lukewarm?'

'Neither hot nor cold. Because if you're lukewarm, neither hot nor cold, I'm gonna spew you out of my mouth, yes sir.'

Home-schooled for Salvation catches my eye, and *Are You Ready for the Rapture?*. 'Ah, yes, I see what you mean. The Book of Revelation, chapter three, verse . . . what? Somewhere towards the end.'

'Revelation, three, sixteen.' He stretches a Band-Aid across the cut. 'So you've read your Bible. And you're out in the darkness running. I sure would like to join up them dots.'

'I wish you wouldn't. I mean it's very kind of you to take care of me like this, but I've got a lot on my mind, and I'm afraid you won't find me very . . . receptive.'

'Stony ground?' He holds the loose edges of the tea towel together and bangs the ice against the table. 'I don't think so. Choked by thorns, maybe. What kind of thorns would they be, I wonder?'

'Mathew. Parable of the sower.'

'Hold it here, against the knee.' He places my hand on the ice-pack. 'And keep pressing till I say. Don't that feel good?'

'Very nice, thank you.'

'How come you know the Bible, David, but ain't taken its truth to your heart?'

This isn't doing anything for my anxiety. 'We're really not going to have this conversation, you know, Wyman. I'm grateful for the coffee and the first aid, but if you try to convert me I'm afraid I'm just going to walk out that door.'

'David.' He gives me a straight look. 'I respect that.'

When I've drunk my coffee and I make to leave, he offers to drive me. 'Gotta go to work, anyways. Sounds like you're on my route.'

'You do a nightshift?'

'I work whatever shift Satan's working.'

The pool-players urge me to me be well and to take care. The girl by the window glances up from her Bible with a shy smile. Josie says, 'You hurry back now,' and, 'God bless.' The bikers are climbing onto their bikes. 'God bless,' they say, zipping their jackets, tightening the straps on their helmets.

Wyman helps me into his truck and hands me the ice-pack. 'Give it another ten minutes. I can take Josie's dish towel back tomorrow.' The engine coughs into life and we set off up the hill.

'What was it like,' I ask him, 'being a soldier?'

'Weren't all killing,' he says, 'and weren't all cleaning latrines, neither. I won some souls for Christ. Went out there heavy with Bibles and came back light. Yes sir, with a light pack and a light spirit, though there was some killing had to be done, and more to be done elsewhere that we ain't attending to. Then I lost my foot, blowed up in a suicide attack. That set me back some. But the Lord gives, David, and it's all his to take. This whole body is on loan, the way I figure it, and every good thing I enjoy in this life. All drawn on God's credit. And that's the only bank that don't foreclose.'

We're winding back towards the broader road, the wealthier houses, and I'm glad I don't have to look Wyman in the eye while he tells his hokey, hair-raising story.

'So I joined the UWC, that's the Urban Warriors for Christ, and came out to Orange County and from there to LA. Cause there's a bigger battle to win right here on American soil, a fight to the death for the soul of our nation, and no place more than here in this city. This is Babylon, my friend, this is sin central. And if you don't believe in Satan and the demons of hell, you ain't got your eyes open. Down there in Hollywood with the whores and the drunks and the drugs and the piercings and the tattoos, down there in the gay bars and the strip joints, there's an air-conditioned elevator straight to the bottomless pit. I know about sin, yes sir I do. Before God found me, you never seen such a sinner as I was, drinking and whoring. I used every cuss word there is and a few I made up, and every time I took the name of Jesus in vain I was spitting on his wounds. Nothing you can tell me about sin I don't already know. But down there in Hollywood the sidewalks burn with the suffering of Christ, the neon lights are aflame with his agony.'

'And that's where you're going now?'

'To the synagogues of Satan, my friend, to confront the sinners with the fierce love of God.'

'Well, thanks for not trying to convert *me*. I should think you're pretty formidable when you get going.'

He grins. 'I figure you ain't ready yet. I found you on your knees. It'll be time enough, I reckon, when you hit rock bottom and you're flat out cold. When you do, you'll know it's God's work. And I hope I'm there to see your soul saved for Jesus, yes sir.'

I'm hoping that if I ever find myself flat out cold, I don't have Wyman to add to my problems. I'm relieved to see Max's mailbox down the road, and I show Wyman where to stop. 'Thanks for the lift. And thanks for patching me up.' I climb down from the pickup, taking the weight on my better leg. I empty the ice into the verge, and hand Wyman the tea towel.

'There's just one thing I will say, David by the wayside. I heared what you said back there in the road outside Josie's about your wife and her Hollywood producer friends. I don't presume to know what's troubling you. But you've read the Bible, David. You know God wants you to have dominion over your wife.'

'Are you married, Wyman?'

'I do not have that blessing.'

'Have you got a girlfriend?'

'See this?' He pulls a slender chain from inside his shirt. A silver ring hangs on the end of it. 'It's my promise ring. Reminds me not to touch a woman, not to look at a woman with lust in my heart, not to lay sinful hands on myself until my wedding night, whenever the Lord chooses to bless me with a wife.'

'Marriage is about compromise, Wyman. Sometimes it's about complicated negotiations in the interests of mutual survival.'

'Neither hot nor cold, David by the wayside, neither hot nor cold.' He grins, toots his horn and pulls away.

There's music coming from the house, but most of the cars have gone.

'It won't last.' Amir Kadivar is standing in the shrubby shadows at the foot of the drive. 'She'll make you feel unique, but it's all a game.' His voice is loud, and there's a wild energy in it I haven't heard before. For a moment I think he's talking about Rebecca. Then I remember his argument with Frankie in the bathroom. 'Because everything with her is a fucking mind game.' He takes a couple of steps towards me. 'Or a game of mind-fucking. She'll seduce you, David Parker from Tufnell Park, and leave you with your dick hanging out.' He turns on the last phrase, shouting it towards the house. There's a diamond of light in a neighbouring window as someone parts the blinds, and I see a pair of eyes looking out.

'I'd better go in. It looks as though the party's winding down.'

'The party never even began.' His laughter is breathy and uneven. 'I should have guessed from all that convoluted hyper-theoretical crap she talks. Do you know anything about Persian miniatures?'

'Not much.'

'Beauty so intoxicating it would have you on your knees. And you know how that cold-hearted bitch spends her time? She deconstructs scraps of third-rate photojournalism. Stick around and she'll deconstruct you.'

'What have I got to do with this?'

'I've watched her watching you. Anyone can see you're the coming attraction. Just don't expect her to be there when you come.' The laughing becomes laboured. There's an uncomfortable wheezing rasp. Then he's raising his shoulders as though it's a physical effort to get the air in his lungs. He's fumbling in his jacket pocket, drawing tight little gasps of breath. He takes out an inhaler and puts it hungrily to his mouth. He reaches out a hand and grips my arm. I hold him steady, and he leans towards me, hunched over, his shoulders rising as he pulls the air in.

'Do you need anything?' I ask him. 'Can I do anything to help?'

Amir shakes his head. He's breathing more easily, holding on to me, his inhaler still in his hand. 'I'll be okay,' he says. 'You'd better get back to the girls. Give the professor a kiss from me. If you ever get that close.'

twelve

'Budge up.'

Before I'm fully awake, I'm aware of the shifting weight on the mattress and the creaking of the bed frame. I like the warmth of Rebecca's body beside me. We've been arguing in my dream. The apartment was open to the sky and as large as a field. The stream running through it grew into a torrent. She sat at her desk on one side. I stood by the kitchen sink on the other. And the bridge between us tipped and creaked when I put my foot on it. I was calling to her, but she'd moved out of range. Now here she is, lying next to me.

'What time is it?'

'Three fifteen.'

It's mid-afternoon. The sun pierces the room in dazzling perforations along the edges of the blinds, and seeps under the door from the hall. I'm fully dressed on top of the quilt. I let my eyes fall shut again, hear the sound of my own breathing, high in the back of my mouth, feel my tongue like an obstruction.

Rebecca pulls herself closer.

I move my lips to speak. 'Must have dozed off.'

'No need to get up.' She strokes my face. Her fingers move gently across the bruise. 'It's still swollen,' she says. I can smell her hand cream. Her breath is warm against my neck.

'I should do something.'

'You already did, remember. You cleaned, went to the launderette, washed the windows, swept the garage. You should get a bang on the head more often.'

'Very funny.'

'Then you lay down to read the paper.'

She doesn't mention my first job of the day, which was to retrieve three tapes from the boot of the car before she was awake. All the rest was filling time – fighting anxiety – until I get a chance to watch them.

'And what have you been up to?'

'I finished that stack of essays.' She kisses my forehead. 'Let's try and have a nice weekend. I just have to get some food organized for the thing this evening.'

'What thing?'

'It's just a potluck, pre-dinner nibbles sort of thing. We don't need to leave for an hour at least.'

'We're going to a party?'

'The ACLU fundraiser, remember. It's on the calendar.'

'Oh, that.' I don't remember, but that doesn't mean she hasn't told me.

Something's happening out on the streets. Sirens approach, wailing above the noise of the traffic, and then from nowhere the clatter of a helicopter.

'Why am I so tired?'

'Because you were awake half the night, probably.'

'Did I disturb you?'

'Not much.' She moves so she can see my face. With her free hand she draws her hair back. The wrinkles have gathered around her eyes. 'Are we okay?'

'I hope so.'

The helicopter sounds close. There must have been an accident, a pile-up, something newsworthy. Or they're searching for someone.

She sighs, letting her head sink onto my chest. I like the

feel of her resting on me, her hands touching me through my shirt and under my shirt. We are okay, then. We must be. The tape is nothing, some other Becks. Unless she's waiting to deliver her bad news, and softening the blow. She runs a hand over my hip, down as far as the knee, and brings it back up between my legs. I roll towards her. Sweeping her hair aside, I kiss the smooth downy spot high on her neck under the ear, then the edge of her mouth, then her mouth, which tastes of lip balm and apple. Her legs are warm. She's wearing black cotton trousers, cut off at mid-calf. Above her hip, uncovered at the waistline where the blouse has slipped loose, there's the soft bulge of her midriff, and higher still the broadening of ribcage and muscle. Her thigh makes space for itself between my thighs. And when I stop looking, thought stutters into fragments. I have an exaggerated sense of the enveloping size of her. My hand rides the luxurious breadth of her back. My mouth drops to her neck, to the curve of her shoulder, to the cushioning warmth of her breasts, which lift and fall under a double layer of fabric textured with ribs of seam and stitching.

'Let's have an early night,' she says, her breath coming uncertainly.

'Why wait?'

I'm lifting the blouse up over her belly, kissing her there where the flesh is malleable, while her hands above my head fumble with buttons. I like this. We both like this. Why is that so hard to remember? I become aware of the sound of a phone. By the time it's got through to me, Rebecca is disentangling herself.

'It'll be nothing,' I tell her. 'It'll be the water company offering us an improved kind of water.'

'It's my mobile.' She's sitting up with the phone to her ear, smiling and saying hi, while she pulls her blouse down, adjusts her trousers, straightens her hair. 'He's fine,' she says.

'It's Frankie,' she tells me. 'Wants to know how you are. Yes . . . yes, I know.' She's talking to Frankie again. 'Still bruised, and tired, I think, but basically fine.'

'Tell her we're busy. Switch it off. People shouldn't phone us when we're having sex. What's the matter with people?'

She's not listening to me. Her face has clouded over. 'Oh, no. What does this one say?' She finds my hand, which rests on her leg, and grips it absent-mindedly. 'But he's all right? Have you told the police?' She listens for a bit, nodding and making sympathetic noises. Then she says okay and bye and see you later, and closes the phone.

'What was it?'

'There is no God but God.'

'She called to tell you that?' I reach out with my other hand and hold her round the waist. 'That's been common gossip for centuries.'

'It was a text message for Max. That's all it said.' She bites her lip. 'I hope he's taking it seriously.'

'Giving up idol-worship, you mean?'

'It's not funny, David.'

'Apparently not.'

'Which reminds me.' She looks at her watch. 'I need to get something for Laura. It's her birthday tomorrow.'

'Who's Laura?'

'You know – Laura. Frankie's Laura.'

'You're buying her a present?'

'I thought some art supplies. She loves all that stuff. If I leave now, I'll have time to do that and some food shopping.'

'But you won't see Frankie till Monday.'

'She'll be there this evening.'

'Is that why we're going?'

'We're going because it's a good cause.'

'The world is full of good causes.'

She leans down and kisses me. 'We'll still have time for an early night.'

'And Max will be there?'

'Yes, probably. I don't know. Does it matter?'

'You tell me.'

She sits up, facing the window. 'What is it with you and Max? Is this still about that stupid documentary?'

'So you agree it was stupid.'

'It's television, David. It's a dog-food factory.' She's putting her shoes on, brushing her hair. 'Whatever you put in comes out as dog food. When did you start caring so much?'

'When you started working as Max's publicist.' This is not what I meant to do – this sniping is so pointless.

'It was cheap and exploitative – all right?' She's on her feet. She's started pulling things out of her handbag onto the bed. 'That's what I thought about it. It was disappointing. But given the way television functions maybe that's the best anyone can do. The women were sad and feeble and deluded. But at least they were better than the men. The men were pathetic.' She's found her keys at the bottom of her handbag and has started stuffing everything back in again. 'That was what redeemed it, actually, that it finally put the men on the spot, the punters and the managers, and the boyfriends, and all the rest of the sleaze-merchants. All the men. You should have stayed for that bit.'

'You were in the garden for half of it.'

'I was in the garden for five minutes with Frankie. I didn't wander off and get in a fight.'

'I fell over – I told you.'

'Yeah, and got saved by Christians.'

'Not saved! For God's sake, I hope I'm past saving.'

She smiles at that. Scepticism is still common ground, at least. 'Rescued, then. Look, I know this isn't working out for you, and I'm sorry I dragged you here.' She sits on the bed and takes my hand. 'But can't you just try and make the most of it?'

'I'll see what I can do.' I say it without conviction.

'I've got to get this shopping done. Will you be ready to leave by four thirty?'

'Yes, fine.'

'Four thirty, then.' She watches me for a moment from the doorway. She's anxious about me, I can see that – my detachment is worse for her than my anger. I hear the front door shutting, the clattering of steps on the concrete stair-case, and the car reversing into the street. We're in trouble, there's no question about that. But how much trouble, and of what kind?

I get up and make myself some coffee and take it back into the bedroom, because that's where the television is. The tapes are in my sock drawer under my socks. I'm about to put the Becks tape in the VCR. I've taken it out of its sleeve. But I change my mind and put in Nat instead. I take the remote and sit at the desk.

There are no titles, just a fuzz of horizontal lines, then Natalie standing in front of a bed. I remember the bedroom from last night, when I was looking for Max's office. Natalie's wearing her peasant frock, the one she died in dancing in the waves. Without the dance or the ocean breeze to give it life, it hangs shapelessly from her shoulders. She's looking side-ways, almost towards the camera. She tightens the ribbon in her hair, raises her chin and sucks her cheeks in. She's alone, studying her profile in a mirror. There's Latin jazz playing, which I'm guessing is Max's choice. She pulls up the front of the dress, bunching it above the waist, and begins to prod her stomach and her thighs, pinching the wasted muscles. It's painful to watch her uncovered like this, taking so little pleasure in her own image.

There's a sound from another room and she lets the skirt

fall, smoothing the fabric over her skinny figure. 'Hey, babe,' she says, and Max comes into view, walking away from the camera in a black silk dressing gown, padding on naked feet. He's carrying a champagne bottle and two glasses. 'Where d'you go?' 'I thought we should celebrate,' he says. 'You're so sweet,' she says. She kisses him, and for a moment there are only her bony arms clinging to him, her fingers in his hair, and the black silk of his robe. With the bottle still in one hand and the two glasses clinking in the other, he lifts her arms from his neck and walks past her towards the bed. Turning, he fills the glasses and hands her one. I see the bottle is only half full. It's a leftover from some other party. If Natalie notices she doesn't complain. It makes me want to punch him in the mouth, that he's so sure of himself. Her mind's on other things, of course. I get that a moment later, when she does a twirl around the room, pausing with her back to him to dribble her mouthful back into the glass, before pulling her hair free from its ribbon and shaking it loose. He's refilled his own, meanwhile, and put the bottle on the bedside table. With his free hand he pulls the cord of his robe and lets it slither to the floor. And I see that his mind, also, is on other things. He knows where the camera is. He knows which way to face as he unveils the main attraction. He's impressively muscular, with an unbroken tan, and thick black hair across his chest and around his cock, and a confident little paunch, the paunch of a man who knows what he's worth. It's like clothing, it seems to me, like armour, all this muscle, all this sun-weathered, sunlamp-darkened skin, like tree bark, like snakeskin. He looks somehow less naked than any naked man has a right to look. Beside him, Natalie seems already too naked even with her clothes on. It's not particularly long, his cock, since I've mentioned his cock, though it's rising even as I look at it, but it's

177

thick, I can't deny its thickness. I wonder if Rebecca has been called upon to deny herself its thickness.

I shake the thought out of my head, with a snarl. Soon enough I'll know about Rebecca. This is about Natalie. And as the thought comes to me, I'm already questioning it. What is this about, really? I found the tape where Natalie said it would be. Rochester's identity is established beyond doubt. What more is there to learn that I have any right to learn? He's sitting now, and she's kneeling astride him, and he's pulling her dress up over her skinny body, over her head, disentangling it from her hair, and the rest is who does what to whom. Could I say I'm watching this for Jake, that I'm the designated viewer? No need to watch it, Jake, I can tell him. It's neither more nor less than you'd expect. It's what it is. No special cruelty, except that Max like Narcissus gazes at himself while Natalie, unnoticed, dwindles to nothing. We've reclaimed the stolen image, you and me together, and now we can erase it, and our duty to the dead is discharged. I could say that. It's a story I could tell myself and it's maybe half true. Instead for some reason I find I'm quoting St Paul, clinging to the words like a talisman. *Whatsoever things are true, whatsoever things are honest, whatsoever things are just, whatsoever things are pure* . . . I press the eject button and the tape pops out. *Whatsoever things are lovely, whatsoever things are of good report* . . . A hunk with a six-pack is demonstrating an exercise machine. *If there be any virtue and if there be any praise, think on these things.* 'Only five minutes a day,' the hunk says, 'to tone those quads.' Behind him three models in Lycra are busy toning.

I pick up the tape called Evie. I can't remember why I took it and I can't think of a good reason to watch it, but I put it in anyway. I know what I'm doing. I'm leaving Becks till last. Evie will be a pause for breath while I recover from Natalie and before I face whatever has to be faced. I have no

particular feeling for Evie. I've pictured her dumpy and awkward, a little bit in love with Max and too shy to show it,
except by labouring over that replacement pawn. As soon as
the tape starts playing, I see how far I've been misled by the
name. Evie has long blonde hair. She's wearing a loose angora
sweater and not much else. She spends her moment alone
rubbing lotion on her legs. I have a feeling that her quads,
when she reveals them, will turn out to be nicely toned.
'Okay, Max,' she says, 'get your ass in here.' The accent also
takes me by surprise. She's from Eastern Europe. 'What are
you doing, Max? Taking your Viagra? You have to pump it
up maybe like an old man?' And the name must be Eva. Evie
is just the Maxified version, the Maxwellian diminutive.

Max has said something in response to her teasing that
makes her laugh. It's a mannered laugh that involves a lot
of hair-tossing. And here he comes with pornographic pre-
dictability in his black silk robe. This time he gives the back
view, the silk feathering from the shoulders, down over the
sculpted buttocks to the floor. If he was hoping for a reaction, he must have been disappointed – when he watched
the tape, if not at the time – because here's Evie, even as
the robe falls, glancing off to the side to check herself out
in the mirror. 'Now you lie down like a nice boy,' she says,
'and do as I tell you.' And she's on her feet, pushing him
down onto the bed, crawling on top of him in a smooth
feline motion. She's done this before. Even if she doesn't
know there's a camera, she's performing as though there
might be. I rewind the tape and watch her wriggle backwards
to her feet, drawing Max up after her with the flat of her
hand. I press play and there's the same prod, the same predatory crawl. I rewind, and play it again, watching her lithe
movements, and the sweater riding up as she leans forward
to clamber across the bed. There's definitely something
there. One more time, and I'm sure of it. There's a tattoo at

the base of her spine. I've seen it before. It's a swallow in flight. Evie is the second stripper from Max's documentary, unpixelated for private viewing. *I work with my hands*, she said in the film. *This is not a joke actually.*

I stop the tape. She's too good at what she does. I want very much not to be turned on by Max's personal pawn-maker.

There are men in suits shouting at each other in a television studio. 'Mel, Mel,' one of them says, 'we've heard all this before. When is this administration . . . No, Mel, you've had your say. When are they gonna to get that whatever America does for the world, the world is not gonna show one ounce of gratitude? We're talking democracy on a plate, freedom delivered at immense cost to us and no charge to them. Haven't the American people earned a break?'

And at more or less the same time, the other one is saying, 'You sure have heard it all before, Harry, and you're gonna hear it all again because your only answer . . . because you never listen, like you're not listening now. Your only answer, Harry, is to cut and run. Face it, you woulda given Hitler a pass.'

I press the mute button and sit for a minute watching Mel and Harry mouthing at each other. My coffee's cold. I'd like a drink, but I want to keep a clear head. I don't know what I'm going to have to cope with. Already I feel the desperate melancholy of the voyeur.

My heart is pounding as I put in the last tape. My life is about to unravel. Or not. I've seen the pattern. I'll know within seconds. I press play. There's the grey horizontal fuzz, then the familiar bedroom, and the bed, but no people. She must be just off camera, my Rebecca or this other Rebecca. I strain to hear something, some dialogue. I wait, but there's nothing. I'm watching a film of an empty bedroom, and an empty bed. Is this Max's joke, a meditation on unfulfilled desire? Is this the space into which he'd like Rebecca to walk? Does Max aspire to art? I feel myself grow light with relief. I'm about to eject the tape. But just to be sure I put it on fast-forward. For a minute or so there's nothing. Then something begins to happen. I recognize Rebecca – the old Rebecca with long hair and her hem just above the knees, so that dates it. She has her back to the camera, and her blouse is coming off in rapid twitching movements. She's doing it one-handed, holding a cigarette. A cigarette? She's never been a smoker. I press rewind and watch her speed-walk backwards, hoisting her blouse back over her shoulders, towards the camera and out of sight. I press play. And here she comes, walking away from me at a leisurely pace, towards the bed, left hand holding the cigarette, right elbow out to the side, the forearm dropping as her unseen fingers release one button at a time. She's a good mover. She carries her weight always with a natural grace. Then, the blouse unbuttoned, she pulls it down over her right shoulder, and wriggles her arm and hand free. She's by the bed. The blouse dangles from her left shoulder, the empty sleeve reaching almost to the hem of her skirt. It isn't a cigarette, of course – it's looser and more ragged at the end. She's smoking a joint. The hands move in front of her and out of sight. The joint reappears in the right hand, while the left shakes the blouse, sending it shimmering to the floor. As she turns and settles onto the bed, her breasts shift in her bra, and the fleshy bulge broadens above the waistband. And I think I've never seen anything so beautiful. And how could she? And why Max? She's looking up with a shy smile. 'I'm not sure this is such a good idea.' She giggles and raises the joint to her lips, and the look says, *But it's not such a bad idea either*.

A shadow passes in front of the camera. I can't bear the thought of Max one more time in his bloody silk dressing gown, with his tight buttocks and his hairy back. I try to stop the tape, but I'm gripping the remote so hard, my finger doesn't connect. I fumble for a moment while the dark shape in the bedroom hardens into human form, then the tape stops. And I'm watching a group of black teenagers hanging around on a street corner, and I'm listening to the voice of a reporter, '. . . where gang violence is never more than a heart-beat away.' And here he is, shouting above the noise of the traffic. 'A revenge killing, or an initiation that went horribly wrong? We may never know. This is Jeb Nordquist in South Central Los Angeles. Kimberly?' Back in the studio, Kimberly looks up from her monitor. 'Thanks, Jeb. Jeb Nordquist there with a special report on minority violence.' For a second she holds the camera, with the earnest look of a Miss World con-testant who longs for world peace, then she relaxes into a smile. 'Now, we've all heard of talking chimpanzees, but how about a fish that can do math?'

Turning it off seems as pointless as not turning it off. I let the images flash in front of me. I watch a commercial for some drug that allows old people to go windsurfing and ball-room dancing and to ride horses through forests. They're all white-haired and tanned, these old people. They're all smil-ing and married and not one of them looks lonely. I watch the weather. We're about to have a lot of it, if the time spent on it and the quality of the graphics are anything to go by. Horace the weatherman strides through a virtual landscape showing us where it's going to be hot and dry, and where it's going to be hotter and drier. We can expect the surf to be up all along the coast. Tomorrow will be just great for the family barbecue. Except for the wind. The wind might just be the fly in the ointment – Santa Anas, apparently, blowing straight in from the desert. That means lower levels of pollution, but zero humidity, and I'm to take particular care if I'm driving a high-sided vehicle.

I press the off switch, pick up the phone on the desk and

call Astrid. There's an answering machine, so I hang up. I wait about twenty seconds, and call her again. I'd call someone else if there was someone else to call. I imagine her tentative questions – *What's happening? How have you been?* – feeling her way towards an assessment of how things stand between us – are we lovers yet, or nothing already? I don't know, I want to tell her, but please stay on the line.

She's breathless when she answers. Between gasps, she tells me she's playing tennis with her coach, BJ. 'Did I tell you about BJ? He's an amazing guy. He wrote the book.'

'On tennis?'

'On everything. It's been the coaching bible for like thirty years.'

'Tennis coaching?'

'Business coaching, life coaching. Envisioning for Success with BJ Bradstock. That's the subtitle.'

'And what's the title?'

'Over the Net. To begin with, I didn't even get the tennis connection. I bought it thinking it would help with web-searches. Then I met BJ.'

'And now he's your tennis coach.'

'He's my everything coach. The tennis is just for fun.'

'For him or for you?'

'Both, I hope.'

'You must be good.'

'Are you kidding? He's had knee surgery, a hip replace-ment and a four-way bypass. And he still beats me.'

'You'd better get back to it, then. You obviously need more coaching.'

'You okay, honey? You sound kind of edgy.'

I'm relieved that she chatters as freely as ever. Her friendship is what I need. But I register a twinge of loss as well. I thought it was me whose brilliance amazed her, not BJ bloody Bradstock. 'Have you got a minute?'

'Sweetheart, I'm right here.'

'I found the tape.'

'Don't hang up.' She's talking to BJ, suggesting they take a break. There's some clatter and background noise. Then it goes quiet, and I hear Astrid clearing her throat. 'You found it, you say?'

'Yes.'

'In Max's office?' She's talking more quietly, holding the phone closer to her mouth.

'Yes, in a locked cupboard, behind some files.'

'Wow, just as Natalie promised. Did you watch it?'

'Enough.'

'Creepy, huh?'

'Yes. Quite upsetting, actually. And something even more upsetting. I don't know even if I should tell you this.'

'Well, you'd better tell me after that teaser.'

'Haven't you got a game to finish?'

'David, do you have plans for the rest of your life?'

'Not really. Why?'

'Because if you don't tell me what else you found, you'll probably be dead because I'll have beaten the crap out of you.'

I laugh, and the momentary release opens a space inside me that fills up with misery. 'He has other tapes.'

'Wouldn't you just know it.'

'Rebecca's on one of them.'

'Rebecca who?'

'My wife, Rebecca.'

'She's on the tape?'

'She's the star.'

'You watched it?'

'Enough of it.'

'Your wife and Max? Jesus, how long has that been in production?'

'I don't know.' There's a pause. Now that I've told her, I don't know what else there is to say. 'And we're supposed to go to some ACLU thing this evening. I'm not sure I can face it. I'm not in the mood for civil liberties.'

'It sounds like this is rough for you, huh.'

'Pretty rough, yes.' And we're no further forward.

'Listen, David, there's something I have to ask you – just to cut to the chase, you know? And because I like to know where I stand?'

For some reason, I'm not looking forward to the question.

'Did you call me,' Astrid says, 'about me or about her?'

'How do you mean?'

'Think about it, David. You're not that dumb.'

My capacity to amaze really has taken a tumble – it's less than a week since I was a genius. 'You're right,' I tell her, 'you're absolutely right. I shouldn't have called.'

'Hey, don't get snarky, okay?'

'I'm sorry. Really, I'm sorry if I sounded . . . snarky. It's not what I meant . . .'

'So . . . okay . . . you called me why?'

I'm getting flashes of Astrid in my head, like a high-speed slide show. Astrid's hands in strangling position, her legs under the rising hem of the burka, her face framed in silk. And there's a soundtrack with it – the electric crackle of her conversation, sparking between sense and nonsense, and my own half-incredulous laughter. I remember the warmth of her breath on my face at the Bluegrass Café. I remember kissing her. If I want her, this is the time to say. And now that adultery's in fashion, what could be easier? Except that the desire seems suddenly theoretical. I can't focus on it with Rebecca's betrayal weighing on me. 'I wanted to let you know about Natalie's tape,' I tell her. 'And, I suppose, to talk to you . . . about Rebecca. About the fact that my wife is sleeping with – has slept with – someone else. I didn't know who else to call.'

I listen to the silence as she takes this in. Then she says, 'My dear fellow, that's perfectly all right. I shall instruct my valet to put the champagne back in the ice bucket.'

I manage a grunt of laughter. Even though I'm not quite ready to walk through it, I hate the sound of the door shutting. 'That English accent,' I tell her, 'it really is remarkably good. Are you honestly all right with this?'

'Hey, it's not like you're my only prospect . . .'

'This phone call, I mean. Because I'm feeling sort of out on a limb.'

'So quit apologizing already. Jesus, David, if you need to talk, talk.'

This time the laughter is spontaneous, but it's only the sound of my physical tension easing. And the silence that follows is just me staring dumbly at my own unhappiness. Astrid is breathing and then, after a moment, something else happens – a new kind of noise, as though someone's turned up the volume.

'Astrid, are you still there?'

'Sure I am, honey.'

'I thought I heard something. I thought you'd gone.'

'I'm not going anywhere.'

'Thanks. Really, though. Thanks for being so incredibly generous and easy about everything.'

'You're pretty incredible too, David – thoughtful and gentle, you know? You should remember that. You deserve better than you're getting from your marriage. You need to stand up for yourself.'

I detect the influence of Bradstock in this bracing pep-talk. Assertiveness training isn't what I need right now. I'm still trying to work out what I feel about this tape – Rebecca stripping off for Max, getting high with Max, being fucked by Max. 'The thing is I feel somehow I've made it real. It's like something Natalie says in her journal – I can't unknow what I know, however much I wish I could. I've looked and now it's somehow irrevocably there.'

'Like Schrödinger's cat, you mean? Until you opened the box it could have been alive or dead?'

'Maybe. I don't know.'

'The universe has divided and you're on the wrong side of the divide?'

'Christ, I don't know what I mean.' I haven't phoned Astrid to discuss Schrödinger's cat and multiple frigging universes. I make another attempt to express some of what's whirling through my head. 'I just keep thinking about how transparent Rebecca and I have always been to each other. We're not used to this sneaking around. There's never been anything like this before. It's nonsense what I said about wishing I hadn't looked. I have to face the truth. What happened the other day, between you and me – I look back on it now like a dream. It was very nice, but I wasn't paying attention to what I had, and now I wish I still had it. Does any of this make sense?'

'Every day is its own illusion, David. Today is no more real than yesterday.'

'But I can't erase today, just because I preferred yesterday.'

'Okay. So you know what I think? You've just got to confront her with it. It mightn't be so bad. Just ask her what she's going to do. Put the ball in her court.'

'Is that the kind of coaching you get from your friend BJ?'

'You could do worse. He'd help you see this isn't your fault. Guilt is terribly disempowering. Deal with her, and then maybe you can start dealing with us.'

The bedroom door opens and Rebecca stands with the kitchen phone in her hand. She's pale with fury.

I tell Astrid, 'I'd better go.'

'Are you okay?'

'We're fine, thanks,' Rebecca says, 'but we're hanging up now.' There's a beep and she tosses the phone onto the bed.

I stand up to face her. 'You were listening.'

'I thought you might still be asleep.' She's shaking with the effort to stay calm. 'I was going to check for messages.'

'I think we need to talk . . .'

'No, I got the whole thing, thanks very much. You reckon you deserve better than me, now you've discovered what an incredible time you can have with that dolled-up little fuck machine, her being so generous and everything – I bet she is. Such a dream, in fact, that you'd like to erase me, and maybe it won't be so bad if you tell me straight out because guilt is terribly disempowering. Oh yes, and your big mistake was sneaking around – you got that bit right, anyway, because your sneaking days are over, mate. Now I'm going to this fundraiser, and you can go to hell.'

And she's gone. And I'm left wondering what just happened. Perhaps what persuades me to follow her is the fear that she might not come back. Perhaps I'm just too angry not to. I'd like to throw some of her words back at her, to say *You can go to hell too*, to tell Max to keep his squat little dick to himself and *Get the fuck out of my life*. Perhaps I've just got nowhere else to go. I know where to find her, because she's left the flyer on the dining table. There's the name of the place – the Rosenberg Memorial Library – with the address and a phone number.

It takes me a minute to find my wallet and my mobile phone. I wasn't thinking too clearly when we got home last night. The wallet's on the coffee table. The phone's in the bathroom and probably needs recharging, but it'll get me as far as the library, in case I need to call for directions.

The neighbour's wind chimes are clanging tunelessly. A loose section of wooden fencing knocks against a post. Down on the street I feel the dust in my eyes and taste it on my tongue. I get in the car and put the key in the ignition. I take another look at the flyer. The Rosenberg Memorial Library is in a part of the city called South Central. I was just hearing about South Central in Jeb Nordquist's TV report – where gang violence is never more than a heartbeat away. Maybe we'll all be shot. It would solve a lot of problems.

thirteen

I've escaped Frankie, who was curious to see me arrive without Rebecca. I'd paid my $25 donation and was making a
start on the red wine. Frankie was doing that look she's so
good at – the head tilted, one eyebrow raised. 'Oh, you know
Rebecca,' I told her between mouthfuls, which wasn't any
kind of an answer to whatever it was she'd asked me. I took
another plastic glass and wandered into the stacks. Thank
God for books, which allow me to turn my face to the wall.
I pretend to browse while I deal with waves of panic. And
thank God for these ill-lit passageways. What's happening to
me? I hold myself steady against a bookshelf while I register
sensations that I associate with fear or grief – disturbances
in the bowels and stomach, rising behind the ribcage and
towards the throat. A pulsing in the diaphragm, causing a
spasmodic sucking in of air – for a while this is as close as I
get to breathing. I feel weightless. There's a sense of levitation that attaches itself to a thought: I know no one, am
known by no one. Except by Rebecca, if she comes. Rebecca
knows me. Which, I suppose, is why I followed her. I drink,
and the drink calms me.

A woman with a kind face approaches so I turn and keep
moving. Serious left-wing literature, I discover, is what this
library specializes in; coated seriously with dust, most of it.
Trotskyism is demarcated from Marxist-Leninism in one
direction and from anarcho-syndicalism in another. Among

the books there are pamphlets and journals from a time when workers were expected to unite in the struggle and the oppressed to break at any moment from their shackles. There are sections on civil rights and the new left. I turn past a bank of filing cabinets labelled Oral Histories and find the spiral staircase to the mezzanine.

Rebecca should be here by now. She should have arrived before me. She might be lost. It's a part of the city we haven't seen before – a flat expanse of low-grade housing, the major streets lined with barricaded storefronts, and this place like a concrete bunker in the middle of it. She would have been depending on me to drive, or to navigate while she drove, all this way eastward into the downtown smog. But she should have thought of that before joining the list of Max's other women. Max is coming straight from work, Frankie says. Maybe neither of them will show up. That will clarify things.

From the balcony I can see who comes and goes, without having to talk to anyone. I recognize one or two faces from the faculty party, but no one from last night's TV crowd. There are more old people here, more of the invisibly unglamorous and the waywardly attractive, fewer taut faces and pumped-up lips. Among the denim caps and the canvas jackets and the boiler suits, the beards and the pot bellies and the flabby necks and the frizzy mops of iron-grey hair, there are bursts of colour and outbreaks of uncoordinated style. I wonder where some of these people have come from, the older baggier ones. They seem so foreign to this city and this time. The librarian has opened the filing cabinets and they've stepped from the dust of their own oral histories. The racial variety is also unfamiliar. I don't mean the Asians or the elegantly suited African-Americans, who would have looked at home at any of Max and Frankie's parties. It's the handful of Mexicans who establish the social inclusiveness of this event. I'm struck by how rapidly I've adjusted to their ubiquity and their otherness, these bit-players in this city of stars, the maids and gardeners and busboys, the casual day labourers who congregate outside the timber yards and the U-Haul depots of the Westside, squatting by walls and under eucalyptus trees for the shade, the building workers in the uniforms of their trades, paint-spattered overalls and canvas tool-belts, gathering on the sidewalks by the catering trucks. Already I'm registering this as an integration, these Mexican couples plump and smiling in their Sunday best, being welcomed and offered wine in faltering Spanish.

Then a grizzled elder with a Lenin beard is raising his voice above the chatter. Something's about to happen. They're shuffling towards the seats, breaking off conversation, promising to catch each other later. The projector screen is a rectangle of blue light, decorated with familiar desktop icons. A fey young woman in a shapeless dress has stood up to tell us that Stu Selznick needs no introduction. I recognize Stu. *Your hatchet-faced friend*, Amir called him, complaining to Frankie that he'd been canvassed for the Palestinian cause. Bending over a table, Stu touches a laptop keyboard and the screen is filled with a still image of a windblown Stars and Stripes. Someone dims the lights.

'Do you remember when the Berlin Wall came down?' Stu looks up from his computer. He has a script or a page of notes in one hand, and reading glasses in the other. 'What excitement.'

There are grunts of recognition from the audience.

'We couldn't get over that this was happening. The end of the cold war. The nuclear threat lifted. Then my mother called.'

People laugh as though they know his mother, which maybe some of them do.

'Stuart, she says to me' – he puts on a mid-European

accent – 'such celebrations on the television, Stuart. Yes, Mother, I said, the Berlin Wall came down. Stuart, she says, this is not good for the Jews.'

This goes down well. I hear the rhythm of the joke, the flight it takes through the air, though I'm not sure I know why it's funny.

'What can I tell you? My mother had a narrow focus. She also couldn't see a silver lining without looking for the cloud. I happen to think she was looking out for the wrong victim, and with the life she'd led that was maybe not so surprising. But she was right about the cloud. Reports of the end of history were premature. Which of us could have guessed that not so many years later, with communism defeated and the Soviet Union dismantled, we'd be facing a new kind of McCarthyism in this country? A threat that has particular resonance here in the Rosenberg Memorial Library.' He presses the key for the next slide. It's a list of names, three columns to the page. He's put his glasses on to look at his notes. 'Here are some of the people affected. Some of the detained, the deported, the disappeared. Not many Jewish names here. My mother would have been relieved to see that. Not many Irish or Norwegian names either. A lot of Arabic names, though, Farsi names, Indian and Pakistani names.' He clicks again and the page becomes one of nine pages, miniaturized on the screen. 'We've had to learn a lot of new words these past few years, as the newspeak of the neo-McCarthyites has gotten cosily embedded in our brains.' He chuckles, leaving time for some of the audience to join in. 'The innocuous-sounding verb to render is one of my favourites. We don't approve of torture, not officially, not in so many words, not on US soil. We *render* our political prisoners. We farm them out to client states. We remove them to bases abroad. We deal with them in their own neighbourhood. Hang a US flag over the torture chambers of the defeated enemy and it's business as usual. How did it come to this?' He looks up, taking his glasses off. 'You know, I remember when my cousin Louie played The Flight of the Bumblebee at my bar mitzvah. Rabbi Goldman thanked him for his extraordinary rendition. Well, it might have been torture for me, but I don't think that's what the rabbi had in mind.' There are grunts of dutiful laughter. 'Innocent times.'

He clicks, and the columns of names are replaced by a naked man cowering from a dog.

'I feel uneasy about showing these pictures. They are, in the deepest sense imaginable, obscene.'

Another man squats at the end of a leash.

'What is the provenance of these images?' He's reading now, and his delivery becomes stiffer. 'Are they the work of undercover journalists with hidden cameras? The grinning poses of the torturers suggest not. Happy snaps, then? Something to show the folks back home, or the grand-kids? Like those sepia photos of white men gathered around a lynching, proud of their work? That seems closer to the mark. Might the photographers be motivated also by an urge to record, like Nazi bureaucrats keeping meticulous records in the midst of carnage? That too, maybe. But we shouldn't forget another crucial element – that the pictures themselves are part of the process, part of the humiliation. The interro-gation hasn't started yet. This is the warm-up act.' He looks up, letting the incongruous phrase sink in. 'Who are these low-status soldiers, by the way, little more than children some of them, who are being inducted here into the sacred mysteries of empire? Because let's remember, like the abattoir at the heart of the bucolic idyll, this is not an aber-ration, but the rough end of a business that couldn't manage without rough ends. In a sense, these are the fall guys, the nebbishes who take the rap when international outrage demands a sacrifice. But they're also the fallen, our fallen selves, challenging us to take a stand for what is good in human nature.'

The reference to the fall brings Rebecca into my mind. It's been all of two minutes since I thought about her. But now, as I remember that this sick feeling has a cause, it occurs to me that they should make me feel better, these dirty pictures, so much dirtier than Max's videos. They should put my mundane distress in perspective. But they're losing their power even to distract. I'm bored already – feverishly, ferociously bored. I've seen them before, of course, or something like them. But my rejection is more than indifference. In my head, I'm telling Stu Selznick to shut up. I'm muttering it under my breath – shut up with your whining decency. I want Rebecca to walk through the door, so I can tell her what I think of her, so I can say it's him or me, so I can say unforgivably hurtful things, and ask her to forgive me, so I can hold her and she can hold me, so I can stop feeling weightless and adrift. I want to get Max out of my head. He's there now, with some girl on a leash, disrobing for the camera with that smirking self-regard that makes me want to punch him. I want to put his head in a bag and set the dogs on him. I've got him by the throat, pushing him backwards over the railings, until he falls head first among Stu Selznick's audience, lying with a broken neck in a tangle of plastic furniture.

And there he is suddenly, no longer a figment, standing in the doorway, dark against the daylight. He has a haunted look. Stu is still talking. Max glances at the screen and at the audience. He works his way around the back of the room, nodding perfunctorily to a few people in passing. Then he moves out of sight underneath me. Perhaps it's guilt, that troubled look of his. The door opens again and it's Rebecca. She looks sad. If they've been together, things haven't been

going so well. Unless they've decided it's the real thing and
they'll smash everything that needs to be smashed to make
space for it. She looks around vaguely, hoping for a friendly
face, or just looking for Max. I wait for her to notice me.
When she does, I get a glare that makes me feel like a stalker.
She crosses her arms and turns towards the projector screen.

I move away from the balustrade and hurry through the
stacks towards the staircase. I'm thinking I'll approach her
now, while she's by the door, and ask her to step outside, to
walk round the block with me, and I'll ask her why Max of
all people, and what the fuck's happened to her, and can't
we just put everything back the way it was. My footsteps
are noisy on the iron staircase. I stumble near the bottom,
misjudging the gaps, and land awkwardly. I turn a corner
between shelves, and I'm facing him, my wife's boyfriend,
with his strong face, tanned and pock-marked.

He stops, and I see the knowledge in his eyes that I
haven't seen before, like a consciousness of me as a factor
that has to be worked into his calculations. He approaches
warily, speaking in a hoarse undertone.

'Can we talk?'

'Are you sure you want to risk it?'

He searches my face for meaning. I realize that for once
I know more than he knows, and that there's power in this.

'Listen, Dave, there's some weird stuff happening.'

'These threatening text messages, you mean?'

'You've heard about them?'

'There is no God but God.'

'Am I being paranoid about all that, Dave? Is that a
threat, do you think, in the circumstances?' His eyes are all
over the place, as if an enemy might be lurking among the
stacks.

'If you're a worshipper of Belial or Moloch, I'd think it
could be.'

'Pardon me?'

'Monotheism, Max. I'm beginning to think it's been the problem all along. I hope you don't mind me saying this, and I don't mean any disrespect to the Jewish people, but was it such a good idea, really, in retrospect?'

He stares blankly at me. 'Look, that's all very interesting. I know you're a very bright guy, Dave, don't get me wrong, but I have more immediate problems.'

'Yes, I think you probably have.'

There's a shushing sound. At the end of a corridor of books, one of Stu's acolytes is peering over her spectacles at us with a finger to her lips.

We're a few feet from a door outlined in yellow light. Max opens it and jerks his head for me to go in. He follows, shutting the door behind him. We're in a storage room stacked with boxes and filing cabinets.

Max stands with his feet apart, adjusting his neck and shoulders as though preparing to deliver a blow. 'The thing is, Dave,' he says, 'someone broke into my office last night.'

'Really?'

'Really. I have to ask you this. That car you were driving the other night, the Bug with the flowers.'

'Attractive, don't you think?'

'Yeah, yeah, very summer of love. I need to know where it came from.'

'Why would you need to know that?'

'You borrowed it, you said. Someone had it lying around.'

'That's more or less it.'

'Because I'm gonna level with you now, Dave. Truth is I've seen that vehicle before. I know the person who used to drive it.'

'You amaze me.'

He peers at me, checking for signs of amazement. 'Some coincidence, right?'

'I would say so.'

'Particularly if you know this person too. See what's going through my mind is . . . and I'm asking you this as a friend, Dave . . . are you being used in some way, is someone using you to get to me?'

'Get to you how?'

'By breaking into my office, for example.'

He's making himself look me in the eye, and I feel a flush of shame at what I've done, before outrage reasserts itself and, with it, the urge to watch him sweat.

'Why would I do that?'

He clears his throat. 'Maybe that's not it, you see, because maybe this person is getting to me in various ways and you driving that car is just one of them. Maybe. But you gotta understand, Dave, there are a couple of things point to you.'

'A couple?'

'Three, as a matter of fact, the car being one, your sudden disappearance last night possibly being another . . .'

'And the third?'

Then there's a look on his face as though my insolence is suddenly unmistakeable, or as though he just can't stand the tension any more. 'Look, you fucker,' he says. His index finger is pointing towards my face and his hand shakes. 'Is this about Natalie?'

'Is that the part that worries you? You're incredible, Max, you really are.'

'All I wanna know, Dave, okay, is what's in it for you. The car should have told me. I should never have been taken in by that friend of a friend crap . . . So what's the deal? She wanna job, or what? She gonna sue? If this is some attempt to blackmail me I'll break your fucking neck. What the hell does that mean, anyway, *is that the part that worries me*? Is that some kind of a threat? Do you think I'm intimidated by you? I've got the Muslim Brotherhood on my back. So you can go to hell.'

'I mean, why Natalie? Why not Evie, for example?'

'So it *was* you.'

'Don't you think, perhaps, I might actually be more concerned about what you did to Rebecca?'

'Oh, so you got that one too. Well, sure, I took a liberty. I'm embarrassed about it. What do you want me to say?'

'You're embarrassed!'

'So sue me. Fuck it, Dave, there are worse things. You've got the tape, so forget it. I'd love to know how you knew about it, nobody else did.'

'I'm married to her.'

'Yeah, I've apologized already, whaddya want me to do? Slit my throat? I won't last through the weekend in any case, if the local jihadists have their way. So you can wait in line. And Natalie can wait in line too, tell her.'

'Natalie's dead, Max.'

He doesn't take it in at first.

'Natalie's waiting in line for the resurrection. Or reincarnation. Or eternal oneness with the universe or something . . .'

'My God,' he says. Strange things are happening to his face. 'That's terrible.' He stares at the floor, then at me. 'How can she be dead? What happened?'

'She killed herself. She stood in the ocean and slashed her wrist with a razor blade.'

'I can't believe it.'

'I've read her journal, by the way. You get a mention.'

'It can't have been my fault. Okay, we had a fight. People fight all the time – it doesn't mean anything. Why would she do a thing like that?'

The colour has drained from his face. He seems to be taking it hard, unless it's just television. Either way, I can't stand to watch. I need a drink. And I need to talk to Rebecca, find out where I stand. The meeting's still on. Someone's talking, an elderly man, it sounds like, irascible and short-winded.

'. . . because the way I see it, Stu, you wanna know the truth, I think you should have listened to your mother.'

That makes people laugh. I catch sight of his stooped figure between the bookstacks. Rebecca has moved from the door. I walk past the stacks, trying to locate her.

'I'm telling you,' the old man says, 'you wouldn't credit how much anti-Semitism there is over there in Europe, in so-called respectable newspapers, on the BBC. Unspeakable lies about Israel being hawked all over the world. If we are not for ourselves, who else will be for us?'

'Nicely put, Irving,' Stu says. 'But I think this is something we can talk about another time.'

'What's wrong with now? Because I'm frankly tired of people wanting America to solve their problems for them. First they want a Marshall Plan for Russia. Then they want a Marshall Plan for Africa. Now they want a Marshall Plan for the Middle East. George Marshall must be turning in his grave. It's just another way of bullying America into coughing up. And for what? For everybody else's mistakes. I mean, for chrissake, what did these people ever do for us?'

There's a noisy response to that, laughter and yelling and an upsurge of local arguments. Somebody shouts, 'I think, people, we're maybe getting off the point here . . .'

I'm facing sideways as I walk, still trying to spot Rebecca. At the edge of my vision, from around a corner, there's something red. Then my skull is rebounding from a collision and my shoulder blade is against the edge of a bookshelf. Then I'm walking away with my hands pressed to my temple and

I'm saying, 'Ow, ow, ow.' I turn again, still walking through the pain, and the patch of red comes into focus. It's Jake's baseball cap. Jake's sitting on the ground, holding the cap in one hand, and rubbing his head with the other.

'Jake, are you all right?'

'Jesus, can't you watch where you're going?'

'Did you hurt yourself?'

'It's nothing.' He lets me help him up. 'I came for the tape,' he says.

'What are you doing here?'

'Astro says you found the tape, you know who Rochester is.'

'Not now, Jake, I've got to talk to my wife.'

He pulls his cap back on, rolling his eyes in exasperation. 'Why are you holding out on me, David? All I'm asking here is that you act with some integrity. Is that too much for you?'

'How did you know where to find me?'

'Astro said it was an ACLU thing. I Googled it.'

Someone hushes us from the other end of the bookstack. Things are quietening down. Stu is taking questions.

Jake lowers his voice. 'So just give me the tape,' he says.

'Fine. We'll go somewhere and talk about it. First I have to find Rebecca.'

'There's nothing for us to talk about. I told you about the tape. If you've got it, you should give it to me. It's nothing to do with you.'

'Just give me a minute, Jake, all right.'

He glares at me. Then he slumps into silence.

'I was wondering . . .' It's a voice from the audience. 'Perhaps I missed something . . .' It's an English voice, with a resonance that cuts through the noise – the voice of someone who's used to being listened to. 'Was there, I wonder, a single reference in your pornographic slide show to the possibility that some of these people you mendaciously describe as the Disappeared might in fact be the mortal enemies of every liberal value you and I presumably share?'

'I showed my gold, didn't I,' Jake says quietly.

'What?'

The Englishman is still talking, and he's getting a noisy response.

Jake says, 'Nat used to say to me, don't show your gold. Show your gold and they'll rob you. She used to say, there's a trickster in you, Jake. You can't be a hero in the world unless you first honour the trickster in you. But I showed my gold, didn't I, and you robbed me.'

I put my hand on his arm. 'I never robbed you, Jake. I'll tell you anything you want to know. It's just that I've got problems of my own right now.'

Leaving Jake, I reach the edge of the audience, and start searching for Rebecca. Frankie is standing near the back, watching me. Her detachment is unnerving. I find my legs are shaking. I seem to be having some kind of delayed reaction to my collision with Jake, or my confrontation with Max. I lean back against a bookcase and close my eyes.

'You may seek to make common cause with the Islamo-fascists,' the Englishman is saying, 'but, make no mistake, there is no common cause to be found. If you choose to ally yourselves with those who despise the freedom of speech of which you make such tedious use, do not be surprised if the day comes when you yourselves are silenced.'

There's a mixture of laughter and booing. Someone says, 'Siddown.' Someone else says, 'Let the guy talk.'

'Is there a question here?'

'The question, Mr Selznick, is whether you are capable of being serious, you, and all those of your audience who are so quick to laugh and so slow to think. I find it frankly pitiable to observe the intellectual contortions of the left – the left of which I once considered myself to be a part. What other president has been willing to stake his place in history on Jefferson's promise that the American experiment would finally be spread to all nations of the world? All our adult lives, you and I have railed against the self-defeating stupidity of US foreign policy in shoring up murderous juntas, funding death squads, doing secret deals with terrorist organizations with agendas entirely incompatible with our own. At the point when, if I can put it like this, some of these chickens have come home very forcibly to roost, we are fortunate to have an administration in power that is willing to overthrow half a century of precedent and fight openly in support of the values we all espouse. And what is your response? To make the solipsistic error of assuming – to the point of choosing fascists as your bedfellows – that the enemies of America, always and everywhere, are your friends.' I open my eyes. The Englishman is good-looking in a jowly kind of way, with a mop of sandy brown hair. He's having to raise his voice to be heard above the din. 'Well, your reluctance to hear a dissenting view is at least consistent.'

'Please make your point.'

There's a lull, during which I hear a metallic grinding and a cascade of water as someone flushes a toilet.

'While Mr Selznick was talking, I was imagining this meeting transported back to 1945 . . .'

Rebecca comes through a doorway at the back of the room, drying her hands on a paper towel. I make my way towards her, between the rows of chairs on one side and the bookstacks on the other.

'Our armies are in Germany and Poland, opening the concentration camps. And you lot are sitting here watching slides of Dresden, beating your breasts over Allied atrocities.'

There are shouts of protest. Chairs slide and topple as people jump to their feet. Stu Selznick is visibly angry.

'There's nothing you can teach me about the death camps, or a lot of other people here.'

'Ah yes, the one-upmanship of suffering.'

I feel a hand gripping my shoulder, pulling me round. I find myself facing Max. 'I don't know what sick game you're playing,' he hisses at me, 'but I want what you took from me.' I watch him push his way along a disorderly row of people towards the door.

Turning back to locate Rebecca, I catch a glimpse of Frankie's eyes, wide with anxiety, and then her head bobbing among the throng as she hurries after her husband. Rebecca is just behind her. I edge my way in their direction. A fat, grey-haired woman is berating the Englishman for selling out to the forces of neo-colonialism. A surge of movement behind me drives me between them. They're quoting Orwell at each other. I apologize to the woman for stepping on her feet.

'You're welcome,' she says drily. 'Orwell was a socialist,' she tells the Englishman. 'He saw how the British upper class were undermining the war effort.'

'What Orwell saw,' the Englishman says, 'was the masochism of the intellectual left.' And the whiskey fumes blow warm and moist against my face.

A space opens in front of me and there's Rebecca.

'What the hell have you done to Max?' she says.

'What about what Max has done to me? And what about what he's done to you? Is still doing to you, for all I know.'

'I think you've got a real problem, you know that?' She pushes past me.

'Can we talk about this?'

An elderly man peers through half-moon spectacles into my face, blocking my way.

'Rebecca,' I shout over his shoulder, 'please don't go like this.'

'I fought against the Nazis, you know,' the old man tells me. 'You don't get to lecture me on tyranny.'

When I reach the door, Jake is waiting for me.

'Was that him? Was that Rochester, the guy in the linen suit? He said you took something from him. Was that the tape?'

'Just, for God's sake, Jake, give me five bloody minutes to talk to my wife, and I'll tell you everything I know. All right?'

'Always the brush off, always the putdown with you, isn't it. One authentic exchange, is that too much to ask for?' His eyes begin to glisten, and I see he's fighting tears.

'Don't get agitated, Jake. I'm not putting you down, I've just a lot on my plate at the moment.'

'Well, fuck your plate, is all I can say, and fuck you.' He walks out, slamming the door behind him.

His anger has attracted attention. People have turned from their political debates and their socializing to see what's going on. I make some apologetic noises and follow him out. It's quiet in the street when I pull the door shut. Jake is striding off along the sidewalk. Beyond him, Frankie is just visible in the early evening gloom, turning a corner by a liquor store. Max is gone. Rebecca is standing in the road, about to get into her car.

'Rebecca, wait!'

Two beaten-up cars cruise towards us, as wide and flat as barges, and I step back to let them pass – a Chevrolet and a Cadillac, pulsing with competing rhythms – while Rebecca fidgets with her keys. Behind her the Evangelical Mission of the Apostles and Prophets announces itself in uneven letters under a tilting cross.

I walk towards Rebecca. She looks shaken. I say, 'Why don't you tell me what's going on?'

'Are you going to apologize?'

'Is this how you're going to do it, then? Make it my fault?'

'And isn't it? What was that with Max, just now?'

'All right, let's talk about Max. I know all about it. I've seen it. I've seen you with him.'

I stop talking because she's just standing there, weeping silently. Her head is down, and her shoulders are moving. Next to the Evangelical Mission is Sunny's New and Used Appliances, with two vacuum cleaners in the window behind an iron grille, and beyond that Pat's Pawnshop. On the other side, there's a car-repair place with room for maybe two cars, and a hairstylist's offering *Tintes Permanentes*. I'm ready to be generous. She can tell me it's over and we can make a new start.

I put my hand out towards her. 'Come home with me.'

'I'm staying the night with Frankie.'

'Does she know?'

'She just invited me.'

'About you and Max. Does she know about you and Max?'

'Is this all just some diversionary tactic?'

'So you're not even going to admit it?'

'Because you've got something going with that woman?'

'That's nothing.'

'But I'd quite like to know if you've screwed her yet.'

'Whereas in your case that isn't even a question.'

'Too right, it isn't a question.'

'Because I know.'

'That's enough!'

I'm startled by her sudden rage – the shaking of her head and the way she covers her ears to shut me out. After a moment, she lets her hands drop and begins speaking again, quietly, articulating with exaggerated care, fighting for control. 'I can be grown-up about this, I don't expect you to be faultless, she's younger and prettier than I am, and it must be flattering, I can see that, except that she's clearly bonkers, which worries me that you seem to be past caring.' She takes a deep breath. 'Because maybe it's just the physical part that matters to you, which wouldn't be so bad, in a way, I mean I've never expected you to not to look at other women, not to be turned on by them, Christ, I know I feel randy sometimes, and some men are nice to look at and some men make me laugh and feel warm and there are times when I could do with some of that, so it's not that I don't understand. And although, to be honest, forty-two is a bit young for a midlife crisis, and you're early for the seven-year bloody itch, if you want to get a few clichés out of the way, I suppose I could live with it if it's just a phase. Because I honestly think that for me it's not so much the thought of her getting her hands on you or you getting your hands on her, as the fact that, to be frank, you don't seem to be able to think straight anymore, and I sincerely hope that whatever you're getting up to you're taking precautions.'

'Precautions?'

'Condoms! Seatbelts! Not leaving your credit cards lying about – precautions!'

I smile at that, and so does she, reluctantly, because she knows it's funny, even though tears are streaming down her face.

'Really, though!' she says. 'Because I really, really don't want you to get screwed in ways you didn't intend, or me for that matter, because it'll be me picking up the pieces in the end, not her, but more than any of that I suppose, I hate the thought that you're telling her things that you're not telling me, having jokes with her that I wouldn't get, giving away our secrets, my secrets, making me ridiculous, talking about how bored you are of me and how overweight I am, and maybe if you could just fuck her and get it over with, and tell me when it's done, or not tell me, well, maybe that would be better, except that I hate knowing about it and I hate not knowing, so maybe you could just stop.'

I'm looking at her, baffled. And she's wiping her face with her sleeve, and then looking at me in this hard challenging way, as though this is a test to see if I can say the right thing. And I'm thinking that her hair really suits her, cut short like that, now I've got used to it. And I suppose there is some justice in her complaints, apart from the bit about her weight which is entirely beside the point, except that she's the last person who has the right to complain, after her coy blouse-removal and her teasing hesitation before the all-conquering, silk-robed porn star. So before I've thought of a reply, she's got in the car and is starting the engine.

I tap on the glass, and say, 'Wait, Rebecca, please.'

She lowers the window a few inches. 'But that's just it, isn't it,' she says. 'I'm thirty-five. Think about that, David, because I've been thinking about it a lot. I haven't got forever to wait for you to grow up. Time is moving faster for me than it is for you.' And she pulls away, leaving me standing in the middle of the street.

I watch the car until it turns the corner by the Celestial Church of Anointed Deliverance. I feel utterly alone, abandoned on an airless planet. There's a pickup truck coming the other way. I feel the heat of its engine as it passes. As its noise diminishes, I'm aware of the voices of people leaving the library, Stu Selznick's audience dispersing.

Three young black men approach from the direction of Sunny's Appliances with that curious loping swagger I recognize from gritty police dramas. In their low-slung pants and unlaced trainers, they seem too hampered for life on the street. How do they run? I wonder. They're looking at me through half-closed eyes, and I'm thinking now would be the perfect time to get mugged, to get beaten and kicked.

I'm so unhappy that my physical well-being makes no sense to me. I'd rather knives or guns weren't involved, though, now I come to think of it. I'm not suicidal. Just enough violence so that Rebecca has to see me in a hospital bed. Then the nearest of them opens his mouth to speak, and I feel my heart beating and I realize I'd rather not get mugged after all.

'You okay, man?' he says without changing pace.

'I'm fine, thanks.'

'You lost, or what?'

'Just getting some air.'

'That's good, that's good, we all need air. Hey, man, you just keep breathing.'

'Thanks, I'll see what I can do.'

'Just keep breathing. We all gotta breathe.' He nods in agreement with himself, and keeps nodding as they lope past.

'Girl trouble?'

I look round and it's the Englishman standing on the pavement outside the library. He's unsteady on his feet, and his hair has flopped down over one eye. The sound of his voice is reassuring, which is a sign of how homesick I am.

He says, 'Was that your ride home I just saw leaving?'

'No, I've got my own car parked round here somewhere.' I cross to his side of the street. 'Tell me something. How do you manage to talk like that? In complete sentences, I mean, complete paragraphs, when you're drunk. I can't even do it when I'm sober.'

'I find the drink helps, actually.' He smiles benignly. 'Except my mouth runs away with me. I only just got out of there alive.'

'Well, you accused them of a solipsistic error. That's fighting talk.'

'Ah yes, I did put a bit of topspin on that one, didn't I.'

He looks at me with renewed interest. 'You were obviously listening.'

'Not really, no. My mind was on other things, I'm afraid.'

'Girl trouble. I know all about girl trouble. Come and have a drink.'

'I shouldn't really.'

'Neither should I, but I'm going to. There's a place, I seem to remember, about three blocks up on the left.'

I walk beside him. 'You've been here before, then?'

'It's a favourite haunt of right-on causes. I'm doing a piece on the anti-war movement.'

'You're a journalist.'

'Apparently.'

'And you live in LA?'

'God, no. Who'd live in this cesspool?'

We walk past a discount store and a welding shop and a scrappy schoolyard behind chain-link fencing. There's another church – Iglesia de Cristo – no bigger than a lock-up, with a bleeding Christ painted straight onto the brickwork. And it strikes me that I'm in a free-enterprise paradise. Even the churches are one-offs. We reach an intersection, where the traffic is heavier. Rusting rail tracks curve across the street into an alley lined with warehouses, a reminder of a forgotten age of communal infrastructure. The Englishman points to a single-storey building on the far corner. The pantiled roof is visible where the parapet wall dips in shallow, curving crenulations. The name, Conchita's Bar, is painted in garish colours beside the door.

fourteen

I think I have a crush on Conchita. I'm guessing this is Conchita, this woman who pours our drinks – she's matronly enough to be the boss. She's short and broad, but shapely in her low-cut, off-the-shoulder dress, and she walks on her heels with an easy motion.

The Englishman is talking to me. He's been talking for some time. It's a bit like waking up and discovering you've left the radio on. His head's full of despots and mullahs and militia leaders. He must have had as much to drink as I have, but the words keep coming – slurred but impressively connected. He's talking of a crescent of theocratic states from Algeria to Kazakhstan, in which debate is silenced, art and literature extinguished, and women invisible, while crazed imams spread terror across the globe. It's not that I can't see the danger, it's just that right now I'd rather watch Conchita quartering limes, which she does with a flexing of muscles from the shoulder to the wrist.

'Don't you think, seriously though,' he says, 'don't you think posterity would judge us to have been criminally irresolute?'

He's waiting for an answer, and I realize I've missed a crucial part of the question. I open my mouth to speak. Conchita has turned her broad back to reach for a bottle, and the effort involves such tilting and tightening and rebalancing that I forget what I wanted to say. I turn to the Englishman, making an effort to bring his face into focus. 'That's all very well,' I tell him, 'but really, when it gets down to it, what are the chances that you'll be blown up compared with the chances of some big-shot TV producer sleeping with your wife?'

He looks puzzled, then exasperated. 'You're being completely illogical. This isn't about me!'

'Am I really, though? I mean, the way I see it, we can manage all the big stuff, the kind of stuff we read in the papers. Or write in the papers, in your case. It's our private lives that really screw us up.'

'Now you're just playing with words. That stuff you read in the papers, as you call it – that stuff *would* be your private life if it happened to *you*. Might well be, one day. And meanwhile it's other people's private lives.'

'Right, right.' And he probably is right. He's right about so many things, and then so bafflingly wrong, like a Tube train that stops with relentless logic at every station on the Central Line and then suddenly shows up in Cockfosters. And he's looking at me so earnestly, so eager for me to follow his reasoning, that I feel I have to respond, however reluctant I am to dredge up all these thoughts from wherever they've been while I haven't been thinking them. Because it's not as though I haven't agonized about all this. I'm quite good at thinking, in a theoretical kind of way – on the one hand this, on the other hand that. But I can't do the debating thing, the knockabout, table-banging, last-man-standing thing. I lack the speed, the killer instinct.

She's turned towards the bar again, Conchita, mixing some greenish cocktail. The front of her dress shifts against her skin as she breathes, like sea water on sand.

'Look,' I say to the Englishman. 'It's not that I don't agree with you about the problem. About tyranny and all that, and the lunatic ideologies that lead to tyranny. I mean, how can we do nothing and still look ourselves in the face? I get that. It's just that I'm not convinced we know how to stop it. And then I wonder why this problem and why not all the other problems, like poverty and sweatshops and children forced into prostitution. And I can't help thinking that we've got these armies in all their staggering wondrousness, and to a man with a mallet everything looks like . . . you know what I mean . . . a thing you hit with a mallet . . .'

'But can't you see we're a facing a unique threat?'

'. . . a tent peg.'

'A tent peg? What the hell are you talking about? You just haven't grasped the urgency of it, have you? This is an epoch-making moment. The times are presenting us with a stark choice – either to confront tyranny or to collude with it. It's the historic challenge to our generation. It forces us to declare ourselves.'

'I get it!'

'You see?'

'Yes, I get it.' And I do. It comes to me like a shaft of light through cigarette smoke. It's not war the Englishman is addicted to. It's what divides us on the way to war. It's having his back to the wall in support of a position. It's the dream of posthumous vindication. A hammer is what I was thinking of, of course, not a mallet. Same kind of thing, except you wouldn't hit a nail with a mallet. Which is why I can't play this debating game. I'm too slow on the buzzer. I notice his glass is empty. 'Have another drink,' I say. 'We're a long way from home.'

He lets out a long sigh. 'All right,' he says, 'I won't say no.'

Conchita fills our glasses. She tilts her head in a shy smile and moves off along the bar.

'So you think,' I ask him, 'posterity will judge us?'

'Of course, whether we like it or not.'

'But what if posterity's wrong?'

'If we're defeated, you mean, and the fascists get to write the history books.'

'Or if we win, but there's nothing left but reality TV, and posterity's judgement is just billions of people texting in their votes.'

The Englishman looks disgusted. 'You really think the West has so little to lose?'

'Or the icecaps melt and posterity's under water.'

'But for God's sake, we have to go on as though what we do matters.'

'For God's sake being why a lot of people do. Which is perhaps what God is for – for those of us who can't wait for posterity.'

He looks at me sharply. 'You're not religious, are you?'

'Sadly, no.'

'What's sad about it?'

'Oh, I don't know. Religion seems to give people comfort. To make sense of things.'

He snorts, and raises his glass. 'I'll stick to other opiates, if it's all the same to you.' When he's had a drink, he says, 'So do you honestly never wonder what history will make of us?'

'I can't say I do.'

'What about your children, then, or your grandchildren?'

'Haven't got any. You?'

'Oh, yes, I've got children.'

'Back in New York?'

'Oh, various places, you know. Here and there, living with their mothers. Eating up alimony.'

'I think mainly about Rebecca. Rebecca's my wife. If something funny happens I always say to myself, Rebecca would love this. I used to. Or some drama at work, and I'd wonder what would Rebecca make of it, and I couldn't wait to tell her.'

'The woman in the road? She seemed seriously hacked off.'

'Yes. We didn't use to shout so much. But we used to talk about everything. Which is why everything seems to have gone flat. As though there's a dimension missing. This conversation, for example. Sitting here, talking to you – who's going to be interested in this, afterwards? Who's going to explain it to me?'

'She's left you?'

'I'm not really sure.'

'Ditto.'

'You're not sure if your wife left you?'

'Or if I left her. I wasn't paying attention.'

'Back in England, is she?'

'Here, in LA, last thing I heard. We met in New York. We got hitched. We'd almost worked out how to live together, then it all came unglued. I blame bin Laden. Queues at the airport, plastic cutlery, my marriage shot to hell.'

'I see what you mean.'

'Do you?'

'Not really, no.'

'September eleventh changed everything, you see. For me, it changed everything. I know everyone says that, but it happens to be true. I'd lived here a dozen years by then, on and off, but for the first time, really in a way I never had before, I felt like an American. It wasn't just that that America was the best place to live – it was something I felt in my gut, an attachment. And that's ironic, actually – that the moment I started thinking viscerally, which is what she does all the time, that was when everything fell apart. She thought I was off my head, you see, and I thought she was. We'd been married for eighteen months. It had been our own little outbreak of millennial madness – to finally deal with this intermittent trans-global flirtation of ours. So we'd closed our eyes and taken the leap. My friends couldn't see it working. What the hell do you two talk about, they wanted to know. Matthew – he was my best man – he challenged me to name a single book we'd both read. My book, I told him – my book on Reagan.'

His face lights up as he says it, and I see that what he's remembering is not just a clever retort, but the best kind of joke, the best punchline life has to offer – the knowledge of being loved.

'She read it on our second date – stayed up all night reading it. Climbed into bed as the winter sun was rising over Manhattan, quoting from my chapter on Iran–Contra – "Intended Crimes and Unintended Consequences". She doesn't read in the way other people read. She sort of inhales and makes it her own. It was a marriage of opposites, of course, I knew that. Hopelessly unsuitable, my mother called her, and I knew she was right. But that's why I came here, to America, in the first place, to escape the tyranny of the suitable. So I knew what I was letting myself in for. For one thing, she's never really internalized the concept of rational thought, my wife. Stop being so linear, she says, as if one can simply suspend the rules of sequential logic. How to fit our books into one apartment was an issue for a while. She accused me of three-dimensional thinking, and I had to point out that, in this particular case, three was precisely the number of dimensions we had to play with.'

He raises his glass to his mouth, and I think of him with this unlikely wife, their cultural differences transformed into stand-up routines, each one setting up the other's jokes.

'But we muddled along. Until nine-eleven. And suddenly terrorism is everyone's special interest. She's jumping in with the worst of them, muddling everything with her ill-informed preconceptions and her vague notions of healing. This is my subject, you understand, I'd been following this mess for years. And we're suddenly staring at each other over the newspapers in mutual bafflement. The moment I'm ready to commit myself utterly to this country and all it stands for, and our marriage is a train wreck. It was as though we'd woken up in the Tower of Babel, speaking two different languages. Understand your enemy – all right, I can go along with that, but understand them to know how to fight them. Not to accommodate tyranny, not to throw all the cards of history and culture in the air and see where they land. There aren't a dozen ways of looking at this. There's enlightened thinking – ideas, competing on grounds of evidence and reason – and there's everything that threatens it – ignorance and superstition and repression. What had seemed comically muddled in her way of talking, exotically fanciful, and generally girlish, began to shock me. And I suppose she must have felt something similar. We didn't break up exactly. We just sort of shifted gear, and convergence turned into divergence. Absences lengthened. We stopped phoning. Then we stopped emailing. We stopped updating our address books. And at some point I could no longer be sure where she was.'

'I'm sorry,' I tell him. 'Have another drink.'

He empties his glass. 'Does that seem stupid to you, that I should care that much about an idea?'

'I suppose if you care that much about it, you'll want her to care about it too. If you care that much about *her*.'

There's an eruption of laughter on the television behind the bar. It's some kind of game show. The host has said something funny. As the laughter subsides, he winks and smoothes his moustache, which makes the contestants laugh all over again. The drinkers at the bar are muttering. One of them taps his watch. They point at the television. Conchita reaches up to change the channel. Her sleeve slips, exposing the soft dark flesh of her upper arm. We watch disconnected glimpses of news in Spanish, news in Korean, some film star's drug problem. Then a blonde woman and a cop are kissing. Behind them, out of focus, a car is in flames. Conchita hesitates, watching the kiss. Her hand hovers by the control panel. The drinkers protest, but she speaks sharply without turning, and the voices falter and fall silent. She's fierce like that, Conchita – fierce but romantic. The cop draws the woman away from the flames, holding her close as they walk. She's beautiful in spite of the gash on her cheek. She smiles and her hair blows across her face. The shot widens, and we see in the background the bad guys in handcuffs being manhandled into the back of a police car. Wider still, and there's the burning wreckage of a dozen vehicles scattered across a road and up an embankment. It strikes me that people must be dead back there. There must be a lot of injuries, at least. But none of that matters, because they aren't part of the story. Only the cop and the blonde woman matter. The orchestra is telling us this.

The credits roll and are immediately squeezed to make way for a picture of a woman in a veil. 'Coming up after the break,' says a television voice, 'a country singer who abandons her family to go on the road, a high-rise construction worker whose husband wants her grounded and an abortionist kidnapped by her pro-life dad. Classic American tales. The twist? All these women come from strict Muslim families. Disturbing footage and startlingly frank interviews in *Dropping the Veil*, tonight's groundbreaking film in Outreach TV's all-new weekend miniseries, Women Speak Out.' Then there's a burst of a Mozart aria as an SUV lurches into view, bouncing across a mountain stream, and Conchita changes the channel again. It's soccer – what the drinkers have been waiting for. The Spanish commentary rises hysterically above the roar from the stadium.

I turn to the Englishman. 'I have to go,' I say.

'Stay for one more.'

He'll be up there now, Max – up in the hills, with his TV friends, maybe, like last night, gathered laughing around the big screen, ready to watch groundbreaking footage of women not wearing veils. This is the one he's proud of – the meat in the sandwich, he called it. Maybe it'll be just him and Rebecca. With or without Frankie, who's obviously in on it – I heard her in the garden, after all, urging Rebecca to come clean. So if I want to talk to Rebecca, that's where I'll find her.

'I'm sorry, I really have to go.' I brace myself against the bar.

'Here, have one of these.' He takes a card out of his wallet and hands it to me. 'It's got my number on it. In case you fancy a drink some time.'

'Thanks.'

'I'll try not to be such a bore. I'm drunk, you see, and when I'm drunk I sometimes talk a lot of drivel.'

'Did you say drivel?' The word has some particular significance that I can't quite grasp. I look at the card. A name swims up out of the blur and sinks again. I slip the card into my pocket.

The Englishman's eyes focus on my mine briefly, then slide off to look at nothing. 'Bugger off, then,' he says.

I step off my stool, and wait while my legs take control. I feel bad walking out on him. And I'm sorry to leave Conchita. She wrinkles her eyes in a smile that hints at depths of disappointment, and picks up my tip. As I turn towards the door, the jukebox and the coloured lights and the crowded pinboard seem to move more slowly than I do, settling into stillness fractionally late. The door pushes open

against me and I hear the hum of air on the move. It ruffles
the flyers and catches the vents of the jackets along the bar,
the archaic jackets of my compadres, who turn now with
hands raised, all shading their eyes and squinting at the disturbance, before the soccer match reclaims their attention. I
pull at the door as I pass, but it escapes me, swinging open
again, and I leave it. Its knocking is drowned by traffic noise
as I step into the street. The intersection is a blur of headlights, and my arrival is greeted with horns and squealing
brakes. I reach the other pavement breathless, with the wind
hot in my mouth.

It's a long way back to my car, which is good, because it
gives me time to think about where I'm going. I could get
home first and set off for Max's house from there. That
would give me the best chance of finding my way. But I'm
guessing this would double the distance I have to travel,
because I don't want to go that far west, not as far as the
ocean – just a bit west and a bit north. Though exactly how
much in either direction I couldn't say. So the short cut
might end up taking me longer. But I know I haven't the
patience to go the long way.

While I'm walking in the shelter of the buildings, the
wind eases off. In the gaps, it gusts from side streets and
across empty lots, pushing me towards the passing traffic. It's
hot and dry, a rasping whisper straight from the desert. The
schoolyard fence is a collage of fluttering paper scraps. When
I find Natalie's Beetle, a magazine is snagged on its windscreen wipers, and a film-star face flaps against the glass.

I rest against the car for a minute, and take out my phone.
I call Rebecca, but her phone's switched off. So it won't interrupt Max's movie, probably, or so it won't disturb her while
she's fucking Max. I call Astrid. I hear the ringing tone and
then Astrid's voice encouraging me to leave a message.

'I'm somewhere, I'm not sure where,' I tell her. 'Sorry

about earlier. What a cock-up. I could do with some moral support, actually, because I went to this meeting and Max was there, and Rebecca, and, well it's a long story . . . and so I'm driving to see Max right now – and Rebecca, obviously – and I'm going to sort it out with both of them in one swoop. It's David by the way. Call me, if you feel like it.'

I drop the phone in my jacket pocket and look up at the sky. If I knew how to navigate by the stars it would help, because there they are for once, laid out on a big plate of nothing. Lying among them is a crisp slice of moon. The sky, as it sinks towards the roofline, sickens into a neon glow. I let my head drop, and when the sidewalk has stopped turning I get in the car.

I have half a block to remind myself how to accelerate and how to change gear before I swing into the flow of traffic, and then it's like a rollercoaster, with the feel of the wind pushing me and letting me go and pushing me again, and the rattle of it against the Beetle's rusting bodywork.

I'm heading back the way I came, with my engine roaring and all my options open. I see up ahead, crossing above the street, the blur of lights on the Santa Monica freeway, and I know it's the big slide home to the ocean – if I can find the slip road, if I can learn to renounce desire and merge with the eternal. But Rebecca won't be there. Rebecca's with Max, up in the hills, and if the ocean is to my left then the hills are somewhere in front, and to my right, I suppose, is the desert from which this wind is blowing, and beyond that the rest of America, all the way to New York, and beyond that, on the far side of the Atlantic, Ireland and England and Tufnell Park. The freeway sweeps out of sight overhead, and I'm committed.

I start crossing streets whose names I know already. It's strange to run into them here, miles from my own neighbourhood, looking so neglected. It makes me wonder where they end. Just run out of steam maybe somewhere in the desert, crumbling into sand and rock, or maybe crawl all the way to the East Coast, dragging themselves unrecognizably through small towns in places I've never been, like Missouri and Arkansas. It makes my head feel huge, this thought, and I'm suddenly laughing with the exhilaration of it – a loose panting kind of laughter. Until the streets start to show up out of order, and a new anxiety stirs inside me, coiling through my intestines, that the fabric of the city is unravelling, or I'm turned around, careering off the map, heading for Mexico. But this passes too. The familiar pattern is restored, and I realize it's only that they've got in a tangle, a couple of these inexhaustible roads, somewhere in that urban vagueness between where we live and where I am now which feels even more like nowhere. The grid is subject to such disturbances.

I have to brake because there's a wall up ahead, ten foot of concrete with barbed wire along the top, so I skid westward and find another way north. There are more abandoned tramlines – I feel them through the sagging seat of the Beetle – and potholes and steel plates bolted to the tarmac. My headlights pick up splashes of white along the gutters like nesting gulls. The splashes grow into snowdrifts, and I see that it's waste paper. A newspaper slides across the passenger window and flaps out of sight. There are boarded-up warehouses, a rash of Greyhound buses and a few shops. Towers shoot up around me, dazzling each other with their bronzed and smoky glass. The street levitates, and the storefronts shimmer with money.

Crossing another freeway, I see rising ground where the patterns of moving lights fracture and are obscured by vegetation. The sign in front of me says Sunset Boulevard. I feel vindicated as I pull up to the red light. I am laughing again, breathlessly, weak with relief. I have mastered the grid. I have won the freedom of the city. A left turn here will bring me in no time to the canyon where the Kleinmans live, and whatever resolution the night has to offer. I am omniscient and immortal and ridiculously drunk.

The lights change and I swing westward with the wind behind me, whistling tunelessly and feeling at one with the Beetle as it rattles along. Cross-streets come and go. I'm learning not to be intimidated by the amber light, but to do what the other drivers do, hurtling across intersections while the lights change against me – there's an excitement to this that I begin to appreciate. I still have only the vaguest sense of where I am. But just when I'm thinking that maybe there's more than one Sunset Boulevard, or I've already passed the canyon, the place begins to identify itself. The lights get brighter and the store fronts flashier. There are limos as long as buses. And mixed up among all the other stuff there's a Hollywood Lingerie Store and Hank's Hollywood Hardware and The Hollywood Diner.

As the city blocks pass, even the figures on the sidewalk begin to look emblematic, as though they've been placed here for the tourists. There's a cluster of them up ahead, towards the next intersection – a Goth on a skateboard, a pair of whores, a bag lady with a shopping cart full of poodles. I take it all in with exaggerated clarity, like a snap-shot for the album. The skateboarder is in the foreground, crouching with his arms out for balance, the studs of his gauntlet glinting. I gain on him, as he speeds towards the girls. There's a skinny one in leather shorts and a crop top, leaning in at the passenger window of a Lexus, and another back on the sidewalk, plump-thighed in fishnet tights, talk-ing on a cellphone. Beyond them, waiting for the lights to change, is the bag lady, twisting a strand of her moth-eaten wig and pouting at the traffic. The girl on the cellphone pushes her face into the wind in open-mouthed laughter.

Straightening his legs, the skateboarder sweeps in front of me, and I have time to admire his skill, before I see that the girl is no longer laughing, but pointing after him with an empty hand, and her friend has raised her head from the Lexus. These two, who were small and distinct a minute ago, have swollen into a smudge at the edge of my vision. In a moment they'll be glimpses of movement in my rear-view mirror, then nothing. And the Goth is about to join them, when he collides with the shopping cart, scattering the poodles into the gutter. His skateboard flips out of sight, and he tumbles in front of me, rolling onto his shoulders and over again onto his knees, while the snatched phone slithers towards the oncoming traffic.

Jerking the wheel to avoid him, I swerve away from the sidewalk, and then towards it again. I hit the kerb with brake and clutch pedals hard to the floor. There's a grinding of steel on concrete and a squeal of rubber. My cheekbone is against the side window and everything is shifting from right to left. And here they are again, the whores blown about in attitudes of fury, the boy scrambling to his feet, and the bag lady, who I see now is a man in drag, dodging traffic with a poodle clutched to his chest and his skirt rising in the wind – the whole panorama of the street passing slowly across my windscreen, while I twist away from one corner and towards another. I cower, anticipating the next collision. It comes as a thud that I feel in my stomach and a scratching noise, and I'm pushed back into my seat, until everything judders to a stop. I open my eyes and sit listening to the horns. I breathe out and in again and feel the shuddering motion of it. I switch the engine off and pull on the handbrake. When I let my feet slide from the pedals, my legs are shaking. I turn my head and see that the car has backed up onto the kerb, slid against the corner of a skip and parked itself, facing more or less downhill.

Ahead of me, on Sunset, a stalled pickup truck coughs into motion. It feels its way out of the intersection, releasing the flow. Life resumes. My survival is miraculous. I seem not to have killed anyone. The thought brings fear like a wave of heat. And when the wave passes, I know where I am. For the first time on this cross-town journey, I'm on familiar ground. This is the turning I was looking for. It can't have been long since we waited here for a green light, on our way home from dinner with Max and Frankie. If the lights had been against us last night, after the TV party, I might have noticed then what I notice now. At the corner of the building, below on the street beyond the skip, is a plaster nymph. She gestures towards her own nakedness, preening in a pink spotlight. I saw her in Max's film, and knew then that I'd seen her before, and her sisters out of sight around the corner. The night of the faculty party, the night of Astrid and the swimming pool, it was in front of this building, just there below on the corner, that the SUV landed against the van and the Mercedes, while the blonde girl staggered bleeding from her Porsche.

And this strikes me as the strangest thing of all, stranger than my survival, stranger than the survival of the phone-thief and the poodles, because it feels as though the event has repeated itself, and I'm just experiencing it from a different angle. And Astrid's talk of multiple universes, which seemed at the time like a colourful eccentricity, comes back to me as revelation. I have the dizzying sensation of looking down on my own life. I look across Sunset and expect to see myself, frozen at the wheel with Rebecca beside me. Then this wave passes, too. And I'm just a drunk in a car who's lucky not to be locked up.

Checking that there's nothing coming down the hill, I push the door open and step out into a gale. The noise of it competes with the traffic, humming at a higher pitch. My knees are stiff and my face hurts. The car is a sad sight, with a buckle in the front bumper and the hood opening in a snarl. The passenger door is up against the skip. Natalie's flowers are defaced with horizontal scratches. Everything is spoilt.

I'm in no state to drive. Confronting Max seems futile anyway. Maybe I should just unleash Jake, phone him now and give him Max's address, so he doesn't have to waste time on Internet research. Instead I call Rebecca. Her phone is still switched off. So I call Astrid again and get her message.

'I was hoping to talk to you,' I say. 'I'm drunk, to be honest. It's me again, in case you were wondering. I thought I was the gridmaster or something, but I'm just drunk. So I was hoping we might talk. Sorry about what happened earlier, with Rebecca. She sort of got things upside down. So anyway – call if you get this. Or not, if you'd prefer. I'm afraid I've made a mess of Natalie's car. And I've upset Jake again. I don't seem to be having much of a day, actually. I hope yours is going well.'

A young woman is coming out of an alley pulling a small suitcase. She notices the car as she passes. She glances at me and back at the car and shrugs, and I remember Evie. This isn't Evie, this dark-haired girl, but she has something of Evie's manner, walking away from me with her ponytail bouncing. She turns the corner by the plaster nymph. I'm thinking of Evie as she appeared in the documentary, walking to work while she explains in voice-over about the tips and the flexible hours. Then I'm thinking of Evie on the video tape, climbing on top of Max in her angora sweater, naked from the waist down. And I follow this girl who isn't Evie to the corner of the street to watch her. There's the row of plaster nymphs with the doorway in the middle and the bouncer cracking his knuckles, and the bar next door done up like a Wild West saloon, and people passing on the pavement, but no sign of the girl. She's gone inside, of course. She's gone to work. It's called the Seven Veils, this club. And it comes to me that if I wanted to talk to Evie this is where I'd find her. I'm too wasted to chase Max, and I've lost the energy for it. Rebecca won't answer my calls. Natalie's dead. If I want to know what goes on with Max, what he does, what gives him this power over every woman he meets, Evie's the one to ask. This is why I've landed here, I tell myself, bruised but alive, right outside the Seven Veils. I don't believe it, of course. I might as well say God brought me here. But I'm here, anyway, so why not. I feel my pulse racing as I pass the bouncer and walk through the open door-way.

fifteen

The girl on the stage raises her legs to pull the last shred of clothing from around her ankles. And I'm thinking, Is that it? Is that all there is – just nakedness after all? With nothing more to hide, the knowingness of the performance gives way to a kind of innocence. The girl's face relaxes into a grin. She crouches to gather her underwear, and a scattering of dollar bills. The music fades into taped applause. Which is thoughtful, I think – that those of us who watch are relieved of the task of responding, of rousing ourselves from our separate states of absorption or indifference.

I'm here to find Evie, of course, so how I like the show is beside the point. Except that I'm also here because my wife's walked out on me and it's a Saturday night and I'm a long way from home. And I'm here because I've had too much to drink and my car has dumped itself on the sidewalk with the garbage. So maybe I'm here just because I'm here. What makes me different from the rest of the crowd? I can't deny there have been moments of engagement, surges of heightened awareness. Lifted by an unexpected gesture or an uncovering subtle enough to cause an intake of breath, I've briefly forgotten to think. But twenty minutes of this, and already I know the cycle of expectation and disappointment, and I'm feeling its waves diminish like a weakening pulse.

I've found a table out on the edges, near a wall. I've mentioned Evie's name to a couple of the girls – Evie or Eva

– peering into faces in the semi-darkness, raising my voice above the music. They maybe know who I mean. She'll probably be in later. They're more predatory offstage, these girls – laced and corseted for combat, and too close for comfort. 'You wanna play?' they say, or 'Mind if I join you?' or 'Haven't seen you before – this your first time?' They murmur endearments, with a hand lightly touching my knee or my elbow. 'Hey, handsome,' they say, 'looking for company?' or 'Shouldn't be sitting alone, good-looking guy like you.' I shake my head, and they drift past leaving their scent behind.

Harder to cope with is the one who doesn't get it right, who brings her vulnerability with her – the eyes not cool enough, not enough flesh on her bones. I want to put my jacket round her angular frame, tell her to put some clothes on, eat something. 'Do you want a private dance?' she asks me. 'I'm real good. You won't be sorry.' But I'm sorry already – that she has to pretend to be alluring, and I have to pretend to be tempted, that she hasn't found a job that suits her better.

There's another part of the room, off to one side through an archway. From time to time a girl leads some guy by the hand into its red glow, and they move out of sight behind a curtain, except sometimes the curtain sways and there's a sinuous movement of a head or an arm.

Meanwhile, they take their turns on the stage, showing what they've got. There are half a dozen men sitting up close, younger than me, most of them, and better dressed. Their heads catch the moving lights or are lifted into silhouette. More sit out in the semi-darkness, alone or grouped around tables. Some of them are talking to girls, who laugh and whisper, or lounge in attitudes of boredom, playing with their long hair. A couple of men sit with women wearing normal clothes, their wives or girlfriends. One of the dancers, watching the stage as she weaves among the tables, applauds a particularly athletic move, whooping and clapping. Heads turn, and the performer blushes, her face lighting up with the pleasure of being acknowledged.

The dancers have begun to leave me alone, preferring to invest their energy elsewhere. The waitress, at least, wants nothing from me. Her hand on my arm is reassuring. 'Got everything you need, honey?' she asks. And her face expresses concern for my condition, as though to suggest that in walking into this place of gaudy lights and dark corners, I have uncovered myself and made my need visible. She does that thing with a tray of drinks, carrying it at shoulder height with one hand, and swinging it down to a table, while her free hand slides the wallet from her belt. In passing, with a single move of the hip, she slides an empty chair against a table. She exchanges a joke with the barman, a tall muscular guy with a hands-free phone attached to his ear. There's a change of music. The volume rises. The pace drops. The DJ asks us to give a big welcome to a very lovely lady called Starlight, and Evie appears. I think it's Evie. She's long and pale, this girl, with straw-blonde hair. Of course I've only seen Evie's face briefly on the small screen. In my head I have an image of her from the video, in a sweater, rubbing lotion into her legs, and an image of her climbing on top of Max. Last night's documentary has left me with vaguer impressions. Starlight is wearing a cocktail dress and her hair is up, so there isn't much to go on.

I take my drink and move to a seat at the edge of the stage. I want to be sure this is the woman I've come to see. She stoops at the top of the steps to put down a small handbag, and glances round to assess her audience. Her eyes meet mine, flicker away, and return. Then they shift elsewhere. The dress is black with traces of silver. She stands up and it glistens in rivulets of colour from the neckline to the hem.

If this is Evie, what shall I ask her? To explain Max to me? To explain Rebecca? What is it my wife sees in your boss, your boyfriend, your agent? What does he have to offer other than a leg-up in the movie business? What's in it for a nice middle-class English girl with more cerebral aspirations? You'd better know what you want to ask her, I tell myself, because she's why you're here. Unless you're here, after all, just because you're here.

And suddenly I'm hoping it isn't her, and that I'm not reduced to asking this stripper why my marriage is in trouble. There won't be a tattoo on her back. She'll open her mouth to talk and she'll be from Brooklyn or Texas. Because the accent would clinch it. I could leave now. But I've just sat down. I'm a marked man. To leave would be too stark a rejection, like walking out of a cello recital in a church hall, or turning my back on the office bore. She's made an effort to look nice, this young woman who might be Evie, coordinating her shoes with her dress, and her dress with the scarf in her hair, and to walk away, as you would from the wrong piece of furniture in a showroom, would signal too directly the crude nature of the transaction. Which is, when you get down to it, that I owe her not one second of polite attention, since her interest in me is only as deep as my wallet. I'm beginning to hyperventilate, and it might be because my mind is spinning with contradictory thoughts. Unless this spinning is merely a symptom, and what I'm suffering from is a sense of exposure that has tripped me up like vertigo – sitting here being watched by the girl I'm supposed to be watching, because she has detected in me some hunger. Tell me, Evie, I want to ask her, tell me, what it's like to move in the circle of love from which I'm excluded.

The other guys are tossing bills onto the stage and she begins to follow the money. After a while, my breathing returns to something like normal. I'm slumped in my seat trying to be all right with what's happening to me, trying not to mind that I'm enjoying this. Whatever discomfort it brings, pleasure is preferable to boredom, after all. Pleasure at least pushes other thoughts aside. It isn't a space waiting to be crowded with regret and distaste and a clawing sense of having been robbed of time. Pleasure is its own justification.

She's attractive, there's no question about that, and she knows how to move. But she projects something more potent than either of these, a kind of mingling of opposites – of the demure with the whorish, and later when she's lost the dress, of the insolent with the abject. For a minute, I forget that she might be Evie. I forget about Evie. It's while she's spinning on the pole, and her long hair freed from its scarf is trailing across her face, that the tattoo becomes unmistakeable, a bluish blur settling as she slows into the image of a swallow in flight.

When she finds me afterwards and says, 'Do you want a lap dance now?' I hesitate, and so she sits next to me. 'It's nothing, you know. It's sexy, but it isn't sex.' She leans closer, lowering her voice. 'So I get wet maybe, and you get hard. This is not so bad actually.' Her tone hovers between reassurance and challenge. She has an expressive face. She does sudden things with her mouth and her eyebrows. She's put her underwear back on, and also a sort of skirt and something around her shoulders in some kind of gauzy material – not clothes exactly, but enough to soften the edges.

'Perhaps we could talk first,' I say.

She shrugs. 'Why not? This is normal.'

'I think you know Max Kleinman.'

Her face mimes surprise. 'You know Max? You're his friend?'

'You could say I'm his friend, yes.'

'And did Max say I work here?'

I wonder what lie to tell, and decide not this one. 'No,' I say. 'You were in his documentary. I watched it last night.'

She looks away, muttering something in Czech. Then she says, 'Those bastards. They told me they will hide my face.'

'Oh, no, they did. I almost didn't recognize you. It was only the tattoo.'

'The bird.' She looks relieved. 'Perhaps I have it taken off when I have money. Some of these girls, you know, they are saving money for boob job. Or they have one already. Do I need boob job? What do you think?'

'You look fine to me.'

'Forget it anyway, this dancing is just for now, to pay rent.' Her eyes have begun to wander. She crosses her legs, and her foot bounces in its high-heeled sandal.

There's a dancer kneeling at the edge of the stage with her bra around some boy's neck.

'Is this sexy, what this girl does? I should do this maybe.'

The boy is leering self-consciously, hamming it up for his mates – students out on the town.

'Tell me about Max,' I say.

'About Max?'

'About you and Max.'

She gives me a sideways look. 'What about me and Max? There is nothing about me and Max.'

'I understood you were close. That there was something between you.'

'So now you are policeman? Why does this interest you, about me and Max?'

'It's hard to explain.'

She laughs. 'Of course. I think maybe you are friend of Frankie.'

'No, really.'

'Frankie sends you to dig up dirt on her husband.'

'It's nothing like that, honestly. This is just for me. I promise I won't repeat anything you say.'

'You promise! And why should I believe you? This is not a place to believe people. I say to some guy, oh how hand-some you are, and I laugh at his jokes. And he tells me he is big producer and can maybe give me job. And what do you think – this is not all one big lie?'

'Why do you work here, then?'

She shrugs. 'What place is different? Really! Here nobody pretends they are telling the truth, which is better actually.' She gets up. 'And now I have to work.'

'How much?'

'It is why I am here, to work.'

'How much for a dance, I mean?'

'Oh. You want dance now?'

I take out my wallet.

'Twenty dollars,' she says. 'Plus tip. Tip is normal.'

'Twenty dollars, then, plus tip, for five minutes of your time.' I throw down a twenty-dollar bill and a ten.

She looks at the money as though it isn't worth picking up.

'I just want to hear your story.'

She watches me for a moment, then shrugs and sits down. 'So you want to know about me and Max. What about it? It was nothing. I teach the girl, once a week. I give her lesson, and Frankie treats me like she's doing me this big favour because the girl is so talented, but I don't see this talent. And I only do this because Frankie will give me extra studio space and things like this. Of course, I earn more money dancing. And she never tells me about the little boy when she gives me this job, who is a monster by the way. But Laura is okay. And then Max is nice to me when I'm there, and comes in to bring me coffee or a glass of water. And I make some things for him, because I like making things, and we have some good times. He makes me laugh. He is funny man. Don't you think he is funny man?'

'Yes, I suppose he's funny.'

'One day you will meet him maybe, your friend Max, and you will know what I mean.'

'I've met him. I know him.'

'And this is not for some divorce case or something like that?' She studies my face.

'This is for me.'

'You're a strange boy.'

'I want to hear the rest.'

'It was nothing, all right? One week the children don't come because they are with their grandmother and Frankie has gone to some meeting in San Francisco, and no one tells me. But Max is there, you know. Perhaps he has even thought of this, because he has some gift for me, some perfume. And so we have sex and it is nice, actually. He tells me Frankie doesn't mind. She likes him to do this, because she doesn't like sex so much. What do you think? It may be true, but, you know, men say these things. Then nothing happens for a few weeks or a month or so, because Frankie is back, and the children are always there. Except he puts me in this film he's making about strip clubs. Then another time Frankie is away. This time she tells me, but I come anyway to see Max. And so it goes on. Then one day I'm with him and I take his wallet – I'm teasing him, you know, and he's chasing me to get it back, and I'm looking at what he keeps inside. There's a photo of a woman, and she's written a message for him on the back, all about how wonderful he is and how he's changed her life. And I am really shocked, because he has this other girl. And I say some hurtful things, and we fight. But I'm relieved in a way because it's not my plan to have some big love affair. After a while we kiss and make up and this is the last time I see him, because I tell Frankie I am too

busy to teach her little girl. So there is no big scandal actually. Maybe you think now you waste your money.' She picks
up the notes and puts them in her purse. 'Dance would have
been better for you.'

'What was she like, this other woman?'

'I don't know. Why do I care what she was like? She was
nothing.' Evie looks around the club. 'Here she would get a
job serving drinks maybe.' It doesn't seem to have given her
pleasure to tell this story. She's restless, distracted by the
activity around the stage.

I know this other woman could be anyone, but I can't
help seeing a picture of Rebecca in Max's hand, and a message of love in Rebecca's artistic scrawl. 'You saw her picture.
Surely you can remember something about it. It was a shock,
you said.'

'Yes, he showed me picture, but I didn't look. Now I
must work.'

'And what did the words say?'

'Nothing. All about love.' She gets up. 'So you want
dance or do I find some other guy? I am very popular girl,
actually. One minute it takes me. I will show you.'

She's looking around the room, swinging her purse,
deciding who to approach. I want her not to go. I want her
to describe this picture, to tell me enough so I know if it was
Rebecca.

'What about the film?' I say. 'Did you know Max was
filming you?'

'I don't understand.' She laughs. 'How do you think they
make movie without people know? They bring their own
lights. And men crawling everywhere with cameras. And
these other men pretend to watch and we pretend to work.
It was too early in the morning. What, you think they make
film and people don't know?'

'Not the movie. The video of you and Max in bed.'

She looks puzzled. I've got her attention again.

'He was filming it. You in your sweater and him in his black silk robe. I've seen it.'

Her mouth opens in shock. 'What are you talking about? You're sick, I think.'

'I just need to know about this picture.'

'What picture? You're a creep. You should find some whore who will say dirty things to you. I don't do this, as a matter of fact. I am just dancer.'

I watch her walk away. She weaves among the tables, but I see where she's heading. There's a big man, built like a wrestler, sitting alone. The waitress is onstage in her sensible shoes, giving the mirror a quick polish. Something in the reflection catches her eye. The bartender is applauding her performance. She turns round and giggles. The music pulses around her and the lights fade from pink to mauve. Out in the shadows, Evie has draped herself around the wrestler and is whispering in his ear. He says something and she laughs, throwing her head back. The wrestler pushes himself up out of his chair. Evie takes his arm and dips her head towards his shoulder as they cross the room. He's got this slow smile on his face and she's laughing. They stroll past me towards the red glow of the archway. I feel my whole life hanging on this single question. I know it's not everything. Whatever the answer, more questions will follow. But it feels like everything. I get up and walk after them. My foot catches the leg of a chair and I stumble against the waitress, who is on her way back to the bar with her paper towel and her cleaning fluid.

'You okay, honey?' she asks. I catch her look of concern as I hurry past her towards the archway. There are seven or eight curtained booths, like a changing room in a department store. I see Evie's fingers slip from the edge of a curtain that swings and settles against its frame.

'Hey, man, you taken a wrong turning.' It's the bartender. Up close he looks even taller.

'I just have to ask Evie something.'

'You don't have to do nothing, man, 'cept get the fuck outta here.'

'Just a couple of questions.' And I pull the curtain back. The wrestler is sitting against the wall. Evie is facing him, straddling his huge thighs. She turns her head. Her mouth opens and her eyebrows shoot up in alarm.

'Please, Evie,' I say, 'the picture . . .'

The wrestler raises a hand towards me. 'No fucking pictures,' he says.

'I just have to know if it was my wife.'

The shock on Evie's face intensifies, and I feel myself lifted from the ground, my clothes yanked up between the legs and under the armpits. Evie and the wrestler revolve in front of me. There's a red light shining in my eyes, a green Exit light the wrong way up, then I'm breathing the musty smell of my own jacket. I recognize the metallic clattering of an emergency door, and the warmth and noise of the street. I'm dazzled by headlights. My head and shoulder hit something hard, but otherwise it's a soft landing. Then I'm looking at the barman sideways on. He's standing in the doorway, feeling his shoulder, shifting his arm in its socket. He's adjusting his neck. He's waiting to see if I've had enough. He's talking to someone, responding to the voice in his ear. There's a stink of rotting vegetables. I lift my head and struggle to get up, but my feet and elbows sink into the softness of the garbage bags. I'm still lying there as the door slams shut. I'm on the pavement up against the skip, listening to the rattling progress of the wind and the anxious horns.

'David by the wayside.'

I know that voice and that gurgling chuckle. It's Wyman.

He's lolloping up the street from Sunset, with his cowboy hat in his hand.

'I prayed mightily, yes sir, that I might have the saving of your soul, and the Lord has answered me, delivering you like a lost sheep into my care.' He limps towards me, and reaches out an arm. His grin wrinkles the grafted patch on his cheek.

'Do you think that ape works for Jesus, then?'

'He takes his wages from Satan but he moonlights for Jesus. He just don't know it.' He pulls me off the garbage and onto my knees. I'm trying to get up, but he drops down beside me, kneeling with his hands on my shoulders. 'The Lord fashions us as his instruments, David, and we don't have no say in it. Even in the days of my sin, I was a pickup truck for Jesus and I felt his foot on my throttle. That's the way of it, David by the wayside. We're all of us moonlighting for the Lord, though there's not so many sign on for the day job.'

'Can I get up now?'

'Well, that ain't a question for me, no sir. Are you ready to rise up out of your sinfulness and drop the chains of drink and fornication? Because until you do, you are a stench in the nostrils of the Lord.'

'Yes, I need to clean myself up a bit, don't I.' I'm feeling in my jacket pocket for my phone. If it's not too late, I should try Rebecca again. Wyman has closed his eyes. He still has me by the shoulders and we've begun to rock from side to side.

'Dear Lord, if it be thy will, bring this sinner to repentance. And for the sake of this one soul, Lord, pulled from the mire, stay thy hand from the destruction of this city, as thou promised Abraham at the gates of Sodom, lest thou destroy the righteous with the wicked . . .'

I'm looking over Wyman's shoulder, down to where the first of the plaster nymphs looks out over the intersection.

Wyman has turned down the volume, but his grip is fierce. He seems to have gone into a kind of trance. I'm beginning to feel queasy with the rocking motion, but I haven't yet found the energy to fight him off. A young woman has turned the corner and she's walking towards us. It's Evie in a dressing gown.

'Already, Lord,' Wyman says, 'this nation has felt the sharpness of thy two-edged sword . . .'

Evie takes out a packet of cigarettes and puts one in her mouth. 'What is this? You are in love now? You turn down dance with me, but you will dance with this crazy person. You are a strange boy.' She lights the cigarette, inhales deeply and leans back against the wall.

'Why do you call me a boy? I'm old enough to be your father.'

'Old enough, maybe. But you are still a boy.'

'Three thousand souls,' Wyman says, 'cut down even in the ripeness of their sin – moneylenders and adulterers and worshippers of false gods . . .'

'You dropped your phone.' She takes it out of the pocket of her dressing gown. 'So I come to find you.'

'Thank you.'

'Your wife called.'

'Rebecca?'

'She said she was your wife. I heard it ringing, that's how I find it, lying on the floor.'

'Wyman, I have to talk to this woman,' I say to him. 'Really, Wyman, I'm getting up now.' I have my hands on his wrists, and I'm trying to pull him off me.

'Turn away from harlotry,' Wyman says, 'leave wallowing in lust.'

'Tell me, Evie, what did you say to her?'

'What do you think? I say I am a stripper, but it's okay

because you don't like me so much and only give me thirty dollars.'

'Christ, Evie!'

Wyman has moved on to the Book of Revelation, and I'm thinking that I'd probably rather face the four horsemen of the Apocalypse right now than another earful from Rebecca.

'That's it, Wyman,' I say to him. 'Really. It's very nice of you to try and save me from eternal damnation but right now I've got more immediate problems.' And I push him off and get to my feet. All this praying hasn't done my sore knee any good. I support myself against the corner of the skip while I rub it.

Evie is laughing. Little gusts of smoke come out of her mouth and curl off in the wind. 'You think I would say this, really? To your wife? As a matter of fact I say I work in a bar, because the music is loud, you know. I tell her you were here and left your phone by mistake. And she wanted to know if you were very drunk. And I tell her not so drunk, actually, but sad maybe because you were all alone on a Saturday night, boo hoo. And I said should I take message. And she said it wasn't so important.' Evie hands me the phone.

'Thanks. That was thoughtful of you, to cover for me like that.'

'She smells real good, don't she, David by the wayside.' Wyman has come up behind me and is murmuring in my ear. 'Yes sir, she smells like an apple orchard in blossom. But she's a whited sepulchre, a corpse stinking with the corruption of sin.'

'That's not a very nice thing to say, Wyman. She came out to give me my phone back.'

'Tell me this then, David. What numbers you got stored on that thing? Can you call Jesus? Can you order up a delivery of salvation when your spirit is hungry?'

'Hey, you,' Evie says, 'crazy person. We're talking.'

'Or is it just the Whore of Babylon you get through to?'

'The guy on the door is friend of mine,' Evie says. 'You better run away or I tell him you call me whore, and he might break your other leg.'

Wyman whistles. 'She's ready to blow, David by the wayside. She's wired to Satan's detonator, and she's taking you down.' He puts a hand on my shoulder. 'May the Lord shine his halogen light on you until your eyes burn open. Praying for you, David. Maybe I'll catch you later.' And I watch him hobble down towards Sunset and out of sight.

'I have to go. It's my turn on stage, maybe, by now.' Evie blows out a cloud of smoke, drops the butt and grinds it into the pavement. 'How do you know this crazy guy, a nice boy like you?'

'There are a lot of crazy people in this town.'

'There are crazy people everywhere.' She turns to go. 'Did Rebecca sound okay?'

'She sounded, I don't know, busy. I don't think she's the girl in Max's photo, by the way. That girl was too young. Is your wife young?'

'Younger than me.'

'Skinny like a teenage boy, with big sad eyes?'

'Definitely not.'

'She's like a boy, I said to Max. Maybe you like boys now. That made him so mad. Maybe if she is pole dancer, the guys will think she is the pole.' She laughs. Then she shrugs her shoulders. 'She was pretty enough, though, with too much hair for a boy.'

'That was Natalie, I think. Her name was Natalie.'

'And do you think maybe Max is a bit in love with this Natalie?'

'A bit, maybe.'

'And is she in love with him?'

'Not anymore.'

'So she says. But Max is too comfortable with Frankie, anyway, and there will always be other girls for sex, so too bad for Natalie.'

My phone starts ringing. 'I'd better answer that.'

'So, I'll see you around maybe.'

'Yes. Maybe.' I put the phone to my ear. 'Rebecca. Are you all right?'

'It's Astrid. Where are you?'

'Astrid, thanks for calling back.'

It's a bad connection. I watch Evie walking away in her dressing gown, and the heads turning down on Sunset as she reaches the corner.

There's some noise and Astrid says, 'Are you at home?'

'I'm in Hollywood. Look, Astrid – about what happened earlier. Rebecca was listening on the extension . . .'

'David, find a television.'

'What?'

'A television. Something's happened to your friend Kleinman.'

'It's on television?'

There's more crackling and then Astrid says something about the police. 'Makes no sense,' she says, and, 'all over the news.' Then there's nothing.

'Astrid . . . Astrid, are you there?' I'm listening to a car alarm, and some sirens in the distance, and the blaring of horns on Sunset Boulevard. I can't hear anything on the phone. I call Astrid's number. There's silence. The battery's dead.

sixteen

The strip along the bottom of the computer screen says
Breaking News, and something in smaller print I can't read
from this distance. The main picture is an aerial shot of a jeep
moving at speed. It flits in and out of the searchlight, through
the shifting shadows of billboards and palm trees. If there's
sound, it doesn't reach me out here on the street. The laptop
is neglected on the table, with a paper mug and half a muffin
on a plate. My own face, hovering over the screen, stares back
at me through the coffee-shop window. Sunset's late-night
traffic scuttles behind me, and the dry wind crawls under my
clothes. The jeep makes an erratic turn, two of its wheels
bouncing silently onto the sidewalk and back onto the road.
The view widens, taking in the street scene and the police
cars in pursuit. The camera swings sideways, zooming in
until only the side of the jeep is visible. Through the tinted
glass, the driver's recklessness is readable in the shadowy
movements of his upper body.

The rattle of a helicopter distracts me. Turning from the
window, I find it in the sky to the west, dragging a cone of
light. Another one swoops up into view and circles noisily.
There are sirens. People come out of nightclubs, step from
limos, push along the pavement with the heat blowing in
their faces. I'm the only one watching the sky. The transvestite with the poodles is crossing the road. He's talking,
probably to himself, but he seems to have me in his sights.

When I turn back to the coffee-shop window, back to the screen, I'm looking at Max. It's a still photo. His mouth is open and his hands are raised in an expansive gesture. He's there for less than a second. Then I'm watching the jeep again, following its wayward progress and its curving tail of police cars. I didn't imagine it. It was definitely Max. Which explains Astrid's phone call. Get to a television. Not to watch some random police chase, obviously, but because something important has happened.

I have my hand on the coffee-shop door when the transvestite reaches me.

'You're so hot,' he says, 'baby, baby, gimme whatcha got.'

'Not just now,' I tell him. 'I'm rather busy.'

'Your thousand-dollar shoes, baby, gimme summa that, cos you know what's on my mind, uh! baby, baby, all the time.'

The shopping cart is in the doorway. The poodles rest their jaws along the edge or on each other's heads, panting and swaying in the heat.

'I have to talk to someone in the cafe,' I tell him.

'Well, it's always nice to talk.'

I push open the door, easing my way round the end of the cart.

'Your black silk shirt,' the transvestite says, touching the sleeve of my jacket with the long scarlet nail of his index finger, 'baby, gimme summa that.'

The door swings shut and the air-conditioning is like a cool hand on my neck. There are half a dozen people sitting at tables, alone or in pairs, and another three up at the counter. I sit down in front of the laptop. I glance around, but nobody's reacting.

On the screen, there are two people talking in a studio, a bearded man and a woman with big hair. The car chase has been diminished to a rectangle on the man's lapel.

A fat man turns from the counter holding a bagel. He notices me, probably because I'm watching him, waiting to be noticed, but he sits down alone, puts the bagel to his face, and lowers his eyes to his newspaper. Next to be served is a handsome woman, who takes her coffee and heads straight for the door. That leaves the young man who's chatting with the girl behind the counter. The girl's voice is wispy and melodic and she gestures like a dancer.

'Well, I think I may be French,' the young man says, 'because I love French food, though my mom once told me that my birth parents were from the Midwest.'

'You should honour that, totally,' the girl says. 'I'm only one-quarter Korean, but I'm like one hundred per cent Asian in my soul.'

'And do you love Korean food?'

'I love any kind of food.'

'I love mainly French food.'

'I love French food so long as it's vegan.'

Lying on the table, wired to the laptop, are silver discs the size of dimes. Anxiety is gathering inside me. Something's happened to Max, or Max has done something, and someone's on the run from the police. I pick up one of the discs, wipe it on the sleeve of my jacket, and put it to my ear.

The beard is talking. 'That, Corinne, is the question the police have to be asking themselves right now.'

'Because if they knew that . . . ?'

'Well, it would make their job a whole lot easier. Anticipating this guy's next move has to be their number-one priority.'

'And if you had to make the call? Where do you suppose he's heading?'

'Back to the scene of the crime is one likelihood. That may not make sense to you or me, Corinne, but remember we're dealing with an Islamic extremist here. There's a different psychology at work. You've gotta factor in the whole martyrdom thing. You have to think, here's a guy . . . there's been a shooting, which we don't know the result of the shooting.'

'We should remind viewers that these are as yet unconfirmed reports.'

'But assuming, A, it occurred as reported and, B, it didn't go entirely according to plan, which is what the evidence points to, here's a guy who maybe ought to have gone down with his ship. He can't expect a whole lotta kudos among the brotherhood if he just walks.'

'So east on Wilshire, or Sunset . . .'

'Or San Vicente . . .'

'Or whichever, but heading you think eventually for the Hollywood Hills?'

'Where the shooting occurred. If that theory is correct, this would have to be his aim.'

'But if not?'

'If not, Corinne . . .' If not, the beard has another theory, but I can't take it in. If Max has been shot and if it happened at his house, where was Rebecca? And where is she now? I'm thinking about her phone call. It didn't sound as though she was in trouble, but I only heard Evie's version. And how long ago was the shooting? I try to connect these events, but I can't handle the mental arithmetic.

The beard is talking about a mosque in the valley, north beyond the hills, and another one somewhere east of downtown.

'And he'd be going to a mosque in search of . . . what?' Corinne asks. 'Sanctuary?'

'Or a symbolic moment,' the beard says. 'You've gotta figure this guy's thinking symbolically, assuming the attack was in fact religiously motivated.'

'As, I think, we are assuming that.'

'Well, sure, given the death threats Kleinman was getting.'

'And those messages we've heard about – you would read them as death threats? There is no God but God, for example?'

'Well, in context . . .'

'In context, of course . . .'

'Sure, I mean, what the heck else is that, if you read it in context?'

'Thanks for those insights, Brett. We'd like you to stay with us, if you wouldn't mind, while we see how this story plays out.'

I'd like to take the beard's insights and shove them down his throat. He's telling Corinne it would be his pleasure, looking pleased with himself as though Corinne's big-eyed stare is meant for him, rather than the camera. I'm muttering at the screen, 'Who the fuck cares about your half-witted insights, you convoluted fucker, if you can't even tell us who shot who?'

The fat man looks up from his newspaper with cream cheese on his chin. He blinks a couple of times and goes back to his reading. The young man is telling the girl about his screenplay, which is sad, apparently, but ultimately redemptive. It must be his laptop I've borrowed, but he hasn't noticed yet.

Corinne has switched off the smile and is trying to look the way someone ought to look who talks about matters of life and death, though her taut face doesn't give her much to play with. 'Brett Spurling there,' she says, 'from the Department of Oriental Studies at St Aloysius College, Yorba Linda. Chuck?'

'Food for thought, there, from Professor Spurling.' Chuck twitches his head in a folksy sort of way. He's white-haired and leather-skinned and has a voice like tyres on gravel. 'You know, Corinne, you have to wonder what's going through the terrorist's mind at a moment like this.'

'Well, Chuck, he has to be calculating whether or not to give himself up.'

'I doubt he's ready to give up on those seventy-two virgins, Corinne, that'd be my bet. I'm Chuck Broderick.'

'And I'm Corinne Dupont.'

'And this is SBC, interrupting our regular broadcasting for breaking news here on the Westside.'

'And for those of you who have just joined us, news at the top of this hour.'

'Following unconfirmed reports of a shooting at the home of TV producer Max Kleinman, suspect Amir Cadaver is leading police on a high-speed chase . . .'

Amir *Cadaver*. Not Frankie's Amir, then, whose last name is . . . something else. Something I can't remember. I'd certainly remember if it was Cadaver. And anyway, Frankie's Amir is no religious fanatic.

'According to witnesses,' Chuck says, 'police officers were attempting to apprehend Cadaver at his Westwood apartment . . .'

Then I remember Amir's name, and I know it's him. '*Kadi*var,' I mutter through my teeth. 'His name is *Kadi*var.'

'Excuse me?' The young man with the redemptive screenplay is looking at me. He's got his arms out, hands open. His head turns sideways, his whole body miming a question mark.

'I know these people.'

'And this entitles you how?'

'Someone's shot my wife's boss's husband, some religious nut, or might have shot him, and they're trying to arrest this Amir, which doesn't make any sense, because

Amir's an atheist, and they can't even get his name right, and I've no idea where my wife is.'

'Slow down, you're hyperventilating. Jesus!' The screenwriter takes the chair next to me. 'You know this guy?'

Corinne is talking about Max Kleinman's controversial film *Dropping the Veil*. She's promising up-to-the-minute insights from LA Terrorism Tsar Carmen Rodriguez after the break. Then it's some other car chase, advertising a movie or a video game. I pull out the earpiece and set it down on the table. The screenwriter's got a point, I should get a hold of myself, look at things rationally. But it's beginning to overshadow everything else, this fear for Rebecca. It's like an obstruction that makes it hard to breathe.

'Hey, Kia!' the screenwriter says, turning to the girl behind the counter. 'He knows the guy in the jeep.' He opens his eyes wide when he tells her this, and lets his jaw drop to signal amazement. Then his eyes are on me again. 'How do you even meet people like that? I never meet people like that.'

Kia bites her lip. 'What do you think he'll do?'

'Yeah, I mean wow, I hope he has a plan?'

'He should drive and drive,' Kia says, 'until it's just him and the desert and the stars.'

'You talking about the guy in the jeep?' It's the fat man. He shakes his head with a snigger. 'I give him ten minutes, tops.' And he goes back to his newspaper.

Struggling to control my breathing, I say to the screenwriter, 'I wonder if I could borrow your phone?'

'You're going to call him? How cool is that?' He takes the phone from his back pocket and hands it to me. 'Wow!'

I tap in Rebecca's number and listen while it rings.

'I'd kill to meet a terrorist. I've got like major writer's block. I'm so bored with self-obsessed little stories about guys getting drunk and sleeping with other guys' girlfriends and the dumbass boss and the cute neighbour and who said what to who and yada-yada-yada . . . And I don't mean like some superficial thriller, either, I mean getting totally under the guy's skin and making it real. Is he going to answer, do you think?'

I hear Rebecca's voice.

'It's David,' I say.

The screenwriter can hardly control his excitement.

'David, I'm at the hospital.' There are other voices. She's talking to someone, apologizing. 'Yes, sorry, of course. David, they're telling me to turn my phone off. Listen, I'm fine. I don't know when I'll be back. Sorry, yes, right now. I've got to get off now, David.'

'All right.'

'All right?'

'All right.'

'Bye, then.'

The screenwriter's staring at me as I hand him the phone. 'That's it? What happened? What did he say? Is he going to give himself up, or what?' He checks the screen, but it's just some piece of cartoon countryside with a flock of tampons settling on the branch of a tree.

Rebecca's at the hospital, which isn't good, but she's fine, so that's all right, then. And the police think Amir shot Max. 'It's all an absurd mistake,' I tell them. 'It must be.'

'Which is potentially even more interesting, if there's like a major twist. Not just a plot device, not just something to jerk the audience around, I mean. But something that comes right out of who he is, some secret in his past maybe. Like two roads diverged in a yellow wood and he took the one less travelled by. Which is totally my poem, by the way.'

'You wrote that?'

'Oh God, I wish!'

Out on Sunset, an ambulance goes past with its siren screaming, and as the noise diminishes there's the rattle of the helicopters louder than before.

The commercials have finished and Corinne's back. The jeep is skidding through another turn. We seem to be getting edited highlights. I recognize the moment where the wheels bounce across the corner of the pavement, and the sideways swoop of the camera. Corinne's in her box in the corner of the screen. Then she's joined by Chuck and a raven-haired woman who must be Carmen the Terrorism Tsar.

The screenwriter picks up one of his earpieces and starts listening. He offers me the other one.

Carmen Rodriguez is talking about the homeland-security budget. I should probably go home, assuming I can get the car to start. But if I stop watching now, I'm afraid I'll miss something.

'Here he is,' the screenwriter says, 'here's your friend.'

It's another close-up, jerky and flattened by the telescopic lens. I recognize Amir in spite of the smoked glass.

'And have you been picking up any chatter about Amir Cadaver, or any of his associates?'

'Intelligence often isn't as specific as that, Chuck.'

'So are we looking at a sleeper cell here, would you say?'

'I couldn't confirm that at this time.'

'Sounds like the authorities are playing catch-up.'

'That would be an unwarranted supposition, Chuck, in the light of today's developments.'

'You really know this guy?' It's the fat man. He's come round behind us to look at the screen. He's started on another bagel.

'He's called Amir Cadaver,' the screenwriter says. 'Can you believe that? Cadaver! What a name. This guy is so not destined to live.'

'Sounds kind of like a magic spell.' The fat man laughs,

spraying cream cheese and bagel crumbs. 'Amir Cadaver! Open Sesame!'

'His name is *Kad*ivar,' I tell them, but the door swings open behind me and my voice is drowned by the racket from the street.

'Hey!' Kia says, protesting at something. She's working her mouth, but there's not enough volume. I turn round, and I see she's talking to the transvestite, who's backing into the coffee shop, pulling his shopping cart, and letting in the hot air and the punchy clatter of helicopters.

'You're right,' the screenwriter says. 'It's the perfect name. You could have like a flashback of the other kids ragging him on the school bus, back in Arabia, or wherever. They'd be like, Yo, Cadabra, where's your magic carpet? It would be this pure experience of pain that he keeps going back to in his mind while he's planning and making his bombs. Then there'd be this guy on the subway, an Arab guy, commuting to work. And Cadaver would recognize him as one of the bullies, the ringleader even. Just as he's about to blow everything up, and their eyes would meet, and they'd be like, Wow, it's you! and, What was that all about? and there'd be this moment of like total redemption. And then Kapow! Special-effects time.'

I pull out the earpiece, silencing Chuck and Carmen. 'He's never blown anyone up,' I tell the screenwriter. 'He probably didn't shoot anyone. He's not from anywhere called Arabia, and he's not a religious fucking fanatic.' I get up, knocking my chair over behind me.

'If he isn't a terrorist,' Kia says, 'why are they chasing him?'

The transvestite rolls his eyes. 'Those jerk-offs,' he says. 'They'll chase anything in a skirt.'

The screenwriter's still watching the screen. 'Hey, I know

where that is. I totally know that store. It's like three blocks from here.'

'Yup,' the fat man says, 'the circus is coming to town.'

The screenwriter grips my arm. 'Let's go.'

'What?'

'Let's follow them, see how it ends.'

'How it ends?'

'He's your friend. Aren't you curious?'

I must be something, but curious is too light a word for whatever it is. The screenwriter's got his car out the back. He's got Kia to look after his laptop. He's got a plan. And I've got nothing but this unfocused sense of dread.

While he drives, he rewrites his latest screenplay. He wants the terrorist to meet his childhood tormentor earlier, at least by act three. He's navigating by the lights from the helicopters, peering up through his windscreen, turning left or right on sudden impulses. The traffic signals and the street lights and the flashing neon signs sweep across the windscreen as we move, darting and hovering like living things in the darkness.

We shoot across a junction and I see up ahead a couple of policemen on motorbikes blocking the road. One of them climbs off his bike, with one hand casually on his holster. I watch them swing past, and we're in an alley, tilting in and out of potholes. And for a while there are just the blank corners of buildings and colonies of garbage bins sucked up in our headlights.

I'm thinking about Rebecca, about how my life is suddenly without form or direction now I can no longer rely on her being where I am. And Max's death, if that's what it is, or his injury, and her vigil in the hospital feels less like the end of whatever they are together than an apotheosis. If I can't compete with Max in the full flow of his bullshit, how am I going to compete with the Max the martyr?

'They've stopped moving,' the screenwriter says. 'Look.'

The helicopters are circling. Underneath them, the conical shafts of light sway and settle. We pull into the side of the alley, scattering dust. Through its haze we can see the red lights flashing on the roofs of the police cars. As we open the doors, the whooping of sirens hits us, and a new sound – an amplified voice, barking warnings and instructions.

We reach the end of the alley as more police cars appear, each one swerving to find an empty stretch of road, and behind them the fire engines and ambulances and TV vans. The screenwriter's ahead of me as we turn onto the pavement and are flooded in light.

The jeep is just fifty yards down, on the far side of the street, up against a mailbox. There's steam rising from the edges of the hood. All around cops are leaping from cars and taking positions with guns. Further away, beyond the glare, there are other lights and other kinds of movement. Firemen and paramedics unload equipment. Pushing in among the emergency vehicles, TV crews are setting up cameras. Reporters place themselves in relation to the action, straightening their jackets, adjusting their hair. The amplified voice echoes from the buildings, harsher than the throbbing of helicopter blades.

There's a cop running sideways towards me from the direction of the jeep. 'Get back off the road,' he says.

'He didn't do it,' I tell him, 'it can't have been him.'

'Off the fucking road, asshole.' And he pushes me back into a doorway.

There's glass on either side of me. I'm surrounded by stainless-steel mannequins in black leather.

'You're making a mistake,' I shout after him. 'He's not even a Muslim.' My voice is swallowed by noise.

I've lost sight of the screenwriter. I turn back to find him, and see the door of the jeep move. It opens a couple of inches and stops. Just audible above the din, there's a sound like a field full of crickets as the guns are cocked. The door moves a few more inches then swings wide open. Unsteadily, Amir climbs out into the road. The lights have bleached all the colour from his face. He holds his hands unsteadily in front of him, as though he's feeling his way in the dark. His eyes are wild, the way they were last night, outside Max and Frankie's. And I know why he hit the accelerator when he saw the police in Westwood. He's high as a kite. And he's probably got a fresh supply in the glove compartment. He was working his mouth that way too, last night, taking every breath like a drag on a cigarette, his shoulders rolling with the effort to breathe. He puts his left hand on the side of the car to steady himself. Someone gives a shout of warning, to him or to the police. The hand on the car tightens into a fist. For a few seconds he just stands there, swaying slightly.

And I'm thinking that someone else should be here to witness this, somebody who knows him better than me, someone who likes him.

His right hand shakes as it settles on his waist and begins to feel its way down. The amplified voice is barking at him not to move, to keep his hand in the air. But the hand has found the side pocket of his jacket, of his sleek black thousand-dollar suit. *Baby, baby*, I hear the transvestite singing in my head, *gimme whatcha got*. I see the hand close around something. It's his inhaler. I'm ten yards from the nearest cop. He's on one knee by the open door of his car, his gun held out in both hands. 'It's his inhaler,' I say, but so quietly that I can barely hear it myself. I have an impulse to run towards the cop and tell him, shouting above the din, He's asthmatic, it's his inhaler. But what about the rest of them? I'd have to run under the lights towards Amir to get their attention. The scene spools through my mind, one take after another. I'm a hero, a buffoon, a dead man. But I'm paralysed in the doorway, because a breath might disturb the street's precarious equilibrium.

Then something changes in Amir's posture – a slight tilt to the left, a minimal upward movement of the right elbow. Half an inch of skin shows between the cuff and the edge of the pocket. And there's a shot, then a burst of shots, too many to count. He sprawls against the jeep, his right arm still in his pocket, his left arm twisted back behind his head. The side window is white as though with a sudden frost. I hear voices saying things that make no sense. Someone close by says, 'Oh, Jesus God, this isn't happening,' and the screenwriter who drove me here emerges from the next doorway. He looks older than he used to. And why not, I think – that's what happens with the passing of time. I'm older too. Even the television reporters look grey and skeletal off in the distance, mouthing their reports. They gesture towards the centre of the action, where Amir has finished sliding to the ground and policemen sprint towards him, warily, as though he might bite.

'Are you all right?' It's my voice. I'm talking to the screenwriter, who's looking around, deciding which direction to take. He looks at me but doesn't say anything because maybe he's forgotten who I am. 'We should get out of here.' I say this without moving. The screenwriter nods, and the nodding spreads down his body, and he stumbles towards the glass, putting his hands out to steady himself. Then there are people around us and a woman is looking at me. She has hair like spun sugar. She pushes something at me, and it's a microphone. The man beside her is adjusting something on his camera.

'Did you see what happened, sir?'
'Yes.'

'Would you mind speaking up. You say you witnessed the shooting.'

'Yes.'

'What words come to your mind to describe what happened?'

'They shot him.'

'And that made you feel how?'

'I've never seen someone shot before.'

'Was he armed?' It's someone else, a man with another microphone, elbowing his way towards me, shouting above the din. 'Police say the suspect was armed. Did you see the gun?' He's jostled by other reporters, all pushing their microphones towards me.

'He couldn't breathe.'

'Before they shot him, did he have a gun?'

'He had one of those . . . you know . . . I've forgotten the name.'

'You know the make? You got that good a look at it?'

'One of those inhalers.'

'Inhalers?'

'Did he say an inhaler? What kind of a gun is that?'

'Is that a make, or just some kind of a nickname?'

'How about you, sir, did you see anything?'

The screenwriter is beside me, rolling his face against the glass.

'Are you all right?' I ask him.

He stares at me out of the corner of one eye. His cheek looks waxy. The mannequins, absorbed by their own elegance, are paying no attention.

'Did he see anything, sir?'

'Could we ask him some questions?'

The woman with hair like spun sugar is talking to the camera. 'Sources close to the police,' she says, 'are suggesting that the suspect was armed. This eyewitness has identified the gun as an inhaler. Whether this was the weapon used against TV producer Max Kleinman is not known at this time . . .' She seems to have more to say. But the screenwriter, who has rolled his face from the shop window and leant forward with his hand on my shoulder, chooses this moment to vomit on her shoes.

'Cut!' someone says. 'I said cut. Jesus, what are you filming that for?'

They're shuffling backwards, the journalists and the cameramen. The screenwriter looks as though he might throw up again.

'Come on,' I tell him, 'I'll get you back to the coffee shop.' I put my hands on his shoulders, to help him up. I'm trying to remember how we got here, where we left his car. I put an arm round him, and steer him towards the alleyway.

Some of the reporters follow us. A cameraman scuttles ahead, walking backwards. One of the reporters is flipping through his notebook. 'The mayor's just said that this puts the enemies of freedom on notice that freedom is not negotiable, and that . . . that the time to worry is when we are no longer free to take out those who would destroy our freedoms. Do you have any comment on that?'

'What I'm mainly worried about is my wife.'

'Excuse me?'

'I'd just like to know that my wife's okay. When they shot Max was anyone else hurt? Can you tell me that?' I turn round at the mob of TV reporters. 'Can anyone tell me if anyone else was hurt when they shot Max Kleinman?' The reporters look blankly at each other. The woman with hair like spun sugar has leant against a lamp post to pull off her tights. A couple of cameras are still pointing at me. 'I want to be sure that my wife is all right. Is that really impossible for you to understand?' The reporter with the notebook is riffling through the pages as though he might have written the answer down somewhere.

When we reach the car, the screenwriter's in no state to drive. I back along the alley with a couple of reporters still in pursuit until I find a place to turn. Then I lose them. The screenwriter looks catatonic, but I drag enough out of him to get us back to the coffee shop, where Kia's eager to hear his story. And it's time for me to go home.

seventeen

I'm sprawled on the bed. I've thought about taking my shoes off but I haven't got round to it yet. Television parades itself in front of me and I notice it in a vague kind of way. I'm exhausted, in a state between drunk and hungover that captures the worst features of both – shaky, dry-mouthed, eyes unfocused, limbs inert, head protesting as though squeezed in a vice.

The news channels are replaying the night's major story, with key moments in slow motion. The commentators and pundits and anchor-people furrow their brows to tell us how weighty this is. By now most of them have worked out how to pronounce Amir's name, but every development brings with it new absurdities. I waste energy swearing at some square-jawed reporter and feel like the inmate of a lunatic asylum protesting my sanity. That's Rebecca's job, it occurs to me – to reassure me that I'm sane. And mine to reassure her. That might be the bedrock definition of marriage, come to think of it. In which case we're finished. I feel more cut off from Rebecca than I've ever been. And I feel ridiculous for feeling that, not because it isn't true, but because Amir is dead and he probably has a father somewhere, and a mother, and other people who care about him, whose pain dwarfs mine. And I feel even sorrier for myself for being reduced to such an undignified state of self-pity.

The highlights reach their inevitable climax. Footage of

the killing is disappointing as money-shots go – too unsteady, too distant. They should have picked a better location. As it is, the action is crowded by tall buildings, and the stark lighting washes the contrast out of everything. I can't quite predict the moment of impact, the moment when Amir's body will move backwards, jerking against the jeep, but here it comes anyway, ready or not. And it's a relief, for these few seconds, to have it out there instead of playing in my head.

And here's me again, blinking at the glare – some old actor who's wandered in from the gas-lit costume drama next door to complain about the noise – which is my cue to change channels. Over on SBC, my friend with the candy-floss hair, in new tights and vomit-free shoes, is wrapping up her report. 'According to some who knew him,' she tells us, 'he called it the Inhaler, a chillingly ironic name for such a deadly weapon. For SBC News, this is Katrina Cantrell.'

'Thanks, Katrina. Katrina Cantrell there, reporting live from midtown, where Amir Kadivar, prime suspect in the Kleinman shooting case, was shot and killed by police earlier this evening. And in a related story, *another* of Max Kleinman's documentary films is tonight mired in controversy. *Breaking the Mould*, an exploration of the hidden world of cosmetic surgery, is due to air Sunday, concluding Kleinman's Women Speak Out series. But already one of the featured Women *has* Spoken Out . . . *against* the film. Soap actress Katherine O'Donnell claims that her admission that she had ribs removed in her bid for stardom was quoted out of context . . .'

There's something in the scrolling news about an attack by Islamic extremists . . . a crowded Cairo shopping mall . . . hundreds feared dead. I should know more about this, I should pay attention. But while I wait for details, I'm distracted by a picture of Max and Frankie's house and a reporter standing in front of it with nothing very definite to report. It's a rehash of the canyon gossip – the suspect seen by one neighbour shouting outside the house during yesterday evening's premier party, the gunshots heard this evening by a second neighbour and the paramedics spotted while loading a man believed to be Max Kleinman into an ambulance – restless on his stretcher according to one report, zipped into a body bag according to another. Then something new about a veiled woman seen driving at reckless speed from the property. An accomplice? Or Kadivar himself, in female disguise? A photo of the clean-shaven Amir digitally inserted into a hijab allows the rugged reporter to comment on the suspect's effeminate appearance. I check the bottom of the screen for more news of the Egyptian bombing. A school board somewhere is pasting a verse from Genesis over the picture of Darwin in its biology textbooks. Some senator has said that taxing the rich out of existence would be equivalent to genocide. But there's no more news from Cairo.

Another reporter poses outside a hospital to tell us that Max Kleinman is said to be in a stable condition and receiving the best possible care. And then a police spokesman pops up on a screen in the studio to assure Chuck Broderick that the suspect was not only armed, but well supplied with cocaine.

'And has any female clothing been found in his jeep?'

The police spokesman is unwilling to commit himself on this question.

And here's Professor bloody Spurling from the Department of Oriental Studies to tell us, on the one hand, what the Koran has to say about drug abuse and, on the other, how far the terrorist is willing to go to infiltrate secular society.

'Would the demands of jihad allow a devout Muslim to use cocaine, for example?' Chuck Broderick asks, the gravel thickening in his voice.

'You've gotta figure that such prohibitions would be waived for a member of a sleeper cell wanting to move in celebrity circles, Chuck.'

'And would the need to infiltrate override proscriptions against the wearing of women's clothing?'

This is when I hurl the remote. As it hits the dressing table, the sound dies and the picture changes. For a couple of seconds I don't know what I'm watching. I see Rebecca's face and wonder if this is more bad news. A shadow passes like an unveiling. And here's Rebecca again, smiling shyly. She's sitting on Max's bed, joint in one hand, the other hand resting on the covers. It's Max's tape, of course, the one with Rebecca's name on. It's just where I left it when I switched off this afternoon, waiting for me like an abandoned dog. The shadow passes back the other way. It's the man himself, this blur of darkness – the great impresario, who's put himself in the firing line in the cause of free speech. At any moment he's going to take shape, and he will go into his goatish performance. And I will watch, because I have watched a man shot and killed and not to watch my wife being fucked seems disproportionately prudish.

Rebecca's talking, but I don't hear the words. She puts the joint to her mouth, puckering her lips to take a drag. The tip glows and darkens. With the smoke drifting from her nose, she rests it on the ashtray beside her, and breathes out, the pale breath blurring her features. Her face has relaxed into fullness again. She stands up to take her skirt off, unzipping it at the side, easing it down over her haunches and letting it fall to the ground. She's laughing as she steps out of it, but it's apologetic laughter. She's exposed in her unmatched underwear, hunching her shoulders, one knee turned in towards the other. It's this self-conscious pose that catches me with a stab of loss. There are young women roller-skating on the Venice boardwalk more naked than this, who manage, nevertheless, to wear their flesh like armour, hard and gleaming. This city's full of sun-baked Olympians, hiding their vulnerabilities under the skin. Evie would never stand so awkwardly, asking not to be looked at. But for me this glimpse of Rebecca's not-quite nakedness has a greater erotic charge than anything I can remember of Evie's posturing. She raises a hand, reaching out for something, and the twisting of her shoulders shifts the weight at the hips, and the delicate texturing of her thighs is like ripples in wet sand when the tide pulls back, the whole movement easing her into grace. She has no idea how lovely she is, which is part of her loveliness.

The figure comes into focus in the foreground. Not Max, but Frankie. Really, it's Frankie. And before I can formulate a new idea, I see that she's holding something, offering it. It's clothing of some kind. Rebecca takes it, turning it to find the way in. It's a dark-blue dress with a billowing neckline and a flouncy, layered hem. She pulls it over her head and she's laughing when she shows her face again. Frankie, who has retrieved the joint from the ashtray and taken a pull, smiles at Rebecca through the smoke. I'm off the bed and scrabbling under the dressing table for the remote. The back has fallen off it and the batteries have come loose. While I fiddle with it, I watch Rebecca pulling the dress down, wriggling into its tight waist, adjusting the straps on her shoulders. She runs her hands down over the material, smoothing it, assessing the effect in the mirror with a sceptical frown. It looks good on her – festive and pillowy. She turns round for Frankie to do up the zip, lifting her hair up at the back.

I press the mute button and catch the end of Rebecca's question.

'. . . really carry this off?' she says.

'Of course you can. Why not? It looks terrific on you. But I've got a feeling this one's the killer.' Frankie hands her something else. It's black, and I see the sheen of it where it catches the light. I watch the blue dress come off and the black one go on. I recognize it from last night's party.

Something moves inside me like a bubble rising to the surface. Max is in hospital, and Amir is dead, and hundreds have been murdered in Cairo, and Professor Brett Spurling has the ear of the nation, and the world is generally fucked up. But the one small corner of it where I live still works. Tears blur my vision, and it might be for everything that's gone wrong and it might be for the one thing that's gone right, I can't tell. I wipe my eyes with the heel of my hand. I have to agree with Frankie – it's a killer, that black dress. It's so obvious now I think about it that she'd never have bought something so sexually expressive without female encouragement. No man could have talked her into it.

I press fast-forward and I'm whirled through a fashion display – clothes I recognize, clothes I've never seen. I press play to watch Rebecca pulling on a skirt or unbuttoning a blouse, moving each time with greater confidence. And always they're talking about clothes, what look suits her, how much leg she can afford to show, how much cleavage, what's professional and what's dowdy, what distinguishes the trashy from the glamorous, what to keep and what to take back. Then Rebecca's sitting at the foot of the bed, and Frankie is behind her, kneeling on the bedclothes with her shoes off. They're facing the mirror we can't see. Frankie's playing with Rebecca's hair, holding it up to show more of her neck. She's modelling the haircut Rebecca hasn't yet had.

I let the tape run. I'm flooded with conflicting feelings. After the relief comes the shame, hot waves of it, each wave a memory of something I've done or said, each interspersed with little surges of insight. I understand Rebecca's injured outrage, of course, but also Max's oddly blasé attitude to this the least of his crimes, hardly a crime at all from his perspective, just a liberty. That was the word that struck me at the time – liberty. *I'd love to know how you knew about it*, I remember him saying, *nobody else did*. Not even Rebecca – I get that now.

Then Rebecca says, 'Did you always want children?' And something in her tone catches my attention – a steadiness, as though she doesn't want to offend Frankie, though I can't think why Frankie would feel sensitive about her kids. Frankie is on her feet. Rebecca's still on the bed, looking gorgeous in a slinky blue skirt and a cream blouse, and she's folding something she's already tried on, so she doesn't make eye contact when she asks the question. 'I mean, did you always know it was something you were going to do?'

'Hell, no. It was Max more than me.' For a moment, Frankie is a blur in the foreground, obstructing the view. When she comes into focus, she's lighting another joint. 'I could've gotten by without,' she says through a billow of smoke. 'But once we'd decided, it became a thing, you know. Max was all over me, which was reassuring but kind of tedious – I mean you can have too much of a good thing – but nothing happened.' She hands the joint to Rebecca and curls up next to her on the bed. 'We had tests. Max's sperm count was way up there, as he'll tell you if you ask him. So it had to be my problem. Turned out I had fibroid tumours. Which is a totally treatable condition. But by the time I was good to go, he couldn't get it up. Can you imagine? He's not given to performance anxiety.'

'Poor love.'

'It was just the worst, you know. For him it was the worst. I was ready to call it quits. Thanks, hon.' She breaks off to inhale. 'But having gone that far, to be thwarted by a limp dick would have seemed kind of pathetic.' She laughs at this, which makes Rebecca laugh. 'Then someone in the

Women's Studies Department recommended this therapist. Of course, getting Max to go was like pulling teeth.'

'It must have been difficult for him.'

'You could say that. It was his favourite fantasy remade as a horror movie. Max and a couple of women – Let's all talk about what turns us on and by the way I've got this problem with erectile dysfunction. He was a complete bear about it.'

'Men always treat it like some major tragedy, though, don't they. You tell them it's not important, but it's just one of those things they can't get in proportion.'

'Something you want to talk about, honey?' Frankie has propped herself up on one elbow to study Rebecca's face.

Rebecca raises her head to blow out smoke. 'How do you mean?'

'David has a problem?'

Rebecca looks genuinely surprised. 'No! God no, not David.' Then she laughs. It's an earthy, lascivious gurgle of laughter that could cure anyone's erectile dysfunction. 'David is . . . well, David is . . . fine.'

And the way she says it, no one could think she meant good enough, or moderately satisfactory. There's the slightest hesitation, then a lingering on the word itself, and it's already become my favourite part of the whole tape. So I rewind it until Rebecca has swallowed her laughter and looked up to suck in the smoke above her face, and Frankie has dropped her head down onto the pillow. And when I press play, there's the same bubble of contentment in Rebecca's voice that's so like her, and that always makes me think of sex but can't make everyone think of sex or she'd be turning people on all the time. 'David is . . . well, David is . . . fine.'

'Fine?'

'Yes,' she says, 'in that way – sexually – David's always

been absolutely fine.' And I can see she still means it. She's not withdrawing her endorsement, exactly. But there's some sadness there, some dissatisfaction that Frankie doesn't pick up on, some flicker of on-the-other-hand regret that pulls me down with her. She looks as though she's tempted to talk about this, but puts the joint to her mouth instead.

Frankie lies back and stares at the ceiling. 'Well, good for David.'

Rebecca has only taken a small breath when she starts coughing. 'No, really,' she says, 'I was thinking about someone else. Murkier times. Ancient history, thank God.' And she laughs, but her laughter is different now, shaded with irony. She smiles defensively, waving the smoke away, and passes Frankie the joint. 'So this therapist. She sorted Max's problem, I'm assuming.'

'Well, she was a nut, as it turned out, but I guess it worked.'

'What was her secret?'

'Hardly a secret. She had some half-baked theory about intensifying one's consciousness, heightening the moment, that kind of thing. Nowness Enhancement, she called it. But that was all pseudo-academic window dressing, it seemed to me. When it came down to it, we just had to film ourselves fucking.'

'Oh!' This has taken Rebecca by surprise. 'Well, I suppose that could be a turn-on.'

'I guess. Or a turn-off. Frankly, it did nothing for me either way. But Max got into it. Must have added some missing element of transgression.'

'And you were supposed to watch these tapes?'

'God knows. We never got that far. I left all that to Max, anyway. Maybe he watched them. I was pregnant already, which was a whole other thing. And then he got into fatherhood in a big way, like he was the first guy who'd ever fathered a kid. As soon as Laura was born, he was telling everyone we were going for five.'

'Five!'

'You know Max. Everything's a competition.'

'Five, though! You'd be on permanent maternity leave.'

'Trust me, we never got down to details. The idea was nixed before it got off the drawing board.'

'Yes, of course.' Rebecca's got this intense look, as though she's studying a picture, but all she's looking at is the space in front of her. 'But if he'd really wanted another – I mean if having another kid, a third one after Noah, had been the most important thing in the world to him, you wouldn't have done it?'

'Honey, I'd already done more than my share. He wasn't the one getting pregnant.'

'And what if it was the other way round?' She's looking at Frankie now. 'If you wanted kids and he didn't.'

'What are we talking about here?'

'Good question,' I tell Frankie. 'What exactly *are* we talking about?'

Me, it turns out, is what we're talking about – all my good qualities. I'm funny, apparently, and easy to be with, and I have this wonderful way of calming Rebecca down when she gets crazy, all of which makes me distinctly nervous, because preambles of this kind have a way of leading to dimly lit backstreets where you could get beaten up and left for dead.

'I've never felt so comfortable with anyone,' Rebecca says, and I brace myself for the turning where the glowing streetlights end. 'It's only that . . . well, it's just me, really . . . it's not his fault.'

'What's not his fault?'

'This thing about children.'

'Ah.'

And here it is. Not a blow, after all – just a feeling of levitation as though my head is no longer in contact with my body.

'And it *is* my fault,' Rebecca says, 'because I'm the one who's changed. It's always been sort of assumed between us that we don't want children, that we don't like them very much. All those years when I was working on my PhD my sisters used to dump their kids on me, like I had nothing better to do, or needed reminding of my destined role or something. When I met David, he became my excuse to be selfish. He doesn't actually like children, you know, I'd tell them. And then I didn't have to explain that I didn't much like them either. We had a kind of agreement. It just happened without either of us even having to talk about it. Then we came here, and it's been so unsettling.' For some reason she's crying.

Frankie is smoothing her hair away from her face. 'I'm sorry,' she says.

'No, you've been great, the work's been great. It's exactly what I needed. It's sort of thrown everything up in the air, though, forced me to think about where I'm going. I've loved working with you. And getting to know Laura . . .'

'She's really taken to you . . .'

'She's a lovely child. I don't know why I'm crying. And then Noah nearly drowned and I saw how frantic everyone was. It did something to me. I'm thirty-five, thirty-six next month, and I'm suddenly thinking I'd better get on with it. And I look at David, and he seems to be reverting to adolescence or something. I mean, jumping in the pool with that woman, while everyone else was in a panic. Well, you know, it just seemed to sum it up.'

'Noah was okay. For him it was like nothing happened.'

'David can't even cope with being *here* for a few months.

I know it's a disruption to his tidy little routine and all that, but if he can't do this, how's he going to do children?'

'He'll cope. You just have to be straight with him. You've as much right to have kids as anyone else, you can tell him that from me.'

Rebecca is laughing and crying at the same time. I can see it's some relief to her to talk about it, and I feel crushed that she didn't feel able to talk to me. Because although it makes me breathless what she's just said, as though someone's just sucked all the air out of the room – and it's true that I've never given it any thought before – I can see it makes sense, which is also what scares me to death now some of the implications are beginning to sink in.

'Call him up,' Frankie says. 'Call him now and tell him. David, I want children. You've got a problem with that, get over it.'

'Yes,' I say out loud, 'call me up, talk to me about it.'

'He'll understand.'

'Of course I will,' I say to the television, 'of course I'll understand.' It hurts me to see her like this, sad and unable to tell me why she's sad. And I know if I could comfort her, hold her tight, I'd feel better too, and everything would stop shifting around me and my heart would stop racing.

They're still talking, Frankie encouraging Rebecca to deal with me as though I'm some kind of problem. Rebecca's blowing her nose. Then Frankie hands her the phone and she dials the number, my number presumably, though I must have had my phone turned off because I don't recall the phone conversation about her wanting a baby, and I think it would have stuck in my mind.

'David, it's Rebecca.'

So I must have answered.

'Am I interrupting? Are you writing?'

And maybe I was, but I don't think so, because I haven't been, most of the time.

'I just wanted to talk. Where are you? I thought you'd be at home.'

So where was I? And when was this?

'Are you with someone? We could talk later if you're with someone . . .'

Which is when I remember. I was in Malibu, in Moon-glows with Astrid, the day I met Jake and Mo and Natalie. And listening to Rebecca's problems wasn't at the top of my list of things to do. How long ago that seems, when it was fine with Rebecca if I was with someone, before the thought had really entered her head that my being with someone might be a problem.

She's still talking on Frankie's phone, getting tearful, wanting to know where I am, whether I'm drinking, what's going on. It makes me cringe now to be confronted with this conversation, even though I can't hear my end of it. Thank God for that, at least – that I don't have to listen to myself being evasive and defensive and getting shirty about nothing.

'Oh, David, this is pointless.' She's crying. Frankie hands her a tissue. 'Don't bother, David, if it's that much of a prob-lem.' She closes the phone with an angry snap. Frankie takes it and pulls her into a hug.

'Well, I made a mess of that,' Rebecca says, sniffing against Frankie's shoulder.

'No, you didn't.'

'What a waste of time.'

'You'll work it out. Talk to him tonight. Or go some-where for the weekend.'

'You don't suppose he's with that woman, do you?'

'What woman?'

'The trollop. You know – the skinny-dipper.'

'She went in with her dress on, honey. Skinny-dipping requires a little more forethought.'

'Did you see it when she came out?' Rebecca says, laughing. 'She might as well have been naked.'

'You don't really think he's with her, though? I mean, is that what he does?'

'No, of course not! David? I don't even know why I said it. Really, it's not in his nature.'

'I'm glad to hear it.'

'It would never occur to me not to trust him. Absolutely not.' It sounds as if she's taken a vote in her head and it's not unanimous exactly but there's a majority in my favour. There was, at least, back then, when this tape was made. She's drying her eyes, putting her grown-up face back on.

'So,' Frankie says, 'are we ready for more work?'

'Yes. Yes, of course. Sorry. Should I get my briefcase?'

'To hell with that. I mean we haven't done the underwear yet . . .' She lifts a carrier bag onto the bed. 'Now I know you weren't sure about this, but trust me, honey, you'll be a knockout in this bra.' She has it in her hand, dangling from one of its straps, twisting from its solid underside to its lacy upper edge. There's a bang from somewhere that makes her start. 'What the hell was that?'

'It came from the office,' Rebecca says with a giggle. 'Max must be home.'

'No, he said he had meetings all afternoon. I told him we'd be trying on clothes, and he said we'd have the house to ourselves.'

'It must be him. Who else could it be?'

'Max?'

Rebecca lies back on the bed, helpless with laughter for no obvious reason.

'Max, is that you?' Frankie moves towards the camera, grows into a blur, and disappears from view.

And that's where it stops. There's just the black-and-white fuzz of blank tape.

'Bad luck, Max,' I say to the flickering screen. 'And you never even got to see her with her top off.' I switch off the television and sink backwards onto the bed. 'Which is too bad for you, Max, because her breasts really are something.' The ceiling's been done in that textured plaster. A light from the street moves across it, agitating all the shadows. When I close my eyes it's my own blood I can see, pulsing through the vessels in my eyelids.

eighteen

It's still dark when I wake up. I've been dreaming, and I'm not ready to let the dream go. I'm in bed with Rebecca. My whole body is buzzing with the texture of her skin. Frankie smiles down at us while we make love. There's a banging noise and it's Max in the next room, hammering on the wall to be let in. He's shouting my name. Can't you see I'm busy, I tell him. Look at all these children I have to take care of. And there they are, lifting their hands from a pit in the centre of the bed – famine victims with flies crawling across their faces. I'm still holding the dream, still on the edge of sleep, when the knocking starts again and I hear my name. It's quieter than in the dream, but the tone is urgent.

I get up off the bed so fast I lose my balance. I have to hold on to the dressing table to stay on my feet. I check my watch. It's four thirty. There's a dog yapping out in the street, and the scattered coughing of early morning traffic. I feel my way to the kitchen window and look out at the staircase. Odd rectangles of light identify the insomniacs and the early risers in the neighbouring apartments. When I turn the latch, the door pushes open against me and the hot air stings my eyes. Jake's down in the alley, standing by his car. He's got the door open. He's looking away from me, towards the traffic lights on the main road, which turn from green to red, signalling to nobody. There's a pinging sound because he's left his keys in the ignition. I can't see his face under his baseball cap, but he's hunched over, with his hands deep in his pockets. His canvas bag is slung across his back. A bin tips over in the wind and rolls towards him. He turns to watch as it clatters past, spilling garbage. He's got his hand on the shoulder strap, about to lift the bag over his head, so that he can sling it on the passenger seat and drive off, when I shout his name.

He looks up, and I see the fear in his face, and it comes to me that it was Jake who shot Max. Once he'd worked out that Max was Rochester, he only had to follow him home from the library. It's a weight, this thought. It's not like the image of Amir's death, which leaps without warning from the edge of my vision, making me flinch. It's a dull weight pulling me down inside.

Jake's on his way up towards me, head down, taking two steps at a time. When he reaches the top, he's breathing hard. 'I don't know what I'm going to do,' he says. 'I couldn't think where else to go.'

'Come inside. You look terrible. Where have you been?'

'Just driving around. Just doing the only thing this city is any fucking good for. What should I do, David? You always know what to do. Jesus, this is all so fucked up.'

'Stay calm, Jake.' I put my hands on his shoulders to hold him steady. He lurches towards me, putting his arms round my waist, clinging to me with his head against my face. I hesitate for a moment. Then I let my hands slide across his back. I can feel his ribs. There's nothing to him. His breathing could shake him apart. Now he's this close, it's like a stab of grief, the thought that this child has done something he'll never recover from.

'I was thinking of going to the police,' he says, 'telling them I did it.'

'Come in and sit down.' I take him by the arm and lead him through the hall and towards the couch. When I switch the light on I see how pale he is. 'If that's what you want to do,' I tell him, 'I'll come with you. But we should find someone to represent you, someone who understands how things work.'

'I was ready to do it. Then they started chasing that Arab guy.'

'Amir.'

'They shot him.'

'I know.'

'I mean, how messed up is that?' He's on the move, too agitated to sit. He pulls the strap of his bag up over his head and dumps the bag on the dining table, next to my laptop and some books I've been meaning to look at.

'Which is why you need a solicitor, a lawyer I mean, so there's some control over what happens, someone who'll speak to the police first and explain.'

'But what if he did it?' He crosses to the sink, resting his hands on the taps.

'How do you mean? I don't understand.'

'Well, maybe he did. And maybe no one'll ever know whether he did it or not.'

I'm struggling to keep up. 'You think you could live with that? Wouldn't it be better just to tell the truth?'

'How can I be sure what the truth is? I'm not God.' He faces me again, leans back against the sink with his arms crossed, rocking back and forward. 'Maybe I got it wrong, what I thought happened never happened and that Muslim coke-head really deserved to die.'

'He wasn't a coke-head. Well, maybe he was a coke-head, but he wasn't a Muslim, and he certainly didn't deserve to die.'

'Because he wasn't a Muslim?'

'Because he didn't do it.'

'And you know this because?' He gives me an anguished

278

look. He's got his hands up as though he's ready to drag an answer out of me. And I realize this is a real question. He genuinely wants to know if it was Amir who shot Max.

'But I thought you said . . . I thought you meant . . .'

He drops his hands and stares miserably at the floor. 'I have to find my mom,' he says.

And I feel a twinge of disappointment that I've let him down, and it comes to me, before I know whether it's a guess I'm making or a promise, that no child of mine will ever be so alone in the world. 'Yes,' I tell him, 'you're right. You should talk to your mother.'

'Because until then it's all just circumstantial. I've got to hear it from her own mouth, what she did or didn't do.'

'Wait a minute . . . you're saying . . .'

'Because until I hear it from her, it's just like this story I've made up and it's driving me out of my fucking mind.'

'Are you saying you think your mother did it?'

'Well, obviously, David. That's what I've been telling you. Look.' He starts rummaging through his bag. 'When I got home this evening, she was gone, which is like the first time in weeks she's left the apartment, and Natalie's journals were scattered all over the couch and on the floor, all lying open. And I'm like, Jesus, Mom, what gives you the right? And I'm picking them up and I see she's marked a page with a piece of Kleenex. Here, see, it's from March, way before any of the stuff about Rochester.' He pulls it out of the bag and opens it at the marked page. 'Look at this bit.' He holds it where I can see, and runs his finger under Natalie's words as he reads. '*Mo is such a star, a beautiful BEAUTIFUL five-pointed star. And she is going to turn my life round through five hundred and seventy degrees! Yay! Because this guy she sent me to see – who is like this real heavy weight TV producer according to . . . hello! EVERYBODY practically – thinks I have a quote unquote . . .*' Jake stops to clear his throat. When he starts reading again, his voice is unsteady. '. . . *thinks I have a quote unquote luminous quality.*' Impatiently he wipes his sleeve across his eyes. 'She did too, didn't she,' he says to me. 'She did have a luminous quality.'

'Yes, Jake,' I tell him, 'she did.'

He puts the book down on the table and walks away to blow his nose.

'I'll put the kettle on.' It makes me smile to catch myself saying something that would be understood in faraway places such as Tufnell Park to mean *Never mind*, and *Let's get this sorted*, and *What can I do to help?* but probably has none of those resonances for Jake.

In fact, he's looking at me, while I fill the kettle, as though he's about to say, *What the hell are you talking about?* But what he actually says is, 'Did you know Mom had a gun?'

'Yes, I found it under the couch the first time I went there.'

'Well, it's not there now. It's not anywhere that I can see. She bought it when all this terrorist stuff began. As if a gun would help. They're taking down skyscrapers. They're releasing poisonous gas in the subway. Kaboom! There's a fucking pipe-bomb scattering four-inch nails, but hey! I'm not scared, I've got a gun. And you see what this means, don't you.' He picks up the journal again. 'She knew this Rochester guy, this Max Kleinman. It was her idea in the first place for Natalie to meet him.'

'Yes, of course. She was his therapist.' I switch the kettle on and take a couple of mugs off the draining board.

Jake is staring at me with his mouth open. 'You knew this?'

'Not really.'

'His fucking therapist? You knew this and you didn't tell me?'

'I've only just found out. I mean I've only just thought

of it. I hadn't really made the connection until you read that page. Your mother was filming Natalie, wasn't she. What did she call it . . . ?'

He does his rabbit-ear quote marks. 'Nowness Enhancement Work.'

'That's it. Five or six years ago, it must have been, she was doing her Nowness Enhancement number on Max.'

'Man, how come you always somehow know these things? Are you channelling this stuff?'

'How about a cup of tea?'

'Are you completely out of your fucking mind?'

'Stay calm, Jake, and let's try and be practical.'

'She knows he's the guy, she's taken the gun – is this practical enough for you?'

'Let's not leap to conclusions.'

'Someone shot him. It's not that much of a leap. You've seen her in that Arab outfit.'

'When were you last at home?'

'You must have heard the news. The mysterious veiled accomplice – could it have been Kadivar in drag? Or was it some nut-job therapist doing a house call?' He's got his back to the wall, arms down by his sides, and he's drumming with his fingers. He's still wearing his cap. The only time I've seen him take it off was when we banged heads in the library.

'Try and focus, Jake. Have you been home?'

'Couple of hours ago.'

'So she might be back by now.'

'Astrid's there. She's gonna call me.'

'And your mother hasn't got a phone with her.'

'If she has, it's switched off.'

'She hasn't been missing long enough for us to start calling the hospitals. And it's too early to report it to the police.'

'I'm not turning her in!'

'Right. Exactly. So there's nothing for you to do. You've got it covered.'

He looks unconvinced.

'And anyway, I'm pretty sure Max is going to be all right.'

'How can you even know that? They said nothing on the radio.'

'Rebecca phoned me . . . my wife . . . she called me from the hospital. She couldn't talk for long but she sounded okay.'

'With all respect to your wife, I mean, like, where did that come from? I mean, is your brain tuned in to the right station here, because according to what I'm hearing it wasn't your wife who got shot.'

'She was there with Max, I'm assuming. I'm sure she would've told me if it was serious.'

His eyes are glazed for a moment then hyper-alert again. 'Did he tell you my mom was his therapist? Is that what Kleinman told you? Because he's a lying fuck – I don't know anything about him but I know that, so there's no reason to believe one fucking word he says.'

'When did you last get any sleep?'

'I can't sleep.'

'You must be exhausted. Your mother's going to show up at some point and you'll be more use to her if you've had some sleep.'

'Did you hear what I said?'

'Eat something, then. When did you last eat?'

'What is your fucking problem? Why are you always telling me to eat?'

'You look undernourished.'

'When did *you* last eat?'

'Now you mention it, I can't remember.'

'So!' He raises his hands in support of this clinching argument.

I respond with a nod and a shrug to indicate that he's got a point. I'm happy to let him have the last word, because it allows me to start organizing breakfast.

I check the fridge. Stocks are running low but there's plenty to work with. Luckily I can do breakfast – breakfast is one of my things. I take out the remains of a packet of sliced ham, an oddment of cheese, an onion, a red pepper and an egg carton with five eggs in it. I put a piece of butter in the frying pan and turn on the gas. Jake has slumped into a chair and is staring into space. I carve up the pepper, cut a few slices off the onion, dump the seeds and the onion skins and chop the rest. When it's all squeaking and spitting in the pan, my hunger hits me. I give it a stir, holding the spoon in my left hand because I'm using my right hand to spoon coffee into the machine and put a couple of slices of bread in the toaster. Then I whip the eggs up a bit, throw in a splash of milk, salt and pepper, some cheese in thick curls straight off the grater and, thinking Jake probably likes his food spicy, a sprinkle of Tabasco. Meanwhile I'm running hot water in the sink – ready for washing up, but mainly so I don't have to serve the omelette on cold plates, because I want this to be as tempting as possible.

As it happens, the temperature of the plates probably doesn't matter that much. Jake gives his omelette a blank stare as though it might be a piece of conceptual art. He picks up his fork, sighs, tears off a piece the size of a broad bean and lifts it to his mouth. He chews in an absent-minded kind of way. Then he starts shovelling it in. Which is gratifying. And I would set this compliment to my cooking against all his earlier rudeness, if I weren't already inclined to forgive him on the grounds that he is clearly carrying more of a load than should ever be dropped on anyone so young.

When he slows down enough to start talking again, I'm

surprised to discover that he's aware of his own rudeness. 'Yesterday,' he says, 'at that ACLU thing?'

'Yes?'

'I was out of line.'

'Were you?'

'I said some things I totally shouldn't have said.'

He was angry, I remember that much, but right now the details elude me. I'd like to remember, if I can, because it must have been really something for him to pick it out, among all the other things he's said to me, as something to apologize for. 'You shouldn't worry about it,' I tell him. 'Really, it's not important.'

'There's a lot of bad shit going down, you know?'

'I know there is.'

He's still eating, but he looks distracted. His knee has started jiggling up and down. He takes his cellphone out of his pocket, flips it open, flips it shut, and puts it back in his pocket. It reminds me that I should plug mine in. He points towards my laptop with his fork. 'Is that where you work?'

It sits at the other end of the table, rebuking me with its silence.

'I'd say it's one of the places where I don't work. Sometimes I don't work on the deck, which has a nice view of the ocean by the way, if you stand in the right place, and occasionally I don't work in a corner of the bedroom, but these past few days this is mainly where I've not been working. It's handy for the fridge.'

'The book's not going well, huh?'

'Just not going, would be more accurate.'

He waves his fork at me. 'Maybe you're standing in your own light. That's what happens to me a lot. I mean, I listen to you talk about it and it's like you're a clearing for failure. You're like, This isn't gonna work, and you're already fucked.'

'I see what you mean.'

'And you've got this word thing.'

'What word thing?'

'Like the words are more important than whatever the hell it is you're trying to say. Like the medium is the message or whatever, which if you think about it, the medium is just the medium.'

'Yes, I see that.'

'So what is it you wanna say?'

'In my book, you mean?'

'Yeah, in your book.'

'Well, it's just a secondary-school textbook, of course, so what I want to say personally doesn't actually come into it, not in that sense. I mean, not like in what you're doing.' I'm disconcerted at how rapidly I've reverted to this fumbling apologetic manner at the thought of the book, even in front of this nineteen-year-old boy.

Jake's shaking his head from side to side and frowning earnestly. 'Man, are you ever down on yourself! I mean you're the writer, okay, so you'd better know what you're writing.'

'Yes, sorry, you're absolutely right.'

He's checking his cellphone again.

I'm touched that it occurred to him to ask about my work, particularly when he's got so much else on his mind, and I feel he deserves a better answer. I take a deep breath. 'Okay. It's about the major world religions. In this chapter, I have to do Islam – the historic origins, basic tenets, major rites and festivals, some later cultural accretions, that kind of thing. Which should be easy enough. Except that, with all that's happening in the world right now, it feels as though I'm inspecting the upholstery on a runaway train. To be perfectly honest, the whole project seems that way to me at the moment. What about a book called "Religion: can't live with it, can't live without it". Wouldn't that be more to the point? Or "Christianity: is it better than a hole in the head?" '

Jake's staring into his coffee. I've lost him. He's worried about his mother, of course, waiting for the catastrophic phone call.

'In addition to which, there has, as you say, Jake, been a lot of bad shit going down.'

He looks up. 'So, assume I know nothing about Islam, and tell me about it. Tell *me* about it, I mean. Then the writing'll be about communicating something to some other person.' He looks down at his plate and spears a few scraps of omelette. 'Do it by email if you like.' When he glances up at me, he's scowling. 'But you probably think that's a stupid idea.'

'Jake, it's brilliant.'

He looks at me doubtfully, reluctant to let go of the scowl. 'Are you kidding around, because I really have got enough of my own crap to deal with . . .'

'Really, Jake. You'll hear from me, I promise. How was the omelette?'

He shrugs. 'Hey, you know. It was an omelette.'

And I'm not kidding around, truly. I'm going to spend Monday telling Jake what I think he needs to know about Muhammad and the Koran and dietary restrictions and the call to prayer and whatever else comes to mind. I feel good about this – it's a glimmer of hope, at least. And I feel good about the fact that my omelette was unquestionably an omelette, which is the highest praise I could have expected. I gather up the plates and take them to the sink. I'm about to ask Jake about his own project, but his head is down on the table, sideways to accommodate his peak. So I start washing up, trying not to make too much noise, and in less than a minute he's snoring.

When his cellphone starts playing its tune, he wakes up

with a start and has the thing to his ear with impressive speed. It's Mo. From Jake's reaction, it sounds as though she's in some kind of state, and as far I can tell Jake isn't doing much to calm her down. He's still trying to find out where the hell she is when the apartment phone starts ringing. I answer it with wet hands. It's Astrid trying to find Jake. She can't get through on his cellphone and wonders if I've heard from him. She's just heard from Mo who is, she tells me, pretty spaced. These two conversations start playing across each other like jazz – the kind of jazz that gives you a headache – me asking Astrid, 'Where do you think she is?' and Jake saying, 'Where the fuck are you?' and Astrid saying, 'She's on her way to the pier,' and Jake saying, 'The pier? Why the fuck . . . ?' and Jake saying, 'I'm with David, you remember David,' and Astrid saying, 'I'm glad he's with you, David – somebody better be looking out for him.'

'So I guess I'll see you on the pier,' Jake says.

'That's all I could get out of her,' Astrid says, 'that she's on her way to the pier. She wasn't making much sense. She kept saying she had to let Nattie go.'

'What does that mean – let her go?'

'Let her spirit move on, I guess.'

'Just don't go wandering off, Mom, okay?'

'In practice, though, what does it mean?'

'Fuck, Mom!'

'Who knows?'

When I hang up there's a message waiting. 'You're probably asleep.' It's Rebecca. 'At least, I hope you're asleep. I can only talk for a minute anyway.'

I have to press the phone closer to my ear, because Jake is still trying to drag some sense out of his mother, and since his main tactic is to say fuck a lot he isn't making much headway.

'I've offered to pick up the kids from the nanny,' Rebecca

says, 'and take them to their grandma's. I'll be home in an hour, maybe, by the time I've got out of here. So I'll see you soon, then.' I hear her breathing in and out and in again.

'Come on,' Jake says, 'we've gotta go.' He's putting his phone back in his pocket and slinging his bag over his shoulder.

'What happened earlier, David . . . Well, maybe we can talk about it.' There's an explosive sound in my ear as she blows her nose. 'Anyway, Frankie's drawing me a map.' She starts talking to Frankie, telling her she'll find the place, no problem. 'All right, then,' she says to me, 'we'll talk later.' There's a pause before she hangs up as though she has more to say.

'All right,' I say into the silent phone, 'so we'll talk later.' And I follow Jake out the door.

nineteen

The wind is behind us as we cross the road, and still eerily warm. It's strange to face this dark mass of water without the cool air of a landward breeze, but for once the thirsty tilt of the palm trees along the shoreline looks right. On the pier, the shutters of the food and trinket stalls rattle their padlocks, and the canvas awnings strain and flap. All nervous energy, Jake moves beside me with shorter, quicker strides so that our footsteps hit the boards like an unsteady heartbeat. We can hear the water shifting underneath, slapping the wooden piles and flumping onto the sand. Among the cries of the gulls, through the wind's hum, a human voice seems to be saying, 'Oh . . . oh . . . oh . . .' It's an unnerving sound, coming at us out of the darkness, until Jake says, 'It's Astrid,' and I realize she's calling Mo's name.

The rails of the rollercoaster loom above us, silvery on the turn where the moonlight catches them. Underneath is a building with signs advertising beer and hotdogs, and a coffee shop, and an entrance between them to the fairground.

The shadows stir under the archway, and Astrid comes out towards us. Her hair is dishevelled, straggling free from a scarf. 'Her car's back there,' she says, 'sort of abandoned next to the carousel. And I found these.' We stop to look. There's enough moonlight for us all to recognize Mo's shoes.

'She wouldn't have jumped in, would she?' I ask.

'She sounded buzzed, David – she's on a high.'

'Have you been to the end yet?'

'I've just got here.'

Jake starts walking again, and we catch him up. Astrid takes his arm. 'They have it in the south of France, this hot wind. They call it the mistral. It can make people a little crazy.'

'And she couldn't go home?' Jake says.

'Couldn't face it, is what she said to me.'

'Couldn't face what, though – the place, the cops, whatever it is she's done? Jesus, Astro, what is it she's done?'

'We didn't get that far. She didn't tell *you*?'

Jake pulls away from her. 'She wasn't making much sense. Just said where she'd be.' There's the hollow thump of his shoes on the boards as he breaks into a jog, and a dozen seagulls racket up around him.

'They understand what the weather can do to a person in France,' Astrid tells me.

Jake is ten yards ahead of us already, loping between the last buildings on the pier. We hurry after him past a Mexican eating place and an information booth with its shutters down.

'In Nice or Marseilles, you know, this wind would be like a mitigating circumstance.'

'It sounds as though Max is going to be all right,' I tell her. 'Stable's the word the reporters have been using.'

'God, I hope you're right.' I hear the catch in her voice. 'They use these words – stable, comfortable – and they put on these grown-up voices, like it's okay now, we're in charge, but it doesn't mean you're not paralysed or in a coma.'

'You think she did it?'

'I've known her like ten years, David. Jake was a kid when we met. She's a dear friend and a really loving person, but her receptors have always been kind of out of alignment.'

Jake's up ahead, calling out. His voice is distorted by the wind. Then we see Mo. She's sitting on a bench with her back to the ocean. The water glitters between them, the moon splashing its light in horizontal streaks. As we get closer, I see that Mo's wearing a slip and her feet are bare. There's a turbulent flow of words from her mouth. Half of what she says is snatched up by the wind and blown off the end of the pier to flap across the water with the gulls. The other half doesn't make much sense. But she repeats herself enough for me to catch the drift. She's telling Jake she's an instrument of the eternal. She's captured the flame. The flame is the flame of the eternal, which is abundantly present in every moment, being a flame of dazzling brightness that burns forever unconsumed. She gestures as she talks. Her fingers glimmer with silver and turquoise, and the heavy sway of her breasts is visible through the flimsy material. Too long out of the light, and stripped of make-up, her face looks doughy. But she holds herself with regal self-confidence. The video camera is in her lap. She did it for Nattie, she says. Nattie needed closure. She captured the flame, but the flame remains undiminished. Jake is beside himself, pleading with her to stop talking shit.

'What's up, Mo?' Astrid asks.

Mo brightens at the sight of her. 'You came!' she says, and puts out a hand as though expecting it to be kissed. 'Can you believe this weather? This city would be unbearable, wouldn't it, if we didn't have the ocean. All that misery with nothing to wash its face in.' I have to watch her lips to catch this, so much of the sound is swept away.

Astrid takes the hand and holds it to her waist. 'Are you okay, Mo?'

'I'm thinking of moving north, as a matter of fact. Santa Rosa, maybe. But what would happen to you, sweetie, who'd take care of you?'

'I'd be fine.'

'And so much healing here still to be done.'

'You'd miss the sunshine.'

'Yeah, Mom,' Jake says, 'and you'll miss the sunshine when you're locked up.'

'Such darkness in that boy's soul! Such lack of faith!'

'Who's been sitting with a hood over her head? Who's been out all night with a fucking gun?'

'Is it me, Astrid honey, or is it getting warmer?'

There's a clatter behind me, and I turn to watch a piece of wood the size of a cafeteria tray somersault towards us along the boards. It dances past the Mexican restaurant and snags on the end of a bench ten yards away, where it stays, wedged between slats, and I see that it's decorated with silver stars. *MADAME ZORA Palmistry Tarot Readings $15* it says, and *Your FUTURE in the PALM of your HAND.* A crack has opened up along its length.

'Mom,' Jake says, 'for fuck sake.'

Mo is standing with the slip pulled up around her belly, her soft thighs exposed. 'So hot, though, sweetie.' She's left the video camera on the bench. Astrid is holding her, pulling her slip down.

'Have you been filming, Mo?' I ask her.

And she starts again about capturing the flame and letting Nattie go. 'Jakey might watch it,' she says, 'but that boy thinks if he stops running, the earth won't turn under his feet.'

'What the fuck are you talking about, Mom?'

I've picked up the camera. 'Astrid, do you know how to work this thing?'

'Sure I do.'

'Sit here and see what's on it. Jake, calm down. Try and keep your mother from doing anything crazy.'

Astrid pulls out the miniature screen on the side of the

camera and presses some buttons. Obediently, Jake has positioned himself next to Mo. She turns away from us, holding up a hand, palm outward, two fingers pointing to the sky, and makes the sign of a blessing over the water. There are seabirds riding the buoys, lifting their wings for balance. Back along the pier, the restaurant windows rattle in their frames. I sit next to Astrid and she turns the camera so we can all see. There's a shaky image of a house. It's Max and Frankie's place, viewed from the driveway – the shallow eaves and the uncluttered panels of glass obscured only by vegetation.

'This is it,' Astrid says, 'this is definitely it.' And her hand tightens around the camera.

The screen goes white as the sensor light comes on. When the image adjusts, we're scanning the front of the building, dipping for no obvious reason towards the slate path and the rustling skirts of the burka, and then up again to a featureless stretch of wall.

Astrid's muttering, 'Oh my God, Mo, what have you done?'

When we reach the side gate, a grey sleeve rises into the frame, and a jewelled hand appears at the end of it to push the gate open. It's unbolted, of course, just as I left it when I smuggled the stolen tapes out to the car. Another light comes on in the back garden. I recognize bits of the house and the swimming pool as Mo swishes through the foliage. We hear a scraping noise – she's walked into a tree, and there's nothing to see for a while except leaves and sky. When the camera jerks back out of the branches, the lounge doors swing into view. We're listening to music that might be Indian and a woman talking. It's the sound of television coming out into the garden. The music cuts to laughter. We see the sliding glass doors, and the stones under Mo's feet, and an upside-down view of the swimming pool, as Mo wrestles with the camera. And here's the door again, with an opening into the darkness. Only the television is visible. Then fragments of the Kleinman lounge grow out of the gloom around it – the mirror by the front door, and the horizontal fireplace, and the coffee table with the chess pieces still in mid-game. On the huge flat television screen there's a woman in a sari doing stand-up, and we hear the tinny sound of audience laughter twice recorded. From somewhere else we hear Max saying, 'Hey, who the hell are you? Get the fuck out of my house.' The camera finds him standing in front of the couch in his robe and slippers.

Under his breath Jake is saying, 'Oh, Jesus, Mom, no, no, no . . .'

Astrid reaches for my hand, and I feel her nails cutting into my palm.

There's fear in Max's face and he's fighting to keep control of his voice. 'Whaddya want? Is this a robbery or what? What's with the fucking camera? Look, if this is about the film, watch the film. I swear if you find anything in it disrespectful to your culture or religion . . . Look, either way, I'll give you a chance to respond – equal airtime. Lady, I respect your traditions, absolutely. I was brought up very traditional. Not in your faith, obviously, but . . . Jesus!' Our view of Max tilts sideways and rights itself again, and we see Mo's hand in its grey sleeve pointing a gun.

'Shit, Mom!'

'As a woman,' Max is saying, 'you must . . . as a woman . . . see that what I'm doing, I'm just supporting other Muslim women in their lifestyle choices . . . Oh God. Fuck, what's happening to me?' Max clutches at his chest. He's taking in little shaky gasps of breath. He staggers backwards onto the couch. His robe has slipped open to reveal his grey-haired chest and his belly and a pair of tight black briefs. The camera turns away, back towards the television, which is advertising an upcoming drama series. A girl in a floaty robe is dragged whimpering to an altar, where a bearded priest sharpens a knife. Naked flames flare around them in the darkness. Over the sound of drums, comes a deep masculine voice: 'Edgy, erotic, meticulously researched. From the team that brought you *Hannibal's Harem*, an all-new historic drama. *Stonehenge*.' There's an explosion and the screen shatters. There's nothing now to compete with Max's voice. 'An ambulance. The fuck yes, it's a fucking emergency. For God's sake, I'm dying here.' The camera turns and hovers for a moment on the mirror. We see the burkaed figure of Mo, with the camera up in one hand by her shoulder and the gun dangling from the other.

'You shot his television, Mom? Is that what you did?'

'He's a deeply, deeply destructive individual.'

'But you didn't shoot *him*.' Jake is hysterical with relief. 'You shot his television. It's not even a federal offence, shooting a television. It's art is what it is, Mom. You should apply for a fucking grant.'

I feel Astrid's grip slacken. 'Mo,' she says, 'you crazy bitch.'

'Is he having a heart attack, or what?' I ask them. 'What's happening to him?'

'He robbed me in Egypt – exquisite artefacts essential for my journey . . .'

'Mom, you were never in Egypt.'

'He desecrated my tomb.'

Max is still making noise on the phone as the camera swings out into the garden. There's a cut. And without any warning we're watching Natalie sinking, her hair swirling on the water. There's screaming on the tape and the sound of an impact, and the camera points at a sliver of sky and the timber struts under Mo's house.

Jake has sobered up. 'You taped over it, Mom.'

'Nattie doesn't need us any more, Jake sweetheart. She has to move on.'

'But you taped over it.'

Mo takes a few paces along the pier. 'I think the wind is dropping.'

'Sure is,' Astrid says. 'Normal smog will resume shortly.'

It's getting lighter. There's a reddish glow above the palm trees and the ocean-front hotels.

'Who's up for breakfast?' Mo takes a twirl back towards us, swinging her arms. 'Tom's Diner on Main Street does the best egg-white omelettes. Did we all come in different cars?'

'We ate already,' Jake says, 'me and David. But, you know, whatever.'

'You should go home, Mo,' I tell her. 'Jake and Astrid are going to take you home. Okay, Astrid?'

To me Astrid says, 'I'll drive her car. They'll tow it if we leave it there.'

'The video camera has to go too,' Mo says.

'Sure, honey, we won't forget the camera.'

Mo takes it from her and hugs it to her bosom, twirling in her ungainly dance.

'Aren't you coming, David?' Jake says.

'No, I'd better get back.'

'But you'll email me, right?'

'Of course I will.'

Mo does a turn towards the railings and, before I can stop her, before I realize what she's doing, she lobs the camera out over the ocean. There's a moment's silence and a soft splash. And Nowness Enhancement is history.

While Jake's settling Mo in the passenger seat of her car, I take Astrid aside.

'Is there a doctor who's dealt with this before?' I ask her.

'Persuading her to see him is the problem. She's got medication. She knows what she should do.'

'And you're going to call the police. I mean, you can't just go on as though nothing happened.'

She sighs. 'I guess not.'

'A lot will depend on how Max is doing.'

'Yeah, and on how vindictive he is.'

Mo's telling Jake how easy he'll find it to access the eternal in Santa Rosa. Jake's telling her they can talk about Santa Rosa when she's taken her meds.

I look at the plastic horses on the carousel, proud and skittish, waiting for the day's performance to begin. 'And they killed Amir,' I tell Astrid. 'Did you see that?'

'God, yes. I met that guy, you know, the same night I met you. An Iranian, right? And you were there when they killed him. Jesus, what a night for you, though. Those racist bastards.'

'Yes, I suppose they probably are, but I can't help feeling somehow . . . I don't know . . . that it's our fault. That we somehow weren't paying attention.'

'What could we have done?'

'Me, then. I contributed to this mess.' I wish I could put this feeling into words. 'If I'd kept out of Max's office . . .'

'It wouldn't have made any difference. Mo knew Max already.'

'I suppose you're right.' But I don't mean anything as mechanistic as that. I don't know how to explain this feeling – that we haven't been watching out for each other, that my mind has been taken up with all the wrong things. The rollercoaster curls above us, red now on its underside. 'I just feel somehow responsible.'

'Because feeling responsible is your default setting. Look at the way you've taken care of Jake. And it's not as though you haven't had problems of your own. Max being hospitalized is liable to bring all that to a head, you want my opinion. A thing like a heart attack causes people to look into their souls.'

She's referring to Rebecca, I assume – Rebecca and Max and their phantom affair. 'Look, Astrid, there's something I have to explain . . . I made a ridiculous mistake . . .'

'Hey, it was just a kiss – a nice kiss, as kisses go, I'll give you that, but no big deal.'

'Not that. What I was saying to you on the phone yesterday afternoon, before Rebecca cut us off . . . I got it all wrong.'

'Oh, honey.' She puts a hand on my arm, her head tilting sympathetically. 'That's sweet of you. But it's really for the best. These things are all in the timing.' And her face relaxes into a smile. 'That was one hell of a bifurcation, though, wasn't it? Somewhere in another dimension you and I are having the best sex.'

That makes us both laugh.

'What an appealing thought. But I meant about Max and Rebecca.'

'Oh!'

'I made a mistake. It wasn't Max on the tape, it was only Frankie. I got all worked up about nothing.'

'Rebecca and Frankie? And Max was taping them? And that's okay with you?'

'No, no, it wasn't like that.'

'Hey, if you're cool with it, who am I to judge? Whatever works, you know?'

And it occurs to me that our friendship has been built on misconceptions, starting with the mirage of my genius, so I might as well leave her with this one.

She's on her way to the car with her hand raised in a wave, when I remember that there's something I meant to ask her. 'Tell me something, Astrid. Is it possible your husband's in town?'

I can see from the way she turns that I've taken her by surprise. 'You know something about him?'

'I found myself drinking with this journalist last night.' I reach into my pocket for the card. 'Jeremy Compton.' I hand it to her. 'You did say your husband's name was Jeremy, didn't you? And a writer. You didn't say he was English, so maybe I got the wrong man.'

But I can see already that I've guessed right.

'I wondered where you learned to do that English accent.'

'I don't suppose he mentioned me?'

'I could hardly get him to talk about anything else.'

'Wow! He's still angry, then.'

'Only about the dire threat of Islamo-fascism and the spinelessness of the left.'

There's a smile of recognition. 'And you were drinking with him? How did that come about?'

'He seemed to be at a loose end.'

She laughs at that. 'Loose is not a word I'd ever use of Jeremy.'

'It was the D-word that gave him away.'

'He accused you of talking drivel?'

'He apologized for his own drivel.'

'Huh! Sounds like progress.' And she slips the card into the pocket of her jeans.

I watch them drive out of the amusement arcade, and follow them, walking quickly back towards the shore. A woman is sweeping the boards, collecting fast-food cartons and sweet wrappers in a long-handled dustpan. In the strip of park along the ocean front, the early morning joggers crunch over palm fronds blown down by the gale. There's a battered pickup waiting at the lights. The driver, an elderly Mexican, smiles at me through his open window. The truck's loaded with flowers.

'How much for a bunch of chrysanths?' I ask him.

He turns his head for me to say it again.

'Can I buy some flowers?'

'You buy flowers for your lady?'

'For my wife,' I tell him.

'Is late to go home.'

'I suppose it is.'

'Six dollars a bunch,' he says. 'Or two for ten dollars. You go home this late, you *need* flowers.' And he wrinkles his eyes, showing me a mouthful of discoloured teeth.

twenty

Rebecca turns from the kitchen counter when I walk in, and stands with her arms crossed. 'What time do you call this, then?' she says. She's sending herself up – doing her mother. Her heart isn't quite in the performance, but I appreciate the gesture. Lines like this aren't meant to be funny. At best, they're comfortable, like old clothes. When we last saw each other she was under the impression that I had something going with Astrid and, with far less justification, I accused her of screwing Max, so she's letting me off lightly. She's opening negotiations, at least. Her eyes are puffy and smudged with eyeliner and exhaustion.

'I was warned you'd be upset,' I tell her.

She raises her eyebrows. 'Who by?'

'The bloke who sold me the flowers.' I hold them up, trying to look as contrite as I feel.

There's a slight easing of tension in her face as she takes them, a relaxing of the shoulders. 'You bought flowers for me?'

'Well, he looked as though he could do with the sale, but yes, mainly, I bought them for you.'

'That's nice. Thank you.' She smells them. Then she turns to lay them on the counter, and stays for moment facing the window. 'We should get flowers for Amir.'

'Yes, we should. That's a good thought.'

'There are some already there, on the pavement near

where it happened. I stopped by on my way home. I promised Frankie . . .'

I'm not sure if she's finished talking or fighting tears. I'm
about to take a step towards her, to put my arms round her,
when she turns to face me again, her eyes bright with anger.
'Half the street's cordoned off and there are police everywhere. I suppose it's a crime scene and they're making sure
no one disturbs the evidence, except they're the criminals,
so what are the chances . . .' She shakes her head, takes a
couple of deep breaths and starts again. 'I promised Frankie
I'd see what was happening and let her know. There were
some students there, and some Iranian families, it looked
like, and some other people. It's a kind of vigil, I suppose, or
a demonstration. Because everyone knows he didn't do it –
the idea's completely ridiculous – I can't make sense of it.'
When she looks into my face, it's as though she's searching
for something. 'And you had to watch it all. That must have
been horrible.'

'You saw me on the news, then?'

'There was a telly on in the emergency room.'

'Not my best side, I'm afraid. It's in the contract, left
profile only, but you can't trust these directors.'

She doesn't respond to the joke – not as a joke. She
doesn't respond to its feebleness either. She just looks past
it. She knows what I've been through without me having to
tell her, maybe better than I do. Her eyes have the exaggerated intensity of someone fighting sleep. 'That was sweet,
what you said, though.'

'They gave me a speaking part?'

'I mean it.' She bites her lip. 'It was sweet.'

'But what did I say?'

'You don't remember?'

'I was in shock.'

'You said you were worried about me.'

'Yes, of course.' It comes back – the microphones and the stupid questions and my fear for Rebecca. And I see why she's softened towards me. 'Of course I was worried.' I reach out and take her hand. 'They must have wondered what the hell I was talking about, though.'

'They've been calling you a bewildered bystander.'

'Bewildered! I'll sue.'

'So you haven't been watching?'

'I changed channels whenever I came on.'

'You're so vain.' She takes my other hand. 'And I spoke to a nice Russian woman who had your phone. That was earlier, when I got to the hospital.'

'Evie. She's Czech.'

'Well, Evie's obviously a fan, if you ever need a character reference.' She looks down and I feel her hands tightening around mine. 'I almost didn't call because I was afraid you'd be busy having it away with your trollop.'

'Well, I wasn't.'

She looks up and her eyes are fixed on mine.

'Never did,' I tell her. 'Never wanted to, not really. That phone conversation – I think you got the wrong end of the stick.'

'But there was a stick of some kind, for me to get the wrong end of?'

'More of a twig, really.'

She manages a faint smile. 'A twig with a tight little bum, and fuck-me-senseless hair.'

'Yes, a bit of a statement, the hair.'

'A statement of the bleeding obvious, if you ask me.'

And it comes to me that this is why I married her, because she was the person I would always want to go home with after the party, if only to hear her say, *What the hell was she talking about?* and *Did you see what that bloke was wearing?* and *Was I missing something or were all those people*

303

completely bonkers? Even though she doesn't have to say any of these things for me to know she's thinking them, because I've caught her eye and I've watched her trying to be good. The pleasure of this collusion makes up for so much that has to be endured. And this judgement on Astrid, though more acerbic than most, is an invitation I'm not going to turn down. 'I always want your opinion,' I tell her. 'How else will I know what to think?'

'David, you talk such crap sometimes.'

'You're right, let's stop talking and go to bed.'

'And what you said about me and Max, outside the library . . .'

'Was bollocks. I know. I'm sorry.' This loosens her up. I can feel it through her hands. 'Really, it was absurd of me to ever think such a ridiculous thing.'

'That someone might fancy me?'

'That you would care, one way or another, given how many of your male students can't concentrate for looking at you.'

'Oh, really. Who told you that?'

'I've got eyes.'

'And an overheated imagination.'

'Tell me I'm wrong – you on the edge of the desk, swinging your legs. All those teenage boys looking up your skirt.'

'You should see some of the girls I teach. I'm no competition. It's a sexy subject, history of art. For most of them it's retail with a veneer of culture – everyone wants to run their own gallery.'

'Beanpoles, though, the lot of them, I bet.'

'Beanpoles with very expensive implants, in some cases.'

And I kiss her. And I'm right about holding her and being held, it does my heart good. It does her good too – her breathing becomes steadier. And when we've held each other for a bit, I kiss her on the neck and on the throat and down to where her blouse is buttoned. I taste the saltiness of the night's heat on her skin and feel a new kind of restlessness in her breathing. 'Come to bed.'

'Good idea.' She runs her hands across my chest. 'Just let me put your lovely flowers in water.'

She turns and reaches for a vase, standing up on naked toes. She's got nicely shaped feet, my Rebecca. Good ankles. She's wearing her blouse with the collar up, untucked and belted at the waist. She puts the vase in the sink to run water into to it, and begins separating the chrysanthemums. I've seen the trousers before – black cotton, cropped below the knee. She was wearing them last night, of course. And I watched her more recently modelling them on Max's tape – pulling them on and peeling them off at fast-forward speed. I'm glad they passed the audition. She's trimming the stalks with the kitchen scissors, arranging the flowers in the vase.

'You haven't told me about Max,' I say.

She looks at me almost shyly. 'I wasn't sure if Max was a safe subject.'

'Tell me, is he going to be all right?'

'Depends who you ask. The diagnosis was still under discussion when I left.' She sniggers and stops herself, and I have a sense of the tension she's been carrying, holding herself together while everything's been spinning out of control. 'Sorry, but it's like a bad joke, what's been going on.'

'Was it his heart?'

'Did they say that on the news?'

'No, only that he was stable. So what happened? What's taking the doctors so long to decide?'

'Not the doctors. The doctors are agreed it was an anxiety attack.'

'You mean there's nothing actually wrong with him?'

'Apparently the main damage was to a small bronze nude. I was rather fond of it. It's worth a lot of money, according to Frankie.'

'So Max demanded another opinion, or what?'

'Not exactly. The hospital had done all these tests and couldn't find any problem with his heart, or with anything else. But by then Max's attorney had turned up, and his publicist, and they decided between them that it must have been a mild cardiac arrest, which the doctor in charge pointed out would be like saying someone was slightly pregnant. Then this creep from the mayor's office started putting his oar in, getting into a strop with everyone.'

'So what happened?'

'I don't know. When I left, the creep was still holding out for a gunshot wound.'

It's timed like a punchline, but the story isn't funny any more.

'That's incredible.'

'It's disgusting, is what it is. There are people responsible for Amir's death, and they're going to weasel out of it any way they can.'

I notice her absent-minded grip on the scissors, her knuckles whitening, so I take them from her, put them on the counter, and draw her towards me.

'And Max got another message,' she says into my shoulder. 'Some people calling themselves the Flame of Islam seem to think he's got the blood of a brother on his hands.'

It's another level of disturbance, this reminder of the madness that's loose in the world. 'God, poor Max.'

'I know. He reckons he's going to hire a bodyguard.' She lifts her head to look at me. 'Imagine needing a bodyguard.'

'He takes it seriously, then?'

She shrugs. 'They got to him once. They can get to him again.'

I should tell her it was Mo who shot the telly. There are a lot of things I should tell her. But just for now I want to tune out the clamour of *You're kidding me!* and *Jesus, no!* and find the unthinking pleasure of *Oh God, yes!*

She's begun tidying up the leaves and scraps of stalk.

Some time soon, later this morning probably, I'll explain everything – about Mo, of course, which will only make sense if I mention Natalie's affair with Max, and Max's secret tapes – including the Becks tape, although I know it'll upset her. I'll explain everything, partly because everything is inter-connected, but mainly because what sense is there in our life together unless we hold in common the stuff that presses on us?

She turns the vase with the chrysanthemums in it. The sun has appeared above the neighbouring apartment block and the room is filled with light. The petals in their intricate clusters glow at their tips. 'What do you think?'

'Beautiful.'

'Aren't they, though. Thank you.' She hugs me, nuzzling my neck. 'Now I'm going to take a shower.'

'You don't need to.'

'And brush my teeth, David, and put my diaphragm in.'

'If you take a shower then I'll have to.'

'Only if you want.'

'And brush my teeth.'

'Okay, you go first. I'll just phone Frankie.'

'Becca, can't it wait?'

'Two minutes, I promise.'

'Okay, how about this? Make the phone call, take the shower, but forget the diaphragm.'

She pulls back. 'David, that's not something to joke about.'

'I just think it's time we started thinking about the future. We can't go on leading this selfish life for ever.'

I see the agitation in her breathing and the colour rising in her face. 'You shouldn't say something like that if you don't mean it.'

'Of course I mean it.'

'Have you actually thought about it, though?'

'Well, don't tell me you've never thought about it?'

'What if I have? It's not something to take on lightly. I mean, what kind of a world is this to bring a child into, really, where innocent people get murdered by the police and lunatics break into people's houses?'

'And there are hundreds dead in some hotel in Cairo . . .'

'Exactly.'

'And hunger and sweatshops and child prostitution . . .'

'And wars that don't ever seem to end. What's it going to be like for her?'

'She'll cope. We coped.'

'And you won't get any sleep for six months, and she'll throw tantrums in the supermarket.'

'It's definitely a girl, then, is it?'

The tears well up in her eyes, brimming over the lower lids and onto her cheeks, which are already mottled with crying. 'I don't think it'll be up to us to choose.'

'So if it's a girl, I suppose she'll get her tongue pierced, and become a vegan, and hate us for ruining her life.'

She gives a shaky, sobbing laugh. 'It sounds exhausting. Just thinking about it is exhausting.'

It's such a relief to be able to make her happy – so much nicer than making her miserable.

'So let's go to bed.'

Which we set about doing – in an orderly kind of way, because we're old enough and are answerable only to each other. She makes her call to Frankie while I take a shower.

And while I wait for her to walk out of the bathroom, pink and lovely and losing her towel, I unplug the phones and turn the blinds to shut out the morning sun. And just for now the only part of the world that has to make sense is this.

Acknowledgements

I am grateful to Andrew Motion for encouraging me in the early stages of this novel, and to Tahmima Anam and Myrlin Hermes for reading it in progress. The book benefited from their astute critical attention. I was fortunate to find Peter Straus, an agent of considerable talent and integrity, and Kate Harvey, a gifted editor.

Thanks also to Andrew Kidd, Camilla Elworthy, Nicholas Blake and Chantal Noël at Picador, Jenny Hewson and Rowan Routh at Rogers, Coleridge and White, Katie Haines at The Agency, Melanie Jackson at the Melanie Jackson Agency, and David Zeiger of Displaced Films for help in Los Angeles.

On a more personal note, I am grateful to David and Jane Kennedy, my first good readers – I'm sorry David died too soon to help me with this book – and to my wife, Leni Wildflower, for her unfailing support.